ROGUE PURSUIT

A MATT JAMES THRILLER

MARK J. HIPP

Black Rose Writing | Texas

ISBN: 978-1-68433-839-9
PUBLISHED BY BLACK ROSE WRITING
www.blackrosewriting.com

Printed in the United States of America
Suggested Retail Price (SRP) $21.95

Rogue Pursuit is printed in Calluna

*As a planet-friendly publisher, Black Rose Writing does its best to eliminate unnecessary waste to reduce paper usage and energy costs, while never compromising the reading experience. As a result, the final word count vs. page count may not meet common expectations.

ACKNOWLEDGEMENTS

Biological terror is an existential threat to America and the rest of the world. The gain of function research on the Coronavirus in Wuhan, China serves as evidence of this danger. Unfortunately, the world saw firsthand the devastation that Coronavirus-19 had on its people, the global economy, the supply chain, and on individual freedoms. Now imagine the catastrophic impact of a virus altered to optimize its transmissibility and lethality by our adversaries and then released on an unsuspecting population. It could crisscross the world in roughly a month and impact nearly everyone on the planet.

Even nature can unleash new and lethal viruses on the world and does so periodically. Historically, pandemics such as the Plague of Justinian, the Black Death and Spanish flu, have brought about more death and destruction than wars. With the deforestation of the Amazon rainforest, the melting of the polar icecap, exposure to alien life from meteorites/other means, and humans advancing into unexplored and remote parts of the world, it is quite possible that humankind will be exposed to something unknown in which people have no immunity and could result in extinction of the human race. Biological virus manipulation and experimentation could be the true Pandora's Box.

This book is dedicated to the scientists, doctors, nurses, and first responders who continue to be on the frontline in creating vaccines, cures, and treating patients while fighting a plethora of viruses and diseases that impact us all. This book is also dedicated to the men and women in local, state, and federal law enforcement who battle to protect the citizenry while preserving our great American country, as well as those who serve in our military, intelligence communities, and national foreign affairs agencies. America can only remain strong with this necessary defense that protects our great country, our democracy, and our way of life. I hope that Americans will unite and appreciate these altruistic, honorable, and selfless men and women. So many talented people have died for the country and there are many who still take our freedoms for granted. We need to remember their sacrifice and our own history or face ignominy.

A divided America weakens our national security, emboldens our enemies, and threatens our way of life. Winston Churchill succinctly stated that "when there is no enemy within, the enemies outside can't hurt you." The threats posed by nuclear, biological, chemical, and radiological are continuous, real, and dangerous. People need to put aside their political differences and band together to conquer these constant threats. For when we work together, we can achieve great things. Martin Luther King once said, "It's time for political leaders across the ideological spectrum to realize that, while partisanship is understandable, hyper-partisanship is destructive to our country. We need more visionary leaders who will earnestly strive for bipartisanship and finding policy solutions that can move America forward."

Rogue Pursuit, albeit fiction, melds current day themes, agencies/organizations, and threats into a fast-paced plot that reflects how a determined and ingenious adversary can threaten America and the world. This book is meant to entertain its reader while providing a look into the origins and plausibility of one of America's true nightmare scenarios involving a biological weapon. Biological weapons do not recognize any boundaries and jeopardizes all of humankind.

This book could not have been accomplished without the support, thoughts, guidance, and encouragement of a special quorum of people led by my close friends and former colleagues Fred Ketchem and Scot Folensbee, as well as Bob Rosenblatt, Dick Sherman, Debbie Hipp, Sylvia Nist, and Sarah Roberts. I would also like to say a special thanks to Fred Burton, Sam Katz, and Robert Booth for their encouragement and support. Last, I would like to thank Black Rose Writing, to include Reagan Rothe and his team of professionals who were instrumental in getting this sequel into its ultimate form and to market.

ROGUE PURSUIT

"Nuclear weapons need large facilities, but genetic engineering can be done in a small lab. You can't regulate every lab in the world. The danger is that either by accident or design, we create a virus that destroys us."

–Stephen Hawking

"Deadly pathogens are the 'next big thing' in terror. It's going to be a defense problem, they will be used in war. They will be used in terrorism."

–Ashton Carter,
Department of Defense's Deputy Secretary of Defense

"An asteroid or a supervolcano could certainly destroy us, but we also face risks the dinosaurs never saw: An engineered virus, nuclear war, inadvertent creation of a micro black hole, or some as-yet-unknown technology could spell the end of us."

–Elon Musk

"Preparing for potential bioterrorist attacks involves unique considerations that are distinct from emergency and disaster preparations necessary for other forms of terrorism, such as those that use conventional, chemical, or, possibly nuclear weapons. Bioterrorism does not announce itself with large explosions. One cannot smell, taste, or see biological agents. The attack will not be known until sick patients begin arriving in hospitals and doctor's offices, usually days later—long after the terrorist has left the scene."

–U.S. Senator Bill Frist

"A crude, but effective, terrorist weapon can be made by using a small sample of any number of widely available pathogens, inexpensive equipment, and college-level chemistry and biology. Even as it becomes easier to develop these weapons, it remains extremely difficult – as you know – to detect them, because almost any biological research can serve dual purposes." And "In 2001, we found evidence in Afghanistan that al-Qaida was seeking the ability to conduct bioweapons attacks. And less than a year ago, al-Qaida in the Arabian Peninsula made a call to arms for – and I quote – "brothers with degrees in microbiology or chemistry to develop a weapon of mass destruction."

–Hillary Rodham Clinton, Secretary of State

PROLOGUE: The Winds of Time

El-Amarna, Egypt (1330 BC)

Dusk loomed as the sun descended beyond the Great Sand Sea. The two men trembled, indifferent to the tequila sunset and transfixed on the creature's black lifeless eyes. Its pumpkin-orange skin, long dog-like muzzle, and razor-sharp fangs sent shivers down their spines. The creature's acrid smell magnified its demonic aura; the nocturnal animal's rancid stench churned their stomachs and stuck to the back of their throats. One man ran to the window to gasp for air, but ducked his head into the building.

An oppressive haze swept through the region. A brisk wind wailed as fine grains of sand blasted the sides of the Great Temple. The roofless mud and brick temple provided refuge for the men while they begged for Ra's forgiveness. A white granite altar and offering tables stood prominently in the temple that once hosted the city's elite.

Abdul Hassan Asfur had practiced medicine for forty years and earned a reputation as a superior healer throughout greater Egypt. People journeyed for days to seek his legendary treatments. His quiet confidence endowed his patients with renewed optimism. Still, the events of the last three weeks had shaken him to his very core. Despite his scientific faith, the surrounding devastation reminded him chillingly of the essential fragility of the human condition.

Asfur stretched his lean, six-foot frame from side to side and motioned for Marwan Abu El-Ghul to place the comatose bat on the chemical-drenched cloth. The skilled blacksmith's callused, leathery hands shook as he lowered the carcass into the ornate gold case. Asfur dribbled a hot, oily preservative agent over the bat. A pungent odor permeated the room, causing el-Ghul's eyes to burn and water. He gagged almost incessantly while rubbing and peeling at his eyes.

"Breathe," said the doctor, wiping the sweat and dust from his brow with his forearm. "The oil will seal the plague inside the bat, but could've released some of it into the air."

The blacksmith rocked back and forth. "We buried all the king's riches throughout this ravaged city, and it's this flying rat that's going to kill me. I can't take it anymore."

Asfur poked his index finger at el-Ghul. "Don't panic. We must document this last treasure on our scroll. You can fall apart later."

El-Ghul etched the code word for the most significant treasure. The decipher key would protect el-Amarna's secrets from the raiders who would strip the city of its valuables.

"What's so special about this bat? This gold case is worth more than it." El-Ghul flashed a bitter smile and then tucked in his upper lip.

The doctor scratched his temple. "Imagine if this plague spread beyond our city, causing other populations to vanish like ours did. Our absence during the outbreak spared our lives, as the plague spread like wildfire throughout the city, sentencing our citizens to horrific deaths as blood oozed from all their orifices and filled the streets. This infected bat's the key to creating a future man-saving cure, so it's more valuable than all the gold and silver we stashed away these past few days."

"That's comforting." El-Ghul's jaw tightened as he crossed his arms.

Asfur ignored the weary blacksmith, chalking it up to the shock that permeated their souls. Their recently shattered lives tested their patience and longtime friendship. His concentration intensified as he added the sixth and final layer of cloth and preservatives to the bat. The doctor then applied the blacksmith's waxy adhesive sealant to the container.

"Get the trapdoor." Asfur's voice cracked as he lifted the gold case.

"Let me get it." El-Ghul lunged forward and grabbed the case from the healer. His toes gripped the first of the ladder's twenty-five wooden steps; its planks buckled with each step. He descended timidly to avoid slipping and unleashing the contents he feared. The cavern's strategically placed torches on the wall crackled, spreading light and warmth throughout the damp room.

"Why are you stopping?" Asfur glanced at the blacksmith.

El-Ghul peered up at the doctor with bulging eyes and a slacked mouth. "Look at this place." His eyes sparkled as he studied the chamber's artisanship and the riches it held. A golden sarcophagus rested in the center of the room.

As his feet touched solid ground, el-Ghul sidestepped so the doctor could follow. Seconds later, Asfur's feet landed on the firm sandy surface. The men welcomed the reprieve from above, where the chilly night air rolled in from the northwest.

"Follow me." Asfur motioned as he stopped at the face of the solid gold encasement, bowed, settled his eyes on the upper part of the sarcophagus, and prayed.

The blacksmith treaded in the doctor's footsteps. "Why didn't the priestess shield our families from the plague?" El-Ghul scowled.

Asfur froze him with a steely glance, causing him to regret his off-handed remark. "Show respect for the dead. She protected this city through war, pestilence, and famine. Ra's power is far greater than the priestess, and his actions can be mystifying and not easily understood."

El-Ghul considered the doctor's ruminations and found it unusual that a man of pure science could be so religious. He had abandoned religion early in his life, and this recent tragedy had served only to galvanize his skepticism.

"How can you be so forgiving after what we suffered? What kind of deity would obliterate twenty-thousand men, women, and innocent children?" His eyes turned cold prior to him lowering his chin.

The doctor interrupted el-Ghul before he began his next tirade; his faced reddened. "Take care when you question Ra's wisdom. This disrespect probably brought his vengeance to our city. You deplored the debauchery that preceded the plague. We lost our sense of values, morals, and community. This is the price we pay as collective sinners." The doctor tugged on his collar.

El-Ghul's mouth fell open. He had known the doctor for forty years, but had never considered his stubborn religious faith. He misunderstood the dichotomy of his character, which somehow balanced the laws of science and nature with religion. This contradiction mystified him and underscored the complexity of this man he admired but never truly understood.

"There's no time to linger. We must finish and leave the city." The doctor's unassuming voice diffused the situation. "The plague may still be airborne."

"I'm sorry." El-Ghul looked down and away. He regretted his sudden outburst and scrubbed his hand over his face. "We've witnessed so many horrors this week." His body sagged as he reflected on the doctor's nobility.

"Are you okay, Marwan?" The doctor snapped him from his reverie.

El-Ghul nodded. "You've saved countless people over the years, including my family. I appreciate your friendship. Do you recall my father's illness?" His eyes softened as he covered his heart with his hand.

"How could I forget that week as your father almost died on the second night?" The doctor sucked in a quick breath as his eyes blinked rapidly before morphing into an open stare.

El-Ghul's eyes sparkled. "I never told you what he said upon wakening."

"The community appreciated your father's wisdom." Asfur's eyes enlarged.

The blacksmith cleared his throat. "He told me how much he respected your counsel, friendship, and wisdom. He also had me promise him one thing."

Asfur leaned forward. "What did he ask of you?"

"He instructed me to look after you. My father believed you brought the community together."

"I just served the community like your father." The doctor gave him a playful swat.

"That's enough reminiscing. Let's finish and get some sleep. Tomorrow will be another long day." El-Ghul walked to the room's corner.

The two placed the gold case on the table's countertop near the chamber's ground floor exit. With the treasure secured, they packed the food, water, blankets, and clothing required for the arduous journey. A new beginning waited for them in Qumran. The doctor had once saved an aristocrat who gave him some land instead of his customary fee. He would now take the grateful patient's offer.

"Let's recheck our work." The doctor peered at the blacksmith.

El-Ghul unfurled the one-millimeter thick copper scroll. It measured a third of a meter in width and two-and-a-half meters in length. The text identified the gold, silver, jewelry, ritual clothing, and parchments that they had stashed in sixty-four locations. The two scanned the scrolls.

"Can I see your decipher code?" He turned toward the blacksmith.

El-Ghul reached into his bag and passed it to his friend. Asfur placed the scroll and code key alongside one another. The scroll listed the prized items with no reference to location. The decipher key appeared empty, unless they applied it to the scroll to unlock el-Amarna's secrets.

"I'll transport the scroll. You take the key code in your pack." The doctor nodded while sliding the copper scroll into his saddlebag.

El-Ghul placed the code key inside his bag and retracted a blanket. He found a spacious spot in the room's corner to sleep while bidding the doctor goodnight. Despite the hard damp ground, they both slept soundly given their physical and mental exhaustion. Waking up at daybreak, the blacksmith opened up his pack and retrieved two small portions of dried meat, handing the doctor his ration.

"It's not much, but it will satisfy your hunger." The blacksmith chewed the tough, flavorless piece of meat.

The doctor grabbed two green bananas from his bag and tossed one to his companion. "Eat this fruit. It's good for you."

The blacksmith ate the banana in four bites. After finishing their scant meal, the two walked to the chamber door and pushed it open. The sun's rays filled the tunnel's entrance with a fiery whitish light which caused them to turn sideways while their pupils readjusted. They grabbed their packs and passed through the entrance, sealing it behind them. About fifty feet up, they had sheltered their horses from the inclement weather. The blacksmith examined the horses' hooves to prepare for their strenuous journey. He fed them some straw and water before departing. Given the scorching desert heat and lack of shade, the men's survival depended upon their horses' resilience.

"Are you ready?" El-Ghul helped the doctor onto his horse. The old man's agility surprised him.

El-Ghul mounted his horse and then looked at the doctor who gave a quick nod; the two vaulted forward and emerged from the cave's exit as the sun's rays parted their faces. As they eased away from the city, the two peered over their shoulders to see a desolate city. A few minutes afterward, they reached the Nile, where they turned and followed it north toward the Mediterranean Sea.

The two galloped past the North Palace and stared at the site; it stirred memories of grand events hosted by the queen. A garden court sat in the northeast corner of the property. The central chamber stood nearby and displayed a continuous frieze representing the natural life of the marshes. Each room had a window to highlight the sunken central garden.

"Look at Nefertiti's Palace." Asfur pointed. "The queen often hosted magnificent receptions with people and royalty from all over Egypt."

"We've seen the last of these receptions. What a waste." El-Ghul pressed his fist against his mouth and puffed out his cheeks.

Their pace quickened to a slow trot as they passed the North City, which marked the great city's end. They glanced back one last time to remember the city as it once stood. One of fourteen huge tablets carved into the surrounding cliffs reminded them that el-Amarna was a distant memory. The two men galloped alongside the powerful north-flowing Nile River. As dusk approached, they stopped at the outskirts of Cairo, finding shelter from a local farmer. The blacksmith examined the farmer's horses for a bed, some dried fish, water, and overripe bananas; it reminded him of the good in people.

The two woke up at dawn to relish the cool night air. They mounted their horses, followed the east fork of the Nile, and reached the Mediterranean Sea by nightfall. The two halted their horses and sat mesmerized by the fiery orange and red sunset over a clear blue sea. El-Ghul inhaled air so fresh that it infused him with energy.

The blacksmith jumped from his horse and scampered out waist deep into the sea. "Come join me. The water feels great."

"I'll pass." The doctor slouched while gazing at the last remnants of a pinkish sky as twilight emerged. Asfur's mind calmed as he sucked in the crisp sea air. His mind wandered to his family and then he envisioned their course ahead. Their journey would take them by Gaza and onto the southern portion of the Dead Sea, where they would then turn north and follow it to its end.

The next couple of days passed without incident. Asfur knew the sites from previous trips. However, el-Ghul found everything new and exciting, enjoying the sights, sounds, and tastes of a new area. El-Ghul's sudden zest for life delighted the doctor. This unique part of him surfaced only with the death of his family. The doctor admired this metamorphosis and his resilience.

Upon reaching the Dead Sea, they stopped for the night. The doctor instructed el-Ghul to swim in the salt-ridden water. As the blacksmith entered the sea, its high salinity caused him to float in amazement. El-Ghul approached the shoreline as the doctor joined him this time.

"It's rumored that the sea can cure many ailments. People travel for weeks just to experience it." The doctor stretched his neck. "You must bathe for about twenty minutes for the sea to heal your mosquito bites, relax your muscles, and relieve your body's tension."

"If we stayed here, we wouldn't need doctors." El-Ghul slapped his knees.

Asfur remained still and silent as grief from the loss of his family permeated his soul, something he had brushed aside until now. He knew the salt solution would not revive his heart or soul.

"What's wrong?" El-Ghul patted him between his shoulder blades.

"I'm fine." The doctor's eyes appeared sunken and dim. "I'm just reflecting on the past week. It's all surreal."

"More like a nightmare." El-Ghul floated on his back and splashed water at him. "Where's your faith now? Everything has a reason, or so you used to say."

"We could live a lifetime without understanding the senseless killing of twenty-thousand people. I'm sorry that you lost your family. I wish I could've saved them."

El-Ghul scuttled from the water and toweled off. "Not even you could've saved them. We just need to accept Ra's wrath and actions."

The blacksmith surprised him with his sudden realization; the trials of recent days had somehow transformed this simple artisan into a man of faith. Asfur would ponder this metamorphosis all night. He realized tomorrow's arrival at Qumran would bring a fresh beginning.

After waking and breakfasting on smoked fish, bread, and oranges, the two girded themselves for the day ahead. Sleeping on the banks of the Dead Sea, they had awakened refreshed by the night air. Perhaps the Dead Sea's healing properties had revived them in body and spirit.

The two mounted their horses and bolted off, excited about their imminent arrival at their new home. The relentless wind masked the heat radiating from the desert floor. About midway into the day's journey, they spotted several horses approaching them from the rear. They quickened their pace to a brisk gallop, but their pursuers closed the distance. Fearing robbers, the two searched for a safe place to hide the copper scroll and the key code.

They glanced off to the west and saw the hazy outline of Qumran. Dust clouds from their chaser's horses appeared much more visible now. El-Ghul stumbled upon a cave, dismounted his horse, and removed the decipher key from his pack. He sprinted into the cave as the doctor monitored the approaching band. Minutes later, the blacksmith emerged after hiding the key within the cavern beneath a pile of rocks. He remounted his horse and led Asfur down the hillside where they encountered yet another cave. This time, they both entered the cave to bury the copper scroll. Unable to determine how much time they had over their pursuers, they hastily buried the scroll. The limited light and myriad tributary tunnels made it difficult to find the cave's exit. The men stumbled out of the cave, accepting the scroll's safety.

Upon exiting, the doctor and blacksmith encountered six brutal looking horsemen. The ruffian in the middle appeared to be their boss, given the others' deference toward him. He bore a small scar underneath his right eye and spoke in a deep voice.

Dismounting his horse, the leader addressed the two travelers in menacing tones. "Give us all your valuables."

El-Ghul stepped forward, shielding the doctor. "We only have food and clothing."

The thug drew his knife and waved it at the blacksmith. "That's the wrong answer."

As the man lunged, el-Ghul blocked the knife with one hand and grabbed the attacker's wrist with the other. The powerful blacksmith snapped the ruffian's wrist downward and tossed him to the ground. Distracted, he didn't spot another thug dismount his horse and creep up from behind. He thrusted his knife into the blacksmith's kidney and retracted a blood-soaked blade. El-Ghul collapsed to his knees as the man stepped in front and slashed his knife across his throat. Blood spewed from his neck as the blacksmith fell face forward to the sandy ground.

The doctor glanced at el-Ghul and then turned to run, but the four on horseback surrounded him. Spinning in time to see the criminal boss thrust his knife at his heart, Asfur sidestepped to the left, drew his knife, and slit the inner part of the bandit's bicep. Blood gushed out of the brachial artery, spurting sporadically as his heart flushed his lifeblood from his body.

Puzzled by the blow, the leader glanced at his arm. "Kill him."

Asfur fought valiantly, killing two other attackers before succumbing to a fatal chest wound. Before he died, Asfur took comfort knowing that the leader had bled out and died. With one last breath by the doctor, the secrets of the copper scroll appeared lost forever.

CHAPTER 1: Ultimate Betrayal

Northeastern Syria

A dense fog wafted over the jagged rock ledge, engulfing the ridge with a dampening cold. Concealed behind several large boulders, a dozen men huddled around a blazing campfire; its florescent embers radiated warmth while casting dancing shadows across their hideout's main entrance. Near the crest of the mountaintop, the cave provided a protective buffer; its steep slope and rocky terrain served as a natural defense against intruders. It also shielded the Islamic State's operational base from the peering eyes of satellites, attack drones outfitted with hellfire missiles, and high-tech aircraft armed with laser-guided smart bombs. However, it lacked the material comforts and luxuries of his native Iraq, but Northeastern Syria's mountains now served as his abode and command post. The legendary figure would plot his next move from this frozen and desolate landscape.

Seated close to the fire, Sheikh Ibrahim al-Sammarri lifted his head to address his top lieutenants. Known as the Invisible Sheikh, al-Sammarri's once muscular six-foot, one inch frame had thickened around the waist. A self-proclaimed descendent of the prophet Muhammad, he strayed away from the prophet's mainstream teachings. At forty-three, his graying beard, sallow complexion and facial wrinkles portrayed an elderly man. His pasty skin reflected a poor diet from living on the run and hiding from his many enemies.

Al-Sammarri stood and brushed an ashy dust off his pants. "Magnificent warriors, after we defeated Syria and forced America's withdrawal from Iraq, the US lies and claims they're defeating us. Their latest surge of military advisors to Iraq and drawdown in Syria attests to our vast gains. They're losing and we'll together deliver a vital blow. We've deployed three of our warriors to America; they'll attack at a set time." His hands dangled behind his back as his chin remained erect.

The venerated sheikh sipped his sweet tea with mint leaves. He scanned his men. His eyes pierced each of them, as if he were examining their souls.

"We're on the verge of a major victory." Al-Sammarri waved his index finger.

"I won't go into specifics because of operational security reasons. We've positioned our warriors in three separate American cities. They each have five drones carrying gas canisters that contain enough chemicals to blanket their targeted sports arenas. One arena will attract ninety-thousand people, including the US president.

The sheikh surveyed his men. Their luminous expressions spoke volumes. The leader knew he had hit the mark with his twelve closest advisors. Their excitement electrified the air.

"Wait, there's more." His voice boomed. "It's an ingenious plan. Artificial intelligence will control and fly our drones using programmed wave points and environmental factors. The drones will be setup and programmed with GPS coordinates from various stadium maps. Once activated at a predetermined time, the drones will fly on their own to their respective targets. When the drones arrive at their destinations, they'll hover, calculate wind directions and velocity, and fly to the stadium's side from which the wind is blowing. They'll reposition to cover the width of the stadium and then strafe the crowd to provide maximum damage. Thanks to our Syrian brothers, we have enough sarin gas to blanket each stadium twice. Imagine more than a quarter of a million American dogs killed in three major cities. Total chaos will erupt." His wide glowing eyes looked skyward.

Hassan Khalil Hussein eyed his boss. Serving as the sheikh's bodyguard for years, he had an encyclopedic knowledge of his habits, strengths, and weaknesses. Al-Sammarri trusted him with his life and he had repeatedly earned it, most spectacularly, by escaping Iraqi fighter jets that pounded his forward base camp.

The thirty-eight-year-old Hassan stood a half foot shorter than the revered leader. His physical prowess and agility melded a middleweight wrestler's power with an Olympic gymnast's nimbleness. His fierceness and quickness earned him the nickname Cheetah. Unknown to those around him, endurance training and a world-class ability on the soccer field forged his athleticism. Instead, his father sent him to Iraq to fight the Americans, forever sealing his fate.

While in Iraq, Hassan battled his enemies, shooting down some of America's finest aircraft with Stinger missiles. Woven into a dangerous game of cat-and-mouse, the hunters would often become the hunted. Hassan escaped the Apache helicopter's barrage of firepower on four occasions. Somehow, he used the harsh Iraqi terrain to shelter him from the Apache's thirty-millimeter automatic M230 chain gun; a nightmarish weapon that could pulverize anything in its path. Equipped with a bank of antitank and general purpose missiles, surviving any Apache encounter proved unlikely. Hassan had gone head-to-head with these flying arsenals of death and survived these risky encounters. He damaged an unprecedented six of the deadly aircraft; this feat propelled him to the top spot on America's targeting list.

These legendary achievements captured the sheikh's attention, resulting in his transfer and rapid advancement in the leader's elite guard. His soft voice and unassuming demeanor masked his warrior prowess. A trimmed beard reflected an almost compulsive cleanliness. Dressed in desert battle fatigues, he was, despite an almost deferential persona, an intimidating figure who could put fear into his opponents with one steely glance. Now his attention was riveted on his commander.

"Bring me the traitor." Al-Sammarri flicked his wrist.

A burly man wearing a black balaclava parted the crowd, dragging a man in an orange jumpsuit. He approached the sheikh, turned, and kicked the prisoner behind his knee. The man fell forward. "Get on your knees."

"Don't hurt me. I'm loyal to the cause." The prisoner shrieked as his body trembled.

Al-Sammarri stepped toward the captive, backhanding him across his face. "You should've followed my orders and killed all the women and children in Mosul. You betrayed the cause and me."

The prisoner shook his head. "They were helpless and did nothing wrong."

"That's foolish sentiment." The sheikh's eyes turned cold as he spit on the man. "They aided the Americans." He flicked his wrist again.

The balaclava man stepped forward and pushed the man to his stomach before kneeling on his spine. Two other men approached the prisoner, wrenching his hands away from his body. They each stepped on the prisoner's wrists before driving an iron stake through each hand. The man screeched, which echoed throughout the valley. The balaclava man turned the lid of a five-gallon gasoline container and splashed half of it on the prisoner.

Al-Sammarri turned toward the crowd, raising his torch. "We don't tolerate traitors. Allah Akbar!" He grinned before lowering the flame onto the prisoner; orange-yellow flames shot skyward as the man screamed. The sheikh's grin morphed into a broad smile. "Our cause requires our total commitment. We can't show any pity. The smile I bear now is the same one I showed the US commander at Camp Bucca. When I left the prison, I vowed to visit him in New York. I intend to keep that promise as well." Al-Sammarri winced as his features contorted and crumpled. Hassan lunged toward him as the sheikh doubled over, clenching his gut.

"I've got you." Hassan's voice softened. He placed the sheikh down on the cold, hard ground.

The council encircled their leader as Muhammad Ibrahim checked his vitals.

"Back up. I need room to work." The ISIS deputy snapped.

Ibrahim, an Iraqi-trained physician, had known al-Sammarri for more than a decade. His once steady hands now shuddered as he placed the stethoscope to the leader's chest; he listened to the sheikh's shallow and irregular heartbeat before peering into his dilated eyes.

"We have to get him to a hospital now or he'll perish." Ibrahim turned toward Hassan. "There's nothing more I can do for him here. He needs specialized care now."

Hassan nodded, pitying the man. The sheikh's weakened condition had hurt the cause. His torture, beheadings, and public executions of fellow Muslims slowed recruitment efforts required to win a war against the West.

·   ·   ·   ·   ·

Meanwhile, Jamal Abu al-Bayd mesmerized his private audience with his encyclopedic knowledge of ISIS locations, operations, and intentions. The

US Consulate in Erbil had not expected this intelligence bonanza when the ISIS terrorist marched through its front entrance earlier in the day, asking to meet the head of security. Al-Bayd had impressed the regional security officer (RSO) who had discovered the "walk-in's" intentions and credibility. He summoned the FBI's legal attaché to join in on the interview.

RSO Jake O'Reilly, as Irish as his name implied, had served in Erbil for the past eight months. His sixteen-hour workdays taxed his body and mind. Yet, today would be a career maker for him if the luck of the Irish prevailed. The art of interrogation came naturally to him. Articulate and charming, he related to all levels of society. His six-foot two frame and lean, muscular build masked an intelligence often overlooked by his colleagues. Before joining the Diplomatic Security Service (DSS), he had finished a four-year stint in the Army. He then attended law school at Yale, where he graduated with honors. He had worked as a prosecuting attorney in Vermont for several years. After a nasty divorce, he joined the Foreign Service and traveled the world. He had advanced in DS ahead of his peers because of his willingness to serve in myriad hellholes. Some questioned his sanity as he accepted assignments nobody else had wanted. The greater the hardship or danger, the better he loved it.

Determined to vet the asset, O'Reilly glanced over at his FBI counterpart. He disliked him, but valued his Arabic language capabilities and his doggedness to unearth the truth. Already interviewing and establishing rapport with al-Bayd, O'Reilly led the interrogation to locate the world's most sought after terrorist.

"So, you report that al-Sammarri is ill and needs urgent medical attention. And you further claim that his chief bodyguard will trade him for the ten million dollar reward?"

Al-Bayd remained slouched in his chair. "Yes, he'll turn him over to you at the Sinjar Mountain pass for the reward money."

"And how does he propose doing this?" The security chief thumped his right index finger on the table.

Al-Bayd guzzled his glass of water before responding. "It's simple. He'll convince the group's twelve member council to use standard security protocols to escort him for medical care. The best way to protect him during travel would be to use a low profile package. I believe you call it a two car motorcade."

O'Reilly nodded in agreement. "Go on." He motioned to the source.

"Hassan recognizes that the sheikh's true value is in the cash he's worth to Americans through the State Department's Reward for Justice Program."

"Will you take a polygraph test?" The FBI attaché interrupted.

"If that's what it takes, then I'll take your test. You'll be happy with my information." The ISIS informer stuck out his chest and smirked, making direct probing eye contact.

O'Reilly pondered his omissions. His guts churned as he sensed both the truth and a hidden agenda.

The FBI attaché scurried from the room without a word. The RSO glanced at his wristwatch, determined to take advantage of his time alone with al-Bayd. He prodded the ISIS snitch. "What can you inform me about the group's pursuit of weapons of mass destruction? And what are their future intentions and targets?"

Al-Bayd shifted in his chair and folded his arms. "ISIS has long sought weapons of mass destruction. Their buyers are canvassing the former Soviet Republics, North Korea, and Iran for nuclear, biological, radiological, and chemical weapons. It also employs several scientists to create rudimentary poisons." Al-Bayd yawned.

The security chief recognized the terrorist endeavored to show good faith, piecing out recent press reporting. He understood the information's secondary nature and knew he needed to nail the world's most notorious terrorist. O'Reilly had interrogated many persons over his lifetime. None involved the level of importance, as the one who faced him. He wanted a hand in capturing the world's most ruthless and dangerous terrorist.

O'Reilly leaned in toward al-Bayd as the door swung open. His FBI counterpart strode into the room and announced the imminent arrival of a three-person FBI team. The FBI attaché was pushing for the case lead, and perhaps a promotion. The interview continued for another two hours before adjourning for lunch. O'Reilly sensed al-Bayd's weariness from the incessant grilling and efforts to catch him in a lie. Given his consistency and detailed responses, he recognized his sincerity. He didn't require a polygraph for confirmation, but if the FBI wanted proof, then he'd play along.

The FBI team arrived after lunch, carrying several black Pelican hard-plastic cases; they meticulously prepared their electronic equipment on a desk in the interview room. O'Reilly used the reprieve to call DS' Command Center, situated some six-thousand miles away in Rosslyn, Virginia.

On the nineteenth floor in DSS' headquarters building, access to the reinforced vault remained restricted; only those with the requisite top-secret clearance, access card, and pin number could enter and traverse the space. Otherwise, a special agent verifies a person's credentials through a videophone before allowing admittance. Upon entering through a reinforced blast-resistant door, the suite teems with activity. A myriad of display screens, clocks, and other electronic media highlighted the state of affairs throughout the world. Cable news tracks the latest fast-breaking story on two kidnapped journalists in Gaza on a sixty-inch plasma screen. Seven clocks representing different world time zones hang above the plasma screen. Further ahead, an electronic board reflects DS' current and upcoming protective details, including the Secretary of State, the US Ambassador to the United Nations, the Prince of Wales, the Iraqi Foreign Minister, and the Saudi Ambassador to the US. A rectangular ring of desks is located just to the right side and serves as the heart of the Command Center; it's here where several watch officers monitor the night's activities, view protective operations in the field, and report key happenings to the service's hierarchy. Next to each part of the watch area, a series of private offices align the walls. Analytical personnel, senior watch officers, and the deputy director and director of the Command Center sit there.

A series of specialized tactical operations rooms live down a short hall and off to the right. A full video display wall and an assortment of LCD screens provide post specific information. Today, the technician displayed real-time footage of the consulate in Erbil, which included a compound schematic, the front, and vehicular entrances, and the interview room, where the RSO sat facing a video camera.

"Mitch, can you hear me?" O'Reilly stared through the screen; his demeanor calm and focused.

"I have you Lima-Charlie." Mitch Johnson, the regional director for Diplomatic Security's Office of Contingency Operations, acknowledged, meaning loud and clear.

Summoned at a quarter past one in the morning, Johnson listened to the security chief's groundbreaking interview; he realized the information's relevance and alerted his CIA and FBI counterparts. They scrambled to assemble their essential case agents and behavioral scientists to monitor the landmark interview.

The RSO nodded, raising his chin. "Mitch, I've conducted hundreds of interviews in my career. This guy's credible."

"We concur. Both CIA and FBI behavioral scientists opine that al-Bayd is credible. The ramifications are significant." Johnson pressed his lips together.

"I watched al-Bayd's body language and demeanor throughout the interview. I only detected possible deception when I mentioned weapons of mass destruction (WMD)." O'Reilly grinned.

"We second that. CIA's behavioral expert noted that he looked away while crossing his arms in a defensive posture." Johnson leaned back in his armchair and clasped his hands behind his head.

O'Reilly stroked his chin. "Al-Bayd seemed to withhold information on W-M-Ds, which doesn't surprise me."

"I hear you." Johnson's eyes widened. "We should focus on capturing al-Sammarri. After that, we can focus on other hazardous weapons."

"He's reliable, but we should wait for the results of the polygraph. We must be absolutely certain before we act." O'Reilly pressed his lips together. "I have to witness the polygraph. Enjoy the show. We'll score high in the ratings with this episode." The RSO turned and walked away with wide steps as the DS technician muted the microphone.

The FBI polygrapher conducted his test with a methodical and unemotional approach.

"Is your name Jamal Abu al-Bayd?" The polygrapher droned.

"Yes." The ISIS snitch unbuttoned the top button of his shirt and gulped.

The polygrapher examined al-Bayd's blood pressure, pulse, respiration, and skin conductivity on the computer screen. Three oscillating lines moved across the screen. He continued his interview. "Are you from Iraq?"

"Yes, I was raised in Baghdad."

"Just a simple yes or no answer will do." The polygrapher glanced at al-Bayd over his glasses.

"Does al-Sammarri need immediate medical attention?"

"Yes."

"Will Hassan give al-Sammarri to US authorities near the Sinjar Pass?"

"Yes."

"Will Hassan honor the agreement to trade al-Sammarri for ten million dollars?"

"Yes."

The polygrapher observed a minor spike in al-Bayd's heart rate and respiration, indicating possible deception. "Allow me to rephrase. Will Hassan transfer al-Sammarri to American officials at Iraq's Sinjar Pass?"

"Yes." Al-Bayd's head tilted back.

The polygrapher's eyes glimmered as his subject's vitals remained constant. He had conducted thousands of polygraphs during his career and recognized his subject's truthfulness.

O'Reilly pondered the terrorist's answers and the important ramifications of his information. The US had been targeting al-Sammarri for years, but the elusive ISIS mastermind had always evaded capture. He sought to end this trend soon.

CHAPTER 2: Executive Orders

Washington, DC

An impressive bouquet of orange and beige leaves fluttered in the fall breeze. Musty air blew off the Potomac, where a southwesterly cold front sparked the season's first severe thunderstorm. Major Bud Harrison jousted with the sudden updrafts and wind gusts of forty knots; he entered his final approach to the White House in Marine One, a VH-3D Sea King helicopter. His passengers included the president and the first lady who sat quietly during their jarring ride.

The president eyed the first lady who gripped his hand. She pressed her eyelids together and sucked in a breath before opening them. Her fiery eyes focused on the exit door. The president had been resting at Camp David when the secretary of state called him with urgent news. He had been suffering a precipitous dip in the polls, thanks to a slumping economy, sagging unemployment numbers, and Iran's recent proclamation that they joined the nuclear club. He could use a break, and he welcomed the secretary's news.

Known for his sarcastic wit, good nature, and business-like approach, President Sam Baker spoke his mind and to the point. As a reluctant politician, the president always pursued the best interests of the country, despite the political fallout. This moral integrity bordered on stubbornness. Yet, it meant he pursued a goal with a heartfelt zest that made the impossible a reality. A man of his word, President Baker's hallmark remained a rarity in Washington politics; he recognized many legislators played the spin game to distance themselves from an unbridled culture of corruption.

The president leaned forward. "You need some help flying this bird Bud?"

"Are you kidding, sir? This is child's play. I've flown through sandstorms, skirted hurricanes in the Atlantic on search and rescue missions, and braved heavy enemy fire to haul out the wounded in Desert Storm. A little breeze doesn't bother me." The veteran pilot said with a shimmer in his eyes.

"You could've fooled me. The way you're bouncing us around, I figured I was riding Dynamo at the local bull rodeo." The president's grin widened.

"More like a mechanical bull on low speed." Harrison fired back.

The president's grin vanished. "All kidding aside, I sure appreciate your team's work. Please thank them for me."

"I'll do that when we land. Buckle up! It's going to become rough. I'm taking severe crosswinds." Harrison increased pressure on the cyclic pedal to adjust for the sudden gust of wind from the east.

The president looked at his wife, whose dilated pupils and pale face radiated anxiety throughout the cabin. She had been with him for over three decades, but had never savored flying in helicopters.

"Bud, you better get us home soon or I'll be wearing my wife's lunch."

"We're almost there, sir. We'll be landing in a minute." Harrison glanced at his altimeter.

"Do what you have to do, but make it fast." The president eyed his wife before checking his gold Seiko watch.

Harrison landed Marine One within the landing zone circle and in seconds. The president bounced out of his seat and approached his pilot, extending his hand.

"Well done." The commander-in-chief squeezed his pilot's hand. "Let's do it again when my wife's at home. I enjoyed the ride." He nodded, eyes glowing.

"I'm ready anytime you need me, sir." The pilot grinned.

The president grabbed his wife's hand and escorted her down the stairs. A Marine in dress blues stood at attention at the seat of the stairway. As the president passed him, the Marine snapped a crisp salute. The president turned toward the Marine and returned the gesture with two crisp motions. His national security advisor and the secretary of state eyed the commander-in-chief. The president greeted each with his customary firm handshake. "Let's go to work."

Secretary of State James Jackson had been a longtime friend of the president. Attending Harvard Law School with him, he then performed corporate legal services in the family-owned oil enterprise. He litigated more than a hundred high-profile cases, many with international ramifications. This record earned him a seat on the board of advisors and the trust of the president. So, when the president asked him to serve as his secretary of state, he willingly accepted. His wife's reservations and his apparent lack of international experience didn't dissuade him.

His senate confirmation dispelled the myth; it becoming known that he spoke three foreign languages fluently and another two passably. Jackson had brokered over thirty-five major international oil deals, so the president deduced that his skill could be best used in handling key diplomatic initiatives. Congress agreed and confirmed him, albeit along party lines. Jackson proved them right in a year by negotiating an end to the North Korean nuclear standoff. He also reorganized the State Department to handle and compete with the new world order.

As the nation's top diplomat, Jackson even looked the part, meticulously groomed and dressed in tailor-made suits. A polished orator, he could socialize with all segments of society, and across cultural lines. His unique ability to establish immediate rapport had served him well in the corporate world. It now helped him win over presidents, prime ministers, foreign secretaries, and kings. The president's cabinet gravitated to him for his insightful opinions. His candid way of cutting to the root of an issue and his fatherly presentation kept people coming back for more, even if it countered their preconceived notions.

At six feet, two inches, Jackson stood eye-to-eye with the president. His medium build, short light brown hair parted just right of center, and a chiseled chin with a small dimple even resembled the president. His intense brown eyes often masked his hidden charm, particularly to the unacquainted. A man's man, his intellectual prowess didn't overshadow his common sense and easy-going southern charm.

"Jim, you look beat." The president leaned in awkwardly with his hands in his pockets. "Are you okay?"

"Mr. President, it has been a busy twenty-four hours, but the news out of Iraq is very encouraging. We've been hunting al-Sammarri for years, and now we're closing in on him."

"So when can I mount his head on my wall?" The president exuded calm and focus.

"Our regional security officer in Erbil just interviewed a walk-in source who alleges he knows al-Sammarri's whereabouts. Not only does he know his location, but he's willing to deliver him to our people for the ten million dollar bounty."

"This is outstanding news and couldn't have come at a better time." The president patted Jackson's shoulder. "We need to reward these guys for their tenacity and resourcefulness. Let's talk specifics." He dabbed the perspiration from his forehead with a handkerchief.

Jackson glanced at the nearby caged press pool and walked the president to the White House's back door. A stern-looking secret service agent snapped the door open. The secretary remained leery of the inquisitive and often overzealous press. Given the opportunity, the press would smear their confidential conversation in the headlines.

After negotiating a short hallway lined with red carpet, the president entered a secure conference room. "Good afternoon. Please take a seat."

The president examined the room and the assemblage of Washington's elite to ensure proper representation. The vice president and the chairman of the Joint Chiefs sat to the president's right. Jackson sat to his left with the defense secretary next to him. Others assembled around the solid cherry oval conference table included the director of National Intelligence, the secretaries of Treasury, Homeland Security, and Transportation, and the directors of the CIA, the FBI, and the National Security Agency. Overall, twenty key figures sat around the table waiting for the commander-in-chief's instructions. Countless officials monitored the conversation from their chairs, behind the president and other key repositories of power.

Sipping his Colombian coffee from the White House's two-century old, gold-plated china, the president surveyed the room. He pondered the number of times he had convened in the Cabinet Room to discuss national security matters. Like many before him, the president had become accustomed to this venue to solve world events, especially events that could metastasize into the next world war.

A mix of artificial and natural light filled the room. Two refurbished nineteenth century crystal chandeliers hung over the conference table; they provided comprehensive light with minimal shadows. Wall-mounted brass and candle-like lights added to the warmth and splendor of the room; spotlights illuminated the portraits of Dwight Eisenhower and Abraham Lincoln.

The president snapped out of his brief reverie. "We have a unique opportunity to capture al-Sammarri." His face shined. "A credible source just approached our Consulate in Erbil and has offered to exchange al-Sammarri for the multi-million dollar bounty." The president turned toward Jackson. "Fill us in Jim."

Jackson nodded. "Our regional security officer received a walk-in earlier today from a source named Jamal Abu al-Bayd; he's the most trusted confidante of Hassan Khalil Hussein, al-Sammarri's chief of security." He paused, glancing over his right shoulder toward his Assistant Secretary for Diplomatic Security for confirmation. "Al-Sammarri has been suffering from organ damage ever since Iraqi bombs targeted him in Qaim in 2014. His number two man, Muhammad Ibrahim, had been treating him until now. The word is the ISIS leader's condition is dire."

Marsha Larson, the Director for National Intelligence, chimed in, "his condition is terminal. We have both human and signal's intelligence that confirms he's suffering from a severe kidney illness. Our analysts have corroborated this information."

Jackson's eyes glimmered. "Ibrahim announced he couldn't do anything more for him and that the sheikh required emergency surgery. He further informed the council that al-Sammarri must travel to Syria. Hassan then volunteered to take the leader to Syria using a low-profile motorcade. This will allow him to avoid detection from our satellites, drones, and reconnaissance aircraft. The council unanimously agreed with him to use a small cadre of his elite guard."

"And why would a loyal bodyguard betray his boss?" The secretary of defense grumbled.

"If you permit me to finish, I'll explain." Jackson's muscles tensed as a vein in his temple pulsed.

"By all means Jim." The pentagon head motioned.

Jackson scratched his temple. "Hassan believes that al-Sammarri is impeding their cause, diverting critical resources to butcher non-conforming Muslims. The war on extremism has affected their communications and caused a decentralized command structure. The

Islamic State's long-term objectives are being supplanted by a series of violent acts. This undermines their long-range goals and objectives by hindering recruitment. Their decentralized command structure makes it impossible for them to deliver significant successive blows against the West."

Bill Singleton, the Director of the FBI, raised a finger. "Jim," he asked, "what evidence do you have that al-Bayd is telling the truth and that he'll turn over al-Sammarri?"

Jackson raised an eyebrow. An FBI polygrapher conducted the test. "Bill, give me a minute to finish. Hassan will give up al-Sammarri for ten million dollars just south of the Sinjar Mountains. The FBI and CIA behavioral experts and polygraphers deemed al-Bayd credible."

Rising in his seat, the CIA director broke his silence. "So we're going to pay a terrorist ten million dollars for betraying his boss. And we'll trust that he'll use that money for good. He might instead purchase some weapon of mass destruction from the North Koreans, Iranians, or former Soviet republics."

The chief spook shook his head. "We've ample intelligence that ISIS is still trying to get a nuclear or chemical weapon to attack America. I can hear the news now. The US government assists ISIS with acquiring an atomic weapon. Talk about a major catastrophe. It was bad enough when the news media accused us of supplying man-portable missiles to Syrian opposition groups. Imagine the field day the press will have with this one when the word gets out?"

The president raised his hands. "I appreciate your concerns. However, we must show the world and the American people that we're winning against the extremists and that we'll hunt down our enemies, no matter how desolate, remote, or hostile the area. Our resolve must be absolute; we cannot waver in the face of adversity. Now, the intelligence is both clear and persuasive; we must take this opportunity to grab al-Sammarri. The question remains, how do we safely negotiate this exchange and who'll undertake the critical mission?"

"I can muster one-hundred agents from my National Security Division and elite Hostage Rescue Team. They can be there in two days to carry out this mission." Singleton scanned the room.

The CIA director shook his head. "We don't need a large operation to conduct this covert action. This might scare him off. We can't afford to blunder this rare opportunity. I suggest we mobilize my ground branch to conduct the exchange. They're already in theater and can travel from Baghdad to Erbil in four hours. Many are familiar with the terrain and some speak Arabic."

Jackson cleared his throat. "Hassan stressed that he'll only meet with our regional security officer, as he wants to deal with a familiar face. Hence, DS is the logical choice given their rapid deployment capability, jurisdiction over the Reward for Justice Program, vast overseas experience, and tactical expertise. Having trained with America's elite federal and military operational units, they're the best kept secret in our government."

Jackson turned to his Assistant Secretary of State for Diplomatic Security for support. Catherine Chen, a twenty-eight-year veteran with DS, had been at the helm of the service for two years. She glanced at the president, while raising herself in his chair.

"I recommend we send two of my protective intelligence investigations agents, along with six members of our mobile security deployments, to protect the group and make the exchange. As you may recall, DS agents did an extraordinary job in finding and capturing Ramzi Yousef, the mastermind behind the first attack on the World Trade Center. They interviewed the confidential source, coordinated with Pakistani security forces, and conducted surveillance; the DS agents then followed the security forces into the residence and identified Yousef. DS is familiar with Iraq from their endless deployments to the critical threat post. My agents are packed, have visas and flight reservations, and can be on the ground in less than twenty-four hours. The reality is that DS will get the job done capably and with a small signature."

Jackson eyed his colleagues. The CIA and FBI directors grimaced and dipped their heads, but the rest nodded in agreement. Jackson desired a unanimous vote; he recognized it would be problematic to get the two eight-hundred pound guerrillas on board. Each of them would want to claim success for such a high-profile operation.

Turning to the FBI director, Jackson rubbed his chin and motioned with his right hand. "Bill, if you have another recommendation or course of action, then let's hear it."

Singleton pondered Jackson's relationship with the president. "The FBI is the premiere federal law enforcement agency and has investigative jurisdiction over this matter. When al-Sammarri is taken into custody, we'll arrest him for the heinous terrorism acts he committed. The FBI has the criminal case on al-Sammarri, and we must bring him to justice."

"Your points are valid, Bill. I think the FBI should play a major role. However, I'd like to hear from the director of the CIA before we decide." Jackson pivoted in his seat, making strong eye contact with the CIA's top spook.

Patrick O'Malley, a decorated CIA veteran, was known for his extraordinary ability to plan and execute counterinsurgency operations. Even thirty-plus years later, many of his operations remained classified because of their political sensitivities. Following his CIA career, O'Malley ran for Congress and trounced his opponent in his southern Virginia district. He later ran for the Senate on a platform of family values and homeland security, and defeated his opponent. After a decade on the Senate Intelligence Committee, the president tapped him to be his CIA director.

O'Malley's eyes glimmered. "The CIA can handle this mission; however, we must avoid exposing our clandestine people as witnesses in a showcase trial. Therefore, I'd like to volunteer all the resources of my agency in a support capacity."

"That's a very generous offer, Pat." Jackson gave his CIA colleague a crisp nod.

Pressed for time, the president had a multilateral conference to discuss the North Korean nuclear threat. "Gentlemen, DS will meet with Hassan to exchange ten million dollars for al-Sammarri. The FBI will send their plane and a small team to take possession of the ISIS head at the airport in Kirkuk, Erbil, or Baghdad. After making the exchange, DS will give al-Sammarri to the FBI planeside. CIA will provide intelligence support for the entire operation, including the requisite satellite imagery."

The president scanned his advisors with a quick glance to ensure their understanding. He stood up from his chair to signal the meeting's conclusion. "Failure isn't an option. We must hand ISIS another significant blow. We'll win this war on extremism. Let's get the government's business done. Have a good day."

The National Security Council rose to their feet as the president exited. They would now execute his wishes.

CHAPTER 3: The Hazing

Special Agent Matt James was not a pedestrian man by nature. He followed in his uncle's footsteps and joined Diplomatic Security not only for the chance to serve his country but also for the unique adventure and danger that accompanied the job. Throughout his fourteen-year career, his choice of assignments always took him to the world's most dangerous flashpoints. Given his powerful sense of patriotism, or perhaps his need to prove himself, James thrived in chaotic environments. His continued quest for non-stop thrills and full-blown adrenaline rushes drove him to bid on, and later be assigned to, DS' elite Mobile Security Deployments (MSD) office. Although the office itself functioned overtly, it often operated covertly to protect US diplomats and facilities worldwide. Few, even within the inner circle of government, knew of the office's existence.

Rumored to be some of the best-trained and multifaceted government operators, MSD agents perform anti-terrorist training, emergency overseas security support, and enhanced protection for high threat dignitaries. Their adaptability, talents, cross-training, and physical prowess permitted them to conquer missions that most deemed impossible. James possessed all the attributes, and then some. A natural leader, he not only looked the part but also could perform in any situation. The tougher the circumstances, the more he liked it.

At just over six feet tall, his medium build supported strong, muscular shoulders. His black hair and brown, elliptically shaped eyes hinted at his ethnic origin: he was half-Chinese. A natural all-around athlete in his youth, he studied hard in school and earned a scholarship to Stanford. His diligence, motivation and discipline made him a two-time All-American in wrestling. It also earned him a teaching assistantship at Washington State University, where his scholarly efforts netted him a Master's degree in Political Science in only one year.

Life presented the industrious James many opportunities, including a generous Air Force proposition to fly fighters. Declining flight school and his professor's plea to complete a doctoral program, he became a DS special agent. He had been drawn to this profession since childhood and wanted to contribute to the American way of life while providing for the national security of the country he revered. James liked to live life on the edge. The more dangerous, the better he liked it, and today's circumstances would prove his mettle.

Enduring another rough and sleepless night in his damp, cold, three-by-three concrete cell, his lower back ached. The buzz of an approaching helicopter supplanted the constant shrill of Arabic music blasted into his cell. He had somehow slept for twenty minutes, despite the noise tactics used to disorient him. Food and sleep deprivation further withered his battered and fatigued body. James, now in his third day of captivity, dreaded his captors' looming arrival with their customary wake-up call, such as repeated beatings, water-boarding, and endless questioning about the purpose of his recent mission to Afghanistan. As the sound of crunching gravel revealed their imminent arrival, he wiped the soot from his brow and contemplated the fate of his five teammates. James knew everyone had a breaking point; he remained determined that his breaking point wouldn't come today, despite the cruel torture they inflicted on him.

James' current predicament puzzled him. His gut churned as he contemplated his capture by Taliban forces while conducting area familiarization in the highlands. He despised the group's brutal tactics and controlled his impulse to fight back, which spared their lives for the moment.

James' eyes snapped open as he envisioned death as a better alternative. In the last fifty hours, he had been pissed on, beaten, interrogated, and imprisoned in a box befitting for a Rottweiler. Yet, he remained undaunted by his cramped concrete windowless cell; he quavered while slipping his wrists from the binding ropes to remove his cloth hood. He gasped for fresh air. His concentration waned from a lack of sleep and hunger. Random indentations on the walls now revealed familiar family figures. He snapped his head back and forth, blinking to shake this phenomenon. Closing his eyes and breathing deeply, his mind traveled back in time. The sun's rays warmed his face as the fresh mountain air invigorated him. The crystal clear water mirrored the bluest skies imaginable. A three-ton glacier flowed into the lake, reflecting the pureness and freshness of the area. The remote eight-acre lake in the Cascade Mountains remained unspoiled by time. He drew an incredible amount of strength and solitude from this visual imprint.

Crunching gravel broke his trance as one of his captors neared his cell; he dreaded the squeaking of a rusty door hinge. He struggled to get his hood back on when his wooden door flew open. Ordered out of his cell, he absorbed the customary stroke to his head for not moving fast enough.

"What are you doing?" The man bared his teeth. "Idiot, you'll pay for your disobedience." The sweaty hand of a sasquatch-sized man grasped his throat. He struggled to catch his breath, as his body skidded from his cell.

"Get up, you American pig. Today, we have a special treat for you. You'll provide us the correct answers or your friends will die." Another man bounded his wrists with heavy-duty rope. Dragging him by his neck, the guards crossed a courtyard. The fresh, damp air revived him. Its thickness reflected a higher elevation. As they entered a dingy and dank room, his heart pounded. His hood obscured his vision as he gasped for air.

"Sit down." The man slapped James' temple region. Once seated, another captor removed his hood and pointed at one of his teammates.

"Look at her. Unless you cooperate, she'll be killed." James glanced at Jeanna; her sallow look and comatose eyes showed the onset of shock. He pondered their captor's abuse. Even the toughest person could be broken. James wondered when his time would come. A slap across his face jarred him from his reverie.

"Look at me when I'm talking. Now, what are you doing in my country?"

James suspected loose lips as his captors appeared to be seeking corroboration. He stood by his original cover story. "We're agriculture specialists here to conduct soil analysis to determine the best agricultural crops for this environment."

James leaned back as his face tightened. A slap across his cheek jolted him awake. Pain radiated from the front of his jaw to just beneath his ear.

His captor nodded. "Tough guy. We already know what grows well here. The poppy plant brings us unimaginable wealth and poisons your American streets." He turned toward his accomplice and gave a simple nod. Abdullah, his chubby companion, struck Jeanna with an open hand across her face. She let out a plaintive grunt that brought an immediate grin from her captors.

"Now, I'm going to ask you one last time. If you don't tell me the truth, then she'll die. What were you doing in our territory?" The man said, thumping James' chest with his fingers.

James pondered the guard's threat. "I was analyzing some soil samples to determine what crops would produce a high yield in this climate." He glared at his captor before glancing down at the floor.

The man scratched his cheek. "Okay, some people have to learn the hard way." He flicked his wrist at Abdullah. "Take her out back and shoot her." Jeanna's face whitened as the terrorist lifted her into a stance.

Suddenly, from outside the door, a shot rang out.

James sprung up as his eyes bulged, but a kick to his chest propelled him backwards onto the floor.

The guard snorted. "You thought we were bluffing? Get up! I'll tell you when you can rest. Now, I'll ask you once again. What were you and the other Americans doing out in these mountains?"

He cleared the top of his throat. "I already told you. My team and I..."

Abdullah sank a powerful uppercut into his stomach, causing him to double over. James gasped for air. Doubts of his invincibility raced through his head as a backhand brought him back to reality.

Abdullah's patience disappeared as his face flushed. He drew a revolver from his belt and flicked open the cylinder. "Ok American scum, let's test your nerve." Abdullah emptied the chambers, inserted a round, and spun the cylinder before whipping it shut. Waving the revolver in the agent's face, Abdullah spit on him and pushed the muzzle into James' temple. "I'll only ask you one more time. What were you doing in these mountains?"

The MSD leader hesitated before answering. "I was analyzing the soil..."

Click! The hammer fell forward as Abdullah squeezed the trigger. "Less than five more chances." He thrust the revolver's barrel back to James' head.

The door slammed open, interrupting the interrogation. James focused on the approaching man. His clean-shaven head and American clothes reflected a misplaced person. The agent stared through the approaching man.

"Stand down. I'm Captain Smith of the US Army's Special Warfare Center. This SERE (Survival, Evasion, Resistance, Escape) exercise is over now. You have an urgent call from your chief in DC." The captain handed James a cellular telephone, turned, and pulled aside his men to conduct a quick debriefing of the exercise.

It was familiar news that James had heard countless other times. It routinely involved situations that would draw him to the most dangerous and remote parts of the world. He would catch the first available flight back to DC for immediate deployment.

CHAPTER 4: High Stakes

DSS Headquarters, Rosslyn, Virginia

James' eyes panned the director's conference room; its sterile ambiance puzzled him. The twenty-by-fourteen square foot room supported a rectangular walnut table centered in the middle. Its fifteen-person capacity led to its limited use. The director's adjacent office could house as many guests while providing them comfortable seating and a panoramic view of the Potomac, Georgetown, the Kennedy Center, the Washington Monument, and the Lincoln and Jefferson Memorial. His selection of the conference room showed the situation's gravity and an assignment out of the ordinary.

The unadorned walls of the room held a gold inscription that read: "Only with great sacrifice and commitment come significant and worthwhile gains." The director cited the quote during graduation ceremonies for new agents. Photographs of the president, the vice president, and the secretary of state appeared centered on the opposite wall. James snorted, rousing his teammates from their distant stares. The statement resonated, but given the severity of the situation, he found the quote too close to home. His guts twisted as he pondered their summoning downtown to meet with the hierarchy's elite.

The studied solemnity of the six agents saturated the room. James handpicked his team because of the mission's criticality, which violated standard protocol. Preoccupied about the classified briefing, he wiped his sweaty palms on his pants while fidgeting in his chair.

James surveyed his team, whose skills and character complemented one another. He selected Dutch Wagner to be his second in command. Wagner remained a devout bachelor who thrived on travel, adventure, and especially women. If you believed his colorful stories, his escapades could have exhausted a SEAL platoon on vacation in Bogota. A former Marine officer, Wagner's straightforwardness sometimes clashed with a diplomat's patience and sensitivity. He wasn't at all averse to telling the truth, even if it defied the hierarchy's wishes. James valued his directness, along with his technical capabilities and marksmanship. Wagner had carried out other high stakes missions and done it flawlessly.

George Atwell, battle proven and articulate, sat to his immediate right. He had known Atwell for over fourteen years. They had attended basic special agent training together at the Federal Law Enforcement Training Center in Brunswick, Georgia. Atwell and James had ruled both the classroom and the nightlife on nearby St. Simon's Island. James often battled Atwell for top academic honors in the classroom, surprising Atwell on the second legal exam. James scored ninety-eight out of one-hundred, beating him by two points. This achievement resonated with the younger agent, given Atwell's law background and his top honors in class.

A former prosecuting attorney, Atwell possessed impressive oratory skills, a supercomputer's logic, and Winston Churchill's wit. These three attributes earned him the highest conviction rate in the state. It also earned the respect of defense attorneys, politicians, and the entire police apparatus. Had he continued on this career path, he would have been a Senator by now. He longed for greater challenges than verbal jousting with less than worthy adversaries. Determined to use his military roots, legal background, and diplomatic prowess, he had established, through studied research, that few jobs could provide a more unique challenge than Diplomatic Security, which, into the bargain, offered the bonus of serving in exotic and dangerous places around the world.

Rounding out his team, he selected Dave Steele, Jessica White, and Doug Smith; all equipped with exceptional skills, technical knowledge, and physical conditioning, not to mention their uniformly impressive records. Among them, they had earned two awards for heroism, ten superior honor awards, and six meritorious honor awards. They had all gone to hell-and-back in such places as Somalia, Bosnia, Lebanon, Libya, Pakistan,

Afghanistan, and Iraq. They had proven themselves against Muslim extremists and other terrorists around the world.

James recognized these agents as the best, brightest, and most dedicated of all the agents in the service. If any team could accomplish the mission, it would be this group of veterans; they would push themselves to their physical limits and, if necessary, die trying to complete the mission. They stood as modern day Samurai warriors whose strict code of conduct defined their own brand of extremism. But it made sense. It would take this rare breed of individual to beat the most dedicated of the Islamic extremists.

The conference door swung open and interrupted James' reflections. James and his team snapped to attention as the Assistant Secretary (A/S) of State for Diplomatic Security entered the room. She held the diplomatic rank of minister-counselor and certainly looked the part. At a little over five feet, six inches tall, Assistant Secretary Catherine Chen stood an impressive figure; she projected both a politician's smooth demeanor and the confidence of a four-star general. The DSS director, the assistant director for High Threat Programs, and the deputy national security advisor flanked her. This was a high-powered group indeed. This, James concluded, has to be big time serious.

"Gentlemen and lady," said Chen, "You're in luck." She smiled thinly. "Though I'm not sure whether it's good or bad luck. It's definitely your call. Anyway, you've been handpicked for the mission of a lifetime. What we say here stays here. Damn few people outside this room know about it."

James nodded. "Understood."

Chen caressed her chin. "We believe that an individual in ISIS will exchange Ibrahim al-Sammarri for the reward money of ten million dollars. The exchange will take place in three days near the Syrian and Iraqi border on Mount Sinjar. You'll escort the RSO, two PII agents, and ten million dollars to the exchange site and trade the money for al-Sammarri."

"Ms. Chen, are we confident of the informant's credibility? I'd hate to walk into a trap," said Wagner, frowning.

"The walk-in source was deemed completely truthful on the polygraph." Chen's eyes widened. "I shouldn't steal I-T-A's (Intelligence and Threat Analysis) thunder, so I'll let John brief you."

ITA Director John White flicked a toggle switch, which turned off the lights. He pushed two buttons and powered up his computer and monitor.

He summarized al-Sammarri's background and his rise to power in the ISIS organization. A PowerPoint slide depicted the ISIS head in Iraq delivering a speech to his followers.

White cleared his throat with one long, hoarse growl. "As you're aware, al-Sammarri has focused his campaign against Syria, Iraq, America, the UK, and other allies. Lately, this agenda has morphed; it now includes any country that doesn't support his cause or provides the US with any help. There's no mistake about it. This guy's a textbook megalomaniac."

White flashed a series of slides showing torture and crucifixions, including the beheading of a journalist.

"Even with satellite imagery, reconnaissance aircraft, and state-of-the-art drones," White went on, "the intelligence community could not get a lock on his location until now." White nodded. "Our source has pinned down al-Sammarri to an area in Northern Iraq. Now, this strategic ISIS base would be extremely difficult to assault. Fortunately, our source will deliver al-Sammarri to us near the town of Sinjar in Iraq under the guise of seeking treatment."

Quiet until now, Atwell said, "I know we can handle our end of the deal. However, I don't get ISIS freely handing over their respected leader without a nasty fight. He's a true iconic figure." His face turned serious.

"I can understand your reservations," said White. "According to our source, Sheikh al-Sammarri needs urgent medical treatment because of a kidney ailment. His chief bodyguard, a legend amongst the troops, has convinced Islamic State's twelve-member council that the safest method of transporting the sheikh to a hospital is a low visibility motorcade. In this fashion, he has selected eight of his most trusted fighters to accompany him on this mission. Hassan Hussein, al-Sammarri's head bodyguard, sent his most-trusted warrior to broker the exchange. He'll lead their side to ensure a safe and timely transfer."

"Now, we don't expect you guys to assume this is a routine transfer. You should take all necessary precautions to protect yourselves, our personnel, and the reward money. Remember, the source is deemed credible and exhibited no signs of deception on the polygraph test."

"Do you want us to arrest them during the transfer?" James' eyes widened.

"Definitely not. We must keep our word if our rewards program is to maintain its integrity. So, we'll transfer the money to them for al-Sammarri, as promised."

The room became unnervingly quiet. White clicked his remote control and advanced his presentation to the last PowerPoint slide. It showed innocent men, women, and children strewn across the road. ISIS has threatened to turn our lands red with American blood. We must capture or kill al-Sammarri before ISIS carries out something larger than nine-eleven.

"This information is a matter of national security. It's not to leave this room." White peered at each agent.

The assistant secretary stood up and turned to her team. "The capture of al-Sammarri will deliver a significant blow to ISIS and it will be a key victory for the president's war on extremism. In the history of DS, this is our greatest mission. Good luck!" Chen waltzed out of the conference room.

CHAPTER 5: Reflections

James directed his team to recheck their equipment as they loaded it into three dark-blue Chevrolet Suburbans. Each rectangular gray hard case weighed seventy pounds. Smith and Steele hurled them into the well of the car. Careful to protect the sensitive gear, White retrieved the cases and guided them to their final resting spot within the vehicle, stacking them on one another. The cases contained body armor, thermal imagers, ballistic helmets, night vision goggles, assault rifles, and other essential gear. Each team member carried two of these portable tactical cases besides their personal suitcase; they required an additional vehicle just to carry their collective load.

James counted off the team equipment as it passed him. He verified their essential gear, prompting him to recall one of his father's many pithy expressions. He had learned countless lessons from his father during his formative years, such as "you have to pay the price, the wise man learns from other's mistakes, the pressure comes from within, and a person's character can be measured by his heart and head." His father had a saying for every situation in life. None of these truisms was as important to the task ahead as: "you need the right tools to do the job correctly." This advice could apply to everything in life, and he diligently applied it to all his favorite pastimes. James enjoyed woodworking, fishing, hiking, rock climbing, biking, golfing, or, in this case, hunting Islamic extremists.

The damp cloudy day seemed typical for the fall, as children prepared their Halloween costumes for a chance at the sugar-rush Olympics and a trip to the dentist. The air's crispness and thickness resembled morning fog blowing off the ocean. James inhaled the fresh air. He knew that in a day he'd be halfway around the world breathing dust while avoiding the heat. The blazing Iraqi sun could turn one's face lobster-pink in a mere thirty minutes. He recalled his shoe's soles melting when he stood too long on the Baghdad International Airport tarmac.

The light traffic surprised the team as they drove the forty-minute journey to Andrews Air Force Base. They avoided the beltway rush hour and drove east on Route 66 through the nation's capital. James considered the gravity of the mission and brushed aside any doubts as they drove over the Roosevelt Bridge. He eyed the passing parade of monuments as goose bumps peppered his body. Never, he vowed, would he take American exceptionalism, values, and democracy for granted. His work flew him to over seventy countries on five continents and he had witnessed too much carnage, mayhem, human rights violations, and other atrocities. Sentiment aside, he had never lost his visceral appreciation for the country he had chosen to serve.

"Are you alright?" Wagner gripped him on his forearm.

James shrugged. "I was just thinking about the job," he said. "Our ancestors set the bar pretty high, didn't they?"

"What the hell are you saying?" Wagner shook his head. "Don't get soft on me now."

"That's the yin and yang of life." James gave a grave expression.

"You sound like a fortune cookie." Wagner scratched his temple.

He glanced at his friend. "Why did you abandon the Marine Corps for life in the Foreign Service? You could've been a warrior, commanding valiant troops into battle."

The deputy team leader rubbed his temple. "I guess I saw one too many of my guys die before their time, despite my teachings."

"You see Dutch, all of us get sentimental."

"You're a warrior poet." Wagner snickered.

"That I am, Dutch."

The rest of the drive remained quiet as the agents contemplated their mission. James arranged for a military police escort to guide them to their staging area, given the base's vastness and classified operations. The team dropped their gear off for inspection and loading, while James consulted with base officials. They hopped a shuttle to the FBI's jet positioned about five-hundred yards down the field.

James spotted Roger Bishop and Michael Clark on the tarmac next to the staircase as they walked toward the forty-person passenger jet. Bishop had found a home for himself in the office of protective intelligence investigations, converting to Civil Service to avoid the mandatory overseas requirement that DS agents undertook every six years. His wife enjoyed a magnificent job on the Hill; they valued keeping the family together rather than to deploy every six years to satisfy a service requirement. Yet, this compromise furthered his career aspirations while providing continuity and historical knowledge to the office.

In his second year, Clark enjoyed the travel, training, and deployments that came with the job. Clark tapped knuckles with James and directed him up the stairway of the awaiting FBI jet. James rubbed the back of his neck as his eyes wandered the tarmac; he knew the plane came with a steep price, including a ten-person FBI team would accompany the jet in order to take immediate custody of al-Sammarri once James' team had nailed him.

James ignored the curious stares from the FBI agents as he strolled down the aisle. Most of them had limited knowledge of DS' role as shields for US personnel and facilities. He slid into a window seat near the tail of the jet with his team surrounding him. Once seated, the aircraft taxied down the runway and lifted off into the night sky.

The seventeen-hour flight to Iraq passed quickly for the seasoned agent. James summoned his team to a small conference table following their refueling in Germany. He directed their attention to the latest overhead imagery of the Sinjar Pass displayed on his laptop. The team studied the imagery's black contour lines intersecting with a supplementary contour line.

Wagner's fingers swept over the screen. "This represents a flat area near a ridge and is flanked by a steep peak. He pointed to the screen at a dirt road with a gully to the left side. Excellent choice of a defensive position, Matt." Wagner nodded.

"Thanks Dutch. I knew you'd appreciate the exchange point selection." James removed several photographs of Hassan and al-Bayd and placed them on the table. "Look at these two terrorists and don't underestimate them.

They're dangerous. We must maintain the tactical advantage and be ready for a fluid and dynamic encounter."

After briefing his team twice, James slugged down five milligrams of Melatonin and drifted off into a deep slumber, despite his insomnia and the heavy turbulence the jet encountered.

Atwell glanced at James, chuckled, and turned up the volume on his phone. He rejoined his music in the middle of Beethoven's Fifth. Atwell, aka "the Doc" to his teammates, cleared his mind with music to achieve greater focus. The Doc enriched the team with his medical knowledge and real-life experience. He hoped the team wouldn't require his expertise.

Hearing the music rattle through Atwell's headphones, James awoke as the plane descended into Baghdad, corkscrewing downward to minimize its profile into the active conflict zone. Clark glanced over at James, lifted two medium-sized suitcases, and tossed one up onto the table and snapped it open. They stared in awe at the five million dollars in hard currency.

"It's a small price to pay for al-Sammarri's head, don't you think?" Clark grinned.

"Imagine the euphoria that will fill the streets when the president announces the apprehension of the world's most dangerous terrorist." James picked up and riffled through a stack of bills.

"It will reassure America that all the commitment and expense of our wars is worth it." Clark rubbed his shoe against the floor.

James pondered Hassan's intended use of the cash and prayed that greed and self-indulgence would get the best of him. Hassan's larger strategic objectives troubled him, and he recognized that the hardcore terrorist's plans would radically affect America, one way or the other.

CHAPTER 6: Deadly Deception

Northeastern Syria

The frigid air whistled through the chasm, melding howling winds with bone chilling temperatures. Hassan remained unfazed as he contemplated his plan; a scheme he contrived following al-Sammarri's brush with death while rushing to forge a new Islamic State. He despised the leader for those predictable habits, which put so many of his followers at risk. After his near death experience, al-Sammarri bolstered his protective arm to ensure his own survival.

The diversion of sparse warriors off the battlefield troubled him. Al-Sammarri had ordered martyrdom operations across the region. Hassan doubted the ISIS head would step down or personally carryout a suicide operation. Al-Sammarri's death would eclipse his life by rallying and banding the Muslim world together. It would skyrocket funding while encouraging millions of Muslims to join the jihad.

His confidence skyrocketed as he recalled al-Sammarri's passionate address to his troops before the battle of Fallujah, in which the sheik pounded home the mantra that no individual surpassed the cause. Only by our concentrated efforts and Allah's wisdom can we defeat our enemy, he intoned. Hassan embraced those words and remained resolute in his conviction to slaughter the infidels in their homeland. His restoration of his group's prestige appeared imminent.

Hassan scanned the horizon with the keen eye of a falcon hunting its prey. He lifted his hand-held radio to his cheek. Depressing the talk button, he called his lookout on a nearby ridge overlooking the valley.

"Nubius one, Nubius one, this is Cheetah. I need an update."

The guard responded instantly. "Cheetah, this is Nubius one. The skies are clear and the ground is still."

"Copy that. Nubius two, Nubius two, what's your situation?" Hassan signaled his driver to hold his position.

Static filled the airwaves for a second. "Cheetah from Nubius two, the backyard is quiet and the birds are singing."

Hassan salivated as his eyes sparkled; his ascension to the ISIS throne appeared imminent. His lookouts had confirmed sparse traffic conditions on his primary and secondary routes, and then cryptically relayed the lack of Kurdish forces and US and coalition aircraft in the area. He radioed for his driver to reposition his vehicle. As the Land Cruiser crept toward him, he smiled at his plan's simplicity. He appreciated the vehicle's reliability and heavy use by the Non-Government Organizations (NGOs) that frequented the area; NGOs brought food, clothing, and other relief to the beleaguered populace. Hassan exploited America's fear of collateral civilian damage, recognizing that a pilot's uncertainty about a potential target could delay a missile strike. These delays would enhance his survivability while tentative pilots radioed their command on NGO activity in the area.

Leaning on his personal assistant, al-Sammarri emerged from the cave walking next to Ibrahim. The two men remained apart from one another because of the necessity of splitting their power base. They couldn't risk coalition forces neutralizing its chief architects with a single blow to further unravel the organization. Hassan understood al-Qaeda's fracturing caused affiliate groups to splinter off to espouse their own principles. Similarly, ISIS' ultra-extreme interpretation of the Koran and its brutality reduced financing and their recruitment of moderate Muslims. His plan to create an enduring caliphate required the involvement of the Muslim masses.

As the sheikh approached the idling vehicle, council members emerged from their caves to encircle their revered leader. Al-Sammarri interrupted his conversation with Ibrahim to survey his men. Many served alongside him, battling the Americans in Iraq. Others had joined him from Baghdad, where they had studied the Koran together in various mosques. Some fought together with him to secure territory in Syria and Iraq to form an Islamic State.

Al-Sammarri gathered his thoughts. "My fellow warriors, our journey to free our Holy Land from the Crusaders began many years ago. The infidels have shown throughout history that they'll destroy, conquer, and plunder our land and resources. They constantly search for opportunities to expand their sphere of influence and their military bases to dominate the world."

He caught his deputy's eye before continuing. "America operates globally with impunity, committing atrocities wherever it pleases. We've seen them spill Muslim blood in Lebanon, Somalia, Pakistan, Afghanistan, Yemen, and Iraq. They're threatening Syria and Iran with targeted strikes, if they don't abandon their nuclear ambitions."

Coughing, he continued. "The Americans preach that they're spreading democracy to empower the people. They're spreading the seeds that corrupt the soul and tempt our people to abandon Allah's way. Not to mention that they dishonor governments with their evil ways and promises of economic rewards. America is the Great Satan; they won't stop until they control the world, ravage its riches, and enslave our people to their ways. They don't want the Muslim world to succeed economically or spiritually."

The ISIS leader's voice took on a sharper edge. "And they've repeatedly shown their dishonesty, as they only back convenient democracy. Just look at the democratically elected Hamas government that came to power in a landslide election. The Americans pushed for democratic elections. When our Palestinian brothers were victorious, they abandoned them and withdrew their support. The Israelis continue to repress and slaughter our Palestinian brothers. The Americans arm the Israelis, who unleash their destructive weapons on innocent civilians. American aircraft patrol Palestinian airspace and rain down their evil cargos of missiles and smart bombs. The Israelis avoid peace and continue to build on Palestinian land, so they control all territorial access. I ask you, what kind of freedom is this? The Crusaders lie and deceive, particularly in their blind support for Israel. They provide billions of dollars and endless military aid to ensure their existence and power over the Palestinians. This is the type of democracy they want for us."

Al-Sammarri extended both arms - palms up and fingers extended - toward his council, and went on, as his voice remained resolute. "If you analyze all the UN resolutions calling for Israel to abandon its attacks on the Palestinians, withdraw from its lands, and permit the opening of its seaports and airport, you'll see that the Americans veto anything that would benefit the Palestinians and disrupt Israel's control over them. These endless atrocities committed against our Palestinian brothers must be stopped. It's our sacred responsibility to protect the Holy Land and save our brothers from annihilation. If we cannot protect Allah's teachings, then we'll lose to the Americans and fail Allah. This cannot happen. We must fight to the end and be victorious."

Hassan nodded, recognizing the infidels must be defeated. He found al-Sammarri's delivery to the infidels he despises ironic; the great Islamic State leader would also become the martyr who would propel his plan into action. The Israelis and the Americans would be hit in a single devastating blow. With Allah's help, he planned to wipe billions of infidels from the planet.

Abruptly, al-Sammarri sagged, his voice faltering. Hassan lunged forward and caught the man before he hit the ground.

"We must get him emergency medical treatment or he'll die." Hassan said, struggling to raise a flimsy al-Sammarri to an upright position.

"Thank you, my good friend." Al-Sammarri rasped as he regained his composure.

Clinging to his chief bodyguard, al-Sammarri's eyes winced as he stood and straightened his posture.

"Noble warriors, if something should happen to me, then brother Ibrahim will lead our fight against the Americans. Allah is with you."

Hassan placed his right hand in between the sheikh's shoulder blades to usher him toward the car. "We must go now." He scanned the area. "We can't risk your safety here in the open any longer. The enemy may be near."

"Wait, a second." Al-Sammarri rasped.

Hassan froze as the leader straightened his hunched posture. He admired his courage.

Al-Sammarri extended his arms out and fraily embraced Ibrahim with a lighthearted hug. He valued their inseparable friendship and his deputy's service, loyalty, and wisdom. He attributed much of their advancement to his close confidant and the man standing beside him. Their symbiotic relationship forged a formidable force that their enemies feared, including the most powerful nation on earth. His vision and Ibrahim's operational planning had dealt America a series of devastating blows.

"My friend, we've endured so much together." Al-Sammarri winced as he attempted to clutch his friend tighter, pain radiating from his left side.

Ibrahim squeezed the fragile leader. "Your vision has rallied the masses and created an Islamic State while advancing our global jihad."

"Allah has led us on this monumental journey. Only through his great wisdom and guidance have we succeeded." Al-Sammarri released his clasp and leaned back, standing upright so he could read his deputy's eyes. The eyes held the soul's secrets. He often allowed others to read his resolute eyes to grasp his commitment to the war.

Ibrahim smiled wryly, agreeing with his leader. "Allah is great and all knowing. Praise be to Allah." The deputy remained more a realist than his friend and appreciated the spiritual and emotional value of Allah. He valued Allah's prodigious ability to attract hordes of followers who would do anything in his name.

The frail sheikh nodded. "Allah's way is our way. His quest is our cause. It's through his great strength that we'll triumph over the Great Satan. America will inevitably fall with each successful battle we wage on them."

The sheikh flipped his wrist toward his bodyguard. "Hassan is the loyal warrior. You must call upon him to mount our greatest attacks on the infidels. If I'm captured or die, promote him to be your deputy and chief strategist. As the head of your international operations, he'll deliver you glorious victories."

The leader's sudden recognition flabbergasted him. It seemed like an odd time for al-Sammarri to promote him to lead the war on the West. The sheikh had never expressed any sort of sentiment in the past. He had occasionally confided in him about some sensitive operations targeting western interests in Europe. This validated his work and expertise in military and protective security operations.

Hassan smiled halfheartedly, as feelings of guilt permeated his soul. "Your confidence in my abilities is appreciated. I won't let you down. I'll perform my extra duties to bring credit to the Islamic State and Allah."

"You'll do an outstanding job supporting our objectives. Aside from Ibrahim, you're my most trusted warrior." The leader's voice thundered as his entire council fixated on him.

Al-Sammarri turned to address his stoic disciples. "It's urgent you work together to fight our great enemy; our enemies are many. The Crusaders have corrupted many Arabic countries, their leaders, and people. We must expand our numbers by appealing to the wider masses."

Ibrahim echoed the ISIS head's guidance. "Absolutely."

"During my absence, Ibrahim will lead our holy war to purge the Crusaders from our land." Al-Sammarri eyed his council.

Hassan glanced at his watch before interrupting. "It's time to go if we're to make it to our destination before nightfall." He opened the rear door of the Land Cruiser, palming al-Sammarri's head to guide him into the car.

With al-Sammarri seated in the backseat, he slammed the door shut and hopped into the front passenger seat. He directed his security team to abandon their circular coverage around the Land Cruiser; they trotted back to their passenger truck, which would shadow them to their ultimate destination. Hassan had studied protective tactics over the years. He disguised his motorcade as two separate vehicles that were traveling in the same direction.

"Let's roll." Hassan pointed forward as al-Sammarri glanced out his window and waved to his council members who were trotting alongside the car; repeated bursts from their assault rifles muffled their steady "Allah Akbar" chants.

"Allah Akbar." Hassan said, stretching his neck. He pondered Allah's punishment for his betrayal of al-Sammarri, but he knew his actions would later be deemed justified for the greater good. This provided him little comfort.

CHAPTER 7: Crossfire

Near misses and dangers plagued the journey from Baghdad to the Sinjar Pass. However, it wasn't the terrorists that James and his team feared the most, but the local Iraqi drivers who either fancied a death wish or liked a friendly game of chicken with a worthy adversary. The road they now traversed had one of the highest traffic fatality rates anywhere in the world. Its pothole-filled roads, endless dust clouds, and aggressive drivers contributed to the phenomenon. Yet, those wacky, caffeine-enriched Iraqi wheelmen posed the greatest danger as they hogged the road and barreled down the middle of it with little regard for anyone else.

"Watch it, Dutch!" James pointed forward as Wagner rounded a blind corner and now headed straight toward a taxi van teeming with people.

"Hold on," Wagner said while steering hard to the right, narrowly missing a head-on collision with the van. His reflexes now put him on the side of the roadway, skidding on the soft sandy surface. He veered toward a guardrail-free edge and a three-hundred foot drop off. Wagner torqued the steering wheel in the skid's direction to avoid the cliff. The front driver's tire sank a foot before rebounding and ejecting its passengers into the ceiling. The pothole's jagged concrete edge pierced the front left tire.

Wagner snapped his head around and steered to the right to prevent the vehicle from spinning out of control. The car darted straight back onto the highway and the stream of traffic it accommodated. He stomped on the accelerator and steered between a taxi van and a sedan traveling in opposite directions.

Wagner disregarded the driver's indifference he just dodged, unfazed by their near miss. His eyes scanned forward while pondering his options as he headed toward a colossal tree. A three-hundred foot cliff sat to the left and a family of eight to the right. Wagner slammed down on his brakes just prior to the point of locking them up. His threshold breaking technique mimicked the work of an on-board computer system and modern vehicle's antilock braking systems. He then yanked the steering wheel to the left, putting the vehicle into a controlled spin. Screeching to a stop, they had avoided the tree, the family, and the drop-off.

Atwell patted him on the back. "That was fun. With your skills, you could hire on as a local taxi driver."

James felt the ground tremor and leaned back in his seat. "Nobody move! We're not clear yet."

"Can't we catch a break?" Wagner said as he felt the right rear wheel teeter. The loose rock underneath the wheel gave way and plunged to the ground far below.

James' hand edged down to the vehicle's car radio to depress the push-to-talk button without raising the microphone. "Smith, Smith, this is James. Get up here now. Our car's on the right-hand side of the road and we're about to go over a cliff."

"Copy that, James. We'll be there in a minute," said Smith, instructing Steele to punch it. Steele stomped on the gas pedal and sped up the fully armored Suburban to seventy miles per hour. The vehicle shuddered given the poor road conditions, and an engine handicapped by impure locally purchased gasoline.

"Over there." Smith pointed to the right shoulder and side of the highway. Steele stomped down on the brakes while turning to the right; he slid to a stop while angling the car forty-five degrees toward the bumper of the disabled vehicle.

Smith vaulted from the car, dashed rearward, and opened the Suburban's tailgate. He grabbed a twenty-foot steel chain with an anchoring hook on each end and secured it to his vehicle before scuttling toward the teetering car. Centering the chain, Smith threaded it between the grill and the bumper, and looped it around the front, but before he could secure it, the car slid rearward. He slapped the hook around the chain, removing his hands a split-second before it snapped tight. Steele's eyes widened as he flung the gear selector into reverse and punched the accelerator, pitting gravity against horsepower.

The stir of a revving engine, sliding rock, and flinging gravel filled the air. As Steele unleashed the horses, the Suburban inched forward; gravity took a backseat to Steele's V-8 engine. After an initial struggle, his car pulled the near fallen vehicle to safety. Smith released the chain from each bumper while Steele flipped his hazard lights on. Steele then backed up his car about ten yards, parking it just off the highway.

The team scurried from their vehicles and gave each other high-fives, having defied death once again. James crept to the cliff's edge and gazed downward before looking skyward.

"I told you to ride with me." Steele said, grimacing.

Wagner shook his head. "And stroll down the road like an old geezer? Where's the fun in that? It's better to ride fast and take chances."

"Sure and end up at the belly of a ravine as a barbecue vulture snack. I won't always be there to save your sorry ass," said Steele, smirking.

As O'Reilly approached the group, James directed Atwell and Smith to assume front and rear protective positions. Wagner and the others broke out the jack and changed the flat tire.

"Let's get this vehicle back on the road. We've an important rendezvous and need to scout the area." James said, smiling and waving to the family of eight.

The team collaboratively changed the tire while protecting their teammates, vehicles, and technical equipment. Clark and Bishop hovered near their vehicle to safeguard the reward money. They valued their careers and disliked the prospect of filing a multi-million dollar loss on his government voucher.

Ten minutes later, the two cars left the sandy surface and scooted back into a blitz of traffic. Wagner raced to recoup lost time; his vehicle shuddered as it neared its physical limits. Steele blinked his eyes as he struggled to shadow the lead car. He employed the high-speed driving techniques he learned at Bill Scott Raceway in rural West Virginia. The Iraqi highway tested his abilities with its poor road conditions, steep grade, winding turns, and unfamiliarity.

James monitored the group's progress via the newly installed GPS tracking system. Within seventy-five minutes, the team neared the Syrian border and the dry, desolate Sinjar Pass. James verified their destination's GPS coordinates, scanning the area for a tactical advantage.

"Wagner, park the car near that fallen tree and position it for a quick get-away." James said, glancing at his watch.

In two seamless maneuvers, Wagner and Steele backed their cars against a steep rock incline and left about one-hundred and fifty feet between them to limit their chances of being neutralized by a single attack. James liked the enhanced visibility of the area. Its three-hundred and sixty degrees of coverage and alternate firing positions provided them a tactical advantage. He pointed up the rock incline. "Smith and Steele, get your butts up the hill to cover us."

A former Marine Corps sniper, Smith lugged his H&K G-3 rifle with four one-hundred round drums. Steele grabbed his Colt assault rifle and a set of high-powered binoculars. The two trotted to the hill while the others stood behind their vehicles' engine blocks. James cautioned them to drink plenty of water given their present elevation and the sun's intensity. Dehydration could wane their concentration, and he needed his team at their best. Downing a bottle of water and tossing its plastic carcass into the Suburban, James peeked at his watch. He expected Hassan's imminent arrival with al-Sammarri.

James scanned the area with an expressionless face, confident in the positioning of his agents. Bishop, Clark, and O'Reilly remained with him, as did Wagner, who kept the vehicle running. Atwell and White covered the middle ground and to the right. Shielded to the rear by the cliff, they concentrated on a mere one-hundred and eighty degrees of responsibility.

The lack of shade and jagged rocks made Steele and Smith's climb arduous. Their heavy, bullet-proof vests exacerbated their hike. Sweat poured from the two agents as they reached their perch.

Steele crumpled his nose. "What's that smell? You're going to give away our position."

Smith's nostrils flared. "You smell like crap and could make a pig run."

Time seemed frozen for the two, even though an hour had passed. The two agents wiped the salty perspiration from their foreheads before it could sting their eyes. Their panoramic view of the nearby peaks and valleys overshadowed their present hardship.

With another hour's passing, James feared the mission's futility. An approaching Land Cruiser quelled his negative thoughts. He keyed his radio's microphone to alert his team. The car glided to a halt about twenty yards from James' vehicle. It became eerily quiet except for the sporadic whispering wind blowing through the plateau. The vehicle's tinted glass obscured James' view of its occupants.

Inside the white Land Cruiser, Hassan scanned the positions, armament, and nearby terrain of his opponents as he spotted Steele and Smith perched atop a nearby ridge. Hassan radioed his men, "Move right and push toward the ridgeline." He gestured to his driver. "Prepare for a hasty departure." Hassan reached for his pistol tucked under his thigh.

"Wagner, something's wrong." James panned the area. "Hassan's stalling. He might attempt to flank us."

Wagner keyed his microphone. "Smith, do you see anything?"

"Wait one," Smith replied as Steele scanned the area with his binoculars. Steele nodded negatively.

"There's nothing," said Smith, looking at his partner. "Hold on, Steele's activating our thermals."

Steele lifted the state-of-the-art viewer to his eye and scanned the shadow-ridden, dense brush. After a few seconds, Steele discovered four faint heat signatures attempting to flank them.

Smith lifted his radio. "James, you have four hostiles approaching from your left."

"Copy that," said James as he blew out three quick breaths and plodded to the operator's side of the Land Cruiser; he drew his Sig Sauer 9mm pistol and pointed it at the driver's head. "Get out of the car."

Hassan scanned the surrounding area as al-Bayd's foot hovered over the accelerator; al-Bayd cracked his window. "Where's Jake O'Reilly? He was supposed to make the exchange."

James pressed the button for his microphone. "O'Reilly, can you show yourself?"

O'Reilly stepped from the Suburban and walked toward James. Al-Bayd turned to his boss. "It's him."

Hassan opened his door and stood up, turning back toward James. "I'm unarmed. Could you lower your weapon?" He stared at the agent. "Did you bring the ten-million dollars?"

James nodded. "We have your money. Where's al-Sammarri? You better have brought him or this is going to turn bad."

"I have him nearby." Hassan raised his chin. "Only a fool would trust an American. You screwed the Palestinians by facilitating Israeli oppression. You blindly back them despite significant Arab backlash."

James gave a hard smile. "And ISIS cares about the Muslims as a whole? Look what you're doing in the Middle East. Muslims are killing one another for religious reasons. We could debate politics all day, but that's not why we're here. Is it?"

The ambitious terrorist shook his head. "Indeed. Let's do business. I recommend you show me the money and then I'll bring up al-Sammarri."

"Fair enough." James peered at his colleague. "Bishop, can you bring the money?"

The protective intelligence agent slid two medium-sized suitcases out of the Suburban and approached the Land Cruiser. As he came to the car's hood, Bishop placed the two suitcases on top of it. He inserted a key and twisted it as the locks clicked open. He flipped open the two lids.

Hassan's eyes glimmered as he radioed for the second vehicle. Within thirty seconds, a flatbed truck trailed by dust pulled up behind the Land Cruiser. Al-Bayd marched back to the truck, flung open the door, and assisted al-Sammarri to his feet.

Al-Sammarri's eyes went wide. He glared first at James and then openly stared at his chief bodyguard. "What are you doing, Hassan? How can you deal with the Crusaders? They occupy our lands, plunder our resources, and poison our people with their corruption."

"That speech would've worked in the past, but we're at war and you're hurting the cause." Hassan barked at the frail leader.

"As much as I'm enjoying this conversation, our prisoner requires some medical attention," said James, signaling for White to bring the Suburban forward. James studied Hassan's face. "Have we met before?" His eyebrows crumpled.

Hassan shrugged. "You look familiar."

James' recollection surfaced. He drew his weapon and aimed it at Hassan. "You went by Al-Mujahid; your twelve-man team attempted to assault our embassy in Cairo five years ago."

"So it's you." Hassan replied, shaking his head. "I should've taken you out when I had the chance. You were in my sights. I instead aborted our mission."

James' eyes bulged. "I should've killed you with a single shot as you fled in defeat. I won't make the same mistake again."

"Take it easy, Matt." Bishop raised a hand. "Remember Assistant Secretary Chen's instructions. We're to honor our agreement, make the exchange, and turn over al-Sammarri to the FBI. We should go now."

James' face reddened as his finger shifted off the trigger. As he lowered his weapon, gunfire erupted from his left. Smith and Steele fired at Hassan's men as a barrage of gunshots peppered the area and echoed throughout the plateau.

In the ensuing chaos, al-Bayd pointed his pistol at Bishop and pulled the trigger. James hastily pushed Bishop aside; a round grazed his left shoulder. Undeterred, he spun around and fired from right to left, downing two and sending a third to cover. He pivoted his sights to al-Bayd, who stepped behind al-Sammarri and fired four shots. James dove behind the car as bullets whizzed by his head and body.

Using the diversion, Hassan shut the lids on the two suitcases and scurried behind al-Bayd and al-Sammarri. The three terrorists walked backwards to the truck.

Smith swept his scope over the four bodies he had just culled and then pivoted his rifle to center Hassan's head in its crosshairs. The terrorist reached into his pocket and removed a detonator.

"I have al-Bayd partially in my sights." James heard Steele's voice through his earpiece and sensed an opportunity. "Freeze Hassan, you won't leave here alive unless you cooperate." His brow furrowed.

"You're wrong. You'll let me go or we'll die together." Hassan lifted his detonator.

James lowered his pistol forty-five degrees to the ground and stepped rearward. His stomach churned from the concession as he despised losing, but couldn't afford to martyr al-Sammarri today. He contemplated his options, needing to salvage the game or at least play to a draw. "Steele and Smith, prepare to take out the hostiles on my order." He radioed.

"Copy that." Steele's index finger rested on his rifle's trigger.

One of Hassan's fallen comrades broke the impasse, stood, and scurried back toward the truck. Al-Bayd pushed al-Sammarri forward and dashed into the driver's side of the truck as Hassan depressed the detonator. The Land Cruiser erupted as the blast's percussion blew those around it to the ground. Thick green smoke bellowed out of the car, obscuring visibility. Al-Bayd shifted into reverse and floored the accelerator. Loose gravel and dirt filled the air.

"What's happening?" Smith scowled. He pulled the trigger and riddled the truck's windshield with bullets. Glass fragments peppered al-Bayd's face as a round tore through his shoulder; he jerked the wheel to the left, swerved sideways, and slammed into a large, white boulder. The vehicle's low revving engine permeated the air.

Smith and Steele snatched their gear and charged down the hill to determine their colleagues' fate. Nearing the burning Land Cruiser, its scorching heat seared their skin. James sprang to his feet to survey the area; his ears ringing. White and Atwell ran to al-Sammarri's side, observing his shallow breaths. James hurried over to cover a dazed hostile and handcuffed the unknown terrorist in seconds. Using a circular motion, he lifted the hostile to his feet and inadvertently removed their head cover. His mouth fell open as he eyed a Middle Eastern woman. Her olive complexion, jet black flowing hair down to her sculpted buttocks, and mystical hazel eyes captivated him. The woman's eyes flashed defiantly at him.

James glanced away from the woman to avoid staring at her. "How's al-Sammarri?" He inquired as Atwell assessed the terrorist's wounds.

"He only sustained minor abrasions from the blast, but he doesn't look well. We must go to a hospital immediately or we'll lose him," said Atwell, examining the terrorist's eyes.

"Let's saddle up." James shouted as he escorted the mute woman to his Suburban, placing her in the rear passenger seat. "Make yourself comfortable." He glanced at Wagner.

"You have no right to hold me." She said defiantly with a British accent. "I'm an archaeologist and not a terrorist."

James smirked. "I don't care if you're the Queen of Sheba. You're a suspected terrorist, or at least a material witness. I don't have time for this discussion now."

"Let's go check on Hassan." James turned to Wagner. They pulled their vehicle beside the shattered truck, where they found Smith and Steele rummaging through it for clues. Other than splattered blood left on the driver's side front seat, Hassan and al-Bayd had vanished.

"There's nothing left for us here. We don't have extra time to search the area. We must transport al-Sammarri for treatment and then ensure that he receives his free courtesy upgrade to America. Mount up." James signaled as the team loaded up into the two running Suburbans. Given the urgency, the motorcade sped off to Erbil.

CHAPTER 8: Revelations

Northern Iraq

The two extra passengers, one wounded and the other a material witness, stretched the vehicle's capacity. Wagner weaved in and out of traffic in his ninety-five hundred pound armored vehicle as he pushed the vehicle's physical abilities to race back to the US Consulate in Erbil. Familiar with the traffic conditions, O'Reilly rode shotgun to identify possible traffic problems or dangers ahead of them as obstacles, taxi vans, and sharp turns came up fast at their freeway speeds. Even with the upsurge in traffic, Wagner remained undeterred and floored the accelerator. His intense concentration dimmed his auditory senses, distracting him from James' conversation with the exotic beauty behind him.

Bishop and Clark sat in the elevated rear seat, which caused their heads to hit the roof. Bishop adjusted the contrast and backlighting on the computer for their GPS tracking equipment as they monitored a map reflecting the reward money's movement across the border into Syria. DS technicians had implanted two dime-sized beacons in each suitcase with one sewn in the liner and the other buried within the bills. Bishop hoped the high-tech equipment would remain concealed, but in viewing the computer screen, he observed only two distinct slow-moving dots. Hassan must have transferred the money to another case as a precaution against tracking.

Keeping pace with Wagner, Smith tailed the Suburban while maintaining a fifty-foot buffer for reactive purposes. Smith focused through the flying gravel and dust, concentrating on Wagner's brake lights. Smith balanced speed for smoothness as Atwell worked feverishly on al-Sammarri, providing him the fluids and pain medications through an IV. Atwell had studied his intelligence folder and knew the dangers of his liver condition without prompt treatment. White held the IV up over al-Sammarri's head while ensuring it remained stable by acting as a human shock absorber.

The stillness of the air permeated both vehicles as the agents battled their physical and mental fatigue. James reflected on his recent interaction with Hassan; he sought answers, and his prisoner likely had them.

The seasoned agent gazed into her mesmeric brown eyes. "My name is Matt James. Are these handcuffs bothering you?" He said, removing a key chain from his pocket.

"They're a little tight," she whimpered, displaying her wrists.

"If I remove them, will you behave and tell me your name?" James leaned in, aware that flirting with the woman could be the fastest way to disarm her.

"My name is Suhar Atallah. I promise to behave. Besides, there's nowhere to go." She returned a trembling smile.

James recognized her rattled state and admired her composure after a heated gun battle and her capture. Only the slight tremor in her hands and voice revealed her fright. He contemplated his next series of questions. He removed the handcuffs and placed them back into his leather cuff holder on his belt. "So Suhar, where are you from? I'm guessing you're Egyptian."

"You're close. I'm Jordanian, but I grew up in many locations, including Iraq, the United Kingdom, and America."

"That would explain your perfect English then." He said, smiling. "Suhar is a pretty name. Is that spelled S-u-h-a-r?"

"Yes it is." Her eyes sparkled.

"Doesn't Suhar mean Dawn?" His eyes widened.

"Not quite." She smiled. "You're thinking about Sahar with an A. That's pretty good."

"Let me try another one then." His eyebrows rose. "Atallah means a gift from Allah."

"That's right." She beamed.

"I should be on Jeopardy. Now I'll guess two hard things, your age and sign. I'm guessing you're an Aries like me and you're twenty-eight years old. He purposely guessed low to elicit a response.

"I appreciate the compliment. I'm an Aries, but I'm thirty-five years old." She chuckled.

"Forgive me, Suhar. Your youthful appearance masks your life experience." James tapped O'Reilly on the shoulder.

O'Reilly nodded as he continued typing on his iPhone. Upon finishing the last sentence, O'Reilly reviewed his text message: *"Al-Sammarri is in custody and is being transported to our official facility in Erbil. Request immediate name trace on Suhar Atallah, 35-year-old female, born in Jordan."* He tapped the send button and his message shot through the electronic airwaves to land at the DS Command Center seconds later. O'Reilly tapped his thigh with his finger while staring at his phone's screen.

"Suhar, I bet you've lived an exciting life, and I can tell by the way you carry yourself that you're no terrorist. I'd like to learn more about your upbringing and how you met Hassan?" James canted his head.

"I was born and raised in Amman. As the daughter of a top Jordanian diplomat, I attended schools in the UK and later in America. My father served as the ambassador to the US and then to the United Nations. This occurred in my formative years, so I remained in America to study at Harvard, majoring in archeology. My ten years in America provided me an excellent grasp of western culture, so I elected to stay following my graduation to work on a dinosaur excavation in Kansas. There I helped to unearth a full, well-preserved fossil of Tyrannosaurus Rex. It provided me the hands-on experience I needed, but dinosaurs weren't my primary interest, so I returned to Jordan to study ancient Egyptian civilizations." Her heart palpitated as butterflies erupted in her gut.

"So tell me Suhar. When and how did you meet Hassan and what did he want you to do?" He leaned in toward her.

"I've known him since early childhood. We grew up in the same neighborhood." She smiled as her cheeks reddened.

"What are you thinking about?" He touched her hand.

"A... A... We were romantically involved for a short time before I left for America. I'm sure my father took the job there to separate us. Hassan's family moved shortly afterwards to Iraq. I hadn't seen nor heard from him since. That was until he called and asked me to work an excavation in Palestine and Egypt. I would've worked the dig for free, but he even offered to pay me. He knew all about me, my work, and must've kept tabs on me throughout the years." She touched her throat and sighed. "You can see that I'm not a terrorist, but a victim of circumstance."

"That's the story of my life. I'm often in the wrong place at the wrong time. It nearly got me killed several times." He glanced at the floor before peering back into her eyes.

"So was your father right to move you far away from him?" His eyebrows rose.

She nodded. "Even in our teens, Hassan hated the West and stressed that King Hussein was too close to the United States. And if he disliked America, he despised Israel and blamed them for all the region's troubles. Hassan staunchly defended the Palestinian cause and their terrorist actions. He also cheered Hezbollah's attacks in Lebanon and al-Qaeda's East African embassy bombings."

"The man doesn't sound very nice." James slumped in his seat.

"He's very charming, athletic, handsome, and smart." She rubbed her temple. "He's also passionate about his cause and in that he's ruthless." She glanced out the window.

"He doesn't sound like your type. And frankly, with your ties to the West, you don't sound like his. Why did you reunite with him? There must've been more than the opportunity to work on a couple of digs." James wanted to retract his sentence, recognizing that her work was ingrained in her soul.

"You don't understand, Mr. James." She threw him a flat look with narrowed eyes. "Yes, I was curious about my childhood sweetheart, but those digs, as you called them, have important historical significance. The excavation in Palestine involved the legendary copper scrolls. Fable has it that one scroll documents the many riches of el-Amarna as an ancient city annihilated by a virulent plague. It purportedly had a mountain of riches, but it's not the treasure that's important. It's what it represents and the story behind the city's demise." Her eyes pierced his.

"Did you find what you sought in Palestine?" He stroked his cheeks.

She nodded. "We unearthed a deciphering key that pinpoints the treasures secretly entered on the copper scroll." She tossed her hair back over her shoulder.

His right eyebrow rose. "Are you referring to the recently stolen copper scroll taken from the Natural History Museum back in July? That created quite a stir when the Israel Antiquities Authority accused the US government of ineptitude. We failed to both secure the artifact and then in its subsequent investigation. It was rumored to be an inside job, and they've never recovered the scroll, nor do they have any leads in the case."

"I couldn't say if there's a connection." She looked down, contemplating the possibility. "If the stolen artifact was the el-Amarna scroll, it would explain Hassan's enthusiasm when we found the decipher key."

James curled his lip. "He's just a common thief."

She drew in a deep breath. "He isn't interested in the treasure. At least not in the riches that greed would evoke. He only wants one particular prize in el-Amarna, and I wouldn't call it that. It's more of a Pandora's Box, and I fear I've done a terrible thing by helping him." Her face turned pale.

"Why is it considered a Pandora's Box?" He touched the base of his neck.

"Folklore reflects that a terrible plague killed the inhabitants of the once thriving ancient Egyptian city of el-Amarna. Only a blacksmith and a doctor survived and purportedly hid all the riches throughout the city, creating a decipher key to mark their locations. They also mummified a bat responsible for the plague. According to legend, they stored the bat in one of the queen's cherished gold-plated decorated chests and then placed it in a secret chamber beneath the Great Temple." She crossed her legs and then uncrossed them.

"So Hassan's after a bat that carried a more virulent form of Ebola?" He glanced at his hands as a lump formed in his throat.

James hated being wrong, but not in this case as he had reviewed the latest Ebola studies and literature. Scientists linked the bat to two of the planet's most lethal viruses—Marburg and Ebola. Both forms caused hemorrhagic fever, illnesses marked by severe bleeding, organ failure, and high mortality rates. Ebola struck everyone's consciousness, particularly with its recent arrival in the United States. Despite CDC assurances that Ebola could not go airborne, he knew otherwise. The 1989 Ebola outbreak at Reston's animal quarantine facility remained etched in his head. The facility sat within the DC metropolitan area with its six and a half million inhabitants. Even though he worked for the federal government, he doubted their honesty.

"It's more than just the bat. I overheard him talking with an associate. He wants to find the bat, resurrect the virus with modern science, and release it on Israel and America." She covered her mouth with her hand.

"And you knowingly assisted him in discovering the decipher key. If this virus is unleashed, nobody is safe as it will wipe out everything in its path. Are you sure?" He raised a single eyebrow.

She leaned away as her mouth turned dry. "I didn't know about the connection between the key and what Hassan intended to do with it. Once I did, I objected to it and that's when he became upset and threatened to kill me. I had no choice, as he's ten times more fanatical than when I knew him as a teenager, so he'll carry out his plan. I've never met a more determined man." Her lips trembled.

"I bet I could give him a run for his money." James offered a curt nod. "I have to stop him, so will you help me Suhar before he starts his attack? Millions of innocent people will die if he's successful."

"More like billions." She jerked her head back. "The plague in el-Amarna supposedly had a one-hundred percent mortality rate. This rate is easy to imagine, as Ebola-Zaire has roughly a ninety percent fatality rate."

"This just gets better and better." He mumbled.

O'Reilly leaned over the chair. "Look here, Matt."

James glanced down at O'Reilly's iPhone screen showing the DS Command Center's response: *"Suspect has no criminal record or known terrorist affiliations. All NCIC checks were negative. Attended Harvard and earned a BA degree in archeology. No outstanding warrants."* James contemplated her anonymity in the United States as she didn't even have a traffic ticket registered to her name.

"There's more." She undid the top button of her shirt while an empty feeling in the pit of her stomach suddenly surfaced. "The plague will devastate America, so it cannot aid Israel, who will suffer the same horrible fate. The Islamic State would then attack Israel and retake the holy land in the name of Allah."

"We have problems, Wagner." James tapped him on the shoulder. "Can you pick up the pace? We have to go to the consulate, so I can alert headquarters and get guidance."

CHAPTER 9: Under Siege

Erbil, Iraq

"Slow down, Dutch. We're approaching the outskirts of Erbil." O'Reilly said, scanning the horizon. "The last thing we need is an accident, which could bring a large crowd."

As the gateway to Kurdistan, Erbil appeared a classic frontier city and one that defied time. From its ancient architectural flavor to its backstreet bazaars, Erbil was unlike anything the team had ever seen. With nearly a million inhabitants, the city hummed with action as people worked, shopped, and brokered trade. They believed deeply in their core values and nurtured their own sense of right and wrong. Any news contrary to their belief system could spark controversy and provoke a significant backlash. A ten-thousand powerful demonstration could emerge in a blink of an eye. James looked out the car's window, recognizing that something had stirred the populace into action.

O'Reilly picked up the mic on the Suburban's radio to contact the consulate. "Post One, Post One, this is the RSO. I need a situation report?"

"RSO, this is Post One. Be advised that you have a small gathering of agitated people at the front of the consulate. The local police are holding their positions and are being reinforced."

O'Reilly turned to James. "It's going to get ugly." He stroked his chin while pondering his options.

"Post One from RSO, react the detachment and advise me of any threats. I'll be at your position in ten minutes. RSO out."

He had seen similar past demonstrations for Guantanamo prisoner abuse stories, the perceived desecration of the Koran, and even a caricature of the Prophet Mohamed. There was no prior intelligence of any problems today, so he called his local Kurdish police contact, who advised that the local radio station announced al-Sammarri's capture by the Americans near the Syrian border. It sparked joy until they learned the US took him into protective custody.

The security chief informed the consul general about the hostile protest. Given its late hour, only a few employees remained in the consulate. However, America couldn't afford another Benghazi as the consulate's secrets required protection. O'Reilly had studied the Benghazi attack and vowed that nothing like that would happen on his watch. Tonight would test his mettle.

"I must go to the consulate and take charge of the situation." O'Reilly said, peering at James.

"Deal my team in," said James, nodding. "We can operate alongside your Marines to safeguard the building and serve as a react team."

"Let's get some." Wagner grinned.

O'Reilly radioed his surveillance detection team to infiltrate, monitor, and identify any hostile intentions by the crowd. He then ordered his guard force inside and a lockdown of the consulate perimeter; the Kurdish police had now fielded a one-hundred strong riot team bearing shields and batons.

"We have to get inside the grounds before the crowd fully assembles. Cover and hide al-Sammarri," James barked, glancing at Atallah as her pale face reflected her understanding of the situation. "And let's not put Suhar in the line of fire, either. Do you have a back entrance, O'Reilly?" He picked up his rifle and placed it between his legs.

O'Reilly radioed his guard force commander. "Get guards to the service gate now." The crowd would inevitably focus on the front and the American flag that fluttered in the faint breeze. As Wagner rounded their last turn, he looked down four-blocks of asphalt and gravel road strewn with potholes and garbage.

"We're one minute out." O'Reilly radioed his guards. "Lower the delta barrier and open the gates." As they closed within two blocks of the consulate, a throng of wild-eyed demonstrators spotted them and rushed toward the service gate. It was a race to the gate, with no points for the runner-up.

An ISIS infiltrator leveled his assault rifle at the rear Suburban and fired as the vehicles came within range of the back gate. Rounds peppered the Suburban's windows, imbedding into them and forming cloudy, ragged, hardball-sized circles. White understood the glass' limitations and stepped up into the turret, aimed her assault rifle, and pressed the trigger. A three-round burst struck the gun-wielding man in the chest. The attacker dropped onto the grass.

As the Suburbans sped through the gate, the guard raised the delta barrier and shut the steel gate. The agitated crowd swarmed the fence, causing it to flex back-and-forth. Approaching the consulate's side entrance, their ears rang as the duck-and-cover alarm wailed over the loudspeakers. Marines scurried up the stairs to their elevated positions on the second floor.

"Smith, Steele, and White," said James, "Can you get to the roof? Take your equipment and weapons and get up there pronto."

James turned to Atwell. "Can you bring al-Sammarri to the health unit and help the doctor check him out?"

Atwell nodded. "I could use Bishop and Clark for security and help me move al-Sammarri if the consulate gets overrun."

"That makes sense." James nodded. "Protect Suhar as well."

"Wagner, you're with O'Reilly and me. Let's head to Post One to find out what the hell's happening."

They bumped into the FBI's legal attaché as they trotted to Post One. How did it go with the exchange? The attaché crossed his arms.

"We made the exchange, but encountered some resistance," said O'Reilly, barely breaking stride. "I'll brief you later. We have an emerging crisis."

The FBI agent's face reddened as he shrugged.

Upon entering Post One, a young corporal briefed the RSO, as James scanned its ten monitors; thousands surrounded the consulate as the crowd swelled by the minute. Give us al-Sammarri chants echoed throughout the building.

James activated his microphone. "Steele, Steele, this is James. What's your read on the situation? The crowd appears to be growing in size and volatility. Please confirm."

Steele wiped the perspiration from his brow and activated his throat microphone with the push of a button. "It's bad out there. Local riot police are being challenged by about two-thousand demonstrators, and they can only hold them back for a few more minutes." Steele's eyebrows drew together as his stomach churned.

James' concentration waned as he recalled the 2012 Benghazi attack; a raging fire billowing black smoke supplanted his thoughts. He twisted his watch and eyed the doorway. "We must stop them. If they get over the walls, it's all over. We're obligated to protect al-Sammarri, even though I'd gladly hand him over for them to extract justice. I understand their animosity toward him as he slaughtered so many of their fellow countrymen." His lips drew together in a mild grimace.

James watched the monitor. Several protestors skirted the police and converged on the west wall as three consulate guards swung their batons. He understood the inherent danger.

"Grab the pepper spray Wagner and follow me," James trotted out the door and down the hallway. "Smith, you guys cover us from the rooftop. Wagner and I are going out to the west wall to stop these bastards."

"Overwatch has your back," said Steele, raising his rifle.

James and Wagner sprinted by several fleeing guards as they approached the west wall. They intercepted the first protester who had climbed over the perimeter fence. Wagner dodged a punch and then struck him in the neck with a brachial chop. The man's legs wobbled as Wagner threw him to the asphalt, snapped his wrists together, and cuffed him. James pointed his rifle into the cloudy gray sky and depressed the trigger, releasing a three-round burst. Wagner raised the nozzle of the fire-extinguisher sized pepper spray and pointed it at those remaining on the wall. He aimed at their faces and unleashed the spray. One by one, they dropped from the wall as Wagner moved from person to person. Ear-piercing screams followed as he continued spraying the throng. James noted the pepper spray's effectiveness, pulled a smaller bottle of it from his belt, flipped off the safety switch, and targeted select people, dropping them like flies.

The two agents focused on those climbing the fence. A shot rang out from behind them, whizzed by James' head, and found its mark on an armed protester who had raised his rifle at James. The man dropped lifeless, White's round striking him between the eyes. As the crowd regrouped, ten military trucks arrived at the scene, carrying over two-hundred reinforcements. The sullen crowd dispersed.

James and Wagner sighed. The two turned from the crowd and trotted toward the consulate as a voice emanated from their earpieces.

"We have a dozen well-armed men who breached the eastern wall." A Marine broadcasted over the radio. "They just shot three guards and are approaching the consulate's side door."

Steele, White, and Smith dashed to the far side of the roof. Rounds peppered the building as they each dove behind some air vents. They crawled behind concrete wall partitions. White sprinted to an elevator shaft as rounds whizzed by her head. She dove behind the wall, escaping a barrage of bullets that trailed her. Steele and Smith observed the faint muzzle flashes that originated from the shell of a commercial building about five-hundred meters away. They kneeled, aimed and squeezed their assault rifles' triggers, sending a dozen rounds at the sniper. The muzzle flashes ceased. Steele rolled over on his stomach and back to take up a better tactical position; he then kneeled behind a backup generator and scanned the building shell.

Meanwhile, James and Wagner sprinted toward the consulate's side entrance as the Marine manning Post One dispensed a cloud of tear gas at the door. They ducked behind a container, put on their gas masks, and advanced toward the terrorists. The terrorists donned their gas masks and then set up in a three-person formation on the door. One man removed a satchel charge from a man's backpack ahead of him, set the timer, and placed the charge on the door's locking mechanism. The other team members fanned out, covering rooftops and any area around the team.

O'Reilly studied the monitors and then turned to the Detachment Commander. "Get everyone to the vault." The hardened and windowless space already housed all the employees within the consulate. Only Atwell, Bishop, Clark, al-Sammarri, Atallah, and the medical doctor remained outside of it. The six of them scurried up the back stairwell. Their hearts pounded faster with each set of stairs they conquered, but the group arrived at the vault only minutes later.

The RSO counted them, comparing notes from the Marines' after-hours log to the people inside the concrete-encased vault. "Sergeant Stock," said O'Reilly, "what's the status of the hostiles?"

A wide-eyed Marine monitoring a screen shook his head. "It looks bad."

It didn't take the Marine's answer to know their status. A loud explosion rocked the building seconds later. Dust from the ceiling and lights wafted downward as the building shook.

"We've been breached," O'Reilly barked. "Seal the vault." He glanced at the Sergeant, giving him a curt nod.

"What about James and Wagner?" Atwell tugged his ear as his stomach sank.

"It's too late for them. The terrorists could be here in minutes. My priority is keeping my staff and al-Sammarri safe." O'Reilly gritted his teeth.

Atwell understood the RSO's rationale, recalling an adage that the needs of the many outweigh the few. "Let me out. I should help James. Atwell's fiery eyes narrowed as he tapped his foot on the floor.

"I can't do that. I need you here to help protect everyone." O'Reilly's face tensed.

"There's a facility breach." The Marine proclaimed over the radio. James pondered Wagner's shooting prowess as the service's best shot and relished his twelve to two odds. He once witnessed him go head-to-head with the Army's Special Operations Task Force champion. In the end, Wagner tied him as they shot metal plates with their pistols from one-hundred feet. Yet, today would test his true grit.

Rounding a corner, they backpedaled and ducked back around the edge of the building as terrorists peppered them with rounds.

"That was fun, Wagner." James grinned.

"Watch this." Wagner smiled while pulling out a flash-bang grenade from one of his pouches on his belt. He stepped backwards, using the angle and the wall of the building to shield him from the terrorists. He pulled the safety-pin on the flash-bang grenade and hurled it toward the attackers.

"Once it explodes, you go high and I'll go low." James said, squatting.

Wagner displayed his fist and pointed his thumb skyward. The flash-bang detonated seconds later. Its percussion rocked the area. James lunged out, using the building to cover the bulk of his body. Wagner simultaneously took a half step out. They engaged the three disoriented targets, dropping them to the ground.

James radioed the vault. "Three tangos neutralized."

As they stepped over the downed assailants, Wagner fired one round into each of their heads. James scowled while shaking his head and peering up at the consulate's operational camera. His stomach churned as he deduced the scrutiny of their tactics.

Wagner crept into a back stairwell. As Wagner raised his foot to step through the door's threshold, James grabbed him by the shoulder.

"Halt, Dutch." He pointed down at a thin line that spanned the entire doorway at six inches off the ground. "These guys are good."

They stepped over the tripwire and started up the first flight of stairs; three terrorists unleashed rounds from their submachine guns, causing the two agents to retrace their steps. James kneeled and traced the line to a US fragmentary grenade. He snapped open his side pouch and retracted his knife, clipping the line and stabilizing the pin in place. The grenade had a four to five second delay. He pulled the pin, counted off two seconds, and lobbed it upward. The grenade ricocheted off the wall and bounced on the first landing. The two agents scooted behind the doorframe. A split-second later, the blast launched shrapnel in all directions; it blew holes through two of the terrorists' major organs and sliced through a femoral artery on the third.

The two agents barreled up the stairwell with their weapons aimed in front and above them. Wagner reached the landing and pointed his rifle at the fading terrorist who raised his weapon. He squeezed his trigger. Three-rounds struck the extremist's heart; his eyes snapped closed as his body wilted.

"Damn fanatics," said James, "they're heading for the vault to free al-Sammarri, take hostages or kill our people. We must intercept them." He grabbed a Russian rocket-propelled grenade (RPG) launcher off the stair landing and slung it over his shoulder.

"Come on; you only live once." Wagner winked.

James gripped him by the shoulder. Wagner shifted his focus and his rifle's barrel to the floor above them. James darted to the next landing, cleared it, and then shifted his aim to cover the landing above. Wagner tapped him on the back and dashed to the next landing. Within a half-minute, they arrived at the third floor.

The two agents stopped to listen while catching their breath. Splintering wood and scuffling feet echoed back to the door. James peaked through the rectangular door window. A three-man team was searching the rooms on the left side of the hallway. Wagner gripped the door handle and jerked it open. James lifted the RPG over his shoulder and centered the weapon's crosshairs on the door occupying the terrorists. His finger touched the trigger as his eyes panned the area. Wagner shot a single bullet into the hall, hoping to lure the three out. Seconds later, a face peered from the doorjamb. James depressed the trigger and watched the rocket sizzle down the hallway at the terrorist's feet; it exploded and severed him in half. A fireball engulfed the room and shot out into the hallway.

James glanced at Wagner. "Cover me." He vaulted up the hallway, drawing fire from one of the remaining terrorists. Wagner returned fire at the terrorist's shoulder and arm. James ducked into a nearby office as rounds peppered the wall behind him. James waited for a lull and then emerged from the doorjamb with his weapon pointed down the hall. The sprinkler system spewed water and drenched the area. A high-low wailing rattled their ears. With James aiming and covering down the hall, Wagner sprinted forward; he whisked by James and vaulted into an office on the right side. James' thumb pressed the magazine release button, launching a nearly depleted magazine to the floor; he inserted another one into the bay and charged his rifle.

James picked up his radio. "Post One, Post One, this is Special Agent James. Can you give me an update of the situation?"

"We have three terrorists setting up an explosive charge on the door. Time's running out," said O'Reilly, wringing his hands.

He glanced at Wagner. They advanced forward with James walking upright and Wagner duck walking; their guns aimed forward. As a terrorist emerged from the corner, the two agents unloaded on him, dropping him before he could press his trigger. They continued walking in unison toward the vault. An arm and rifle sprang from around the corner, unloading an entire thirty-round magazine. Rounds whizzed past their heads and bodies, impacting on the walls, floor, and ceiling. The two agents kept walking and firing at the exposed arm. An AK-47 assault rifle fell to the floor as their rounds sliced through the terrorist's arm. Blood spurted from the half severed arm.

James and Wagner ducked into another room and reloaded their weapons; each agent removed a flashbang grenade from their waist belt and lobbed it toward the vault. Two deafening bangs and a yellow flash spiked the area. The agents hurried forward, walking high and low. They rounded the corner and abruptly encountered the two remaining attackers, who fired as they did. James fell backwards as two rounds hit his chest. Wagner sprayed them with several bursts from his rifle. He turned to check on James, who now sat upright.

"I'm lucky. He hit the ballistic plate on my vest. Damn, it hurts." James groaned.

Wagner gripped James's hand to assist him to his feet. A terrorist lunged forward and hit a button to the timer affixed to the explosive. James raised his pistol, took quick aim, and fired one round into the terrorist's head. The man collapsed to the ground. Wagner turned around to notice the timer edge down to twenty seconds.

"Get away from the door and take cover." James radioed O'Reilly.

The two agents scanned the military-grade explosive device, which incorporated shape charge technology designed to channel the blast's energy through the door's locking mechanism.

With the clock edging down to thirteen seconds, they bypassed standard protocol as it involved using a portable x-ray machine to identify the position of the bomb's internal components. Wagner unslung his Remington 870 shotgun and loaded number four buckshot into it. His mind reflected to his explosive manual and the nomenclature of a Russian-made device. He estimated the fusing system's location, aimed his shotgun at the area, and fired with eight seconds remaining. Wagner sighed and inserted another round into the shotgun's chamber. He racked it, aimed at the device, and fired with only three seconds remaining.

The two agents hastily ducked around the corner and waited ten seconds. With the Peshmerga and police securing the consulate grounds and all twelve terrorists neutralized, James radioed O'Reilly. "It's clear. You can come out now."

James leaned against the wall and gasped as the vault door's locking pins clicked open. O'Reilly cracked open the heavy steel door, glanced out, and opened it.

"It's great you survived. Are you alright?" Atwell said, clearing his throat.

James nudged a body on the ground. "We're doing better than this joker and his eleven other buddies. At least we're still alive."

O'Reilly dispatched his eight Marines to search the building and assume their defensive positions. The consul general emerged from the vault, extending his hand. "That was splendid work. I'm going to put your team in for the Heroism Award."

"You guys sure schooled the terrorists," said the base chief, grinning. "We watched you on the vault's monitors. Forgive me for not introducing myself. I'm Dave Mattson, Chief of Base." He extended his hand out to the agent.

James gripped his hand. "It's my pleasure. If you have time, I'd like to brief you on the situation and seek your help."

"Absolutely," said Mattson, "Let's go to my office. We can talk in private."

Mattson, a veteran CIA officer, served his country for over thirty years. As the base chief in Erbil, he worked on America's front line in the war on terrorism. His top secret work entailed finding and neutralizing al-Qaeda and now ISIS leaders, and his relentless resolve made him a legend in the spy agency. Not that he counted, but he had helped to capture six major terrorists in two years. This interrupted two significant terrorist plots on the US homeland, but al-Sammarri had topped his list of capture or kill targets. He had worked day and night to capture the elusive terrorist, and DS had now delivered him to his doorstep.

James glanced at Wagner. "Can you protect our guests? Atwell can help the doctor with al-Sammarri's examination, and Steele and Smith can entertain Suhar, but not too much."

"Give me five minutes, Dave and I'll swing by your office. I have to update my director on the latest developments." James said as he tailed O'Reilly back to his office.

CHAPTER 10: Internal Deception

The solid wood core door had a seal of the Erbil RSO's office on it. O'Reilly entered the three-digit combination to the spin dial lock on the door, releasing its locking mechanism. He then depressed a five-digit sequence into a scramble pad, which released a separate lock. Pulling the hardened door open, he motioned for James to enter and directed him to his office, which resembled a war room with local and regional maps filling two of the four walls. Consulate schematics, a compound map reflecting guard positions, and an aerial photograph of the city lined another wall. A U-shaped desk tucked against the back wall supported two computer monitors, one processed unclassified data, and another for classified information. In the corner next to the desk sat a two-drawer safe with a secure telephone placed on top.

James walked behind O'Reilly's desk, moved a chair next to the safe, sat down and dialed the office of the DSS director. After a couple of rings, a soothing voice answered.

"Director Jacobs' office, this is Patricia Hartwell speaking."

"Pat, this is Matt James." He pulled the receiver tight against his ear. "Is the director available?"

"You guys have been very busy, as the Kurdish rioting is being flashed all over the news." She glanced down at her phone.

"Indeed, I can't remember the last time I had so much fun." James pinched the bridge of his nose and squeezed his eyes together.

After a pause, she transferred the call to Diplomatic Security's top cop. "Are you guys alright?"

James jittered his foot against the floor. "Yes, we swapped al-Sammarri for the cash. The doctor advised that it's dire, but he's stabilized now. We also detained a material witness who accompanied Hassan. She's provided critical information about his intentions."

"Wait a second, did I hear that correctly? You detained a witness?"

O'Reilly entered the room, so James depressed the speakerphone button. "That's correct, sir. She's stressed that Hassan plans to use the money to excavate a treasure in el-Amarna."

"How does treasure hunting relate?" The director rubbed the side of his neck.

"If you allow me to explain, it will become apparent." James rolled his eyes.

"By all means." The director's face tightened.

James relayed the money transfer for al-Sammarri, the ensuing firefight, and the capturing of the witness. "I'll get more information once I consult with the base chief and the FBI's legal attaché, but I'm running late for their meeting." He raised his watch to confirm the time.

"Call me when you have something more definitive. That was a marvelous job today." The director's eyes brightened. "We watched you guys neutralize the terrorists from our command center. The odds were against you, but you kicked their asses while demonstrating America's tenacity. DS would've suffered some serious blowback had the terrorists taken hostages or killed our people, as we're still plagued by Benghazi."

"Thanks, we were only doing our jobs, but I'll relay your praise to the entire team. I have to run, but I'll call you in an hour." James hung up.

O'Reilly reclined in his chair. "The base chief is a great guy, as he's a straight shooter, provides accurate intelligence, and doesn't play political games. The FBI attaché is another story, as he's a self-promoter who seeks credit for a successful operation, but points his finger when something goes south."

"I know the type." James grinned. "Don't worry as I know how to handle these guys."

O'Reilly walked James to the CIA's office space, which had been expanded to accommodate an influx of officers sent to neutralize the resurging ISIS threat. As they came to the CIA's suite door, the RSO glanced at the wall-mounted camera and pressed a buzzer. An officer pushed the door open and escorted them to a secure conference room. Upon entering the room, the base chief stood up to greet them.

"We haven't been formally introduced. I'm Dave Mattson, and this is Bart Johnson from the FBI. That was incredible work out there today."

The CIA officer motioned his guest to a black leather chair. James sat down, glanced at a top secret file on the table, and refrained from grabbing it.

"So how well do you understand Hassan Khalil Hussein? That's his classified CIA file. He's a slippery bastard." Mattson leaned in, scuffing his chair closer to the table.

James tipped his head back and closed his eyes. "He's tough. There's no doubt about it. His moves are meticulously planned, and he understands security tactics. Hassan's committed and views the end as justifying the means. He's in very good physical shape and is brilliant."

"The man's extraordinary at thinking on his feet. Check out his top secret file." Mattson pointed to the folder.

James opened the dossier and studied Hassan's two-decade old photograph on the file's left side. His eyes swept right to the source of the report; an Apache attack helicopter pilot who had survived an encounter with the terrorist in the hilly Iraqi terrain. Cleverly using a ruse, Hassan lured the veteran pilot into a steep and narrow canyon. Nearly commandeering the helicopter, the decorated pilot shook him off the wheel by dragging him over some rocks. Had Hassan taken the aircraft, he would have attacked the Americans at Baghdad's airport.

"This is an interesting file. Hassan's gutsy. I'll give him that." James shut the folder and slid it toward the base chief. "I've a photo taken during our exchange today, so it's yours if you want it."

Mattson beamed as his faded, grainy, and outdated Polaroid dated back to Hassan's college years. The hardened terrorist was the top priority on his targeting list, and Mattson recognized that his operational involvement spelled trouble for America while threatening large casualties.

"What's Hassan planning to do with the money?" The FBI attaché said, puffing out his chest.

"That's anyone's guess. However, according to a source, he plans to excavate an ancient artifact at el-Amarna. The artifact purportedly contains a virulent and easily transmittable strain of either an Ebola or Marburg virus.

He then intends to alter the virus using science, weaponized it, and unleash it on the Jewish state and the US." James said with an inward gaze.

"And you buy that from one of his associates? You probably just helped ISIS buy a nuclear weapon on the black market. Worse than that, he'll inevitably use it on America. Congratulations, that's a delightful piece of work." Johnson smirked.

James clenched his teeth as he turned toward Mattson. "I believe she's telling the truth, as I can tell when someone's lying, and she showed no signs of deception."

"Let's say for the sake of argument that you're right. What's his next move?" Mattson's eyebrows furrowed and suddenly released.

"We should intercept him at el-Amarna. If we can prevent him from digging up the plague, then we can stop him cold in his tracks." James's eyes gleamed.

Johnson glanced at the base chief. "You can't believe this crap. DS should've never been assigned this mission as they're a second tier law enforcement agency and incapable of carrying out this kind of operation. DS can't even understand and prioritize the intelligence."

James' face flushed. "You arrogant ass," he said. "Tell me the FBI did a wonderful job analyzing the intelligence before nine-eleven, and I can't forget to mention your fine work in thwarting the Boston bombers and the Capitol Hill insurrection. In these instances, you misread the clues or the seriousness of the matter. Your own people even pointed this out in their memorandums to your headquarters recommending action."

"You don't have a clue of what you're talking about." Johnson sputtered; his body rigid as he sucked in his cheeks.

James sensed he had struck a nerve. "The FBI should stick to criminal investigations. Hoover would tremble in his grave if he saw the bureau's blunders before and after nine-eleven. The FBI should concentrate domestically."

"This is our turf, James." Johnson held his elbows wide from his body with his chest thrust out. "Terrorism is our jurisdiction. We're going to prosecute al-Sammarri and when I'm through with you, DS will never chase another terrorist." He flashed a stiff smile.

"Give it your best shot. DS, not the FBI, was instrumental in the capture of Ramzi Yousef. In case you forgot, he was the mastermind behind the 1993

World Trade Center attack. We also just captured al-Sammarri. Yes, we'll turn al-Sammarri over to you, so the bureau can bring him back to the states and claim credit for his arrest. The FBI had little to do with it. You're just glorified transporters and credit hounds." James gave a crisp nod.

"I will not sit here and take this crap." Johnson's face reddened. "I'm going to report to headquarters and tell them we have a possible inbound nuclear weapon." The FBI agent stormed off.

"He's not a bad guy," Mattson shook his head. "He's just a company man."

"You're probably right, but that fumbling, bubbling idiot couldn't find a criminal if the bureau assigned him to a state penitentiary." James cracked his knuckles, eyes hardening as they glared at the door. "We must stop Hassan. Do you have any suggestions?"

The base chief scratched his head. "I've several resources at my disposal. If he's going after the treasure, he must pass through several countries, so I'll alert our people in the Egyptian, Israeli, and Jordanian intelligence services. If Hassan passes any of their borders, they'll know it and will alert us. Other than that, we must wait."

"What about the material witness? I'll try to get more information from her." James stretched his lower back with a twisting motion of his waist.

"Good idea. Let's do it." Mattson motioned to a door.

The two unlikely collaborators used a back stairwell to walk down to the RSO's office. They found O'Reilly typing a cable to his superiors, outlining the day's activities and highlighting the massive demonstration. The head of security waved them in, so they sat as he pushed the enter button on his keyboard to transmit his cable to the consul general for clearance.

"That was an interesting write-up." O'Reilly bowed his head. "It could rival an Ian Fleming novel. I hope I'll never have to write another one like it as long as I live."

"I'm sure it reads more like a Hollywood blockbuster." James grinned.

"How may I assist you guys?" O'Reilly reached down into his mini-refrigerator, retrieved an energy drink, and popped it open.

"You can start by handing me one of those drinks." James pointed. "It's been one hell of a day and I could use a caffeine boost. And one for Dave, if you have an extra one."

Mattson waved off the offer.

"We need to distract Atallah and get her to relax, and we think a drink in a comfortable setting may do the trick. Alcohol has a way of loosening lips." James rubbed his hands together.

"I have just the place." O'Reilly raised his eyebrows twice. "It's close and we can grab a bite to eat as well. And it's easy to find a secluded place to talk."

James nodded. "That sounds good. If I were to bet, then I'd say we're going to the American Club."

"You know the place?" The RSO turned his head sideways.

"You bet I do as I once took part in the best mustache competition there. The women there judged the contest. It got pretty wild in the last round, as a six-member panel of women had to kiss each participant. Can't believe I won, and I'll never know to this day whether it was my mustache or kissing ability." James' eyes widened.

"I've an idea." O'Reilly grabbed his jacket as he headed to the door. "I'll get my assistant regional security officer to join us there as she's sharp and one hell of an investigator. She might get Atallah to speak freely."

As they exited the office, O'Reilly locked and alarmed the door. He had once challenged the Marines to discover an infraction in his office space, and he paid the price when a resourceful Marine, working a midnight shift, located his classified printer, and observed it was out of paper. The young Marine loaded it, pushed the print button, and it spit out a confidential cable. So the corporal nailed the RSO with an infraction and received the coveted case of Foster's for his efforts.

They met Steele, Smith, and Atallah in the lobby and led them to an awaiting white van. O'Reilly's local national investigator greeted them at the vehicle. Mattson opted out, advising them he might meet them later.

"Where are we going?" Atallah raised her eyebrows while stepping into the van.

"I thought you might be hungry and thirsty, so we're going over to the American Club. It's close to here." James clasped his hands together as she slid next to him.

A nervous energy filled the air during the ten-minute silent ride. James' heart fluttered as his mind replayed flashes of his gunfight with Hassan, causing a light bead of sweat to pour from his forehead; its sheen highlighting his thousand-mile stare in the low light.

"Are you okay?" Atallah grabbed his forearm. "We're here."

James nodded. "I'm fine." He peered into her eyes before looking away.

An officious guard reviewed O'Reilly's consulate ID and accepted his word on the others. They passed through the front doors and walked up a flight of stairs to enter the bar. A sparse crowd eyed them before resuming their conversations. James looked off to the bar's left side, where three British journalists threw darts in the corner while a small contingent of aid workers hovered around the bar. The place buzzed with only mild activity and seemed perfect for their rendezvous.

"Over here Pat," a lone female called out from an isolated table near the window.

DS agent Sandra Morales stood up. Serving in her first tour overseas, Morales stood five feet nine inches and towered over most other women, but it wasn't her height that captured most people's attention. Her long flowing blond hair, combined with her exotic Latin features and elliptical eyes, captivated many.

"You guys are off the clock, so enjoy yourselves; you've certainly earned it. We depart for Baghdad at zero-seven hundred tomorrow." James dismissed Steele and Smith, who tilted their heads downward by the news and walked toward the bar. Steele turned to Smith. "Morales is hot." Smith nodded with a glimmer in his eyes.

As they arrived at the table, James pulled out the chair opposite Morales for Atallah. O'Reilly introduced the three to his young apprentice, who had a talent for establishing rapport with her soothing voice that put people at ease.

"I know you've had a tough day, so I ordered drinks. I've a pitcher of beer coming, a Cosmopolitan, and a Boardwalk Breezer," said the Hispanic agent, beaming.

"Nice choices. Did you order our dinners as well?" James casually anchored his right hand on his hip.

"I could have, but I didn't know Suhar's tastes." She brushed the hair out of her face.

"I'm Jordanian, but being a diplomat's daughter, I gained a taste for a variety of international cuisine. My favorite is Italian."

"I love Italian and Mexican," said James, eying the entrance.

Before the conversation could diverge into the mundane, a Kurdish national delivered the drinks and four menus.

"Let me guess." James passed the Cosmopolitan to Atallah, the Breezer to Morales, and the beer glasses to the men.

"Not so fast, as I prefer the beer." Atallah raised a hand, grabbing a frosted mug.

"You're a woman after my heart. You get the Cosmopolitan, Pat. I can get you an umbrella for it." James chuckled, sliding the Martini glass over to him.

After ordering a pizza and several appetizers, the four discussed geopolitics, world events, and recreational activities. Atallah responded to the informal atmosphere as her tautness dissipated.

"If you'll excuse me," said O'Reilly standing, "I should check on our other guests."

James stood. "I should ensure that Smith and Steele are keeping out of trouble." He walked off, understanding that she might relax, conversing solely with a woman who could relate to her visceral feelings.

Morales went right to work. "I don't understand it, as you're beautiful, smart, sophisticated, and compassionate, so how did you get involved with Hassan?"

The archeologist answered without hesitation. "You know how it is as teenagers everywhere need to rebel a bit. I found myself attracted to my childhood friend as he was charismatic, a great athlete, handsome, and passionate about politics. I was naïve and mistook his fanaticism for political enlightenment. My father knew he was trouble from the start and volunteered for assignments in Britain and America."

She chugged the last of her beer before continuing. "I've not heard from him in years. He then out of the blue offered me a unique opportunity to work on an excavation near Qumran. I was surprised that he even knew I was an archaeologist. Well, work was slow, so I jumped at it, but I also wanted to see the man he'd become."

"And did you like the man he became?" Morales' eyes glimmered.

Atallah shook her head. "He looked the same, but his fanaticism had gotten worse. By the time I found out, it was too late, and he said that I knew too much, and if I left, he'd kill me."

"Would he have killed you?" The leggy DS agent leaned in.

"I'm not sure." She shrugged her shoulders. "I hoped it was only a threat, but who knows? His lifeless, shark-like eyes sent shivers down my spine and he's a zealot who would sacrifice his life for the cause. That I know for sure."

Morales beamed. "You know what helps me forget my problems? I like to dance, so I think that I'll go ask Doug to dance. You should ask one of the other guys as they're all nice men. Come on." She said, grabbing her hand.

Approaching Smith's table, Morales asked him to dance, and he obliged with a smile. The two headed off for the bar's dance floor, which left Atallah standing by herself. O'Reilly invited her to sit, but she had other plans.

She glanced at James and beamed. "Would you care to dance with me?"

"Absolutely, but I left my dance shoes at home." He winked.

James stumbled out onto the deserted dance floor, feeling exposed and awkward. A fast-paced mix of 80s and 90s music saturated the air and appealed neither to him nor the half-full bar. The music remained much too fast for his country roots; however, it left plenty of room for the four to dance freely. Atallah capitalized on the fast-paced music to show her moves, which combined the elegance of a professional dancer with the exotic moves of a high-priced stripper. Consistently a step behind her, James eyed the beauty, as did the entire envious male-dominated crowd.

James relaxed as the seemingly everlasting dance finished. His physical prowess paled to hers on the dance floor. Delighted by the DJ's selection of a country love song, he approached the Jordanian beauty. Glancing into her dark-brown eyes, he drew her close to his body. He relished the touch of her soft hand while her hair's subtle strawberry fragrance delighted his olfactory senses. As they swayed back and forth, he twirled the exotic beauty to assuage O'Reilly's disapproving eye. She moved with the grace of a ballerina. The two danced for eight songs straight, working up an incredible full-body, forehead-dripping sweat. Riveted in the moment, James lost track of time. He admired her perfect rhythm as he nearly missed his deadline to call the director. Fortunately, his watch and its multiple beeps snapped him back to reality.

"I have to contact my headquarters. I enjoyed myself tonight, as you're an incredible dancer." He grabbed her hand and walked her back to the safety of his colleagues before trotting upstairs.

His team occupied all the rooms of the American Club. James walked a half-flight of stairs and then traversed a small uncovered walkway that connected the club to the living quarters. He inserted his key into the door, entered his room, and strode over to a gray case. James unlocked the case's combination lock, opened its top, and removed a satellite telephone. After extending the telescoping antenna and dialing the DS director's office, he stood connected and talking to him.

"Director, Suhar Atallah, our cooperating witness, informs that Hassan plans to resurrect a virulent plague, so I recommend she remains with me to help thwart his plans."

The director's tenor elevated. "As you indicated, this is now an investigative matter and outside our jurisdiction."

James let out a loud breath. "She's speaking candidly and we must act now or risk losing the initiative."

"Look, James, I understand your rationale. You make a compelling case. However, I just got a call from the FBI director, who demanded that we transfer custody of both al-Sammarri and Atallah so they can pursue their investigation. It's out of my hands, as the FBI has jurisdiction, so turn them over to the FBI tomorrow at the airport."

"But director, we risk her clamming up if we turn her over, and she's the best chance we have to catch Hassan. The intelligence agencies know little about him, and I've seen him face-to-face; I understand how he thinks. We still have links to the case given our handling of the Rewards for Justice investigation, and with her help, we can drop him before he strikes." James placed a hand on his hip.

"I've made my decision." The director's nostrils flared. "You'll give both terrorists to the FBI tomorrow. You got that?"

"Sir, she's not a terrorist, but an archeologist and a material witness. Hassan threatened her life if she abandoned him."

"Just follow my orders, James, and get your team back to DC as soon as possible, as we have other urgent missions to undertake."

James pressed his palm against his forehead. "Yes sir, I'll provide you a full report tomorrow. Bye."

"Son-of-a-bitch." James hung up the satellite phone and repacked it in his case. The director's alliance with the FBI bothered him, particularly given his persuasiveness. He accepted the jurisdictional issues and acknowledged the FBI's prowess on domestic investigations, but he doubted their overseas abilities, especially when weighed against the CIA and DS.

He returned to the bar to relay the news to the RSO and his team, but Mattson intercepted him as he neared the table.

"Did you learn anything more from our witness?"

James nodded. "She spilled her guts out about Hassan's plan."

The CIA officer grinned. "I've one of our planes on standby, so we can fly with her to el-Amarna tomorrow. We might even beat Hassan there and dig up the treasure ourselves."

"What's the CIA's interest in the el-Amarna treasure?" James glanced uneasily around the bar, pondering his own question.

"We must ensure that no other terrorist entity or foreign government uses it against us. The coronavirus devastated our people and our economy." Mattson knew the military would create a biological weapon and an antidote to its lethal effects.

"That sounds about right. The only problem is that the FBI requested that we handover both al-Sammarri and her tomorrow at the airstrip in Baghdad. My director sided with the FBI, so I've been ordered to do it." James sipped his beer.

"It's too bad that you couldn't fly out of Erbil, but the massive countrywide strike has shut down the airport. Credible intelligence about stinger missiles has grounded our helicopters for the week, and ground transport is dicey, but it's the only way you're getting out of the country this week." Mattson's posture stiffened as he felt a knot in his gut.

James shook his head softly. "Not great options, but I'd rather take my chances on the road.

"Leave it to me." Mattson pulled up his sleeves. "I'll make some calls, coordinate, and get in touch with you tomorrow. I have to go to the consulate for a planning session with my officers. The operation will be rushed, but I'll get it done. Have a safe trip back to Baghdad."

The base chief patted the resolute agent on the back before disappearing. James admired his dedication and courage. Clueless to the CIA's intentions, he hoped for higher intervention to permit his witness' involvement in the operation. He encouraged his team to join him in getting some rest, as there would be little time for it in the upcoming days.

The fully booked hotel left James with only a few options, so he requested Morales to house Atallah for the night. She agreed, motioning for the archeologist to follow her out.

Atallah gave James a pained look. "Can't I stay with you, as today's events are catching up with me and I feel safe with you. It may not be appropriate, but I feel that if I don't stay with you, something bad will happen. Silly, I know."

James glanced at Morales, who nodded, speaking to Atallah. "No problem. It's understandable given what you've been through today, and you're right, as he's a pretty capable guy and I'm sure he'll give up his bed to keep you safe. I know he'll remain a gentleman, isn't that right, Matt?" She eyed him.

James nodded, scratching his ear.

Atallah lacked a change of clothing, so she asked James for a shirt. He surveyed his polo shirts, but opted for one of his long-tailed dress shirts. He tossed her an airline travel pack that he carried for emergency purposes. The well-traveled agent spent many nights without his baggage as it circled some carousel halfway around the world.

Atallah showered, brushed her teeth, and then put on the dress shirt. She sauntered into the room, causing James to repress every emotion in his body. Her natural beauty overpowered him, as the backlighting cast her radiance into the room.

She turned around with her arms extended above her head and beamed. "So how do I look?"

"The shirt looks much better on you than me." He grinned playfully.

"It's very comfortable," she murmured, moving toward the bedroom and stopping at the door's threshold. "I had a great time tonight; it was the best time I've had in years. Thank you." Her faced glowed.

"The pleasure was all mine." He smiled. "You're a magnificent dancer and a talented lady. I hope you sleep well tonight, and I'll see you bright and early tomorrow."

"That couch doesn't look very comfortable. There's plenty of room in this bed for you and I promise not to bite." She grinned.

He welcomed the offer, imagining the warmth of her body and her skin's sweet fragrance. "That's a generous proposition," he said, "and one that I'd love to accept, but I think I'd better decline as Morales, for one, wouldn't approve. I'll come get you in the morning, as we have a busy day tomorrow." He turned aside, but his peripheral vision captured her shutting the door. He knew the image would linger.

CHAPTER 11: Misdirection

The alarm beeped at quarter past five in the morning, jolting James out of his deep slumber. His lower back twinged from the worn, spongy, decade-old sofa mattress. He regretted not sleeping in the queen-sized bed with his exotic companion - paramount, ironically, for better back support. He slipped into the cramped shower and focused the water stream on his back while lathering his body. His muscle soreness subsided after five minutes, so he rinsed his body before exiting and toweling off. He shaved, brushed his teeth, and dressed.

James peered through the doorjamb and eyed the Middle Eastern lady. Her angelic face in sleep masked her enigmatic and guarded character. He maximized his time by trotting downstairs, wolfing down a bowl of cereal, ordering a continental breakfast, and returning to his room, where he knocked on the bedroom door.

Atallah sat up in bed. "Come in. Good morning, Matt. Did you sleep?" She smiled, stretching her arms skyward.

"Not so well, I'm afraid. That sofa killed my back, and the morning call to prayer didn't help either. How did you sleep through it? Anyway, I brought you some breakfast." He pulled an end table to the bed, placing the breakfast tray on it.

"I asked you to share the bed, so you should've joined me." She gazed at him over the lip of her coffee cup.

"I should've taken that offer, as I'm sure I would've gotten a glorious night's sleep." He grinned.

She continued to stare. "Perhaps not. We may have practiced a different dance step."

He pursed his lips. "I have to pack and double check my equipment." He stood and stepped toward the adjoining room.

"You don't have to leave, even if it's getting hot in here." Her smile was eloquent.

He gave her a long, thoughtful look, and then shook his head. Duty, he mused, could be a pain in the ass. "I like the heat, but it's not the time. Besides, there's work to do and daylight is burning."

He resumed packing his equipment, folding his clothes, and organizing them in his suitcase, which had accompanied him to seventy-plus countries on six continents. The black suitcase bore the battered marks and security stickers of extensive travel. He had the routine down, organizing all his personal items and then his government equipment. After clicking the cases shut, he carried them down to a waiting local driver and consulate armored Suburban.

James threw his cases into the Suburban's well and walked over to O'Reilly, extending his hand. "Thanks for the hospitality and babysitting al-Sammarri. He looks comfortable sitting in the rear seat of the van. I like his metal bracelets and the drool coming out of his mouth."

With his team waiting, James trotted upstairs to retrieve Atallah, only to find her nowhere in plain sight, so he searched the bathroom and then checked her room. His eyes wandered the suite without encountering the exotic woman. Opening the closet, he stood mesmerized and speechless.

"I've been waiting for you." She exhaled, inching toward him in a black corset that accented her curvy but slender frame.

He felt her radiance. "You look stunning, but we must go." His eyes shined. "They're waiting for us, but perhaps we can dance another time."

James shrugged, grinned ruefully, picked her clothes off the chair, and handed them to her.

Her smile morphed into a comical pout. "Don't you like it? I expected a much more enthusiastic response."

"And if we were on vacation in France, you'd have seen a much different one. What I do for God and country." He closed the bedroom door behind him. "Hurry, get dressed and pack, as we should be in Baghdad before nightfall."

He left her to dress, perplexed by her forwardness. It was a reaction to either the previous day's adrenaline overdose or a case of hero worship, most likely stemming from her rescue from Hassan and the potent attraction they both felt. He lacked the energy to consider her motivations for coming on to him that way.

She exited the room and appeared just as striking as she had minutes earlier. Her natural beauty and exotic looks made even a pair of jeans and a tee-shirt look great. They ascended the stairs and walked through the lobby, exiting the club. They jumped into the front vehicle, joining O'Reilly, a local Iraqi driver, Bishop, and Clark. His other team members and al-Sammarri occupied the trailing van. As the two-car caravan drove out of the front gate of the American Club and turned right, a marked Kurdish police car pulled out to lead them.

The RSO looked toward the back seat. "I didn't want to be delayed, so the police will escort us to the town's outskirts. He'll drop off at that point and we'll be on our own. Besides, ISIS still may be lurking nearby."

"That's fine." James rested his hand on the grip of his pistol.

The night's activities left dark circles under their eyes. That, combined with the jet lag, contributed to the uneasy silence. Ten minutes into the six-hour journey, the two protective intelligence agents dozed off despite the constant jarring from the pothole-filled roads; their collective snores echoed throughout the vehicle. Minutes later, James received a cryptic call from Mattson, who advised him to stand down when it happened. He questioned him, but the CIA officer cut him off in mid-sentence and advised James to control the situation before hanging up.

"Who was that?" O'Reilly turned around to face James.

"That was Mattson, who wished us bon voyage."

"I told you he was solid and has this placed so wired that a fly couldn't spit without him knowing it?" The Irish-American agent grinned.

"You're right that he's a real pro." James considered the call's meaning as he analyzed the area, buildings, cars, and the terrain around their vehicle. He disliked the unknown, but he suspected that whatever Mattson had planned, it would unfold soon. The sudden change of a traffic light separated the police car from the two car motorcade. A woman in full veil sauntered in front of the car. The sun's backlighting turned the regular dark gown into a see-through garment, which highlighted a perfectly sculpted woman's figure. The driver's eyes went wide as she turned to eye him.

On the opposite side, a taxi van pulled up and its occupants piled out. James gripped his pistol. Just then, one man magnetically affixed a shoe-sized box onto the hood of the Suburban, while six armed wielding thugs drew down on their vehicle. James glanced back and observed a Chinese-made rocket launcher targeting their vehicle, recognizing his tactical disadvantage and the futility of any action.

"We want the girl." One of them tapped on the window. "Hand her over and we'll let you live."

"What now?" O'Reilly turned to James.

James depressed his radio's microphone button and ordered Wagner and the others to stand down. He appreciated the meticulously planned operation as the attackers knew the configuration and contents of the vehicles. They also knew the ballistic capabilities of each car, which made it pointless for James' team to execute a quick counter-attack.

"We comply as there's no other option." James eased the door open and stepped out, raising his hands in the air. "It will be cool, Suhar, as these men are rescuing you." His eyes looked to the side.

Atallah stepped from the car and squared off with James, peering into his eyes. She grabbed his chin and rotated it toward hers. Fear filled her dilated eyes as she grasped James around his lower back, clutching him hard. He hugged her as his eyes scoured the area.

"It's okay. Trust me, you'll be fine." He whispered.

One insurgent pulled her into the van as James threw his hands skyward. His heart remained steady, while his eyes wandered from al-Sammarri to the thugs holding them at gunpoint. They piled into their van and sped off, maneuvering around traffic and leaving a trail of dust in the air.

Wagner leaped from the van to join James. They studied the unusual, remote activated device, which had a small shape charge and affixed cylinders directed at the engine compartment. At first glance, they thought the cylinders might contain some sort of compressed gas to amplify the blast. Upon further inspection, the cylinders held smoke that would obscure visibility. Wagner pulled the device off the car and tossed it well off the roadway where it detonated, sending green smoke skyward that drifted in the light breeze.

"I don't understand." Wagner's face tightened. "This device kept us from pursuing them."

"I wouldn't give it too much thought." James took slow, even breaths as his posture relaxed. "We still have al-Sammarri, so let's get him to Baghdad International Airport, and then we can contemplate our next move."

James hopped back in the car and wiped the dampness from his face. His attitude puzzled the RSO.

"Let's go after them." O'Reilly's eyes hit James.

"No, transferring al-Sammarri to the feds at the airport takes priority." James' lips pressed together in a slight grimace.

The Iraqi driver looked at his boss. O'Reilly nodded and ordered the driver to proceed to the airport, so the two cars departed in unison. The rest of their trip proved uneventful. James pondered Mattson's plan and reflected on the fate of the seductive female archeologist.

CHAPTER 12: Cold Reception

Baghdad, Iraq

Sunset loomed as they neared the south gate at Baghdad International Airport. A DS agent from the US Embassy, accompanied by his local investigator, radioed O'Reilly. The two viewed the approaching two car motorcade and activated their hazard lights. O'Reilly pointed ahead. "There they are."

The DS agent maneuvered ahead of the two-car procession to lead them to the airport side entrance. As the three cars approached the side gate, the DS agent electronically lowered his window. The Iraqi guard matched their license plates to his list before waving the vehicles through the security checkpoint. A police car escorted the convoy out on the tarmac past two taxiing jumbo jets to a US marked jet.

The jet's pilots clicked a series of switches following their preflight checklists; its twin engines hummed as they prepared for takeoff. The US government recognized that Iraqi complicity in the rendition of al-Sammarri, a folk hero throughout Iraq and the Middle East, could spark major civil disturbances and terrorist reprisal attacks. Hence, the US government sheltered the Iraqi government from the operation as they were an important US ally in the battle against ISIS. The president recognized the gamble and deemed the operation well worth the risks.

James relished handing al-Sammarri to the bureau and resting. Headquarters already demanded comprehensive details to the entire operation, and they wanted them yesterday.

"This is it for you, al-Sammarri." James turned toward the man in the next seat. "Its game over. You'll be transported to America to face justice, and you'll be convicted for your heinous crimes. I know you'll burn in hell, but you'll rot in prison first. There'll be no glory or seventy-two virgins for you. You'll, instead, have thousands of America's most dangerous inmates lining up to get a piece of you." James reclined in his seat and stretched his arms forward.

Al-Sammarri, gaunt and hollow-eyed, returned the agent's stare. "No, it's your time that's over. You Americans think you're so superior. Allah will take his revenge on you. It's you who will be wiped off the globe." He turned away, closing his eyes.

"That's where you're wrong," James said as he shot him a flat look. "Your fellow Islamic extremists will be hunted down and killed, so you cannot dictate your will on others. Freedom will ring all over the Middle East and it's a shame that you'll not be around to witness it." He taunted, his stare morphing to a callous look.

As the car stopped, James scanned the grounds to ensure that the area was free of the press. Four FBI agents converged on the vehicle. Upon opening the door, the FBI agent-in-charge greeted him.

"Here's your man, however, we lost the girl," said James, shrugging.

"You did what? How's that possible?" The veteran FBI agent barked over the roar of the jet's engines.

"It's a long story, but our motorcade was ambushed in route by a professional group. They knew our route, vehicle armoring, tactics, and numbers. We couldn't stop it." James' head fell back.

"That's hard to believe, given your group's skill level. I must report to Washington." The G-man glanced at the master terrorist.

"I already did." James smiled.

"We'll take it from here. At least you delivered the ISIS leader." The FBI agent said, taking al-Sammarri by the wrist and leading him up the plane's stairs and into the craft.

After shaking James' hand, Bishop and Clark strode up the stairs, carrying their personal suitcases. The aircraft's hatch closed behind them.

James hopped into the car and they drove several hundred yards away from the aircraft. He envisioned tomorrow's headlines, highlighting the FBI's capture of the world's most wanted terrorist, and expected the slight.

DS often worked in the shadows, avoiding the limelight for both political and operational reasons.

Ten minutes later, the plane lifted off. James and his teammates became, as of this moment, a part of history. It was a transcendent moment, one laden with both a quiet euphoria and a giddy sense of relief.

"A job well done," said James, looking at his team. "Let's hope this capture shakes ISIS right down to its boots."

"I'm not that optimistic," O'Reilly mused. "But for every one of these bastards we neutralize, another one rises."

James gave a single nod. "It's like beheading a three-headed serpent, only to have another grow back. Although it's a futile effort, it has to be done as a serpent will keep destroying all in its path. It's the beast's nature, underscoring, that we have to attack its source of power. We must eliminate the ignorance, hate, poverty, and intolerance, which leads people to seek this destructive path." He said, shrugging off the intensity of his emotion. "Since we've solved the world's problems, let's head to the embassy."

"Right." O'Reilly folded his hands in his lap. "Let's get moving."

As they left the terminal grounds, James remained alert for the thirty minute drive. Staring out at the colorful mosaic that was Baghdad, James broke the silence. "This is an incredible city," he said, "and was considered the center of learning throughout times."

O'Reilly smiled his agreement. A true history buff, he loved to play tour guide. "Baghdad sits along the Tigris River and emerged in the eighth century, evolving into a cultural, commercial, and intellectual center for the Islamic World. Built in a circular design of that period, one-hundred thousand plus architects, designers and artisans merged on the city. They created its three concentric walls and four gates opening towards Basrah, Syria, Kufah, and Khorasan. A major highway sprang from each gate; a deep moat surrounded the city and served as another protective layer."

"Unbelievable," James smiled. "You're a wealth of knowledge. They did a magnificent job planning the city."

Undeterred, the RSO continued. "As you can see, Baghdad has been planned with wide, tree-lined streets. Its large homes, public buildings, organized bazaars, markets, and shopping centers give it a unique flare. Traffic jams only occurred within the last decade. The trees provide plenty of shade and blocked out the traffic; that is until capitalism brought more cars than the roads could accommodate. Baghdad is the heart and soul of Iraq. It's a pleasant blend of the present and the past. If it weren't for the civil war, it's a great assignment."

"That's amazing," James said as they pulled up to the embassy gate. "How long did it take you to memorize the guide book?" He jibed.

O'Reilly grinned, remaining quiet and shaking his head.

A guard circled the vehicle with a bomb-sniffing German Shepherd. After passing the inspection, they parked the cars and proceeded to the RSO's office. The ambassador's special assistant intercepted the DS agents and summoned them to the upstairs conference room, so the RSO and James followed the spry assistant that ushered them into a conference room with six individuals. The ambassador stood, motioning them toward a couple of chairs opposite of him. James shook the ambassador's hand and nodded at his deputy. He then greeted the CIA station chief, Erbil's base chief, the FBI attaché, and Baghdad's senior RSO.

Ambassador Jones rose from his chair. "Outstanding work, guys. This was a monumental achievement. I also want to acknowledge your efforts in defending the Erbil consulate. You prevailed against overwhelming odds."

The ambassador sipped his coffee. "I'm puzzled, though, by the news that you lost your witness. It's inconceivable that the attackers only took the girl and not al-Sammarri. What are your thoughts?"

James scratched his jaw. "The rescue operation was painstakingly planned and executed, showing a very professional group. They were well armed and coordinated, and they knew we were in armored vehicles and unable to return fire. They also knew motorcade tactics and used the element of surprise, and designed the bomb they placed on the vehicle to disable, not destroy it. The group must've prioritized freeing the girl with no collateral damage, so the only logical answer is that it was Hassan's group, as they had no desire to free al-Sammarri, but they needed the girl to finish their work in el-Amarna." James sat back in his chair with his hands clasped behind his head.

The ambassador nodded. "That makes sense to me as well." He turned to the CIA chief of station. "What's your thought John?"

The station chief scratched his forehead. "We had no prior intelligence that there was a group operating here, nor did the local Iraqi or Kurdish intelligence services, so it makes sense that Hassan wanted her back for her archeology skills and her knowledge of their operations. I agree with Matt." He winked at James.

"I'd like to keep your team here in Baghdad just in case the political situation deteriorates. It wouldn't surprise me if word of al-Sammarri's capture sparks massive demonstrations here." The ambassador said.

The FBI agent shook his head. "I can't believe you're buying his explanation for their botched transport operation. DS should never been given this case. The FBI has jurisdiction and should've carried out the arrest and transfer operation."

"The FBI couldn't find a criminal in a penitentiary without the warden's help," James said, "let alone your ass if your hands were in your back pocket."

James stroked his forehead and turned to the man at the end of the table. "Mr. Ambassador, I apologize for my outburst."

The chief of station raised a conciliatory hand and smiled. "OK, guys," he said. "Enough. We can't forget what we accomplished today, but what's next? We must safeguard our missions here in Iraq and around the world. As we witnessed in Erbil, news of al-Sammarri's capture triggered an attempt to overrun our consulate. It's a strong possibility that we'll see that happen here. At a minimum, there will be large, violent, anti-American demonstrations."

"With your permission, Mr. Ambassador," James said, "I can get the go-ahead from my headquarters to assist your RSO in safeguarding your personnel and facilities."

RSO Tom Jenkins acknowledged the agent's suggestion. "I could use the help in compound defense, protecting our dignitaries, and assisting our surveillance detection teams."

"Then it's settled." The ambassador scanned the group. "Tom will request MSD's extension to bolster security. Be sure to include the CIA's assessment regarding the precarious security environment that we're facing. We can't place our personnel in danger or risk our facility being burned and plundered. You guys make sure that this doesn't happen. I have to brief the secretary of state." The ambassador stood and left, signaling the meeting's conclusion.

James and O'Reilly trailed Jenkins back to his office. The DSS director required an update to understand the circumstances and to reallocate additional resources.

Jenkins opened his safe, removed a small two-by-four encryption card, and inserted it into the classified phone on the corner of his desk. "It's all yours. Just dial triple eight and the five digit extension."

James lifted the receiver and punched in eight digits. After five rings, a familiar voice answered. "I'll push to go secure. Stand by." James depressed the button for secure voice.

Within seconds, the phone's teleprompter flashed secret. "Director, I have you in secure voice at the secret level." James glanced at Jenkins.

"How's everything going out there?" Jacobs looked at his calendar.

"We just finished meeting with the ambassador, the deputy chief of mission, the chief of station, the base chief, the FBI's legal attaché, and the RSO. Because of the situation's volatility, the ambassador has insisted that the MSD team remain. A cable will be forthcoming." James pressed the phone to his ear, gritting his teeth.

"What happened during the final transport phase of the operation?" The director barked. "I have the FBI director breathing down my neck, and he's alleging that DS is a second-rate organization incapable of mounting a successful operation. I suspect he'll be taking it to a higher level. How could you lose the material witness?" He snorted.

"I had no choice. Resistance would've resulted in agent casualties, and it wasn't worth the risk given our strong disadvantage, and we couldn't risk losing al-Sammarri. The attack team knew our routes, armoring, weaponry, and tactics. I think the mission was compromised. Al-Sammarri was our primary mission, and we delivered him to the FBI." James picked some lint off his forearm's sleeve.

"It's a good thing you did, or I would've taken a pummeling if you failed that mission. You need to return immediately, so you can appear before congress."

"Sir, the ambassador has requested that we remain in place to help counter a possible volatile situation."

"Leave your team in place and report back to headquarters. I want you on the next flight."

"But director, with all due respect, there's another angle here, so I should remain here to help protect the embassy."

"This isn't up for debate. Just catch the next flight." The director hung up.

The director's intransigence left James little choice. He would have to tread delicately or risk his wrath and an assignment to Ulaanbaatar, Mongolia.

CHAPTER 13: A Higher Calling

Baghdad, Iraq

Rummaging through his backpack to ensure that he had a change of clothes, James rifled through his compass, GPS, utility knife, flashlight, gloves, ball cap, and wrap-around sunglasses. He zipped the pack shut, slung it over his shoulder, exited the RSO's office, and walked out of the embassy. The agent's fiery eyes scanned the compound grounds, its vacant streets, and its residential buildings; his posture relaxed as his eyes shined. Deliberately avoiding his deputy, he provided him plausible deniability as to his whereabouts.

James ambled out of the embassy's pedestrian exit, as daytime turned into night. He walked three blocks, crossed the street, and backtracked one block before shuffling down a side street. After walking several more blocks, he arrived at a modest neighborhood grocery store, where he entered, purchased a bottle of coke, and emerged a minute later sipping it. The buzz of a high-altitude drone interrupted the street's quietness and foreshadowed the perils that still lurked within the city. Kids played soccer down the street until a dark blue Mercedes sedan drove by them and pulled up in front of the store. The area appeared quiet other than a few passing cars and some local Iraqis smoking a hookah pipe, drinking coffee, and debating politics at a nearby internet café. The Hookah's mint tobacco flavor wafted into the air. James' eyes panned the neighborhood once more before he jumped into the car.

"Were you followed?" Dave Mattson glanced at him before looking forward.

"I doubt it as I ran a surveillance detection route with no glitches. Nobody from the embassy asked questions, so I don't expect any problems. I told my team that I was going back to my room to rest. They won't know that I'm missing until mid-morning."

"Excellent, we'll be long gone by then." The Erbil CIA base chief grinned.

Mattson punched the accelerator to his armored vehicle and sped down a narrow side street.

"This is dicey for me as I'm disobeying a direct order." James rubbed his eyes.

"Don't worry about protocol," Mattson said, tapping his fist against his heart. "The highest levels of government sanctioned this operation. The president believes the information you elicited from Atallah and sees Hassan's plan to resurrect a plague as a threat to our national security. We've captured several intercepts that corroborate your information, so he wants us to go to el-Amarna and either get the treasure first or intercept Hassan. The operation is compartmentalized. Your assistant secretary won't even be informed about your activities. Only the secretary of state has been apprised and he endorsed your participation."

"Say no more." James nodded. "Let's get it done."

The CIA counter-terrorism expert traversed the heart of the city and then backtracked into a modern residential area. He eyed his rearview mirror and noticed a black Range Rover for the second time. Driving down a narrow road, a car abruptly backed out into the street after the CIA officer passed. The driver of the Range Rover pounded his horn as Mattson sped off. Convinced that his tail was clear, he drove toward Yarmouk in the Mansour District, which was an upscale residential area that sat between the airport and the Green Zone. The drive, even with all the detours, took only thirty-five minutes in moderate traffic. As they approached their destination, the landscape changed from urban to rural and the area became more spacious, with large, professionally landscaped yards. Mattson pulled up to a black iron gate. James noticed an elaborate camera system, which monitored all the grounds and the vehicular and pedestrian entrances. This, he mused, was no ordinary residence.

Mattson depressed a remote control button and watched the iron gate opened into two sections. As they cleared the gate, it closed behind them. The DS agent scanned the vast grounds; it boasted a pool, tennis courts, and a spacious Japanese garden. A nine foot high concrete wall surrounded the two-acre lot. It was a mansion by anyone's standards. He deduced the CIA paid much better than DS. They kept their budget hidden for a reason, and it became increasingly clearer with each passing minute.

"I see the CIA has some nice perks." His eyes widened.

"This," Mattson said, "is one of our safe houses. We use it for special meetings and extended interviews." He smiled.

James analyzed the technological features of the grounds while walking toward the front door. The multiple layers of security fortified the residence. An elaborate camera system blanketed the grounds and the perimeter's exterior. His eyes counted nine cameras. Atop the nine-foot concrete wall sat a two-foot high electrified fence. Microwave alarms ran the entire length of the wall, creating a two-foot wide, six feet high virtual fence. Both fixed and motion-activated lights illuminated the entire grounds like a football stadium at night. All ground-floor and accessible windows on the second and upper floors contained iron grates.

The CIA base chief opened the front door and punched in a five-digit code into the alarm panel. James scanned the metallic door with a reinforced frame. Multiple deadbolt locks ensured the door remained closed unless its occupants desired company. Its advanced security features could thwart a person from either entering or escaping.

The house's subtle elegance impressed the DS agent as he stood in the foyer and eyed a spiral staircase that connected the vast entryway to the top floors. A ballroom and study sat to the left. He looked toward the rear and noticed a formal dining room, a large kitchen, and a breakfast nook that led to the back yard and a covered glass sun room. A formal living room with an enormous fireplace appeared to the right. He scrutinized a series of closed doors next to the living room. No doubt that the place once hosted the elite of Iraqi society. Every detail had been addressed, from the study's grand piano to the china in the dining area.

"Nice place, Dave." James examined a jade oriental vase perched atop of a three-foot-high Roman pillar.

"Saddam's favorite uncle owned this place and entertained the rich and famous, such as the royals, parliamentary members, and film stars, but that was decades ago." Mattson gave a slow, disbelieving shake of his head.

"Why am I here?" James' voice softened. "I don't qualify for the red carpet."

Mattson glanced to the side. "Follow me. You've established great rapport, which isn't always easy. The CIA figures you're the best person to convince Atallah to help us nail Hassan."

Walking into the living room, Mattson depressed a hidden button on an eighteen century vintage grandfather clock. A door-sized panel slid open, exposing a stairwell. James admired the craftsmanship as the panel's crown molding and other features hid the passageway from plain view. The two descended a staircase to its base, where Mattson placed his hand on a door's electronic reader. A green light swept across the small screen; it scanned his fingerprints, analyzed them against a database, and affirmed his clearance. A lock disengaged, allowing them to enter a security room. Two men greeted the base chief with subtle deference.

"How's our girl? Has she behaved?" Mattson extended his hand to the veteran security officer.

"All's quiet." The officer gripped Mattson's hand.

Mattson patted James on the shoulder. "This is where you come in. Atallah's the key to grabbing Hassan. She understands how he thinks and what he's after in el-Amarna. We need her cooperation and it's up to you my friend."

James quirked an eyebrow. "You don't ask for much."

Mattson nodded to his officer, who opened a side door by depressing a rectangular button on his control panel. James passed through the door and found Atallah sitting on a bed. A local channel station displayed the weather on a forty-two-inch HDTV.

"Are you okay?" His eyes captured hers.

"What's going on?" She sprang off the bed to meet him halfway.

He peered into her brown eyes, while grabbing both of her hands.

"Your information's correct. Hassan's off to el-Amarna to push his plan, so make no mistake, Suhar, if he succeeds, the world could end. He may intend to release the plague on only America and Israel, but a virus knows no borders. Even if our doctors develop an effective antidote and vaccine, it doesn't mean it will work as its resilience and adaptability may make it unstoppable. A virus has an amazing ability to mutate. It's a dangerous leap of faith if Hassan thinks the virus will only kill westerners."

She nodded. "As I told you, he's a fanatic. He'll follow through with his plans, even if it costs him his life. He's a deeply religious man, and I'm sure he thinks Allah will protect the innocent."

"Then he's flat out insane." His stomach hardened. "Our scientists have created a computer-generated model that shows how fast the virus will advance with their initial projections showing the sickness will spread worldwide in months and be airborne for over a year. Billions of people will die. Do you understand that number as it's one-sixth of the earth's population?" His eyes darkened.

She covered her eyes with both hands, stepped back, and sat on the bed. "What have I done and how can I help?"

"You know his thought process and he'll certainly try to find the gold chest without you. Will he be able to locate it?" His lips parted slightly.

She shrugged. "He had a map and a general idea where he should look. Given his determination, it's likely that he'll succeed with sufficient time. I also shared my thoughts with him and he has a photographic mind, so he'll discover it. I can guarantee that."

"We have to act now." His voice elevated.

"I'll help you anyway I can, but we must get to the treasure first and excavate it." Her legs felt restless.

"Then that's what we'll do." He pulled her tight to his chest. As he released his embrace, she pulled him closer. Long moments passed before the two parted, causing his heart to hammer against his chest.

James recognized the need to prepare for the journey to Egypt. Fortunately, Mattson's staff had handled all the logistical details, as he instructed them to purchase clothes and a large backpack for Atallah. They would board a small aircraft within the hour.

CHAPTER 14: Hourglass

El-Amarna, Egypt

With the sun nearing its peak, Hassan glanced at his watch's thermometer; it registered one-hundred and ten degrees. This didn't bother him. He found the searing heat of the Middle East comforting. He had learned early on how to embrace adverse circumstances, particularly those over which he had no control. Like the Chinese monk, Hassan had trained his mind, body, and soul to handle heat, cold, and extreme pain. Composed, he welcomed the blistering sun while his sweat-drenched colleagues struggled with each passing step.

He scanned the desolate, sandy terrain for a suitable site to unroll his copper scroll. His eyes froze on a nearby sculpted, preserved rectangular two-ton rock from the late Cretaceous period. He recognized the Egyptians' mastery of mummification and envisioned his unspoiled and sought-after treasure. His operation relied on the bat's vitality and viability.

Hassan rolled out the French-produced overhead satellite imagery, eyed it as he examined the surrounding terrain features, and struggled to decipher Atallah's notes scrawled on the imagery that marked the temples, houses, and other notable buildings. By identifying the remaining structures, he could orient the map to calculate the treasure's location. Unveiling the copper scroll, he then removed the cipher key from his backpack. His confidence spiked as he united the two; the fabled gold case now appeared within his grasp. The treasure would level the playing field, permitting him to strike down the infidels.

He placed the cipher key on the scroll; it contained a directory of items on one side and a list of locations on the other. The key's midpoint contained a miniature map of el-Amarna, centered on the Great Temple. Hassan examined the one-hundred plus decorative hieroglyphs on the scroll, but further scrutiny revealed seventy-five exact pairs, so he glided the key over the scroll until two bat hieroglyphs aligned with those on the scroll. The apex of the boomerang-shaped key held a protractor-like device; when manipulated properly, it displayed the same hieroglyph in a pea-sized circle. The rear of the protractor and the apex of the key's main body intersected with a precise location on the map. He pressed his black marker to the map and removed the cipher key.

The cipher key's simplicity astonished him. The scroll was a list of items and unaffiliated locations without it. Upon merging them, he realized el-Amarna's secrets, acknowledging Atallah's analysis of the scroll and the cipher key. She had determined their function, interaction, and which of the many symbols represented the targeted artifact. He trusted her reasoning and powers of deduction. Otherwise, he didn't know which pair of hieroglyphs to try next.

Jubilant and on the verge of discovery, his men pushed him for the other el-Amarna riches. He froze them with a steely glance; principle rather than greed drove him. He had no interest in the vast amounts of gold and silver the ancient city held, but he calmed them with the promise of future riches once he unearthed his artifact.

Hassan removed a magnifying glass from his backpack to analyze the miniature map on the scroll. He placed the scroll side-by-side with the satellite imagery of el-Amarna and compared the scroll's map to the imagery. It was difficult to find common features. He grasped for the answer, but found the imagery's comprehensibility much less precise than the scrolls. His eyes scrutinized each wall, broken pillar, and unique structure for ten minutes. He scratched his head before recognizing a likely corner of the Great Temple. He reoriented his map and identified his precious artifact's location; it rested somewhere in the Aten Temple.

Finished with the cipher key, he repacked it in his rucksack. "We're on the brink of the world's greatest discovery. The folktale of el-Amarna is true. Even the world's greatest archaeologists have dismissed the treasures of el-Amarna as a simple myth. We're about to prove them wrong. Within hours, we alone will discover an artifact that will give us the great equalizer. America and Israel will be brought to their knees. Let's go conquer our fate. Allah will guide us to our victory. Allah is great." He looked toward the sky.

Hassan looked at his compass and then spotted the Great Temple off to a distance. He walked south down the royal road; the sheer size of each structure amazed him. He peered to the right, reviewed his map, and noticed the sparse remains of the Great Palace, a colossal structure spanning six-hundred meters. The palace meandered to the Nile. At four-hundred meters into their walk, he stopped at the King's House. He scrutinized Atallah's notes and realized that the Aten Temple was the next structure on the left.

He approached the temple and reviewed the scroll; this narrowed the search to the temple's southwest corner. As they reached the corner, Hassan and his team unpacked three advanced metal detectors. Hassan assembled his detector by connecting its three sections and then adjusted its sensitivity to the highest level. He swung the detector's search coil back and forth across the ground and listened to the steady chirping of the machine, expecting the imminent discovery of the fabled gold case. Hassan and his two confidantes searched in a grid pattern with meticulous care. The steady beeps of their metal detectors frustrated them.

After scanning the four-hundred square foot area, the lack of hits bewildered him. Hassan ordered his team to re-inspect the area. Upon completing a fruitless second search, his face morphed to red as his temper flared.

"Damn it." He slammed his walking stick to the ground, hitting a solid structure just beneath the surface of the sand. He dropped to his knees and scraped away the sand, exposing a four-by-four foot rock slab. Hassan summoned his men, and they brushed away layers of sand to uncover six more rock slabs. This, he mused, explained the failure of his metal detectors. Perplexed, he pondered the finding's significance and whether the folklore surrounding el-Amarna was nothing more than ancient fiction.

Hassan recalled Atallah's discussion about the ancients' use of hidden chambers and booby traps. He stood and walked from slab to slab, tapping his walking stick against the ground. They all sounded solid with one exception. He hit it again and noted a higher pitch.

"Grab your pry bars, get over here, and use your combined strength to lift this slab." Hassan grinned.

His five disciples wedged their steel bars into the seams surrounding the three-hundred pound slab; they struggled to find a gripping point. They jiggled their pry bars back and forth as they prepared to leverage the weighty slab. Each man pried at one of the slab's corners. After two minutes of wriggling with it, the slab slid.

"Be careful. Move it over to the side." Hassan barked, quirking an eyebrow.

The men grunted in unison; the compressed sand packed into the surrounding seams acted like cement, doubling its actual weight. Determined, the men concentrated their strength and lifted the slab to the side.

Then, to their amazement, the five men peered into a two-story deep underground cavity. Hassan tied a rope to a Coleman lantern and lowered it into the cavern. As the lantern drifted downward, it illuminated a greater portion of the room and its trove of artifacts.

Hassan's wide eyed team rigged two rappelling ropes, tying them off to a nearby solid two-ton column. Mindful of the ancient's booby-traps, Hassan gave two of his men the privilege of going first.

"Al-Ful and Samia, go down and secure the site." He said, rubbing his hands together.

The two hooked up their O-rings and slid down the ropes, making the twenty-five foot descent. Hassan snapped his O-ring to the rope and backed to the edge of the hole, while instructing the others to secure the temple topside. With one backwards leap, he disappeared into the cavern and landed at its base seconds later.

"Be careful down here. Look before you step and try not to disturb any of these items. You could trigger a trap and entomb us forever." Hassan said; his gaze skipping around the room.

"You shouldn't watch American adventure movies and poison your soul." Al-Ful crossed his arms and thrusted-out his chest. "It's not reality."

"Think what you like, but I'll only caution you once." Hassan's head cocked to the side.

Al-Ful removed a flashlight from his vest and scanned the room. Samia and Hassan panned left to right with their flashlights illuminating the cave's secrets; the spectacle amazed them while affirming the legend. Just a cursory glance revealed a gold sarcophagus, an assortment of extravagant vases, precious gems and jewelry. Several colossal marble statues accented in diamonds, rubies, emeralds, pearls, and gold lined a nearby wall. What captivated him rested in the chamber's northeast corner, setting on a table. The small chest appeared two feet long, one foot wide, and one foot high. It differed from what he had imagined, uniquely decorated in gold.

Preoccupied on the gold chest, he failed to notice al-Ful seeking his own riches. A fifty-carat white diamond sat lodged in the hand of a marble statue of Ra. Al-Ful rejoiced as he unknowingly released a pressure switch. Hassan turned to witness a bladed pendulum swinging down from the ceiling and severing al-Ful's head. His head flopped to the side while his neck spurting blood and body fell to the ground.

"I hope this gets your attention. I ordered you guys not to touch anything. This is a sacred place with its own defenses, so I urge you to walk in my footsteps." Hassan pointed at Samia.

"I've got your back, boss. Lead on." Samia clutched his hands together.

Hassan crept toward the small chest; it conjured up his days in Iraq, where he had planted roadside bombs on key access roads against American troops. But the ancients had simple, yet creative ways to end potential threats. Al-Ful's untimely demise reminded him of their ingenuity; their innovation surpassed the explosive devices that he emplaced for an unsuspecting enemy. He contemplated the ancient's other awaiting surprises.

He arrived at the stone table and squatted to search for trip wires or other activation mechanisms. Unfortunately, his move was a detriment to his lifelong friend. *Swish!* A three foot long spear sailed out of the wall and impaled Samia. Perhaps the light source's interruption above or his motion had activated the trap. It didn't matter now. Freeing the cavern of its one veritable treasure rested with him.

Hassan looked down at his fallen friend before rising to his feet. He skulked to the table, skirting the light. A sudden surge of adrenaline heightened his senses. He observed the gold-plated chest, blew the dust off the ornate artifact, and savored the revelation. The chest bore a hieroglyph in each corner; it matched a disease-ridden bat on the copper scroll and his cipher key. His landmark search appeared over. His heart raced as he pondered the chest's removal without triggering another trap.

An eerie quiet swept the room, disrupting his concentration. Hassan contemplated his options as time seemed frozen, and then he realized the answer. He traced the light source to a point on the ceiling; it ended about twenty meters from his two associates positioned above. He had to think like the ancients, but employ modern technology, so he speculated the booby trap would be inactive at night or in the dark.

He unclipped his radio from his belt and depressed a button to trigger his microphone. "Al-Bayd, Al-Bayd, this is Hassan. I need you."

"What do you want?" The devoted disciple said.

"Look for, discover, and cover a light source; it should be about twenty meters northeast of your present position. Look for a softball-size hole. Can you do that for me?" Hassan glanced up through the roof's hatch.

Al-Bayd reviewed his compass and then paced off twenty meters in a northeasterly direction. Arriving at the location, he studied the area, unable to locate anything that resembled a softball sized hole.

He lifted his radio to his mouth. "I can't find it, boss. There's nothing out here. Are you positive that you provided me the correct bearing?"

"Look for anything unusual." Hassan's voice elevated.

After minutes, he observed a quarter-sized hole in a foot high pillar buried in the sand. His right hand covered it; Hassan acknowledged he found it. Al-Bayd examined the small hole and saw a radiant cut diamond imbedded several inches down. It refracted the sunlight to shoot it deep in the chamber. This could explain the difference in the size of the light beam that his boss had observed.

Al-Bayd trotted to the hatch's opening and radioed his boss that he covered it. Hassan instructed him to reduce most of the light entering through the removed slab. His trusted disciple retrieved a tarp from his backpack and rolled it out over the slab. Hassan grabbed his night vision goggles from his backpack and activated them; darkness turned into light. He tested his theory and extended his hands forward. Compensating for his loss of depth perception because of the dated Russian-made devices, he grabbed the chest with both hands and inched the artifact closer to the edge. A final swift motion freed the artifact. He exhaled; his facial muscles relaxed. The sixty pound box surprised him.

He set the artifact on the ground, approached Samia, and grabbed his backpack; it contained a gold-plated chest that was the size of two shoeboxes stacked upon one another. He placed the replica on the table and opened the lid to the chest. He removed the improvised device composed of C-4 high explosive and a dual fusing system. A one-inch thick, rectangular, six-by-twelve-inch piece of plywood held both fuses. He set the timer to one minute and activated the device that served as a safety switch. Once the timer completed its countdown, then the primary fusing system would be activated. He wired in a motion sensor to the lid to trigger the device.

Hassan lowered the lid on the chest and inched the chest back into the middle of the table. By thinking like the ancients, he had beaten them. He retraced his footsteps to the dangling ropes, only stopping to pick up Samia's pack. Hassan removed his goggles and radioed al-Bayd to allow a slight quantity of light into the chamber. He placed the ancient artifact into Samia's backpack, tied the line to the backpack's cloth handle, and tugged on the rope. Al-Bayd's hands pulled the rope to the case. As he watched the backpack edge upward, he smiled, as his plan was advancing, albeit with fewer of his trusted warriors. At least, he mused, they had died for an honorable cause. He hated leaving them behind; they would be entombed with the high priestess of el-Amarna, who lay undisturbed in her sarcophagus.

Once the backpack reached the cavern's hatch and al-Bayd secured it, he started his ascent up the ropes. Minutes later, Hassan retrieved the backpack and recounted the deaths of Samia and al-Ful to the stunned survivors.

Hassan ordered the team to restore the slab to its original position. With a light sheet of sand beneath it, the slab glided back into place. Before leaving, the three men paid tribute to their fallen comrades with a moment of silence. As they walked toward their jeep, Hassan instructed al-Bayd to go back, remove the stone, and allow light to filter back into the chamber. He didn't want to deprive any followers of the opportunity to match wits with the ancients. Al-Bayd trotted back to the foot high pillar and removed the stone he used to cover the quarter-sized hole. A fine beam of sunlight penetrated the chamber.

CHAPTER 15: Destiny

Egypt

Mirroring her previous shopping trips, Dr. Aafia Sukhayla checked off each item that she required for her work. She had been born and raised in Cairo, a sprawling city of sixteen million, and intimately knew its streets. The daughter of aristocrats, she attended the best schools and eventually journeyed to America to study biology at the University of Wisconsin, specializing in genetic engineering. She finished near the top of her class and earned a PhD and received job offers from three prestigious pharmaceutical companies. She declined them and returned home to work with an emerging biotech firm; it pioneered methods to boost crop yields.

Sukhayla loaded her bounty of Petri dishes and beakers into the tail of her Jeep Cherokee. She hopped into her car and drove six hours to the resort town of Taba. After checking into the Marriott hotel, she opted to swim in its luxurious pool. She changed into her two-piece bathing suit, reflecting on her willing adoption of certain explicit aspects of western culture. She valued the footing that women enjoyed in American society. At five feet, five inches, she stood lean and exotic with long, jet black hair, an olive complexion, high cheekbones, full lips, and dark eyes, reflecting her Egyptian roots. Her bright smile could illuminate any room while her eyes could mesmerize the casual passerby who glanced upon them. The generous use of eye make-up amplified the effect.

Careful not to get her hair wet, Sukhayla placed her hair up in a ponytail. She sat at the pool's edge and lowered herself into the temperate water. After her long drive, the water invigorated her. The scorching desert sun warmed her body, so she sprang out of the pool after fifteen minutes to order a drink at the poolside bar. She toweled off, slipped a skirt over her bathing suit, grabbed her bag, and strolled to the bar. She slid onto a bar stool and gazed out at the crystal blue waters of the Red Sea.

"What can I get the beautiful lady?" The Egyptian bartender said.

"I'll have a margarita, please." She smiled.

As the bartender turned to prepare the drink, a finely dressed Middle Eastern man tapped the bar. "Make that two," he said. Turning to the doctor and sitting next to her, he asked, "May I join you? Taba is beautiful this month of the year."

"I prefer the French Riviera in the fall." She gave him the code phrase in response and beamed. "Besides, do I have a choice? Would you leave if I said no?"

"If you asked, then I'd leave, but I'd be disappointed." The man winked.

"Then you should stay." She eyed the man from head to toe.

"Allow me." He dropped a twenty-dollar bill on the bar.

She smiled again. "Thank you, but I only accept drinks from people I know."

The man grinned. "My name is Hanni al-Bayd. And let me guess. You're the lovely Aafia Sukhayla, a renowned genetic biologist. Hassan's waiting for you and has a special artifact that he wants you to analyze. We must leave within the hour if we're to arrive by nightfall."

"Can I get my drink to go?" she turned to the bartender.

"I'm parked near the hotel's front entrance in a Land Cruiser. I'll wait for you there." He stood and shuffled off.

She sauntered upstairs, sipping her drink. She would have preferred to stay and dine by the sea; however, the opportunity to meet with Hassan and analyze the artifact pleased her. Fortunately, her suitcase remained packed, so she gathered all her other belongings and gear. At the front desk, she smiled upon the news that al-Bayd had already settled her bill.

Sukhayla joined her newfound benefactor, curbside, tossed her luggage into the back seat, and then climbed in next to the man and belted herself in. He shifted into drive and depressed the accelerator. The two settled in for the five-hour drive, more than doubling the journey's normal drive time. They drove a circuitous, pockmarked route to prevent any tail. Al-Bayd drove northwest for several hours before cutting back and bearing northeast toward Jebel Hilal. They showed up at the mountain at nine o'clock at night. It would be dangerous to negotiate the winding roadway at night. Instead, the two pulled out their sleeping bags, curled up, and rested in the car.

The sun's rays pierced through the windshield at six in the morning, stirring them from their slumber. After breakfasting on fruit and bread, they donned their hiking clothes, repacked their backpacks, topped off their water bottles, and set out on foot to negotiate the last leg of their journey. Barely breaking a sweat, their strides remained long, as they conquered the first stage of the trek's incline. The two rested, reaching for their water bottles. Sukhayla sat on a large boulder and viewed the horizon. The biblical landscape mesmerized her.

Al-Bayd walked up and touched her on the shoulder. "It's a beautiful view, but you must listen to me. The next leg can be treacherous, so you must follow my instructions and stay at my side."

Her eyes widened. "Why? What's ahead?"

"It's very dangerous. You'll find out soon enough." He slung his backpack over his shoulders. "Let's go."

She trailed him, scanned both sides of the trail, and observed the unusual, prearranged boulders on the hillside, while failing to spot the vigilant ISIS warrior; he could unleash thirty tons of rocks with the flick of a switch. Al-Bayd whispered into his radio, giving the sentry the code word for safe passage.

About four-hundred meters up the path sat another surprise. A thin, clear line crossed their path, a foot off the ground and attached to a Claymore mine. They both stepped over it and continued up the mountain. During the next hour, the two hiked carefully, passing a series of booby-traps, landmines, and battle-hardened warriors. Each one swore an oath to protect the Islamic State's most important base in the Middle East. As they finished the second phase of the hike, eight lighthearted men greeted them.

Al-Bayd embraced the group's leader. "It's great to see you, brother. I've brought you a new Koran, letters from home, and a new watch. Our mission to el-Amarna was a great success. Victory's at hand. Praise Allah."

"I know. Hassan boasted about his success, but mentioned that it came at the expense of two of our soldiers." The ISIS commando said, frowning.

At over seven-thousand feet in elevation, the view overlooking the peninsula captivated the female geneticist. The last phase of the journey, a mere five-hundred feet, remained the tough part of the trek; its three-hundred foot vertical rock cliff challenged even the most seasoned of climbers.

Al-Bayd's brother radioed a vigilant guard who unleashed three climbing ropes over the cliff; the ropes landed next to the newcomers.

"Your ride to the top awaits you, brother." He said, grinning and pointing to the ropes.

Al-Bayd tied the doctor's backpack to the third line and ordered the guard to raise it. After hugging his brother, al-Bayd assisted Sukhayla into her climbing harness. He cinched up the straps and tugged on them to ensure their integrity. He slipped into his harness and instructed her to use the same hand and footholds as him. A newcomer to mountaineering, she learned the basics of rock climbing in the first fifty feet and found it exhilarating.

With each crimp, side-pull, and open handgrip, the two scaled the cliff in an hour. The doctor shadowed and duplicated his hand and footholds. Upon reaching the crest, she pulled herself up over the rim with a glow in her eyes. Sweat poured from her forehead and soaked through her shirt. She stood with her hands on her hips and peered at the nearby hills and valleys. Fascinated by the panoramic sight, she hated to abandon it. However, duty called and Hassan would demand that she get started immediately.

As they climbed a narrow ridgeline, the cave's car-sized entrance appeared. She closed her tired eyes and smiled. Both the mountain's steep grade and final cliff had challenged all her muscle groups. Pain radiated through her shoulders and thighs. The sun's heat had sapped her energy; her arrival at the operational base's entrance and its shade brought a cascade of relief.

"Alhamdulillah (Praise be to God) brother." Al-Bayd shook the guard's hand. "Delta-Echo-Victor-India-Lima-Nine-Eleven."

The password is correct. "Please place your hand on an electronic reader." The guard motioned to the scanner with one hand while his other one remained on his pistol's grip. A small green light emitted as it scanned al-Bayd's hand, matching his palm and fingerprints with the ones in the accompanying computer database. A green light flashed as a large metal vault door opened and disappeared into the cave's ceiling. She admired the base's set up, from its impenetrable location to its impressive array of security measures. Cost, it was clear, was no issue.

As they began their gradual descent into the cave, the light faded. With each passing step, she felt the walls collapsing onto her. The drop in temperature, dampness, and low visibility only amplified the effect. Reaching the mid-point of the tunnel, she observed a bright light at the narrow passage's end. With each footstep, the dampness and her claustrophobic feeling dissipated as it transformed into added warmth and light. She rejoiced as she neared the great opening. She stepped over the door's threshold into a large room, pressing her palms against her eyes. Her eyes scanned to the left where she saw a level III-type bio-hazard facility; it appeared similar to the ones she had used in America.

"Aafia, over here." She snapped her neck to the right. Hassan motioned her to the corner of the cave and pointed to the greatest treasure of el-Amarna.

"Isn't it amazing, Aafia? Look at it." He said, standing frozen with a slack mouth.

Her eyes widened. "It's the most beautiful artifact that I've ever seen. It's magnificent. Where did you discover it?"

"It's one of el-Amarna's many treasures," said Hassan, grinning.

Bouncing from foot to foot, her voice trembled. "Do you have any other artifacts? This is the greatest archaeological discovery ever."

His head shook. "This is the only el-Amarna treasure that I retrieved. It's the most valuable one though, as it will annihilate the Israelis and the United States."

Her brow furrowed. "I don't understand. My degree is in biology, not in archaeology. I'm not sure how to assist you?"

"Most people see this decorated gold chest as a beautiful artifact. Yet, its contents are the genuine treasure and the reason you're here. I'm sure you've heard the story of the ancient plague that wiped out the city of el-Amarna, and how two survivors buried all its riches throughout the ravaged city. I believe this find supports that legend."

"You should go public with this news." She rose on her toes. "You've actual proof that the treasures of el-Amarna exist and that the legend of their demise was true."

He lifted a cautionary hand. "Did you ever wonder what decimated the city? All the people were wiped from the planet in an instant. The story reflects that a great plague descended upon the city as Ra's punishment. Are you familiar with Ebola?"

"Absolutely, it has killed thousands of people throughout the world since 1976 and could balloon to several million if not contained. The fear is that it will soon mutate and become transmitted from human-to-human. It's believed that airborne transmission of Ebola would cull over half of the world's population." Her muscles relaxed as she canted her head.

He beamed. "El-Amarna was lethal to everyone it encountered. The doctor and blacksmith survived because they were away when the plague hit. A mummified bat in the chest has the plague imbedded in its tissues, so I wish you to resurrect this plague and alter it to make it the ultimate biological weapon."

Her mouth fell open. Not that she couldn't do it, as her background and American training made it a straightforward process. The overwhelming ramifications of creating a virulent Ebola strain and releasing it on the world shook her. She despised the Americans, but did she hate them that much to risk humanity's downfall?

CHAPTER 16: Dark Knights

The CIA's C-12 jet rocketed from Iraq to Egypt in the stygian sky. The pilot got a last-minute departure and landing clearances from Iraqi and Egyptian authorities because of the agency's extensive contacts and an outlay of cash. CIA Erbil Base Chief Dave Mattson accompanied James and Atallah, coordinating with Cairo station for support, weapons, and other gear for the journey.

"Cheers, to a successful mission." James raised his glass to his companions. "This Italian red wine and five-course meal are spectacular." He sipped from his crystal glass.

"This tilapia with lobster sauce is exquisite." Atallah's eyes rolled back.

"Why do I feel that this is the condemned man's last meal? Is there something you're not telling me, Dave? These comforts are usually reserved for the rich and shameless, such as dictators, dissidents, and spies." He glanced at the veteran spook while pondering his royal treatment.

"Nothing in life is free. I can't tell you how many spies this plane has flown to safety." Mattson grinned.

"I'm sure that Noriega, Saddam Hussein, al-Qaddafi, and the Shah of Iran enjoyed the luxuries of the friendly skies." James felt a knot in his belly.

The plane shuttered as it experienced a series of rhythmic bumps or chops. Atallah gripped James' arm.

He caressed her hand. "Relax my dear as it's only light turbulence, probably because of our sudden decrease in altitude. Let me tell you about the time I was flying in Iraq to Erbil, where we faced a wall of sand that stretched from the ground to the clouds. It was reminiscent of a scene from a movie where the sandstorm inhaled a biplane. Our pilot made an emergency landing so we could take cover. We eventually landed in Erbil, where our Iraqi hosts regaled us with a feast to honor us. I wanted to build trust by respecting Iraqi customs, so I ate the fish off the colonel's greasy fingers. Resultantly, I had to take a course of antibiotics to deal with the bacteria that flooded my gut."

"Enough of my stories, Suhar, tell me more about Hassan's fanaticism." James poured her another glass of wine.

"Hassan is the most determined man I know and committed to destroying America. It was his zealotry that precipitated our high school break-up." She sighed. "During the Iraq war with America, he loved fighting the infidels. His ingrained psychosis transcended patriotism, and I believe he's the most dangerous man alive." Her lips squeezed together in a slight frown.

James exhaled. "Obviously," he mused, "Hassan has to be stopped, so your help is vital, as you understand how he thinks."

"I'll help you any way I can." She nodded.

"Okay, now let's get some rest. We're going to need it." He smiled knowingly.

Within minutes, they both drifted off. Three hours later, an abrupt change in motion and cabin pressure woke James. The plane veered to the right as it descended upon the city of the ancients. During the journey, Atallah had used his shoulder as a pillow. He turned and gazed at her, transfixed by her angelic countenance and captivated by the faint message of her perfume. What the hell, he thought, is happening here?

When the jet's wheels touched down at Cairo International Airport, she awoke and smiled, as the nap had revitalized and readied her for the arduous journey across the desert to el-Amarna. The name itself quickened her pulse; a place brimming with ancient splendor and an archeologist's dream. The jet taxied for ten minutes, stopping at a remote part of the airport next to a large hanger capable of storing a jumbo jet. Egyptian officials thumbed through their passports and issued them tourist visas. Over to their right, a US Blackhawk helicopter sat with its rotors spinning. Mattson introduced them to Eric Blake, a veteran CIA operations officer with extensive local knowledge.

"This is where I leave you." The base chief smiled. "You're in expert hands. Blake's one of our best. Good luck."

Blake took his cue and provided them with a hasty briefing about their approach to el-Amarna. He also discussed the specific equipment for the mission as he directed them to the helicopter; he cautioned them to lower their heads as they walked under the craft's rotating blades. As they approached the Blackhawk, the crew chief directed them to their places. The passenger compartment had been reconfigured to accommodate two four-wheeled All-Terrain Vehicles (ATVs), weapons, and other essential equipment.

James hopped into the helicopter and helped his female companion into the craft, strapping her into a rear-facing seat behind the pilot. He sat opposite of her, facing forward. James, an adrenaline junky, found night flying invigorating. Blake sat on the aircraft's left side, while the crew chief sat opposite of him.

Midnight loomed as the pilots donned their night vision goggles to prepare for the sixty-minute trek. Masking their imminent arrival, the Blackhawk flew north and to the west, and then landed about ten kilometers northeast of el-Amarna. With the blades spinning, the crew chief and Blake offloaded the ATVs and other gear with dust swirling all around them. Within minutes, the Blackhawk had vanished into the night. Blake hoped their hasty landing had summoned none of the bands of thieves that roamed the area.

The CIA officer handed James an MP-5 submachine gun and distributed the cargo of twenty, thirty-round magazines. The DS agent calculated the total number of rounds at six-hundred. He attributed Blake's wariness as a matter of professional practice. Or was he withholding intelligence? James also received a Sig Sauer 9mm pistol with four magazines, night vision goggles, and pre-programmed GPS.

James loaded his web-gear with a knife, grenades, ammunition, a utility tool, a hydration system, and a compass. He stowed a medical kit, binoculars, and Atallah's belongings into a special compartment on the ATV. James climbed on it, turned the key in the ignition, and the ATV's engine roared to life.

She climbed on the tail of James' four-wheeler and draped her arms around his waist.

He turned and gave her a smile. "We'll take a real vacation once this mission is over. Barbados is nice in the fall."

"You're on and I'll teach you how to relax." She beamed.

She squeezed him once more, and again, his pulse jumped. "Come on, buddy," he chastised himself silently. "This isn't the time…"

Activating his GPS, the instrument shot through its warm-up cycle; its pre-programmed waypoints emerged. He inserted the earpiece to his radio and radioed Blake, who acknowledged with two terse clicks about the transmission. He glanced at his CIA guide and motioned his hand forward. James switched the ATV into gear and charged off into the darkness. Minutes later, Blake directed them to cut their headlights and activate their night vision devices, so James cut his lights off to mask their travels in the desert's heart.

As they sped across the sand, the desert appeared to blossom and come alive. Moonlit shadows concealed hidden rocks in the sand, exacerbating the already perilous passage. Halfway to their destination, motorcycle-mounted bandits swept out of the darkness and surrounded the two US operatives; they instantly drove in opposite directions. Four of the hostiles chased James while the remaining four pursued Blake. James sensed an orchestrated ISIS trap, knowing that robbers operated closer to the highway. Fortunately, his newfound CIA friend came prepared and equipped for the worst.

Although he lacked the horsepower to lose his pursuers, James traversed the dunes to evade them. Every time he thought he lost them, they would reacquire his trail and close the gap, so he had to improvise or they would catch and eliminate him. Land-locked pirates or ISIS, they would slit their throats and feed them to the vultures.

He eyed his GPS and spotted Blake as a dot moving across his screen.

He radioed the CIA operative and instructed him to double back to converge on one another.

"Copy that." Blake said, spinning his ATV around. He only had a minute to position himself prior to the battle.

"Do you have any experience driving these four-wheelers?" James turned toward Atallah.

"Move over," she barked back. "I'll show you how to lose these fools."

He stood on one leg and then slid his other leg back over her head.

She slid forward and grasped both handles of the ATV as he relinquished control of the handlebars and dropped in behind her.

"Steer toward Blake's dot on the GPS." He clutched his submachine gun.

She downshifted and then twisted her wrist for full throttle; the ATV fishtailed back and forth as she prepared to crest the dune. Blake flew up the other side of the steep dune.

"Break right now." James said into his microphone.

The two ATVs whizzed by one another, missing each other by two feet. James extended his left arm and clotheslined the bandit trailing the CIA operative; the thug somersaulted through the air and landed on the hard sandy surface. He gasped for air as James collapsed his windpipe. James pressed the tip of his submachine gun into the robber on the right. He pulled the trigger, firing six rounds into the man's chest. He fell lifeless to the ground as the surrounding sand turned a deep shade of red.

As four bandits collided head on with one another, the scene resembled a medieval jousting match. The thugs crashed against each other and tumbled to the ground. James vaulted off his four-wheeled horse and peppered the four with three-round bursts from his submachine gun. Six down and only two more to go. Unfortunately, two of the terrorists sped after Blake, jockeying their motorcycles to have a clean shot.

He spoke into his microphone. "Six tangos neutralized. What's your situation, Blake?"

Blake's voice shuttered. "I'm in serious trouble. There are two assholes breathing down my back, spraying bullets at me with their assault rifles. I can't shake them and need help."

James jumped onto his four-wheeler and sped toward Blake, but before he could reach him, three rounds struck the veteran CIA officer, knocking him from his ATV. He smacked the ground with a thud and tumbled to a stop. The two terrorists moved in for the kill, dismounted their motorcycles, and strutted toward the downed man. Blake rolled into a sitting position and drew his pistol from his drop holster. Aroused, the terrorists raised their weapons. In that instant, Blake fired, dropping the two men to the ground.

James and Atallah reached him only seconds later. Blake sustained multiple hits to the abdomen, chest, and shoulder. Unless he could control the bleeding, the CIA officer would be dead in minutes. James removed two pressure bandages from his medical pouch and instructed Atallah to open one and apply direct pressure to Blake's stomach wound. He removed another bandage from its protective wrapper and pressed down on his chest wound. It took only seconds for his blood to saturate both bandages.

"We require help and the Blackhawk now." James gave a pained stare off to the horizon.

Blake grabbed the agent's hand. "I won't survive these wounds." He sucked in a sharp breath. "I need a favor. Tell my wife and son I was thinking of them. Can you tell them I love them more than life?"

James nodded. "You got it, buddy," he stated assuredly.

Then his eyes closed, as his head drooped forward.

"Damn it." The DS agent pounded the ground with his fist, shaking his head.

James plotted the GPS and Blake's location. He then poked through his gear, taking his food rations and extra ammunition. His ATV, riddled with bullets, was ruined. James and Atallah would finish the journey on a single four-wheeler. Before they left, he radioed the CIA's station in Cairo to inform them of Blake's demise and grid coordinates, so their man could be retrieved, returned to America, and buried with honors.

CHAPTER 17: Fabrication

El-Amarna, Egypt

The desert storm disappeared as quickly as it had appeared, returning the hills and surrounding sand dunes to their eternal state of tranquility. James tried to repress the fatal images floating through his mind as extinguishing human life left him no joy. He knew it was either them or him. However, Blake's death filled him with remorse, no less painful for the brevity of their acquaintanceship. Like many who had fallen before him, Blake had been an American patriot in the truest sense; he gave his life to protect his homeland.

There was no time to brood, so he gripped Atallah's hand and guided her back to their desert chariot. He climbed onto the four-wheeled ATV and started the ignition, glancing at his companion.

"We should leave now, so we can complete our mission. Are you alright?" His chest tightened.

She awoke from her trance. "I can't believe what just happened. You killed those men. Doesn't it bother you?" She turned away.

"The choice is simple." He shrugged. "Kill or be killed. They deserved their fate."

"I see your point, but I was raised to believe that all life's precious." Her chin quivered.

"Think of it this way. The world's better without them. I can sleep with that. Let's go, as you have a treasure to discover. Your destiny awaits." He said in a flat voice.

She climbed aboard the ATV, wrapped her arms around his upper abdomen, and they drove away into the abyss. With the desert wind rushing through his hair, he buried the throttle, pushing the four-wheeler to its limit. Distraught by the violent episode, she sat quietly behind the relentless agent. It would take her time to accept the night's bizarre turn of events. He knew she would recover as soon as they arrived at el-Amarna. It gave him an added incentive to get her there within the hour.

Following the waypoints on his GPS, James covered the five miles to the outskirts of el-Amarna. Daybreak would occur in another couple of hours, so he searched for an area that would provide them temporary refuge from the frigid desert temperatures and winds. He located a car-sized fissure in a nearby hillside. The crevice and the fallen boulders surrounding it created a natural shelter from the elements. He drove his ATV toward the fissure, navigating between several rows of boulders. James stopped short of a cranny, opened the ATV's hidden compartment, and removed two sleeping bags. He unzipped them both, reassembled them as one, and guided her inside the sleeping bag, joining her once he set down his backpack.

Gently guiding her head on to his shoulder, he draped his muscular arms around the shaken beauty. This provided her additional warmth and much needed comfort. The hard ground acted as its own cooler, radiating its chilliness to all that encountered it. The sleeping bags did little to counter this phenomenon. Yet, their combined body heat fended off the frigidity cast by the surface below. She lay there quietly with her eyes staring toward the stars; her heavy stomach churned. Touched, he turned into her and kissed her forehead.

To his surprise, she responded with a soft, lingering kiss. For an instant, he considered reciprocating, but, feeling ridiculously noble, he aimed another kiss at her forehead.

"What's wrong?" She took his palm and covered her heart with it.

He smiled in the dark. "With all the shooting behind us, I'm still strung pretty tight. When this mission's over, let's give it a better chance."

She shut her eyes and dozed off under the bright desert stars. He could feel her faint heartbeat through her clothes. Damn, he thought. Being a nice guy is no fun at all. Still, he was filled with warm expectations. Perhaps he had finally found the woman who could ease his perennial angst.

Neither the squawking birds nor the light of the sun as it rose over the hill awoke him. He sensed a presence watching him, so he opened his eyes and saw a warm smile and a friendly face gazing down at him.

"I was wondering if you'd sleep all day." She smiled.

"Have you been watching me long?" He smiled back.

"Long enough. You almost look innocent and at peace with yourself."

He nodded. "That has nothing to do with me and everything about being around you. I feel good when I'm with you. Shall we eat and then save the world?"

The two ate a couple of chocolate flavored protein bars, drank a bottle of Gatorade, hopped on their ATV, and headed off into the blistering desert sun. His eyes followed the GPS, leading him by the Great Temple. He then followed it down the royal road and by the King's Palace. It beeped meters from the edge of the Aten Temple. Technology had taken the guesswork out of navigation and made it virtually impossible to get lost, even in the blinding, featureless desert.

Atallah leaped off the ATV, unstrapped her helmet, and dropped it next to the four-wheeler. She examined the expansive and mysterious area, recognizing the obvious advantages of the site. The mighty Nile flanked it on one side and hills sat on the other. The river supplied alternative access, trade and food, while the nearby hills provided shelter from the winds and other hostile elements. Its vast ruins stood as a meager reminder of the once vibrant city. She contemplated the city with a sense of awe, imagining the pace of life thousands of years ago with its bustling streets and teeming crowds flocking to the temples and marketplace.

He broke her reverie. "What's it going to be? Are you dreaming or working?"

"Let's search for the artifact. We should start near the temple's altar." She smiled.

"Show me the way." James scanned the area for hostiles.

He checked his watch and expected few people around at seven-fifteen in the morning. His vibrating senses assessed the surrounding area. As they entered the Aten Temple, she passed the first two sections with only a cursory glance, as she remained certain that any artifacts concealed in the temple would be stored in a hidden chamber. As she approached the altar, its unique design intrigued her. James ignored the splendor of the ruins and searched for Hassan or any other potential threats. His eyes scanned down and followed four distinct and fresh footprints meandering away from the altar. He followed the path to an isolated area of the room. He motioned for her to join him and they converged on the back corner where the footprints congregated.

Atallah rolled open her archeology tool kit, removed a hand brush, and swept away several inches of sand, exposing a rock slab below. She inverted her brush and tapped the rock slab with its handle; its faint higher-pitched tone showed something hollow beneath, so she scraped away the sand from the adjacent slab. As she continued sweeping around the slab's edges, her eyes froze on several fresh tool etchings on a slab. James inserted his pry bar beneath one of the slab's corner and struggled to lift it. She abutted her pry bar to his and assisted him in moving the corner of the slab up; it now rested on top of the adjoining one. The two struggled to slide it sideways. Their eyes widened as they scanned the cavern beneath the temple.

Shining his flashlight deep into the chamber, his jaw dropped because of its expansiveness and depth. James trotted back to the ATV, removed his climbing ropes from the storage compartment, returned to the altar, and looped the rope around the stone structure, tying it off with a fishing knot. James tossed the remaining rope down into the chamber, hooked himself to it with his O-ring, eased himself through the opening, and slid to the cavern's floor in seconds. He disconnected from the rope and held it steady for his companion. As Atallah descended into the cavern, she surveyed the room and its panoply of riches; her eyes glimmered at a gold sarcophagus centered in the chamber. The two moved to the sarcophagus and scanned the room. The untouched cavern was marked by layers of dust, cobwebs, and an eerie dampness.

"This is unbelievable and a magnificent find." Her eyes widened.

He nodded. "It's spectacular, but something's wrong."

"You're paranoid." She grinned.

He re-scanned the chamber with his flashlight beam, moving from point-to-point. His beam then came upon a headless body in a puddle of blood. He turned back toward Atallah and followed the beam of her flashlight as it pierced the chamber's darkness in a semi-circle, freezing on a table.

Focusing on the light's beam, her jaw dropped as she gawked at the small gold-plated artifact. She ambled toward it, stumbled as her foot wedged into an object on the ground, shined her light downward, and gasped at a man's corpse as his bulging eyes and slacked mouth alarmed her. She crept around the body, as her eyes fixated on the ornate chest, now within reach.

James gazed at the gold chest as the hairs on the rear of his neck tingled. His flashlight's beam spotlighted smeared footprints in the sand. The disturbed tracks, downed man, and dust-free chest spelled trouble. But before he could warn her, she stepped closer to the chest. A small red LED light flashed. He lunged forward, pushed her to the ground behind the sarcophagus, and blanketed her with his body.

Seconds later, a powerful blast rocked the cavern. Projectiles shot throughout the chamber. Small portions of the cave's ceiling collapsed, showering jagged rocks to the compacted ground. The blast wave activated a flurry of protective mechanisms. Spears sailed overhead while pendulum-rigged traps powered down from the ceiling. Worse still, the explosive device cast a large fireball that seared off their ropes and with it any hope of escape.

The explosion and the percussion wave that followed had knocked over the sarcophagus, pinning them to the ground. Luckily, the heavy lid hit the ground first, which prevented the ancient coffin from smashing all the way to the floor and crushing them.

"Some guys will do everything to get on top of a lady." Atallah displayed a wide grin.

James laughed, the tension relieved by her joke. "Are you okay?

She grasped the agent's head and pulled it toward her, kissing him on the lips. "That was for saving my life. I'm fine now, as long as I'm in your arms."

"Remind me to save you more often." He reciprocated before pulling back. "We should look for a way out of here."

He knew if he pushed the lid aside, the sarcophagus would continue its tumble and crush them. Fortunately, the Jordanian's petite frame permitted her to inch her way out. She slid herself through a small opening at the end. He remained trapped and suddenly felt alone. She had disappeared, returning minutes later with a marble statute head severed from its body; she placed it underneath the sarcophagus. On the opposite end, she placed a small foot-by-foot brick.

"What are you doing?" He grimaced.

"Just stay silent and remain low. I'll pry the lid off and the sarcophagus should rest on the brick and statute's head. Are you ready?" She gulped as she licked her lip with cautious optimism.

She pushed her pry bar beneath the lid and gave a downward thrust that dislodged the lid from the sarcophagus. As the lid tumbled away from him, the half-ton sarcophagus slammed down on the statute's head and then the brick. It rested there until gravity pulled it downward. She thrust her pry bar up against the statute's head.

"I can only hold it a few more seconds. Move now." She grunted.

He rolled his body away from the sarcophagus, just as the statue's head gave way to gravity. The sarcophagus slammed to the ground, narrowly missing him. A dust cloud flew skyward. He rose to his feet and brushed the dirt off his pants. She crept toward him and hugged him as if she hadn't seen him for years. He gazed over her shoulder, searching for a means of escape.

"Wouldn't they've planned an escape door? Anyone that could design such a magnificent structure as this chamber, along with its elaborate booby-traps, would've also developed an emergency exit." His eyes wandered the room.

"You're on to something." She looked around the chamber. "According to the research, the ancient architects were master builders. If there was an escape route, then it's most likely hidden from plain view."

James gazed at the chamber's corner where the blast had torn away a small nickel-sized opening. He crept to the corner wall to examine the hole. Feeling air push through the aperture, he sensed his likely escape route. The trick would be to exploit it without further compromising the cave's integrity.

They struggled to push open the wall, but centuries of dampness and sandstorms had weathered it shut. The two jostled their pry tools into the crevice and wrestled against the elements without success. James pondered his options, and suddenly the answer popped into his head.

However, he needed a few items and asked her to find some copper stripping. While she foraged through the cave, he dismantled his four grenades by first removing the fusing system and then the explosive. She discovered several sources of copper, to include a thin decorative copper etching. James molded it into a small funnel shape and carefully positioned the explosive.

After placing his makeshift shape charge over the cave door's seam, he improvised a fuse from the grenade and attached his string to the grenade pin. James grasped her hand and moved her behind the sarcophagus, confident that it would shield them from another blast.

"Are you ready? This blast may be louder than the previous one."

She nodded. "I'm ready."

He pulled the string, released the pin, and five seconds later, the blast ripped open the door's seam. They moved to it and pushed it open, seeing light at a distance. They followed the light for about one-hundred yards and emerged from their underground tomb.

CHAPTER 18: Metempsychosis

ISIS Operational Base, Sinai Peninsula
Recalling her genetic engineering methods honed in America, Sukhayla thrived on the science, precision, and methodical approach. The lab, equipment, and the analytical process mirrored one another. She recognized the requirement to take every precaution given the virus' purported virulence, so she followed protocol and donned a self-contained biohazard suit. An assistant taped every seam and then double-checked the geneticist's entire body to guarantee the suit's impermeability. Another associate, who monitored the process from the control room above, unlocked the airtight seal to the door. Sukhayla plodded into the room. Her biohazard suit creaked with each step. Upon clearing the door, the assistant locked her into the clear acrylic chamber.

Hassan stood in his self-contained control room above the lab and observed the geneticist with more than idle curiosity. He lacked a scientific mind, but knew she would follow her protocol with precision, so he repeatedly checked his phone while waiting for his game-changing treasure.

Sukhayla worked inside the level III biohazard laboratory and used one more layer of protection. The ornate gold case lay centered in an airtight, four-by-four-by-six foot glass cube enclosure. Her arms jostled into the reinforced flexible sleeves and gloves centered in the glass, which allowed her to manipulate items within the safety of the chamber. She grabbed a scalpel and pierced the blade through the waxy seal which separated the lid from the container. Thrusting the blade's tip an inch inward, she slid the blade from end-to-end, separating the front and two sides. Her surgical hand remained steady as she set the scalpel on a metallic tray beside several other steel instruments.

The geneticist's heart raced and her body electrified as she gripped the chest, lifting its lid. Her eyes widened. The ancient relic astonished her. A faint winged creature appeared, even though it was hidden by layers of protective bandages. She picked up two sets of forceps and probed the end of the wrap. Seconds later, she found her starting point. She struggled with a sticky adhesive for minutes, before she could finesse the forceps' tips under the unusual cloth. She lifted the cloth up and then back over the object, careful not to damage it. The cloth wrap seemed unbreakable, despite its age. She repeated the procedure, removing layer after layer of the sturdy cloth. Upon removing her sixth layer, an intact and near-perfectly preserved bat appeared. Her eyes blinked several times before morphing into a stare. The artifact's physical properties amazed her; even its orange fur, eye membranes, teeth, and feet remained intact. She had seen several mummies in her life; none of them were as well-preserved as the one in front of her. She pondered the ancients' work and their unmatched knowledge of the mummification process. It appeared far superior to that of present day embalming.

She pivoted right and spoke into her microphone. "It's remarkable. The bat is perfectly preserved. I'll open it up to get some soft tissue. El-Amarna is no longer folklore." She sucked in a calming breath.

"I knew it. This is the great equalizer." Hassan grinned.

"Don't get your hopes up. It may take me months, perhaps years, to sequence the genomes and then reverse engineer the virus." She said, peering back over her shoulder.

"What? Are you serious? We don't have that kind of time. You must speed up the process."

The geneticist chuckled. "American experts took ten years to sequence and reverse engineer the 1918 Spanish flu. I was delighted that your contacts bought a sample of the Ebola-Reston virus from Syrian stocks. I won't have to do much with that virus. Even though I have the requisite sequencing–thanks to your purchased research–and the equipment, it will still take some time to complete the process."

She caught her breath. "Ebola's structure comprises ribonucleic acid (RNA), which can only facilitate rapid genetic changes through one of three means. First, a process known as reassortment mixes genetic material of a species into new combinations. Second, nucleotide substitution can be used, however, that can result in high error rates during RNA synthesis. Last, RNA-RNA recombination between non-segmented RNAs is the best option. I believe that recombination provides the best opportunity to meld the two strains of Ebola virus. All I can say is that the reverse engineering and mapping of the Spanish flu was child's play compared to what I'll have to do," said Sukhayla, rolling her shoulders as her chest tightened.

Hassan snorted. "Speak in simple terms. I don't understand what the hell you're talking about." His eyes tightened as he swatted the air.

Sukhayla's face scrunched up and then relaxed. "I've simplified my explanation. Science isn't as easy as the art of killing."

"Why can't you just mutate the virus?" He tapped his fingers on the table.

"I could do that, but mutations can occur to either increase virulence or transmissibility or reduce them. Unless I can control the mutation to increase its virulence and transmissibility, then the outcome may fall short of your expectations. Mutating Ebola is like playing Russian roulette. The odds will favor an empty result." She scowled.

"Explain again your plan, Aafia." He demanded, knowing that if he was to lead ISIS into the next decade, he needed a foolproof plan. "Tell me your proposal - how you plan to use the dead bat."

She smirked behind her mask. "In simplified terms, I'm going to first sequence the el-Amarna virus, resurrect it using chemical synthesis, and then grow it in a Petri dish. Once I have a small quantity of the virus, I'll complete a process known as recombination. This will meld the spreading efficiency of the 1989 Ebola-Reston strain with the lethality of el-Amarna virus."

She gulped before continuing. "Because the Americans won't have the sequencing pattern of this combined virus, they won't be able to protect their citizens against it. By the time they figure it out, hundreds of millions will have perished. You'll strike your fatal blow and I'll give you the ability to do so."

"Well, what are you waiting for? Get to work." He said, nodding.

She picked up a scalpel and incised the mammal's chest with one steady stroke of the blade. Her concentration increased as she analyzed the bat's inner organs. Again, like the mammal's exterior, the inside of the bat remained well preserved; it appeared soft, as though it had just died. It seemed implausible that anything from 1330 BC could be intact. She wondered if they entombed the bat alive.

She picked up an elongated scissor and dissected parts of the bat's lung and stomach for study. After splicing a thin layer of soft tissue from each organ, she placed each specimen on glass slides. She set the first slide containing lung tissue on the table of the compound microscope. Her hands turned a dial to adjust the microscope's magnification to ten power.

As she viewed the slide of the lung tissue, she rubbed her eyes and then blinked multiple times. Sukhayla took another look and confirmed the subtle movement on the slide. She increased the backlighting, adjusted the microscope to one-hundred power, and peered through the microscope's eyepieces to observe a worm-like virus aggressively invade another normal cell. Flabbergasted by the virus' resurrection, she surmised Allah's divine intervention; it was a scientific miracle that would allow her to produce her unstoppable virus in weeks, not years.

"I've glorious news, Hassan. It's remarkable." Sukhayla felt a sudden tightness in her torso.

His eyebrows rose. "What's it now? It better be promising as I'm refining my plan.

"It's better than good news, but I can't explain it. The bat contains a live virus. All I must do is incubate it in a dish, using a monolayer of human cells." She flipped her hair back.

He stood abruptly and rubbed his hands together. "How long before we can test it?"

"I'll incubate it for fifteen hours at thirty-four degrees Celsius, and then after about thirty-six hours, I'll have the viral plaques. How does that sound? I'll then start the genetic recombination process, allowing for the Ebola-

Reston strain to mix with the el-Amarna virus. Give me three more days and I'll deliver you what I promised. This virus, which I'll name Ebola-Nile, should have a lethality rate far beyond anything we've seen in history. The airborne Ebola virus in Reston devastatingly spread throughout a quarantine facility. Now you add the el-Amarna virus potency into the equation and you'll have something beyond the control of anyone or any government." She winced. "We shouldn't be opening Pandora's Box."

"Let me worry about that, as Allah has called upon us to carry out this attack. He'll protect us as our modern plague wipes out the infidels and our Zionist enemies." He held his chin high.

CHAPTER 19: Black Ops

James' heartbeat sensor spiked and then turned erratic as the CIA station monitored it. Mattson and the Blackhawk team lifted off to provide James help. Banking left, they circled above el-Amarna to locate the DS agent. Hearing the faint sound of the helicopter's rotating blades slicing through the air, James checked his compass, removed his satellite telephone, and called his CIA contact. Within seconds, the helicopter altered its course toward him. He identified a clear landing zone, removed a smoke grenade, and verified the wind's direction. Pulling the grenade's pin, he tossed it twenty feet forward, and it detonated seconds later. A plume of green smoke wafted skyward as the helicopter swooped toward them.

He guided Atallah into a squatting position, facing away from the approaching helicopter. He gave her one of his pairs of wrap-around sunglasses to protect her eyes from the circling dust. As the skids of the Blackhawk settled into the desert sand, Mattson appeared at the doorway, reached out, grabbed Atallah's wrist, and pulled her up into her seat. James clambered in after her and sat opposite of Mattson.

"Glad you made it," Mattson barked over the sound of the whirling blades. "I just wish it would've been more productive."

James shrugged. "Me too. Did you retrieve Blake?"

Mattson nodded. "We got him, but it's a darn shame. He was exceptionally talented and had a loving family."

"The only way to overcome his loss is to finish what we started." James stretched his arms above his head. "Do you have any leads on Hassan? He reached the treasure first, deployed an attack team, and left a booby-trap for us at el-Amarna." James belted himself in as the helicopter lifted off.

The CIA man grinned. "I'm glad you asked as we've unearthed more intelligence on him. For years, the Israelis contended that the precursor to ISIS sat in their backyard and established inroads in the Palestinian territories and the Sinai. They were right, as Hassan has retreated to a strategic ISIS base in the mountains near Jebel Hilal."

James nodded. "I've heard of the place. They say it's more secure than Tora Bora. The Egyptian people attacked it once and were knocked on their asses. The bastards are dug in stronger than a tick on a deer."

Mattson shrugged. "Anyhow, we must breach the place as the intelligence suggests that Hassan has a level III bio-hazard laboratory there. The Israelis advised us that if we don't handle it, they'll send in their fighter jets. Do you realize what will happen if the Israelis invade the Sinai again? We could have another regional war."

Mattson held up his forefinger. "But don't you worry, the CIA has a grand plan."

James cocked his head. "I suppose it involves me doing some sort of suicide mission."

Mattson considered the comment. "It actually involves both of you; we're short archeological experts and the operation requires a minimal signature so it won't be detected."

"You mean you want plausible deniability if something goes wrong." James let out a deep, weighted sigh.

"You're too suspicious, Matt. It's a brilliant plan and we'll brief you when we land. We've a long ride ahead of us, so just relax and enjoy the ride."

"I can't wait to hear your scheme." James smiled.

Quiet until now, Atallah glanced at James. "I'm willing to help, so can you tell me your plan?"

The agency spook grinned. "Okay, I hope you don't mind heights, because the plan involves approaching from the north via a hang-glider. You'll fly at night, so we'll give you all the help we can, but you're going to be on your own."

"This gets better and better." James shoved his hands into his pockets.

"Indeed it does." Mattson nodded once. "The winds are powerful at this time of year and can pull you into the jagged rocks, which would destroy your glider, leading to your deaths. Once you brave the winds and down drafts, you must land near the mountain where you'll encounter two sentries. If you deviate from the designated flight path, you could end up several miles off course, so it's imperative to land near the sentries to neutralize them, as they cover the only passable climb up the cliff."

James gave a downcast expression. "What's so tough about that? You should just blindfold me to make it a real challenge."

Mattson rubbed the dust out of his eyes. "Stow it," he said. "I'd like to finish the brief."

"By all means, please continue." James leaned away.

"The cliff that you must scale is a dangerous and difficult one. It's not a beginner's climb, so you must use all your strength and determination. I understand that you're an accomplished climber and you've climbed both Rainier and McKinley, right?"

He clutched his hands together as his stomach stirred. "I haven't climbed in years since I lost one of my hiking buddies on McKinley. I had to tell his wife and five-year-old kid that his dad died when an ice field we were crossing gave away. One minute he was there, and the next second he was gone, so I haven't climbed since."

"That must've been very difficult for you, Matt." She kissed his hand. "You undertook that hike for the challenge, but this is for humanity. We can only stop Hassan by conquering that cliff. You can do it and you must guide me."

"You're right, Suhar. We'll do this thing together." He clutched her hand.

Mattson cleared his voice. "Once you reach the crest of the mountain, you'll eliminate a two-person react team who rove near the cave's entrance. Our intelligence shows that these men are well trained and equipped. Once you take out these two men, you'll sneak toward your ultimate aim. The last exterior guard can seal the cave's entrance and alert Hassan with a single panic button. You must get to him silently and eliminate him."

"I'm not Rambo. The Delta Force or SEAL Team Six should undertake this mission as this is right up their alley?" James swept his fingers across his brows.

"Unfortunately, the special operations groups are all deployed in Afghanistan, Pakistan, Iraq and Syria, besides probing Iran. The military doubts the intelligence and doesn't consider this enough of a priority to reallocate their troops." Mattson scratched his jaw.

"Okay, say we can scale the cliff and eliminate all three guards. How do I defeat the alarm system, so I can breach the facility to eliminate Hassan?"

"That's the simple part." Mattson shrugged. "We have the alarm type and its specifications, so the agency has developed a special decryption device to defeat it, which will get you inside so you can eliminate the threat." The CIA man looked down at his watch, pointing toward the southwest. "That mountain over there is your aim," he said. "Once we land, one of my guys will bring you to your tent, so you can get some rest. We'll wake you, brief you, go over your equipment, and then assist you in your flight. We'll start the operation around zero-four-hundred. Do you have any questions?"

James shook his head.

As the helicopter touched down, the three exited the craft, stooping down under the helicopter's swirling blades. Whisked away to their respective tents, James' eyes danced as Atallah grabbed his hand and accompanied him to his tent. He pulled over a second cot next to his and they both went to sleep.

CHAPTER 20: Break-Through

ISIS Operational Base, Sinai Peninsula

Hassan examined the geneticist's computer-generated graphs; he beamed at the short incubation period of the combined Ebola-Nile virus. Within one to two days, the microscopic germs would infect healthy cells and kill them. He thumbed through page after page of infection and mortality rates. It astonished him that a healthy person would succumb to the strain in two weeks.

He pondered the killing efficiency of the virus. It could undercut his plan by slaying people too quickly to ensure its widespread transmission. He flipped to the fatality projections. His downturned mouth changed to a smile. Even with a fatality rate of fifty percent, the virus would quell about one-hundred sixty million people in America. His mouth fell open and his skin tingled as he perused the page.

"This is unbelievable, as an eighty-five percent fatality rate would kill over two-hundred and fifty million people in America alone. This will decimate its population, economy, and way of life." Hassan knew if the plague spread as in the el-Amarna legend, then the American populace would become virtually extinct.

He contemplated a special name for his resurrected plague. It only took him seconds to coin the name - Allah's Revenge. His excitement increased as he came closer to realizing his goal. He shouted at Sukhayla to join him in the control room.

"This is remarkable. Will it be as effective as your projection models show?" He grinned.

She nodded. "My calculations are accurate enough. I only question the lethality of the virus. My experiments show it will work, but you never know until it's tested."

"Load two dosages of the virus into a syringe and then come with me." He returned the nod.

He escorted the geneticist to the level III bio-hazard facility. As she grabbed her protective suit, he waved her off. "You won't need it."

She bit her lip in the face of his stare, understanding this plan's dangers. She enjoyed the creative process, but feared the result, understanding the precision of her scientific work. The resurrected virus strain would not discriminate by race, age, gender, or ethnicity. She recognized it would produce the projected fatality figures. Although he failed to elaborate on his plan, she understood its singular purpose. However, unlike him, she knew the virus had no boundaries; only a lunatic would release it on any population.

Sukhayla placed her arms into the sleeves of the bio-containment box. She picked up a syringe, inserted the needle into the lid of the self-sealing bottle, retracted the plunger, and withdrew two small doses of the resurrected plague. She controlled a mild shiver in her hands while placing a safety cap over the needle. Moving the syringe to a removable tray, she swabbed it with bleach.

She opened the tray, grabbed the syringe, and left the lab. Hassan motioned for her to follow him without saying a word. They marched through several connecting hallways. She felt a sudden drop in temperature as they meandered deeper within the base's hideout. The labyrinth within ISIS' strategic base impressed her, as it would have taken an army of workers with digging machinery to create such a spectacular haven.

They walked for a few minutes and arrived at a gymnasium-sized underground chamber. A constructed room with thick protective bullet-resistant glass sat in the corner; it housed two men with only a couple of beanbag chairs. She felt pity for the men and their dreary existence.

Hassan turned. "Look at these two infidels. They were captured in the Gaza Strip and transferred here a couple of days ago. As you can see from their dress, one is an Israeli soldier, and the other one claims to be an American journalist, but we know he's a spy. They're enemies to our cause.

We'll test Ebola-Nile on them, so we'll have absolute proof that it's genuine before I begin my plan."

Her stomach churned. "I can't inject this virus into them. I'm not a killer, but a scientist."

"No problem. I'll do it." He said, snapping his fingers. "Guards, open the door."

Hassan grabbed the syringe from her. "I only need you to watch the effects of the virus and document it by filming its progression. That's not too much to ask?"

Nodding her reply, she watched him walk into the glass enclosure. Her eyes scanned the self-contained room with force-fed air into it. The overpressure guaranteed that any germs, bacteria, or viruses would remain within it. She avoided eye contact with the two men, as she pitied them and understood that once injected, they would die within weeks, courtesy of her work.

As the guard opened the glass door, Hassan ordered two other armed men to enter. The guards shuffled in and pointed their guns at the westerners' faces, so the prisoners complied with their orders, first dropping to their knees and then sprawling out on the floor. They did not know about their pending fate as human guinea pigs. Hassan required test subjects, and terrible circumstances dictated their fate.

Hassan approached the two without remorse as he understood his actions. He didn't view the men as human beings, but as despicable enemies. He kneeled and thrust the needle into the shoulder of the Israeli and pressed the plunger as half of the virus flowed into the soldier. Hassan then pivoted to the American and shot the rest of the virus into his shoulder. The two men remained silent through the entire ordeal as they presumed that the injection involved a sleep inducer or a drug to further disorient them. Hassan didn't dissuade them of this notion. Their plague-ridden bodies would soon convince them otherwise.

The ISIS leader exited the cell and advised the prisoners to stand. The guards secured the door with a large padlock. He approached the female geneticist. "It's done. I'll defer to you regarding the results, so it better be as good as your charts reflect." He turned back toward his living quarters.

"Do you realize what you have done to these men? They'll undergo a painful death." She replied, rubbing her eye.

He spun around. "I hope so, and all thanks to you, your American education, and modern science." Hassan beamed.

Sukhayla shook her head as acid flooded her stomach. She stared down at her feet with a slight frown. The reality of her actions permeated her soul as she also realized that Hassan had grandiose plans that involved unleashing the virus on an unsuspecting population. Her mind raced regarding the outcome. The virus would spread like wildfire, causing the century's second major worldwide pandemic; it would know no borders and devastate all of humankind. Unlike Coronavirus-19, the Ebola-Nile virus would attack everyone in its path and not disproportionately hit the elderly, those with preexisting conditions, and other unhealthy individuals.

Sukhayla recognized that once released, nobody could stop the virus. She saw how governments reacted to avian influenza outbreaks in bird populations. Their overpowering response involved culling all the birds near the outbreak. They had slaughtered hundreds of millions of birds in over ninety different countries. Humankind couldn't stomach levying that remedy on any civilian population. Hence, the fate of the world now stood in jeopardy. Unless she created either a vaccine or a cure to combat the Ebola-Nile virus, and that would take a significant amount of energy.

She walked back to her laboratory to review her notes and contemplate a cure for the unstoppable virus. Her determination now eclipsed her original resurrection of the strain. With so much more at stake, her motivation would guarantee success. The trick would be, however, to complete the research discreetly using algorithms and artificial intelligence as Hassan wouldn't hesitate to kill her for this betrayal. He would let nothing impede fulfilling his mission, even if it doomed him.

CHAPTER 21: Mission Impossible

Sinai Peninsula, Egypt

The alarm sounded at three-forty in the morning, stirring James out of a deep and restful sleep. It had been many years since he had slept so soundly. Perhaps the rigorous pace of the previous week or the crisp and cool mountain air contributed to his slumber. Either way, he remained grateful for the brief respite and the REM sleep that followed, re-energizing him.

He turned back to Atallah and watched her sleep for several seconds before giving her a kiss on the forehead. James rose from the cot and approached a chair where he left his clothing and gear organized. He dressed, recognizing that he required the right gear to complete the mission. Nothing could be left to chance.

After slipping into his black battle dress utilities, he discarded his bullet-proof vest and donned his web gear, which would allow him to carry an assortment of tools, weapons, and ammunition for the task. His load required careful balancing. Too little gear would make it impossible to accomplish his mission, and too much gear would make it difficult to climb the sheer cliff. Like everything in life, he required the right balance.

With all his gear positioned and fitted, James picked up a 9mm Sig Sauer pistol, loaded a magazine, racked the slide to the rear, and released it forward to chamber a round. With a smooth motion that he must have repeated a thousand times, he used his index finger and thumb on his left hand to pull the slide of the pistol one-half inch rearward. His eyes inspected the chamber and the nine millimeter round that sat centered in the barrel. He released the slide forward, de-cocked the hammer, and then slid the pistol into his drop holster. Satisfied with his load, he unzipped the tent and walked over to a camouflaged two-car garage sized tent; it served as a makeshift command post.

"Good morning, Matt. I take it you slept well and found everything you need for the mission." Mattson said, motioning the agent to a nearby chair.

James nodded. "I did, however, I had to balance the equipment load for the specific mission, which proved difficult, not knowing the exact nature of the operation."

"Okay, let's get to it." Mattson jutted his chin. "We only have a short time before we launch this gig."

Mattson pointed to a four-by-four military map on the table which showed terrain features, elevations, distances and the layout of ISIS' strategic operational base. James memorized the time frames required for each phase of the operation. This included a death-defying stealth flight, the precision elimination of two sentries at the mountain's base, a rigorous rock climb, eliminating three ridge guards, a complicated alarm deactivation, a dicey breach of the underground complex, and the capture of Hassan. Each of these stages presented a challenge unto itself, so he had to conquer each of the seven outlined phases within an acceptable time frame. Failure at any of these stages would lead to discovery, ISIS reinforcements, and probable death. Worse yet, Hassan would escape with the dreaded Ebola-Nile virus.

Mattson smiled. "It's hardly impossible. Let's go over each phase." He directed his laser pointer to the map. "The first phase of this operation involves you flying a hang-glider in tandem. You'll start further up our mountain and land at the adjacent mountain's base. The entire flight will take less than eight minutes, so it's critical that you follow the pre-programmed flight path. It considers the latest wind considerations. If you deviate, even marginally, from your approach pattern, you could be off course by miles. If this happens, then you won't make the next two objectives in time. We'll help you every step of the way. Our technicians will monitor your flight to provide you guidance and constant feedback. Do you have any questions?

"No problem. I got it."

"Oh, there's one further thing. There will be constant wind gusts tonight, which could force you against the mountain. You should maneuver your glider carefully." Mattson said; his voice devoid of any emotion.

"Do you have any other splendid news for me?" James cringed.

The veteran spook smiled. "Unfortunately, I do. Two sentries are posted at the bottom of the other mountain. You must take them out or risk them alerting the other guards. If you're lucky, you can arrive undetected and then sneak up to neutralize them. There are simply two of them and they'll be together."

"What if they detect me in the air? It's kind of hard to miss a sixteen foot glider coming at you, and there's no way I can eliminate them with my pistol or submachine gun. This only happens in the movies." James cocked his head while raising his eyebrows.

Mattson snapped his fingers. A technician approached the table. "We expected this problem. Allow me to show you one of the latest weapons in our arsenal." Mattson pointed.

The CIA technician squinted with a hard smile, placing a metallic, cone-shaped pistol on the table. "This weapon," he said, "has a maximum dispersion rate of thirty feet at three-hundred feet. The Radio Frequency Weapon (RFW) emits an ultra-high radio frequency that incapacitates by making an enemy ill. The trigger activates it, and this switch adjusts the field of fire. Just point and pull the trigger. It's that simple."

"This is amazing." James cleared his throat. "Does it work?"

The technician grinned. "You'll be amazed at its speed and effectiveness. You could immobilize all the sentries with it."

Mattson glimpsed at his watch, showing he had only fifteen minutes to get James and Atallah into position. He instructed the technician to show a top secret decryption device, which could break the alarm/access code on the vault door to the ISIS hideout. Mattson summarized the rest of the mission to the agent. He outlined eliminating three guards, the penetration of the facility, and the final mission objectives. Short on time, Mattson finished briefing James while escorting him to fetch Atallah on the way.

James marched into the tent to see a young female CIA officer assisting Atallah with her outfit, including a black jump-suit, a climbing harness, and a nylon pouch to hold other essential gear. The officer had already provided the archeologist with a crash course on rock climbing.

"You look great in black. Somehow I pictured you in a black evening gown, instead of black tactical gear," said James with a beaming expression and glowing cheeks.

"Perhaps you'll see me in that evening gown on our Caribbean vacation. I'm going to hold you to it." She returned the smile.

"Are you prepared to go, Suhar? It's time to fly the unfriendly skies." James leaned toward her with a glint in his eyes.

Mattson shook James' hand and directed his aide to escort the two to the launch site. They walked up a steep rocky incline and reached the launch platform in five minutes. As they topped a small hill, James eyed the vessel that would carry them to their destination with nothing more than wind power. Even with a wingspan of sixteen feet, the black aircraft appeared nearly invisible. He stepped in behind the control bar as two CIA officers helped strap him into the bag-style harness. They then secured Atallah into a strap harness to the agent's upper left. The officer then checked James' radio and placed the latest generation of night vision goggles onto his head. He cinched the strap tight.

After activating the GPS screen, the officer signaled their readiness for flight with a thumbs-up.

James depressed a button to his microphone. "Backbone, Backbone, this is Nighthawk. How do you read me?" James squeezed the control bar.

Mattson replied over the encrypted network. "Nighthawk, this is Backbone. I read you loud and clear. Have a pleasant flight."

James sucked in a heavy breath as the officers stabilized the wings of the glider. He rotated a small dial on his night vision goggles, turning the darkness into daylight. He turned to his left. "Are you ready to fly, Suhar?" He grinned.

She nodded once and patted his hand.

The fearless agent surged forward and lifted off. Veering left, he followed the GPS' waypoints. As he soared aloft in the darkness, his mind calmed as the brisk mountain air reinvigorated him. He reached four-thousand feet and six miles from his destination within minutes and started his controlled descent. James flew at about thirty miles per hour while charting the glide path. An abrupt updraft surprised him, pulling him up and toward the cliff just off his left shoulder. He struggled to compensate, but Atallah's leftward lean compounded the problem. He assessed his options in a split-second as the cliff's edge neared.

James jostled right while pushing his weight away from the control bar to raise the glider's tip. The craft sputtered as it neared its stall point. In avoiding the stall and spin, he pulled his weight forward. The glider shot downward nearly one-hundred feet and fell well below his glide path.

"Backbone, Backbone, I've a minor problem as I'm well below the glide path. I'm going to fall short of my destination." James drew his mouth into a straight line and bit his lip.

"Nighthawk, this is Backbone. Don't worry, as our technicians have spotted a thermal lift about a mile from your position. You must continue on your present course and use the thermal lift to regain your altitude." Mattson said in a deadpan voice.

"Copy that. Just give me a ten-count as I approach the thermal lift." James' eyes scanned forward.

James relaxed, eased rearward from the control bar, and steadied the glider. Peering around, the solid rock structures amazed him. Gusts of howling wind sporadically broke the night's quietness by pounding through the nearby peaks and plateaus. His familiarity with hang gliders did not extend to the night.

"Nighthawk, Nighthawk, this is Backbone. You're approaching the thermal lift. On my count... ten-nine-eight-seven-six-five-four-three-two-one. Push back from the control bar now and ascend to two thousand-four hundred feet."

James shifted his weight back from the control bar. The glider climbed skyward.

The technician watched the monitor. "Damn this guy's good. He's at the desired height now, so he should level off and resume his course, sir."

"Nighthawk, this is Backbone. You're now okay, so adjust your weight forward and level off. You're now back on course. Good luck." Mattson said, patting the technician on the shoulder.

With the wind whipping through his hair, James continued his approach for another three minutes. He crested a small hill, spotted a pickup truck just ahead, drew the RFW, and aimed in on the truck. Before he pulled the trigger, he noticed the men's closed eyes and their sagging postures. His trigger finger relaxed. James eased back from the control bar and cruised above the truck. His eyes scanned forward and spotted a suitable landing area about fifty yards in front of them. He maneuvered the glider to a location just beyond several large boulders. He edged back from the control bar at six feet above the plateau's ground. This stalled the aircraft and floated him to a near-perfect standing landing.

James slipped out of his harness and assisted Atallah out of her strap harness. "Stay here," he said, pulling out his silenced pistol and creeping toward the truck. He aligned his pistol's sights on the driver's head. His eyes bounced back and forth between both targets. He then shuffled to the vehicle's front to better transition from one target to the next. As he came to the hood, the passenger opened his eyes. James fired one shot to his head, parting him between the eyes. In one smooth motion, he pivoted to his right and fired a single shot into the driver's head.

James rifled through the driver's jacket and recovered a small, hand-held radio. He heard crunching gravel, turning to see Atallah staring, benumbed, at the two bodies.

"I instructed you to stay back," he hissed. "If you want to survive this mission, you must listen and do as I say."

"I understand." She shook out her hands while taking a couple of quick breaths.

He glanced up at the near vertical cliff and recognized its difficulty. An experienced rock climber, it appeared to be just as dangerous and demanding as Mount McKinley. He questioned his capability to make it to the summit, let alone with Atallah in tow. She possessed neither the skill nor the endurance to scale the sheer cliff. At the very least, she would slow him down.

"I see the doubt in your eyes. You think I can't make it," She rushed her speech. "Please, I'm a trained gymnast, and I have outstanding balance, strength, and endurance."

"This is nothing like you've ever seen or done before. It's going to take an enormous amount of upper body strength, so I think you should stay back." He turned away and eyed the cliff.

"That's impossible as you need me to handle the artifact. You can't decipher it. And what it reveals could be critical." Her eyes pierced his.

"Don't say that I didn't warn you. We better get moving or we won't make the summit in time." He shrugged.

James studied the rock structure; his eyes scanned its base to the top, searching for the safest path before starting his ascent. He used his thermal binoculars to identify the best course, committed it to memory, and envisioned his climb. She would double his time, as he would forgo his customary risks with her life hanging in the balance; the rope would be secured throughout the climb.

He grabbed a couple of handholds and began his climb. "Just follow me, using the same footholds and handholds. Concentrate on what's above, instead of below you. I'll be anchoring the rope the entire way, so just remember to lock on; you'll only fall a short distance should you lose your grip or footing. If this happens, don't panic. Just climb back up the rope and regain your foothold. You got it?" He turned to focus on the cliff.

He placed the first spring-loaded camming device into a small crack at thirty feet. His strategically placed rope would guide and safeguard Atallah, as it would provide her the security she would need throughout the arduous two-hour long climb.

As he broke the three-hundred foot mark, he glanced back at his climbing companion. Her guts and stamina surprised him. She glided from one transition point to another, keeping her balance like a seasoned climber. Going back to work, he kept free-climbing the cliff. Though he hadn't climbed for years, his mind recalled the heightened sense of focus it brought him. James also relished the peace of mind and the full-blown adrenaline rush that climbing educed. Hanging by a finger with the wind whistling through his hair energized his senses. Life remained in his own hands, and he preferred it that way.

James climbed up several hundred more feet, encountered a small ledge, sat, and watched his protégé scale the distance between them in minutes. As she neared him, her foothold gave way, and she fell about twenty feet; her head slammed against the rock cliff. Fortunately, her helmet took the brunt of the blow. She calmed and focused her mind, gripped the rope, and pulled herself up. Within seconds, she regained her footing, and several minutes later, she crested the ledge without a word.

"That was a great recovery. So, do you like rock climbing?" James peered into her eyes.

"What a rush." She smiled.

He glanced at her arm. "It looks like you cut your arm on the fall. Let me fix it for you." He opened his small medical kit, cleaned the wound with disinfectant, and then bandaged it.

"It's better than new. Should we finish the climb?" She glanced into his eyes.

James withdrew two energy bars from his side pouch and handed her one. "Let's have a snack, catch our breath, and have a drink of water."

"Are you tired? Perhaps I should take the lead." She grinned playfully.

He laughed. "Never become too confident when rock climbing. Look up there. That's what's left for us to conquer." James pointed. "What do you see?"

"It looks a little easier than what we've done so far." She winked, taking a calming breath.

"That's where you would be wrong. Look closer." He pointed again. "Did you notice that fissure? That surface will be difficult because of the loose material surrounding it. Be careful in that area." He glanced at his partner.

"That's excellent advice. Be safe, Matt. Don't waste your energy worrying about me. I'll make it." She winked.

James stood, grabbed a handhold, and concentrated on the rock face and the cliff as he couldn't afford any distractions. Yet, the only distraction remained a few feet away. He added distance between them in order to get his head back in the game. James shook off the alluring vision of the Caribbean and Atallah in a scant bikini and forged ahead. He inserted a Tricam into a larger crack, releasing the handle and locking the device into the mountain.

James climbed to the large fissure, realizing it would be the last actual test of the cliff. At that point, it would be a vertical climb for another two hundred feet. Worried about the loose surface, he planted several nuts and Tricams just ahead of the fissure. He peered down and could see that she had quickened her pace. She displayed a heartening talent for climbing.

At four feet across, the fissure appeared larger than he had calculated. He lacked the time to search for an alternate course. Double-checking his line's integrity, he scrutinized a hand and a foothold on the other side. He inhaled, jumped across the fissure, and seized the handholds, while his feet missed their targets and dangled limply. A light stream of blood dripped down his wrist; the jagged handhold ripped through his flesh on the palm of his left hand. His feet struggled to find their footrests, scuffing up the rock face. Loose rocks tumbled below.

Atallah heard the clamor of rock skipping down the cliff and glanced skyward to witness James in a precarious situation. She watched helplessly as he grasped for a hold, waiting and hoping with bated breath. Within seconds, he found his footholds and regained his balance. He secured a couple of nuts and a Tricam, so she could cross the fissure. James focused upward and began his final ascent to the summit. He spotted his goal and caught his breath to free climb to the mountain's top. By the time he crested the mountain, Atallah had closed the gap to thirty feet.

Peering over the ledge, James spotted a sentry as the sun rose east of him. Daylight loomed, so he increased his pace. Unable to get a clean shot with his silenced pistol, he mulled over his next move. He never questioned his marksmanship, but this would be nothing more than a prayer. He had to accomplish full immobilization with a single bullet. James drew the prototype weapon from his reconfigured drop-holster, aimed, fired on the unsuspecting guard, and watched as the microwaves invaded his body. The terrorist gripped his head, uttered something barely audible in Arabic, and doubled over. An opportunity emerged, so he set down the RFW, pulled himself up over the edge, and crept up the hill, silencing the terrorist with a single shot to the head. The weapon's efficiency delighted him; he felt his empty drop holster. The weapon rested about fifty meters back at the edge of the cliff.

James canted his ear to the left. The howling wind masked what appeared to be crunching gravel. Drawing his pistol, he aimed toward the noise, recalling the intelligence that two commandos patrolled the ridge. He cocked the hammer on the pistol as his eyes focused forward.

Atallah crested the cliff and spotted a second man approaching James. She raised the RFW, sighted in on the target, and squeezed the trigger. The crunching gravel ceased while a series of dry heaves echoed across the mountaintop. James shuffled forward and squeezed off a single round at the man's head. The man fell limp and lifeless to the ground.

As the sun pierced over a neighboring hill, James moved toward the guard protecting the facility's entrance. He hugged the exterior wall of the cave and stalked within ten feet of the man. Listening to the guard pace back and forth, he waited until the tone of his pace softened. Gradually side-stepping left, he centered the front and rear sight of his pistol with the sentry's head. He pressed the trigger. The guard dropped to the ground.

His eyes surveyed the area and spotted a newly installed closed circuit television camera at the hideout's entrance, reflecting old intelligence. He mulled over his options to defeat it without the proper tools while avoiding detection. Fortunately, the downed guard lay outside of the camera's view, which solved one problem. Recognizing that climate could wreak havoc with electronics, he would disable it with either extreme heat or cold. The question became how.

Out of the corner of his eye, he captured Atallah's silhouette moving in behind him.

"We have a minor problem. There's a camera focused on the access pad and its general vicinity." He gave a downcast expression. "I must disable it, but I don't know how."

She shrugged. "Can't you just shoot it?"

"I suppose that's possible, but I risk being detected. At the absolute minimum, other sentries will come investigate the camera's apparent breakdown. The ideal way is to disable it by mimicking a malfunction because of extreme heat or cold. I have nothing I can use to freeze it, so I'm down to heat." He gripped her forearm. "Do you have any thoughts?"

"Could microwaves distort the picture? After all, they're powerful enough to incapacitate a guard."

"Excellent point, but I worry the microwaves may ricochet around the cave and make us sick. However, if we stood under the camera and directed the RFW outside, I believe that we'd be fine. We must maneuver beneath the camera as there's a dead spot right under it. We have to back out and loop over to the other edge of the cave. You must direct the RFW while I work on deactivating the control pad, which will allow us access. Are you ready?" James rubbed his neck.

"Let's go." She smiled.

James crept undetected to the opposite side of the cave, as Atallah shadowed him stride for stride and passed behind him under the camera. She aimed the RFW at the camera, angling it to bounce the waves outside of the cave's entrance. As she squeezed the trigger, he squatted, removed the CIA's decryption device, and used his Leatherman's screwdriver to remove four screws to access the control panel. After attaching two alligator clips to the leads of a green and red wire, he pressed a button with his thumb on his device, which began its successive running of sequential numbers.

"How much time will it take to crack its code?" Her eyebrows rose.

He shrugged. "It could take minutes or hours. It depends on how many numbers they use."

After minutes of the device running various numbers, he heard the latch on the vault door turning and moved toward the door to catch the rifle's barrel extending through the opening. His feet shuffled forward as he confronted the bemused guard. He thrust three of his fingers into the man's brachial plexus origin; a nerve center situated where the bicep and pectoral muscles meet the front part of the shoulder. The guard yelped as his arm went limp. James grabbed the sentry's hand, twisting it back to torque the shoulder. He dropped to the compacted ground and clamped his forearm and bicep on each side of the sentry's throat. Within ten seconds, the sentry lay motionless on the ground as James cut off the oxygen to his brain.

"Is he still alive?" Her voice softened as she stared at the motionless man.

"Yeah, but we won't be if we don't move now." He removed the alligator clips from the control panel and placed the decryption device in his side pouch.

James no longer required the control pad's secret code, as the vault door remained open, courtesy of the man that he had just immobilized. He pushed Atallah through the door, removed his silenced pistol, pivoted, and shot the sentry in the head. James couldn't afford to be surprised from behind, so he entered the cave and slammed the heavy metallic door behind him as an added safety precaution. The determined agent concentrated all of his efforts ahead of him.

CHAPTER 22: Face-Off

ISIS Operational Base, Sinai Peninsula

With Atallah clinging to his side, James crept through the cave's narrow channel. His fingers swept against its wall; the tunnel's smoothness and chilled touch felt like an ice sculpture and reflected professional engineering and artisanship, while the width and height seemed like the many souks he traversed in Libya, Jordan, and Yemen. Only each step deeper into the cave brought increased dampness, darkness, and coolness, instead of the souk's promises of good deals and untold artifacts.

"I don't like this." She slid closer to him.

He looked around. "Just relax, as I have everything under control and the tough part is over." James said, knowing otherwise as he had witnessed the tragedies that occur when one lets their guard down, so he kept his pistol pointed forward.

"I hope it is worth the risk, as an army could ambush us or we could walk into a trap." She gasped.

"Your instincts serve you well. If we survive and succeed in this mission, you'll probably meet our secretary of state." His eyes scanned back and forth.

"Yeah, that makes it worth it, as the odds of us surviving are remote, especially as this is a suicide mission." She snickered.

"You watch too many movies." James gave her a hard smile. "Just stay close, and I'll protect you."

"It's not you I'm worried about. You don't know Hassan like I do as he's fearless, ruthless, and he won't let anything get in his way. He'll kill you if he gets the chance and not even blink an eye." Her eyebrows drew together.

"I like a challenge and a worthy adversary. Besides, I can handle myself." He grinned.

"I know you can, as I've seen your work, so you two have a lot in common." She nodded.

His face reddened. "We're nothing alike, as I only kill to preserve life, and Hassan is a cold-blooded murder who wants to wipe out all traces of western civilization. I'm also wiser than him, as I understand that his biological creation has no boundaries and will kill whoever it contacts. A higher being won't intervene, as Allah won't protect him, if there's such a god."

"That's blasphemy. Of course there's a god." Her voice quivered.

He scowled. "Can we debate this later? I should concentrate on the mission versus our philosophical differences on a higher being."

"We need to talk about it, but you're right that it can wait until later." She sighed.

His exchange with her surprised him as he finally unraveled a new side to her. She devoutly believed in a god, something he had questioned for years. He pondered what kind of god would use religion for such violence and hatred? Aside from that unexpected observation, he respected her instincts about an awaiting army or trap. He marched deeper into the ISIS hideout and embraced the unknown.

James crept forward, scanning the ground for any tripwires that could activate an explosive, as a single misstep could drop tons of rock on them. And he hated to come all this way just to die out of recklessness.

She sensed his trepidation. "Are you alright? You're slowing down, so what's wrong?"

"Nothing's wrong. I'm just being careful, as we've made it this far, so I don't want to take any unnecessary risks." He gritted his teeth.

She gave a double take at the agent. "I don't buy it as I've watched you these last few days, and you haven't hesitated before."

"Don't be absurd. We should be careful as we're walking into a hornet's nest. They'll lop off our heads on television if we're captured." His voice elevated. "Keep quiet or we'll be killed."

"Say no more, as I'll be quiet." She exhaled.

James didn't mind cramped areas; however, her kung-fu grip and increased respiration reflected her anxiety and claustrophobic nature, but she drove on without complaint. He favored it that way, as the critical mission required his full concentration.

Yet, his mind wandered from the mission to the exotic beauty as he admired her intelligence, warmth, charm, wit, determination, and courage. Her internal and external beauty made her unique. He understood that fate worked in mysterious ways.

Continuing down the cave's path, the light diminished until they reached the midpoint, at which time the light gradually increased with each additional step. His senses heightened as the eerie darkness could trick the mind. He favored the clarity of the light, even though he embraced the dark. Through the years, he had learned to trust his vision, recognizing that his sense of smell and hearing required refinement. He understood these senses' importance in discerning the dark's unknown. He stood frozen as his nostrils flared in response to the rancid odor that emanated from the next corner.

"You smell that dead rat or small rodent." He pinched his nose. "Don't be alarmed."

She cringed. "I hate rats! They're despicable, disease-carrying creatures that should all be killed."

"Tell me how you really feel and don't sugarcoat it this time. Let's cut the chatter and move on." He smiled and forged ahead. His steps quickened.

A minute later, the two converged on an expansive chamber and felt its warmth and radiating light. As they pierced the room's entrance, a level III biohazard facility stood in front of them. The eerie quietness troubled him. A nearby desk displayed countless charts and papers strewn across it. His eyes surveyed the desk, knowing the value of a trove of intelligence. He barreled over to the desk and rifled through the loose papers. There had to be evidence of Hassan's activities, intentions, or progress in developing a biological weapon.

Meanwhile, the archeologist strayed from his hand to investigate a gold chest perched atop a nearby table as its splendor intrigued and beckoned her. Atallah walked toward it and studied the ancient and priceless work of art. Hassan had proved the el-Amarna legend by unearthing his cherished artifact. She stared pensively at the ancient relic as her near-death experience beneath the Aten Temple flashed in her mind. The hair on the back of her head straightened as she contemplated Hassan's creative attempt to kill her.

Mesmerized by the artifact, she caressed the gold case. Its craftsmanship intrigued her as she examined the intricate decorative pattern and focused on an ancient Egyptian dialect, recognizing the difficulties in deciphering the ancient writing and hieroglyphs. The symbols mystified her and described the great plague of plagues caused by a sickened bat. As she reached for her magnifying glass, a man seized her from behind.

James spun around as Hassan clutched the archeologist, holding a syringe to her neck. The DS agent drew his handgun from his holster and aligned his sights on the master terrorist. "Let her go or I'll shoot you." James gulped as his mouth became dry.

"You won't shoot as you can't afford to miss and have me inject this innocent lady with this deadly biological agent; it's a gift from Allah, so put down your weapon," said Hassan, smirking.

Atallah froze. "Don't listen to him. Shoot him, as I'm dead either way."

"Shut your mouth, sharmuta (bitch), or I'll inject you now." He tightened his hold on her neck.

"This is your last chance, so let the girl go or I'll kill you." James cocked the hammer on his pistol.

"You're too late, as Allah will have his revenge on Israel and America, and sooner than you think." Hassan grinned mockingly.

"What makes you think that you're walking out of here alive? There's too much at stake." James probed as Hassan nestled behind Atallah's slender frame.

Hassan backpedaled to another door while using Atallah as a shield. "America's weak democracy will be your downfall. Because you play by a distinct set of rules, we'll always defeat you. Besides, Allah will help defeat America and wipe it from this planet. Now what do you have to say?" Hassan taunted him with a sparkle in his eyes.

James smirked. "You don't understand what you're saying and always blame America for the poverty and living conditions that exist in the Middle East, so it's you that's weak as you never take responsibility for your own actions. You bastardize and skew your religion to justify your violence. Good will always prevail over evil, and you're nothing more than murderers who kill innocent civilians. When your fellow terrorists attacked our twin towers, you woke up the sleeping giant. We then kicked the crap out of you in Afghanistan and Iraq and killed tens of thousands of your comrades. We'll stomp your ass in Iraq and Syria and annihilate you." James glared.

Hassan returned a fevered stare. "You'll pay as America and Israel are evil. Your arrogance makes you weak, as does your alliance with the Jews, who control you with their lobby and sense of guilt. They make America vulnerable to the hatred and wrath of the Muslim world, while killing and abusing our brother Palestinians. Your bias has alienated moderate Muslims, and for what, six million Israelis, of which one-third are Russian immigrants. America just needed to be an honest broker in the region, and then you wouldn't be in your current predicament. Once you're destroyed, life will improve on this planet," said Hassan, baring his teeth.

"The Middle East is a complex area as there's no peaceful solution with the Palestinian right of return and Jerusalem's division. People have been fighting over this land for thousands of years, and they'll probably fight for another thousand." James glared back at the terrorist.

Hassan shook his head. "The Israeli scum won't be around another year as I'll see to that with Allah's help."

"You're a crazy bastard. You release that virus and it will also kill your fellow Muslims." James' jaw tightened.

"Allah will protect us. I've talked too long and have other things to do. You've been a worthy adversary, but it's time for me to bid you farewell." Hassan grinned.

Striking a button with his right hand, Hassan scurried through a narrow opening with Atallah in tow. His actions started the destruct sequence, while sealing the American agent inside the chamber.

James raced for the narrow opening, but it sealed him in before he could get there. He gripped the lip of the steel door and pulled, but it wouldn't budge.

CHAPTER 23: Countdown

James' head throbbed as his ears rang from the public address systems' hi-lo wailing. His eyes checked the room from left-to-right and from floor-to-ceiling to locate it. He directed his pistol at the speaker and then lowered and holstered it. An electronic, two-by-one foot countdown timer with bold red numbers sat just above the speaker. It reflected the time remaining until a thermite blast would incinerate the underground base. Other than sterilization, incineration ensured the virus' destruction to prevent it from escaping into the atmosphere. It seemed more like a useful way for Hassan to cover his tracks.

The wall mounted countdown timer with its automated voice flashed four minutes and fifty seconds. He had to do something fast and before it reached zero, otherwise four-thousand degrees of heat would turn him into ashes. Without the experimental subjects and the virus that was running through their veins, a rapid antidote or cure for the virulent Ebola-Nile virus would be nearly impossible. His mind recognized the critical stakes. He also had a score to settle with Hassan. Given the amount of attention to detail the laboratory evinced, he surmised the base contained a control room; there he could override the countdown-and-destruct sequence. He only had to find it.

James' eyes scanned the room again. A female silhouette abruptly appeared when a side door sprang open. She staggered into the chamber and collapsed as blood soaked through her shirt. Her hand covered a gaping wound, but did little to slow the bleeding. Rushing to her side, he laid her on the floor. Hastily removing a bandage from his pocket, he opened it and pressed down on the wound. Blood spewed from the bandage in seconds. He swept his fingers over her clammy skin to her pale face as her enlarged pupils showed shock.

James knew he could do little other than provide her limited comfort. "How do I halt the countdown sequence?" He hissed. "Tell me. We have little time."

Sukhayla's hand slapped the floor. "Hassan betrayed me, and after all I did for him." Her blood-drenched fingers squeezed his hand.

"I won't betray you." He caressed her forehead. "I can help you, but first I have to interrupt the destruct sequence. Where's the control room?"

She lifted her head and pointed to a door. "The control room is one flight up those stairs. Centered in the control panel rests a computer keyboard. You must access the computer and input the correct password to abort the destruct sequence. You merely get three chances and then the system will self-destruct." She gasped for air.

"What's the password?" He removed his pocket notebook and readied his pen.

She winced. "There are thirteen characters total. Enter them, as I tell you. It's capital A-l-l-a-h-s-capital R." Her eyes had sunken deep in their sockets.

James examined his paper pad. He had only seven of the thirteen characters. A bitter tang filled his mouth, as he had never excelled at Wheel-of-Fortune. Yet he knew that he would have to hit the jackpot today.

With limited time remaining, he shook her by the shoulder to revive her, but she remained unresponsive. Without higher intervention, she only had minutes to live. He ran out of the area and ascended the stairs, two steps per stride, as the countdown sequence showed only two minutes and thirty seconds remaining. His heart pounded as he reached the top of the steps and the entrance to the control room. He grasped the door handle, but it remained frozen. Pulling out his eight-piece pick set, he kneeled and inserted the torque wrench. He jabbed a saw pick into the lock and began a steady back-and-forth motion; one-by-one he felt the pins shift upward as he maneuvered the pick. As he hit the last pin, the lock snapped open.

James trotted to the console and scrutinized his written notes, A-l-l-a-h-s-R-x-x-x-x-x-x, and then it dawned on him. He reflected on his recent encounter with Hassan and recalled his last exchange of words as Hassan stressed that Allah would have his revenge. A smile overtook his face by the password's simplicity, which morphed to a grimace as the countdown timer flashed seventy seconds.

James peered at the keyboard as he inputted the seven known characters, and then the final six deduced letters, e-v-e-n-g-e. "***Access Granted***" flashed in green across the computer screen. With twenty seconds left, he used the mouse to scroll through multiple options. He placed the pointer on the abort icon and then clicked it. The computer-automated voice announced, "***Destruction Sequence Aborted***."

James rushed downstairs to the geneticist's side; her flaccid body laid there lifeless. Staggered by both relief and remorse, he hung his head and took several deep, shuddering breaths. Seconds or minutes later, he could never be sure how long he crouched there; he refocused on the questions that remained, beginning with the cave's secrets. He walked through the door and bypassed the stairs leading to the control room. Two doors faced him, one to his right and the other in front of him. His gut told him to march forward, so he ducked to fit through the doorway. A bright light glowed about twenty feet down the corridor. He bit his lip, drew his pistol, and pointed it forward. His slow, careful pace changed to a purposeful trot until he approached the door.

James tiptoed toward the door's threshold and stopped to listen; his stomach churned at the awkward silence. He crouched down and peered around the corner. A glass, prison-like structure containing two men captured his eye. He scrutinized the prisoners.

His senses vibrating, he withdrew a large pen-like device from his waist belt pouch; its tip contained a small, circular mirror about the size of a silver dollar. James extended the telescoping mirror to its full length of two feet; he directed it to the right at about a forty-five degree angle before inserting it into the chamber. Eying the mirror, he manipulated it to provide views from one side to the other, then floor-to-ceiling. He stopped on the midpoint of the far right wall and scrutinized a balcony fifteen feet above him. His eyes squinted as he looked closer. A person crouched behind a machine gun captured his attention. He calculated the distance at thirty yards, giving the gunner a clear advantage. The tenacious agent welcomed the factor of surprise, however brief; he had one chance to shoot the terrorist before being peppered by a barrage of bullets.

James stood, backed away from the cave's inner wall, and extended his pistol forward. Inhaling and holding his breath, he stepped out, exposing one-third of his body. He squeezed the trigger twice, the noise echoing throughout the chamber. Both rounds sliced through the gunner's chest, dropping him to the cold concrete balcony. He looked for other targets, but saw no one.

He holstered his weapon, marched toward the glass enclosure, and studied its design. Two pipes fed into the roof of the glass container, feeding oxygen and overpressure to the enclosure. He sighed, believing he remained safe from the virus the two men carried. There were many pleasant ways to die rather than from a biological weapon which killed a person cell-by-cell.

"Are you guys okay?" James surveyed the men; their lips moving without sound confirmed an airtight enclosure. His brows narrowed as he examined their lips' movement. Their eyes bulged as they pointed over his shoulders.

James snapped his head around; his eyes enlarged as a silhouette emerged from the door behind him. The guy resembled a Russian heavyweight wrestler on steroids. His reddened face and bulging neck veins showed he would pay for taking his comrade's life. The three-hundred pound giant's finger rested on the trigger of his assault rifle; it pointed at the tenacious agent's chest.

James eased his hands skyward. "Easy there, big guy," he said, striving for a reasonable tone. "You don't wish to fire at me and break that glass behind me. That virus is nasty stuff."

The man's mouth twisted into the rictus of a smile; the giant shuffled his feet to the right, seeking a safer line of fire.

James moved in a slow dance, keeping the acrylic enclosure behind him. "We could dance all day, but in the end you must kill me by hand. Are you afraid? You have me by over one-hundred pounds. Don't you want to look into my eyes and strangle me?" James smiled.

"Lay down your weapon. Don't make me shoot you," said the man, smirking.

"You're not too good at poker, as I see you're bluffing." James grinned back.

"Empty your weapon and toss it aside, and then I'll lay my weapon down, so we can settle this the old fashion way, mano-a-mano." The giant growled.

The resolute agent considered his options. He contemplated drawing and firing his weapon, as he questioned his ability to defeat the Sasquatch-sized terrorist who appeared as angry as a raging bull. James recognized his weapon's disadvantage, so he opted for a fight and drew his weapon from his holster. He depressed the magazine release button and watched the magazine fall to the hard surface and then tossed his pistol to the side. "It's your turn to lose your weapon now."

The terrorist unslung his rifle from his neck and set it on the dirty ground, drawing his knife.

James felt a burning in his throat as his eyebrows lowered and pinched together. "I thought this was going to be a fair fight, but I guess you're afraid of me."

"I'm going to slice and dice you." The man grinned. "You'll be sushi when I'm done with you."

"Let's see how tough you really are." James smirked, winking at the man.

The giant lunged forward, thrusting his knife at the agent's chest. James sidestepped leftward and kicked forward, but missed his opponent's wrist as he retracted his knife. Vaulting forward, the man slashed his knife diagonally. As he slashed again, James stepped in, but the blade's tip pierced his wrist. Blood dripped from the wound and onto the floor. He grabbed the Goliath's knife-wielding wrist with his hands, snapping it up and back towards his face. The man yelped as the knife fell to the floor. The commando threw a left jab. It landed on James' cheekbone, rocking him back on his heels.

As the giant bent to grab his knife, James snapped a roundhouse kick to his face, causing the man to teeter and fall to the firm ground. The agent sprang forward; his stomp kick missed the man's torso as he continued to roll. He attempted an overhead strike, but the giant blocked it, catching his wrist. James circled his hand, breaking the man's grasp. His adversary's agility surprised him, as he rolled back to a sitting position and stood. James drew a deep breath and shook his head.

Squaring off again, the man threw a wild left hook, followed by a right jab. James ducked and deflected the left jab downward, using his opponent's forward momentum against him. He snapped a pisiform wrist strike into the center mass of the man's head, jarring his brain. The terrorist's knees buckled, but he appeared only dazed. The man reached over James' arm with his hands, seized him by the throat, and lifted him off the ground. James gasped for air. The giant's viselike grip guaranteed his death in seconds. James cupped his hands and slapped them against the man's ears; air surged down his ear canals and perforated both eardrums. The man dropped the American to the ground as he held his head. He stumbled backward, nearly tripping over his rifle.

James' eyes caught the man's rage-filled eyes; he glanced left, spotting his government pistol only five feet away. As the giant kneeled to retrieve his rifle, James dove to the ground, grabbed his pistol, rolled to his side, and aimed his pistol at the man's heart. He squeezed the trigger. The pistol's sole chambered round fired and struck the giant dead center in the chest. The man staggered, before reaching down for his rifle. James rolled to a standing position and sprang forward, executing a flying front kick. He sailed above the man's rifle. His foot struck the man's chin; it propelled him backward as his finger depressed his rifle's trigger and fired three rounds. The man's head hit the ground with a loud thump. His projectiles ricocheted off the cave's wall and slammed into the acrylic enclosure. James rushed toward the man to check for a pulse. He felt none.

James wiped the sweat from his brow while peering over his shoulder. After retrieving his pistol and magazine, he inserted the magazine into his pistol and chambered a round. He de-cocked the hammer, holstered the pistol, and sashayed over to the glass cell.

"Don't worry. I've deactivated the destruct sequence, so I'll get you medical help as soon as I can." James said, even though he recognized their limited chances for survival.

The American journalist stuttered. "Who, who, who are you? Don't come near us. We've been injected with a biological agent."

James glanced at the journalist, not sure what to say. "I'll have the best American and Israeli doctors here shortly. If anyone can save you, they can." He said with a shining face and a flutter in his belly. He pitied the men.

"You should leave us here to die, as you can't risk spreading whatever we've been injected with," said the Israeli, nodding and looking at the starburst crack in the acrylic enclosure.

"Speak for yourself." The journalist rubbed his chin. "I've a major news story to write as I'm looking for a Pulitzer."

"I'll be right back." James smiled as he disliked the press, but admired the guy's guts.

James trotted off through the cave's hallways. As he emerged from the entrance, a reddish-orange sunrise blessed him; however, his thoughts flashed to Atallah. He recognized now that she mattered to him, and he knew, too, with a sharp twinge in his chest, that Hassan would interpret her cooperation with him as a sign of disloyalty - reason enough to kill her.

He removed his radio from its pouch and depressed the talk button. "Backbone, Backbone, this is Nighthawk. The bird has landed and secured the nest, but be advised that the falcon has flown the coop with my assistant in his talons."

Mattson's voice came across the air. "Is it clear? My team is standing by to launch."

"Send in the biohazard team, Dave. We have two infected victims who require medical attention."

James sat down on the cold ground, looked across the plateau, and contemplated his next move. He wasn't sure what to do, but he would have to do it quickly.

CHAPTER 24: Doomed Fate

Negev Desert, Israel

A blistering sun transformed the desolate expanse of desert into a breathtaking mosaic of orange and reddish hues; its rays cast dense shadows throughout the nearby hills and desert floor. Nothing except the Technicolor scenery seemed to thrive in this barren landscape. Next to the Dead Sea, the desert sat fifty kilometers from the lowest point on earth. The strategic Israel Defense Force base appeared out of place. Yet, this environment produced an ideal location to conduct unsanctioned experiments with bio-agents and other deadly man-made viruses. The facility's remoteness kept its secrets away from prying eyes, while also protecting its citizens from an accidental release of its deadly pathogens.

The fortified base deterred both escape and attack. A twelve-foot fence topped by coils of razor wire surrounded it. An array of sophisticated, ultramodern alarms extended several miles around the base's circumference. The ultrasensitive alarms could detect a rabbit crossing its field and alert the command post. A twelve-person tactical team stood ready to investigate and eliminate any potential threat. The Israeli soldiers often joked that the base's security surpassed that of Area 51 in America, only their facility held petri dishes instead of flying saucers.

Within the perimeter fence laid another barrier secured by both mines and attack dogs. Each corner held an around the clock manned guard tower with a three-hundred and sixty degree view that provided the skilled guards' clear vision and fields of fire. If someone breached the outer layers of security, then the guards could deploy sniper or machine gun fire. Even a mechanized assault could be countered with their Mark-19 grenade launchers and their AT-4 light anti-tank weapons. Inside the wall, over one-hundred and fifty cameras covered every crevice of the facility. Vigilant Israeli soldiers observed everything in and around the compound. During nighttime, motion-activated lights ensured the rapid detection of all movement within the facility. Each building boasted additional levels of security, including a variety of high-tech locks. All doors used a five-digit combination lock, and many more required a thumbprint or a retinal scan.

Apart from its super-secret nuclear research facility, the bioresearch lab remained the best hidden secret in Israel. Not even their closest allies understood the research that was undertaken at the facility to ensure the Jewish state's existence. The Israeli government took no chances with the fragile nature of international politics. Given the secrets the base held, it seemed an unlikely destination for an American agent. Not that James could roam around the ninety acre compound, as he might overhear or witness something that the Israelis desired to hide from their American allies.

The rigorous environment deprived him of sleep, as his six-foot frame eclipsed the hospital bed, which caused him to brush against the cold steel railings. The hospital ward appeared prison-like, and in a way, he was right. Still dozing, a sudden knock at the door jarred him awake. He sat up and scanned his surroundings, as sweat dripped from his forehead. The sensors affixed to his heart and lungs constrained his movement to a hospital bed and examination table.

"Come in." He cleared the back of his throat.

The door opened and a bizarre figure entered. Clad in a full protective mask, oxygen tank, and a biohazard body suit, the figure could have stepped out of a sci-fi film. Glancing at the apparition, the soft, very human, feminine voice that emerged from the face shield startled him.

"How do you feel?"

"Pretty good, all things considered." James stretched his arms skyward.

The Centers for Disease Control (CDC) doctor returned his smile. "I'm surprised, considering your ordeal. Dave Mattson briefed me on your mission."

James nodded. "How are the American journalist and Israeli soldier we rescued?"

"The journalist died a short time ago, and the soldier is in critical condition." The doctor pulled up a chair and sat down. "I've never observed a virus so virulent. It's resistant to everything, including the experimental drug Zmapp. If we don't figure out how it works, we're facing an unstoppable worldwide pandemic. More than that, it reproduces like rabbits. I've been in this business for twelve years, and seen nothing like it, including Peruvian jungle viruses that make dengue fever look like the sniffles."

"That's not surprising," he said, grimacing. "If the tale of el-Amarna is true, Hassan has resurrected a thousand year old virus, and then merged it with the transmissible Ebola-Reston virus. That's pretty scary."

"What's the legend of el-Amarna?" Her eyebrows furrowed before releasing.

"The ancient city was destroyed by a plague. The legend reflects that a bat spread the plague to humans, which decimated the city in two-weeks. So Hassan resurrected this virus, and it's now a lethal threat to the world." He felt a prickling in his scalp.

"This is unbelievable." The CDC doctor's eyebrows drew together. "We've long suspected that the former soviet bloc countries had experimented with this sort of genetic recombination, as they wanted to create a super virus for biological warfare. Our top generals dreaded it because our enemies would possess the antidote and perhaps a vaccine, making America vulnerable to this type of strike. The CDC feared biological agents would fall into terrorists' hands, but they never imagined that it would be this soon and with this lethality."

"I must leave here now, so I can stop him before it's too late," said James as a sheen of perspiration formed on his cheeks, chin, and forehead.

"You're not going anywhere, Agent James, until I finish a few more tests." The CDC expert leaned in.

"Please doctor, the name is Matt. What's your name?"

"That was rude of me. I'm Doctor Sherman."

James folded his arms across his chest. "What's your first name?"

"It's Jillian, but my friends call me Jill."

"Thanks Jill, what's my prognosis? Can you rid my system of any viruses? It's unimaginable that something so microscopic could lead to the end of humanity." He winked.

"You have no worries. Our preliminary tests show you're fine, but I have to draw one more batch of blood, though. Stick out your right arm, please." The doctor's gaze wandered the room.

He rested his right arm down on a table while she prepared the syringe that he was used to receiving. During his career, he had gone to the remotest and harshest places on the planet, so he routinely gave blood for analysis or received a shot for myriad tropical diseases.

"Are you sure that the needle is large and strong enough to pierce steel?" He flexed his bicep. "Did I ever show you which way to the Dead Sea?"

The doc's eyes narrowed as she waggled her head.

Flexing his bicep, he turned his wrist and pointed east. "Did I show you how deep the water is there?"

She nodded. "No, but I sense you will."

James transitioned from his bicep pose to one with both hands on his hips, flexing his pectoral muscles. "Did you realize that there were sharks there, but they're afraid of me?" He executed a Mr. Olympus pose over his head with both of his biceps bulging.

She paused and then burst out laughing. "Do you entertain all your physicians with this show?"

"I reserve it for only my most trusted friends." He grinned.

"Don't quit your day job. I don't think the public will go wild over that routine." She gave him a playful nudge and inserted the needle into his forearm to take three vials of blood for her tests.

James smiled, a little surprised that his muscle routine failed to resonate with the stern doctor. Either this was a more sophisticated audience than he was used to, or he failed on his delivery. He liked the way she had dished it back to him and now saw it as a personal challenge to make her laugh. He discarded his thoughts about her humorless bedside manner as he had other pressing issues to conquer, but first he needed to get out of his quarantine state.

Withdrawing the needle, she advised the weary agent that the results would take between sixteen and twenty-four hours. Only after careful analysis could the CDC provide a definitive answer. His boredom fueled his disappointment with Hassan gaining distance from him with each passing minute.

"You should rest now, but I'll come tomorrow to see if we can release you." She said, nodding before exiting the room and leaving the solemn agent in solitude.

James picked up the remote to a forty-six inch flat screen television and tuned into the local news; it showed the aftermath of an Israeli targeted strike against a Hamas weapons factory in Gaza. The smoldering building and three militant bodies strewn in the doorway served as evidence of the attack's success. The Israelis had learned terrorism lessons the hard way; they discovered it was important to eliminate the terrorists, their supply routes, finances, and support structure, something America now faced as ISIS spread throughout the Middle East while threatening the US homeland.

He recognized the quagmire; however, that in killing each terrorist, another one would soon replace the deceased with increased resolve. Hence, it became a continuous cycle of violence. Palestinian militants would retaliate tit-for-tat, rocketing Israeli towns, including Tel Aviv and beyond thanks to Syrian rocket technology. The Americans faced this sort of guerrilla tactics in Iraq. Each battle success seemed to rally other Muslim extremists to the region and ISIS. James pondered all the world's cruelty because of religion. His faith suffered because of it.

Suddenly, the room's phone rang. His eyes examined the area, looking for the receiver; its location on the end table next to the bed momentarily compounded by the sedative the doctor administered. He picked it up on its fourth ring. "Hello."

"How are you feeling?" Mattson's voice elevated. "We have to spring you loose, as we've got serious work to do."

"Oh, it's you, Dave. You mean that you have more dirty work for me to do." James gave a purposeful shiver.

"Is that how you talk to a friend?" Mattson snorted. "We've come so far together. Besides, we must neutralize Hassan before he does his dirty work."

"You're right. What's our plan, Dave?"

The CIA officer rubbed his chin. "There are a couple of different assessments on his next move. Our analysts think that he's going to make a move on Israel."

James took a calming breath as an inner light appeared in his eyes. "He'll go after America. We're his target. I guarantee it."

"I couldn't agree with you more. The airport's out of the question. He knows he's on our watch list." The veteran spook's posture straightened.

"Hassan could use false documents. Look at how most of the nine-eleven hijackers infiltrated our country. He may use someone else's name or assumed a deceased identity and got authentic documents fraudulently. Hell, he could just cross our southern border and be greeted with open arms, along with a free hotel room courtesy of US taxpayers. The Border Patrol recently interdicted three terrorists on our watch list waltzing across our border." James scratched his head.

Mattson cleared his throat. "I believe he'll travel to America by boat. That will give us time to interdict him."

"That makes sense, Dave. I'm sure that it takes a little time for the bio-weapon to become active in a living human. Hassan's going to want to spread it productively and widely."

"I think you're on to something. He'll also want to spread it simultaneously, so he can overwhelm our healthcare system. This would require countless accomplices." The CIA man rubbed his forehead.

James felt a tingling in his chest. "I thought the not so affordable care act already overwhelmed our healthcare system. I guess we're going to get a double dose. So how do we find a boat in the middle of the Atlantic Ocean? It's like finding a needle in a haystack."

"You leave that to me and I'll have the boys at Langley run it down. I'll give them some underlying assumptions and they'll build a model, tie it into the coastguard database, and provide some hits."

"I hope it's just that easy. If we fail, then there'll be a lot of deaths hanging on our shoulders." James' mouth turned downward.

"Failure isn't an option," Mattson barked. "You get some sleep and I'll pick you up tomorrow. We'll have something definitive by then, but if not, we can solve it together. Bye."

James watched the news for another twenty minutes before retiring for the night. The sedative the doctor provided him knocked him right out. Even the background of the television didn't disturb him. The week's activities exhausted him and his body needed to recuperate.

CHAPTER 25: Arabian Star

Alexandria, Egypt

Perched atop a scenic overlook, Hassan scanned the horizon; he watched several Egyptian-registered freighters take out to sea. Alexandria was a city with a long history as a port town. It was created by the Greek architect Dinocrates in 331 BC under the orders of Alexander the Great. The city immortalized the celebrated leader and flourished into a prominent cultural, political, economic, and intellectual metropolis. Its ancient architecture, combined with its picturesque setting on the Mediterranean Sea, amazed him. It also highlighted the need to protect the ancient world from the crusaders, as they would poison everything with its decadent and corrupt culture. He vowed to stop the spread of western democracy, even if his actions threatened his fellow Muslims.

Weary from the long journey, his patience waned in the one-hundred and ten degree heat. He remained untroubled as his goal emerged. As he surveyed the port's surroundings, he gathered his intricate thoughts. He squinted to see his gold wristwatch and secured his briefcase at his feet. The watch had sentimental value to him, belonging to his father who died fighting the Russians in Afghanistan. The watch served as a stark reminder of the price for following one's convictions. He recognized his duty to serve Allah at all costs.

Hassan felt the light ocean breeze whisk across his face, so he relaxed his mind through deep breathing, but it was short-lived. His colleague's tardiness agitated him. Life had taught him the virtue of patience, but he discarded it for operational matters. He valued precision and meticulous planning and had zero tolerance for carelessness. Not wanting to take any chances, he would abort his plan in five minutes. Suddenly, a man stood shoulder to shoulder with him and placed an identical briefcase on the ground.

"You're late. Did everything go as planned?" He looked at the man.

"There was a slight delay with the money transfer, but I straightened it out." His bagman assured him.

"I don't like excuses." Hassan fingered his collar.

"So I've been told," said the man, "I thought I was followed by the police, so I took a detour through some isolated streets and congested areas, changing my pace. I did exactly what you taught me."

Hassan tapped his index finger against his lip. "You did the right thing, as in our line of business, you can never be too careful. Many of our Muslim brothers have strayed from Allah's path. Wouldn't you agree?"

"Indeed, the stakes are too high to get sloppy, and we can't afford any mistakes now." The man appealed to Hassan's cautious side.

"Did you confirm any surveillance? If so, we must hurry." Hassan checked his watch.

"My tail was clear, as I probably just saw shadows. I'd never risk compromising you. When do you leave for your business trip?" He rubbed his neck.

"I'm leaving right now." Hassan shook the man's hand and then retrieved the other briefcase. "Wait here for ten minutes and watch my back. You'll do that for me?"

"I'll do as you ask. Good luck on your trip. May Allah be with you."

Hassan strolled away, grasped his cellular telephone from his pouch, and held it in his hand. As he turned the corner, he pressed redial on his phone. After two rings, a police dispatcher answered.

"I want to report a suspicious man with a briefcase. I think he's a terrorist who is surveilling ships from the scenic overlook, just above the port, so please hurry before he kills someone." He hung up his phone, discarded it in a nearby trash bin, and continued on his way.

Hassan walked down a set of steps and crossed a major thoroughfare, barely avoiding a Mercedes four-door sedan, as it whizzed by him without swerving. He saw this as a good sign, praising Allah for his watchful eye and protection.

Police sirens wailed in the background, so he turned around and saw six Egyptian police officers surround his bagman. He removed a cigarette pack-sized metallic box from his pocket and extended a telescoping foot-long antenna. Flipping a safety latch out of the way, he depressed a red button. An explosion rocked the nearby overlook, sending a plume of grayish-black smoke skyward. Seven twisted and charred bodies lay dead, including his bagman, who carried out his last delivery. Hassan couldn't risk that he would willingly or unwittingly divulge his plan and he would be in a better place; Allah would reward him for his obedience, or so he convinced himself.

Without remorse, he continued on his mission. His pace quickened as he neared Wharf 3. He glanced over his shoulder, ensured his rear remained clear, and ambled to the gangplank of a nearby two-hundred foot freighter. Peering at the vessel's stern, he read its name in bold print, the "Arabian Star."

He questioned its seaworthiness, given the lack of rudimentary upkeep. Rust swept across the bow and extended aft. Not that it mattered, as he knew the vessel could conquer one last voyage.

As he crested the top of the passageway, the ship's captain extended his hand. "Hassan, I'm Captain Popandropolis. Welcome to my humble ship. I'm at your full disposal and I'll get you to your destination on time."

"You're Greek." Hassan's eyes went wide.

"Last time I checked." Popandropolis pulled in an abrupt breath while puffing his chest out.

"I thought that this was an Egyptian registered vessel." Hassan rubbed his chin.

"It is," said the captain, "I piloted Greek ships for most of my life. My wife is Egyptian, and she wanted to return to Alexandria, so I took my talents over here and was hired within days. It doesn't pay as much as piloting Greek shipping vessels, but I have other lucrative opportunities."

"Indeed you do." Hassan lifted his briefcase skyward. "Let's do business."

"Follow me through here." The captain motioned. "I have a crew of fifteen Egyptian men that are very skilled and loyal to me. Many have been with me for over ten years, and they understand enough not to ask questions while understanding the need for discretion."

"I'm glad to hear that because in my line of work, I can't afford any loose lips. You never know when one of them may say the wrong thing to the wrong person and compromise my mission." He smiled.

The captain grinned. "That's why I required more money, as I'll divvy up half of it to the others. There's nothing like a forty thousand dollar bonus per crewmember to ensure their silence, as I know all too well that loose lips sink ships."

They meandered through several corridors. Hassan trailed the captain to his quarters, where they both sat at a small wooden table.

"Would you like some tea?" The captain poured two cups from a steaming kettle.

"Thanks." The aspiring ISIS leader nodded.

Hassan lifted his briefcase and put it down on the table, depressing two buttons with his thumbs and causing its latches to snap open. He opened the lid and displayed his ticket for his journey. "Here's your two million dollars, as agreed."

The captain smiled as he eyed his retirement bonus. "You've held up your end of the deal, so now let me guide you to your quarters for the next two weeks. It's not lavish by any means, but it's very comfortable, as it has all the basics, including a television, stereo, and a small refrigerator that's stocked, which should ease your journey."

The captain sipped his tea. "Can I do anything else for you?

Hassan nodded. "I'm tired from my long journey, so perhaps you can give me a quick tour of your ship before bringing me to my quarters."

"Absolutely," said Popandropolis as he motioned him to the door.

As they walked through a corridor, Hassan froze. "I assume my men are being treated well, as they're god's warriors and they deserve to have a good place to rest and prepare for their mission?"

"I saw to it." The Greek's head rose. "Do you want to see them before you're taken to your room?"

Hassan pondered the offer.

"I'm sure they would be delighted to hear from you. I have them set up in the cargo hold, so their space is cramped, but they have everything you requested." The captain nodded. "I've provided them with the requested cots, Korans, and food."

"Good idea, as I'd like to address them on their important mission." Hassan puffed out his chest. "I imagine they're experiencing some apprehension from the unknown."

"I bet you're right as they asked me several questions when they boarded."

Hassan leaned away from the captain. "And what did you inform them of our journey, as it's essential that none of them know anything about our eventual destination?"

"I told them you'd be here shortly to answer their questions, which seemed to assuage them." Popandropolis nodded.

"And has my special package been delivered?" Hassan grinned.

The captain smiled. "It arrived earlier today, and I placed it in your quarters."

"Excellent, can I speak to my men now?"

"Follow me this way." The captain pointed down another corridor.

Popandropolis led his guest through several corridors and stairs, culminating near the central portion of the vessel. As they entered the cargo hold, the amplified voices of fifty men echoed throughout the chamber. Seeing Hassan descend on top of a container reduced the commotion to nothing more than several idle whispers. Hassan dismissed the captain, so he closed the door on his way out. A cautious and intelligent man, the captain knew the less he understood, the better it was for him.

Hassan raised his right hand to gain their undivided attention. "Noble Warriors, today's the first day of our great journey together. We, together, will do what no nation could accomplish against the Great White Satan. We'll make the crusaders pay for their sins and bring them to their knees. Allah will reward you with all the riches you can imagine, so enjoy your time together. I'll brief you when we approach America in about twelve days, and remember, no phone calls from this day forward. We can't risk the infidels intercepting them and foiling our plot." He surveyed the group.

The crowd chanted "Allah Akbar" as Hassan departed to his quarters. Knowing that the captain had accommodated his men, he could retire to his room to complete his plans.

As he navigated the corridors, he contemplated his next move. Upon arriving at his suite, he inserted a skeleton key into the door's lock. As he cleared the door, a fiery woman intercepted him.

"I can't believe you locked me in this room." Atallah said in a sharp tone. "You're no different from when we were children, arrogant and convinced of your male superiority. I've always known you were a bastard."

"Don't you ever call me a bastard, you sharmuta." He slapped her face, which knocked her onto a nearby bed.

Her hands sprung skyward to protect her face, as she expected him to levy another slap for her defiance of Arabic customs. "You still think that force is the answer to every situation, particularly if it isn't your way. I thought you would've learned by now, but you haven't." Her eyes watered.

"I should just toss you overboard to feed the sharks, but the more I ponder it, the more I believe that I'll keep you around. I still have a use for you, as I need someone to cook my meals, launder my clothes, and service my other desires." He laughed.

Her face turned lobster red. "Don't count on it."

"Clearly, Suhar, you've been corrupted by western ways, and your defiance is annoying. Perhaps I'll teach you a little respect and your place in society." He smiled.

"Go ahead, if you think you're man enough. I doubt you have the guts." She taunted.

The stout man moved towards her, pushing her flat on her back. "Is this what you want? For someone to show you what a real man is like?" He straddled the exotic beauty, pinning her wrists out to her sides.

She struggled, but his strength made her efforts futile, so she snapped her head back and forth to avoid his kiss, as the bed flexed from the weight of their bodies.

"Get off of me." She hissed.

He stared at her face before turning away. "You fight Suhar, but you know we were meant for each other."

"You're delusional." She barked as her face reddened.

"I can see that you still have feelings for me. It's in your eyes." He sighed.

She reflected. "You're right. My feelings remain unchanged, but being held captive isn't making me feel any closer to you."

He released her arms, rising from the bed.

As she lay on the bed, he became saddened by the turn life had taken. His first crush brought back a deluge of memories, and he relished that simpler time in his life. Somehow life seemed to complicate itself with age. He awoke from his brief reflection.

"You better change your ways, Suhar, or I'll be forced to hurt you." He walked toward the door. "I'll be back for you later, so make yourself comfortable in my quarters. You can sleep in the adjoining room."

"You bastard, let me go," she shrieked.

Hassan exited the room, locking the door with his key. He would make his way topside to get one last glimpse of Allah's land, as business always took him away from his customs and fellow Arabs. He would miss home, but it would be the best and most rewarding trip of his life.

CHAPTER 26: Game Time

Negev Desert, Israel

James' heartbeat raced. His neck hair tingled as he sensed impending danger from behind. He glanced over his shoulder, as thousands of plague-infected men, women, and children converged on him with their arms extended and clutching at him. Their collective murmurs echoed throughout the streets. Thick, reddish pus oozed from their orifices and countless lesions covered their bodies; their decaying flesh permeated the air. His eyes sprang open as droplets of sweat ran down his forehead. He sat up in bed, rubbed his face, and looked to the right, reading the digital clock on the nightstand next to his bed. Twelve hours had passed, but he felt exhausted. He considered his vision as he walked to the bathroom.

James retracted the shower curtain and scowled at the height of the shower head, which landed at his shoulders. He turned the hot and cold knobs to unleash a steady stream of brown water that cleared a minute later. Entering the shower, he pulled the curtain shut, spun around, and let the shiatsu-like jet of the water relieve the muscular tension. Aches radiated throughout his upper back and lower neck. He had forgotten that the most painful part of rock climbing came a day later, as the seldom-used flexor and extensor muscles throughout his upper body, arms, and hands collided with his sedentary life.

He inhaled the hot steam through his nose and mouth, opening his nasal passages. After lathering his legs, arms, and torso with Dead Sea soap, he rinsed every inch of his body. He doubted the hype about the soap's healing properties, but at least the warm water relaxed his muscles and cleared his head. Only with clarity of thought could he outwit Hassan. He wouldn't underestimate him again, as humankind's fate rested on his shoulders. James withdrew the shower curtain and reached for the towel to his right, slipping from the wet surface. He dried off, wrapped the towel around his waist, and then tucked the towel's corner to the inside, covering his lower extremities.

James sprayed shaving cream into the palm of his hand and blotted it on his face. After ensuring the lather covered his jaw-line and front of his neck, he picked up his disposable razor and slid it across his face and neck. He glanced into the mirror to scrutinize his shave while contemplating the ISIS leader's next move. Recalling his encounter with Hasan in the Sinai, he replayed their conversation in his head and pondered how Israel and the West would pay. James doubted Hassan would hit Israel. Still, it puzzled him, given Israel's proximity to the ISIS base; it seemed like a logical next move, but his intuition told him otherwise. He brushed his teeth, further considering Hassan's choice of transport.

James knew that Hassan's global underworld connections provided easy access to false documentation. He only needed money, which he received for handing over the master terrorist to DS. He cringed at the irony, rethinking his last week. His deep reflection caused him to miss the repeated knocks and the eventual door opening.

A soft voice startled him. He peered around the door frame to see a doctor enter.

"Is there anyone here? I'm coming inside," said the doctor, peering around the corner.

"By all means." James' eyebrows rose.

Dr. Jillian Sherman strutted into the room with a luminous smile. He fleetingly didn't recognize her without the biohazard suit. Her girl next door look surprised him with her wavy, shoulder length strawberry-blond hair and light complexion that hinted to her Irish roots. The doctor's petite frame with gradual curves didn't sway many eyes. Even so, her quiet competence and natural beauty aroused him.

She blushed. "Did I catch you at a bad time? I can return later, if it would be better for you." She smiled, eying him from head to toe.

"Do you like what you see? Please examine me, as I'm overdue for my physical." He grinned.

"Oh, that won't be necessary." Sherman reached for a pair of latex gloves next to the door. "I can give you a once over." She placed the glove on her right hand and pulled the glove snuggly over it. She wriggled her fingers back and forth.

"That's funny. My prostrate is just fine and don't forget I work for the US government. They bend you over every chance they get." He chuckled.

"Don't say I didn't offer. You don't know what you're missing, as I have gentle fingers and I cut my fingernails." She beamed.

He sighed. "Regrettably, I have other work to do. Perhaps we could do it another time."

"It's your loss. Since you want to be all business, I've some wonderful news for you. You can leave now, Matt. You're clean."

"That's splendid news." He exhaled and stepped forward to hug her, but refrained at the last minute, as his towel slid from his muscular frame, so he grabbed the towel and held it around his body.

"You should get dressed. Dave Mattson is out in the lobby and he wants to see you." She said, transfixed on his mid-section.

"Thanks, doc. He returned to the bathroom to grab his clothes, when she snatched his hand.

"You have to be careful, Matt, as I read the latest reports and casualty projections of the Ebola-Nile virus. If you get it, you'll die." She pinched the skin at her throat.

Her solemn eyes hinted at more bad news. "You've something else to add?" He cocked his head.

"The Israeli soldier died forty minutes ago. If we don't discover a cure, then humanity is at risk." Her stomach quivered. "Yet even with this prospect, the Israeli doctors seem more interested in developing their own super virus. I'd think they would instead want to find a cure for it."

"That's odd," he said, considering the ramifications.

She cleared her throat. "There's more. I overheard two Israeli doctors commenting that the super virus would backfire on their enemy, and it would spread among them as the rats return to their nest."

"Those stupid bastards." His face reddened. "The Israelis are just as crazy as Hassan for thinking they can control the virus. It's a leap of faith on both their parts."

The CDC expert nodded. "I also heard them discussing that there may be an el-Amarna virus cure hidden in the city. An expedition's departing within the hour."

"It makes sense from their standpoint, as the Israelis could close their borders, vaccinate their six million people, and ride out the pandemic. That is, provided they've found a cure." James scowled. "I have to get ready."

"Wait, I want to ask you one more thing."

"What is it, Jill?"

"Where's the beach?" She flexed her bicep with her index finger pointing.

Perhaps she had a sense of humor after all, he mused. "Thanks again, doc. I've work to do." He dressed and exited the room, while fancying the thought of being quarantined with the good doctor rather than chasing a killer virus. Instead he had to meet Mattson, who obviously intended to place him in harm's way. The CIA remained notorious for getting other people to do their dirty work. He clenched his jaw, ashamed of himself for his disloyal thoughts, when a maniac held Atallah captive. Still, he had to wonder at the injustice, as all those years of meaningless encounters with girls, and suddenly the world threw two intelligent, warm, and attractive women at him at once.

He walked down a small corridor which led to a sterile waiting room. He found his CIA counterpart waiting for him, reading the Wall Street Journal.

"You're working on your next investment? What pharmaceutical company are you investing your hard earned money? Will it be the one that discovers a vaccine to counter the Enola-Nile virus?" James inquired sarcastically; knowing an element of truth existed in his statement, as knowledge was power. He recalled one presidential candidate turning a one-thousand dollar investment into one-hundred thousand in no time. Given the stakes, he recognized Mattson could make one-thousand times his investment. James could use that sort of inside tip, so he could purchase that land on Lake James nestled at the foothills of the Blue Ridge Mountains. He dreamed about retiring to the serenity of the lake and its cool mountain air.

Mattson looked up from his paper. "I'm glad you're okay, as we were worried about you. Shall we discuss our next move?"

"You bet, I've got a score to settle." James bounced from foot to foot.

"Let's go outside, Matt. It's not safe to talk in here, as the walls have ears, if you know what I mean." His eyes widened.

"What? You don't trust our closest ally in the region? They wouldn't spy on us." He smirked, trying to get a rise out of his CIA friend.

Mattson contemplated the agent's cynicism. "Don't get me started. This frustrates the hell out of me. I've shared our intelligence with many members of congress and they believe what they want and refute the facts. So, I stopped caring. Meanwhile, we continue to dump billions in yearly aid to the Israelis, and for what? Our closeness to the Israelis only generates greater animosity from most of the Arab countries."

"This, we can agree on." James nodded. "But nothing can be done, as politics will never change. The only way to forge change is to educate the American people, and that will never happen because it's politically incorrect and it would be political suicide for anyone in congress or anyone who seeks higher office. Hence, it is what it is."

"I can't stand politics or politicians." Mattson eyebrows lowered and pinched together as they stepped outside into a small courtyard, covered from the sun's intense rays.

"I wouldn't count on this being a safe area to talk." James stretched his neck as his muscles tensed. "You can bet they're bouncing microwaves off us at this very minute."

"I feel my brains baking as we speak." The agency man chuckled.

"Perhaps it will knock some sense into you." James snickered. "So where do we go from here?"

Mattson leaned in toward the DS agent. "Our analysts believe Hassan will take a crack at Israel, before hitting America, as Israel's near the Sinai, so it's a logical move."

James let out a deep, weighted sigh. "I doubt it given Israel's security practices, as it's too risky for him, and he wants America. He's ISIS throughout and must mount a successful, catastrophic attack against us to gain respect within his organization. Make no mistake, Hassan wants to lead ISIS and he'll use his catastrophic strike against America to solidify his base."

"When did you deduce this? Did you dream this answer while you slept? We have analysts working on this around the clock, and I think we know what we're doing." Mattson waved his hand in dismissal.

James raised a single eyebrow and contemplated bringing up nine-eleven, but refrained, knowing it could foster bad blood. He understood the need to work together, despite his underlying feelings. "I'll bet you a case of champagne that he'll go after America and is already in the boat."

"You're on, but it better be excellent champagne," said Mattson. "We must go. Come on, my car is over here. We'll go back to the US Embassy in Jerusalem."

The two hopped into the CIA's armored Mercedes and headed back to the sprawling city of Jerusalem. It would take several hours to drive there, but it would give them time to discuss their next move, which would rely heavily on the intelligence apparatuses' tracking capabilities. They hated to let a supercomputer make such an important decision, but they would act once they received actionable intelligence.

CHAPTER 27: Lethal Breach

Negev Desert, Israel

The morning blessed them with a rare southern breeze; it kept the temperature ten degrees cooler than normal for this stage of the year. Yet, the mercury topped eighty-five degrees at eight o'clock in the morning. This did not bother Lieutenant Colonel Joe Levy. He had disciplined his body from childhood to endure conditions ranging from extreme heat to severe cold. A devout mountain climber, he had conquered three of the top four highest peaks in the world; he endured negative thirty-five degree temperatures for hours. Levy could also handle the desert heat when others would run for shade.

Levy commanded an elite team of the border police and remained a legend within the service. Early in his career, he trained under the unit's founder. He gained trust with his technical skill, dedication, and knack for covert operations; so much so that when his instructor retired, he pushed Levy as his replacement. The endorsement met little resistance, and Levy assumed the post three weeks later.

With his men in formation, Levy trooped the line. The procedure was a mere formality: his battle-tested team recognized the art of intimidation rested to a degree on proper appearance and bearing. They had been tested by Palestinian terrorists and radical Israeli settlers; their missions included evacuations from the Gaza Strip and the West Bank.

Other than the cooler climate, it seemed like just another ordinary day of duty. Levy's orders entailed routine patrol along the Israeli and Jordanian border. The colonel planned to send both teams to the border, but they would then split with one heading north while the other one headed south; however, their plan remained fluid to accommodate any problems. Such would be the case today as an alarm sounded at the Border Police central monitoring office, as it showed a breach in their electronic fence.

Unlike the wall which separated Jerusalem from the West Bank, the border between Israel and Jordan remained expansive, desolate, and difficult, so the Israelis devised an electronic fence that could locate an intrusion within a ten foot segment. The system's supercomputer could distinguish subtle variances to identify an intruder with ninety percent accuracy. Here, the alarm generated actual concern, as the computer had identified eight human signatures.

As Levy's team broke from formation, they entered their assigned vehicles. They readied themselves for a jolting ride and hardened terrorists. The men remained calm as they conducted a cursory and systematic check of each other's gear.

Levy picked up the microphone. "We have a breach of multiple targets in section four. Let's roll." He knew that the harsh terrain would limit the progress of even the most determined terrorist. His driver punched the gas pedal as he gripped his steering wheel. The two Suburbans departed the base and kicked up a dust trail that would be visible for miles. Levy remained undaunted, as he adhered to the doctrine of surprise, speed, and violence of action; this proved impossible on the Israeli-Jordanian border, where smugglers, terrorists, and other criminals had the advantage of surprise. Here, Levy recognized that a show of force was the great equalizer. He remained determined to interdict his prey with the ferocity of a tornado.

Levy radioed his operations center as they crested a gradual hill at sixty miles per hour. "Lightning Rod, Lightning Rod, this is Grey Wolf. Please provide a situation report?"

"Grey Wolf from Lightning Rod, we still have eight human signatures in section four. They're staging in place. Proceed with caution."

"Copy that, Lightning Rod."

Levy turned to his driver. "Uri, this is odd. They must know that we're coming. This could be an ambush, so let's spread out."

Levy radioed his deputy in the second Suburban and ordered him to approach section four from the south. Levy turned his head to see his tail gunner peel off and speed south.

"Slow down. We must give him time to get into position for a multi-directional assault." Levy peered at his watch. After two minutes and closing within a mile of their target, Levy's team held their position.

Levy picked up his microphone. "Thunder, Thunder, this is Levy. Are you in position?"

"Grey Wolf from Thunder. We're in position and awaiting your orders," said Avi, turning to his team. "Lock and load."

"Let's get some." Levy grinned as he directed his team to begin its assault.

As they conquered a small hill, the colonel adjusted his rooftop camera with a joystick, zooming in on sector four. His twelve-by-twelve color monitor displayed in high definition eight kids kicking a soccer ball. It seemed surreal to him, but he had long since gotten over surprises, faced with such imponderables as the mindset of a twelve-year-old suicide bomber, all the violence in the name of religion, and Israeli internal politics. Nevertheless, Levy's team advanced vigilantly.

Levy picked up the handset on his radio and pushed the talk button. "Lightning Rod from Grey Wolf. I've eight Palestinian children playing soccer, so we're approaching them with caution and will send them back across the border. We'll advise you when we complete the mission. Levy out."

Avi depressed the transmission button on his radio. "I copy your transmission direct. We're standing by for instructions."

"Avi, continue your approach from the south, but remain in the cars once you're next to the kids. My team will exit and approach on foot, so you guys cover us in case of a contingency." Levy barked.

"Roger that boss. We have your back."

As the two vehicles converged on the youth, they formed a 'V' with the apex facing the kids. Levy's five-man team dismounted the car even before it came to a complete stop; they trotted toward the kids with their M-4 assault rifles angled toward the ground.

"What are you doing out here?" Levy asked, shrugging. "You must be miles from your home. Did you know that you're in Israeli territory? You all must return to Jordan at once."

The eldest kid responded in Arabic. "I'm sorry we troubled you. I guess we're lost." The young Palestinian turned to his friends and motioned for them to leave the area.

As the kids retrieved their ball and scampered over the Jordanian border, Levy turned to Avi and shrugged. "Kids are the same everywhere. I've three of my own and I can hardly understand any of them unless they want more money."

"I know the feeling." Avi grinned.

Shielded until now behind a series of boulders, Abu al-Bayd and his four-person team raised up; they unleashed a barrage of gas from their 40mm launchers. Blanketing Levy's teams with plumes of gas, one canister sliced through the mid-window of Avi's Suburban. Without warning, Levy's elite team had been immobilized by al-Bayd's precisely executed ambush. The unconscious team members laid like rag dolls across the desert floor. The gas dispersed, riding the desert's prevailing northerly winds.

Once the gas cleared the area, al-Bayd waved the kids over. "Here's the twenty dollars I promised you. Now run along and tell no one what you heard or saw."

The Palestinian kids nodded, crossing into their homeland while debating how they would spend their sudden riches.

Al-Bayd's men raised their rifles above their heads and fired off several celebratory rounds for their decisive victory. Their rapid succession of rounds permeated the area. They approached the downed Israelis, while aiming their weapons at their fallen opponents, as they all relished at the prospect of killing their mortal adversaries.

Even though al-Bayd hated the Israelis, he couldn't execute them yet. He raised his weapon and fired a barrage of rounds into the air. "Don't kill them." He shouted. "I have much greater plans for them. Now gather around."

The men huddled in a small semicircle around their leader.

Al-Bayd grinned. "Do you know how the pest exterminator eliminates a colony of ants? He poisons a few and allows them to transport the toxin back to the nest, as it then spreads the poison throughout the colony, wiping out every ant."

His team exchanged perplexed glances.

Al-Bayd scanned his group, pointing his index finger at them. "I have ten syringes filled with a super lethal virus, so here's what you must accomplish. Take two of these syringes and inject two Israelis with the virus, concealing the needle mark. I'd suggest you inject them between their toes and make sure that you wipe away any blood. Then place the shoe back on the foot using the same type of knot, as the Israelis are shrewd and might figure out that something's wrong. Do you understand?" Al-Bayd eyed each man.

His squad nodded in unison.

"Oh, there's one more thing. Use these latex gloves, alcohol wipes, and place the trash in this container. Do not accidentally stick yourself or you'll suffer a painful death." Al-Bayd gave them a curt nod.

He watched his team move from Israeli to Israeli, precisely following his instructions. They finished their work in less than eight minutes. Al-Bayd doubted the injection points would be detected by the Israelis, but he knew it didn't matter. By then it would be over for the police officers, and they would be contagious and infect the rest of their base.

After picking up the spent gas canisters, syringes, and other disposables, al-Bayd ordered his team back to Jordan, so they scurried across the border, sparing the Israelis' lives, but only for the moment.

CHAPTER 28: Doomsday Dawning

Outside New York Bay, Atlantic Ocean
Hassan glanced at the sun setting behind the horizon and stood uninspired by its fiery pink sky. The sunset's splendor would captivate most people, but not him as his mission consumed him. He lifted his binoculars to his eyes, dialed the focus, and peered out at the horizon, as the silhouette of American freedom appeared barely discernible to him. For over a century, the Statue of Liberty had guided pilgrims to the shores of opportunity. Like those that came before him, he found it a welcoming sight, particularly after such an arduous journey.

His decisive moment had come: a rare chance to change the course of history. He would forge a new world order under Allah. As he saw the faint outline of the American coast through his binoculars, he smiled; he would soon strike deep into the vitals of the home of the brave. He glimpsed at his watch and pondered the details of the speech he would soon deliver to his warriors. Once martyred, these men would create more mayhem than five nuclear weapons, and they would accomplish what no country could do, even with their innovative weaponry. His men would be the perfect killing machines with nature's smallest and deadliest weapon; one that had existed since the planet's beginning.

Hassan strolled back to the ship's cargo area, navigating the corridors with the expertise of a seasoned deckhand. He took advantage of his time, learning every facet of the ship, rehearsing his plan, and rejoicing in its catastrophic effects. Approaching the cargo door, he inhaled. He popped the hatch open and felt the stares of a hundred inquiring eyes. His men had been holed up in the vessel's bowels for twelve days. Other than several minutes topside each day, they had spent their days reading, socializing, and sleeping. Now they wanted answers, and he had them.

"The time has come. You're Allah's mighty warriors. You'll bring down America, destroying its way of life. And you'll accomplish this with relative ease," preached Hassan; his chin elevated as he pulled in a sharp breath.

The room remained quiet as his men waited for their instructions; they knew the plan's momentous implications. The last act neared, and they each had front row seats.

Hassan's eyes swept the room. "All of you are loyal warriors. Each of you shall please Allah with your spirit of sacrifice. You'll bring courage and the honor to your homelands. Most of you've been fighting the infidels for years. You fought them courageously, despite their superior firepower. Look at Abdul Samia, who faced the wrath of Israeli tanks, missiles, and fighter jets. He fought them with nothing more than his AK-47 assault rifle.

Hassan glanced down at Abdul Samia. "Tell your fellow warriors about the battle of Beit Hanoun."

Samia stood. "My fellow Hamas warriors," he intoned, "we unleashed a barrage of missiles on the Israeli city of Sederot to punish them for their bombardment of Beit Hanoun. The Israelis had killed many women and children with their American bombs; they believed they could use this vicious technology to cripple our resolve. Let me reassure you. It only strengthened it." He lifted his tight fist.

The rapt crowd responded: "Allah Akbar."

"We prepared and braced for their next wave, a ground invasion," said Samia. "We felt it would be a 'shock and awe' campaign. They had learned from their defeat against Hezbollah in Lebanon. We prepared for their invasion for months. My team buried countless explosive devices to cover all the ingress routes into Beit Hanoun. My men watched the area and waited for the infidels to come. They didn't disappoint us. One morning, the Israeli incursion began, and my men obliterated their targets, neutralizing three out of five of their tanks and disabling two more. This blocked their advance and allowed my men to fire a barrage of rocket-propelled grenades. This brought on the wrath of Israeli jets. Instead of them fighting us like men, they unleashed hundreds of missiles on our fighters. Fortunately, our warriors took refuge in our tunnels and survived their attacks. The rest is history. We achieved a stalemate for months and then watched the Zionist pigs retreat to our stolen land."

"You can see we're defeating our enemies all around the world," said Hassan, raising a hand. "Abdul Samia showed the strength of our mighty warriors in overcoming insurmountable odds. In every war, it's the warriors with the greatest resolve who often are victorious in battle, even against the mightiest of armies. And you're the best. America will soon feel your wrath."

He bounced on his toes as his pulse quickened. "It's time that you learn the details of our plan. We'll annihilate America without firing a single shot. You'll be the ultimate weapon and able to kill millions of Americans. You all remember nine-eleven and the pain inflicted upon America by nineteen of Allah's heroic warriors. It was a masterful attack; they used airplanes as missiles to hit the World Trade Center and the Pentagon. Yet it killed only three-thousand of our enemies. This number will pale compared to what you'll each accomplish." Hassan pointed at the ground. "Look under your cots and pull out a small trunk."

He gave them a moment to withdraw their respective trunks. The screech of metal scraping against the ship's floor echoed throughout the chamber. Puzzled, many of the fighters placed the trunks on their cots while others cradled them in their arms. Each warrior pondered the trunk's contents, but their curiosity would be satisfied shortly. Hassan would provide them the key to their future, and it would drastically alter America's way of life.

"You're pondering the trunk's contents." Hassan said. "You can find out by entering nine-eight-seven-six-five into the combination's lock. You must push the lower left button to activate the device. Once the digital pad stops scrambling the numbers, you'll enter the combination. Then you'll press the keypad in the lower right corner." He paused. He would discover shortly whether he had selected the right men for his unprecedented mission.

His warriors examined the digital scramble pad. Their technological ignorance surfaced as they struggled to follow their leader's instructions. Only a handful would complete this rudimentary procedure successfully; they were rewarded with a click, allowing them to access their boxes. For the rest, Hassan would repeat the instructions one more time.

"Listen up, you only get three attempts before the box locks. After twenty-four hours, you'll have another opportunity to open it, but it will be too late. For those whom opened their trunks, don't disturb its contents until the others are ready. You should help those around you with the lock."

He surveyed the crowd. "First, depress the button in the lower left-hand corner of the scramble pad. This will activate the mechanism. Once the digital numbers stop on one of the twelve buttons, you'll need to enter nine-eight-seven-six-five. You'll then push the enter key in the pad's lower right-hand corner." Hassan watched while the other men gained access to their boxes. Then, one by one, they looked to him for further instructions.

Hassan cleared his throat. "You each have a specific plan, maps, tickets, contact information, and a syringe. You'll each carry out your mission in silence. Don't show anyone else your instructions. If you're caught, then the other missions won't be compromised."

Hassan paused again, staring at his audience. "The syringe's contents are the centerpiece of our plan. Allah has provided us the ability through the liquid in your syringes to strike down millions of infidels."

"Now, pick up the syringe and inject your arm with the needle." Hassan displayed a syringe to his warriors. He injected himself, pushing the plunger inward to release its contents into his veins. He raised his injected arm to display it to his warriors. "Go ahead."

Hassan looked up from his arm. "Push the plunger all the way in."

He again swept the crowd with his gaze. He wasn't disappointed. All of them injected themselves within seconds, glancing up at him for their next orders. His confidence in their resolve surged, as he chose the right people for the mission.

Nodding, Hassan said, "You're each carrying the virus that eliminated the venerable city of el-Amarna. The virus running through your veins is so potent that it wiped out a thriving city. You're the ultimate weapon, even much more powerful than a suicide bomber. Each one of you will kill millions. Yes, you heard me." He smiled. "You'll each kill millions of those blood-sucking, American pigs. You're Allah's greatest warriors. It's an honor to be with you on this historic day." He paused and led a chant. "Allah Akbar, Allah Akbar."

Fifty men's collective voices droned throughout the cargo bay and were audible to the captain. He watched with great interest as an American flagged vessel maneuvered around a buoy and out to sea. The captain recognized something big was happening. He had no desire to know more.

"When you land in New York, you must follow your instructions to the letter. Every one of you will attack different states and infect thousands while traveling to your ultimate destinations; they're major sporting events, passenger terminals, and other areas where people congregate. You must infect areas that people touch, such as door handles, turnstiles, bathroom faucets, countertops and railings. You should cough in public places and spread your germs like bullets, hitting everything in sight. Go forward with Allah."

Allah's mightiest warriors studied their respective instructions with great intensity, as each wanted to do his part to bring the infidels to their knees. Chills filled each of them as their historic moment approached.

Hassan left the room and moved to his sleeping quarters, as he would get some rest before the ship docked in the morning. He had set the plan in motion and the tide of history was about to turn.

CHAPTER 29: Hot Zone

Negev Desert, Israel

As the helicopter descended, Colonel Levy gazed skyward, transfixed by the craft's whirling blades. Groggy and bewildered, he struggled, but couldn't get off his back. Like all worthy leaders, the welfare of his men consumed him. He replayed the attack in his head as his mind raced. His head flopped to see his men lying across the desert floor. The ominous sight sent chills down his spine; he had dreaded this sort of defeat his entire career. The reality of the nightmare eclipsed the pain he felt in his foot.

"Damn, look at this mess, Avi. I never imagined our fighters being defeated like this on our own soil." The veteran pilot declared to his co-pilot. Benjamin Zimmerman had flown helicopters for most of his career. He eliminated countless terrorists in Gaza with his precision-guided missiles. However, age, waning vision and declining reflexes took its toll on his lean body, so he now flew search and rescue missions. He didn't mind the change though, and his wife welcomed it. He remained in the cockpit and it beat sitting behind a desk. Seeing the earth from the sky enthralled him; however, he would soon rather forget today's sight.

"I wonder what happened out here today." Avi said, glancing east. "I'll bet whatever happened came from the Jordanian border. We'll never be at peace with our neighbors."

Zimmerman nodded. "We'll never be free of Islamic extremists. We've been at war with our Palestinian neighbors for far too long. I don't trust them, given their recent attacks against our people at their place of worship."

"Let's land over there, Ben. We need to dispatch our medics to our fallen comrades at once." Avi pointed to the ground.

As the helicopter landed, the door gunners bounded out to cover the medical team. The doctor exited and moved perpendicularly from the helicopter to avoid its tail rotor and main blades. He rushed over to a dazed Colonel Levy.

The doctor kneeled down, leaned the officer over, ran his hands the length of his body, checked him for any booby-traps left by the terrorists, and then visually and physically checked him for any wounds. His fingertips and hands started at the head and worked down to his toes. The lack of wounds on his body surprised the doctor. He scratched his face and then peered over his shoulder as a second helicopter landed nearby with reinforcements.

The doctor examined the colonel's dilated eyes. "Colonel Levy, what happened here? Can you understand me?" Levy remained unresponsive. The doctor gave him a second to respond. He then signaled the corpsmen to retrieve and load Levy into the helicopter.

As the corpsmen picked up the colonel and placed him on the stretcher, Levy barked. "Doc, how are my men?"

The doctor returned to his side. "We're treating them as we speak. They're all alive, but suffering from some unknown event. What happened? All your men are unconscious."

"It's all a little hazy," said the colonel, blinking in quick succession. "One moment we were reacting to kids who had crossed into our territory; the next minute we're out like a light."

"Can you think of anything else that could help with our diagnosis?" The doctor pushed his fingertips into his stomach.

"What, you want to know what happened?" Levy's eyes narrowed. "I recall some gas canisters being shot at us. That's the last thing I remember. I'd like to be more helpful, but that's all I can remember."

"You're doing fine, so just rest and we'll get you back to the base hospital for further analysis." The doctor studied his eyes.

The doctor ordered the corpsmen to secure Levy in the helicopter, as he examined the area; he saw no evidence of any gas canisters. Walking over to the Suburban, the doctor examined a broken side window. He observed only glass remnants scattered on the inside. The sterile crime scene and survivors perplexed him. The combat doctor speculated that Jordanian security forces interrupted the terrorist operation, causing them to abort their mission. He made a mental note to have the Israel Border Police contact their Jordanian counterparts.

After examining each downed officer, the doctor found out that they all suffered a similar ailment as the colonel. Grogginess and pounding headaches exacerbated their vague recollections. He deduced some sort of sleeping agent. A perceptive diagnostician, he knew the root cause would not evade him. The corpsmen loaded all the fallen officers into the transport helicopters in just under ten minutes. Once airborne, they would reach the safety of their base within five minutes. He needed to request a toxicologist upon his return to the base.

Zimmerman pulled back on the throttle as the blades roared louder in response. The helicopter vibrated from the additional thrust and lifted into the air a second later. Zimmerman transported his charges back to the base. He looked over his shoulder to determine his patient's condition. Levy had sat up and now sipped some water. The pilot recognized the positive sign. He only hoped the colonel's entire team would respond similarly. They remained in the best of hands. The doctor had been treating patients for over thirty years.

Flying one-hundred feet above the ground, Zimmerman used his combat tactics to counter a missile threat. Palestinian terrorists had mastered the art of the ruse. They drew in medical, fire, and police responders, and then hit them with another bomb, often with catastrophic results. The Israelis discovered this tactic and applied countermeasures to avoid the ploy. The veteran pilot maneuvered his craft, cranking and banking both left and right. This prevented the terrorists from easily tracking the helicopter. By flying low to the desert floor, it reduced the ground angles to the target. These tactics had been developed and proven during multiple wars.

Now closing in on his target, Zimmerman scanned all around the flight path to ensure its integrity. He now focused on a yellow circle surrounding an "H." As he approached the landing zone, scurrying medical personnel staged for rapid transport to the emergency rooms. He understood the direct correlation between response time and survivability of his patient in trauma situations. This wasn't the case today. The Israeli police were exposed to some unknown gas or worse yet, some form of undetermined nerve agent. Zimmerman received word from his crew chief that both sides remained clear for his approach. He piloted the helicopter squarely into the pad and set the helicopter down so softly that only a slight knock showed they had landed. He eased back on the throttle to slow the spinning blades. Teams of medical technicians rushed in to retrieve their newest patients, which they offloaded in seconds.

As Levy lay on the gurney, he contemplated his survival and brush with death from an unknown enemy. His mind flashed several isolated images of the attack, as he struggled to fill in the gaps; his survival at the hands of terrorists perplexed him. Nothing added up, and he required a reasonable answer to allay his concerns. Expecting a thorough debriefing by intelligence officials once his doctors cleared him, he soon needed the answers. This remained the least of his worries. The ordeal tormented him, and perhaps that's why his unit stood so decorated and fielded an unblemished record until now.

Levy glanced upward at a doctor asking a series of questions. He focused on her words, only picking up about every other one. His splitting headache and blurred vision impaired his thoughts, which raced uncontrollably. "What are you saying?" Levy blinked several times.

"What were you exposed to?" The doctor asked.

The colonel shook his head. "I don't know, as the ambush surprised us. One minute we were responding to a bunch of kids playing soccer and the next minute we were being rescued."

The doctor smiled. "Is there anything else you can recall? Think about it from the beginning. Any specific detail could be quite helpful in your diagnosis."

"I'm sorry," he said, frowning. "The only thing I can remember is the sound of a gas round cutting through the air, the thud of it landing near my feet, the ensuing yellow gas that permeated the air, and its pungent odor."

"Okay, don't worry. We have you now." The doctor pivoted to her assistants. "Take him to the observation room, stat."

A veteran trauma surgeon, Donna Hengal normally treated visible gunshot and fragmentation wounds instead of possible chemical exposure. She sought more information and turned to get it from her longtime associate and colleague.

Hengal approached the pilot as he leaped from the cockpit. "What the hell happened out there, Ben?" The doctor barked over the rotating blades.

"Beats me, but it was the oddest thing I've ever seen. As we approached the scene, the colonel's men were strewn across the ground. No signs of blood; they were just out and it was eerily quiet." He felt a tightening in his chest.

"Levy's a legend in his unit, so it's hard to believe that he would be defeated without a shot fired. It would take a well-organized and disciplined adversary to defeat him." Hengal's fingers touched her parted lips.

"You're right there. The colonel has responded to hundreds of hostile events and always triumphed," said Zimmerman, "He's one of the most notable and decorated police officers in the history of the border police."

The doctor patted Zimmerman on the back, before dashing off to the emergency rooms to examine her new priority patients. She would uncover what happened and would run several toxin screens first to unravel this painful chapter in the history of the border police. As the doctor entered the emergency room, her assistants were drawing blood from Levy's right arm.

"Are you feeling any better, colonel?" The doctor said, placing her stethoscope on his heart.

"Other than a splitting migraine, I'm very groggy and disoriented," said Levy. "It makes little sense, doctor. What terrorist would leave us alive? There must be more." He didn't realize the truth of his statement, as the doctor would eventually discover that Levy was ground zero for the most lethal virus known to man. The only question was whether she would catch it before it metastasized and spread like wildfire.

CHAPTER 30: Journey Back in Time

Tel Aviv, Israel

Dr. Jacob Weinberg scurried into the room, troubled over the ongoing debate between the US and Israeli scientists. Although their verbal jousting suggested opposing views, Weinberg could distinguish the multiple conversations, and could focus his thoughts around the two most pertinent themes; those surrounding the ramifications of failure and the merits of the expedition to el-Amarna. Like most geniuses, Weinberg could simultaneously process multiple complex issues, but common sense eluded him. He could explain an Einstein theory in simple terms and found wormholes and their effects completely understandable. Conversely, directions to the neighborhood store could baffle him. Fortunately for Weinberg, a national hero, the State of Israel handled most of his routine matters. His time and life were much too valuable, so people surrounded him around the clock. This included his security detail from Israel's Security Service, the Shin Bet.

Weinberg was an American by birth, but an Israeli by choice. He had immigrated to Israel after the 1973 war and had sworn allegiance to protect the homeland, serving in the Israel Defense Forces. Given his academic credentials and his Jewish roots, Israeli society accepted him; he made a name for himself when he pioneered Israel's atomic bomb.

Weinberg raised his hand. "Listen here. We don't have time to debate our mission's significance. We must accept it as fate. I've studied the folklore of el-Amarna since college, and a great plague decimated the city in days. It also reflects that there's a clue in the Aten Temple that could shed light on the virus and a potential cure."

"This expedition is a waste of valuable time. We should work together to develop a vaccine and a cure." Dr. Josh Cutler said. Cutler was from the Center for Disease Control and the ranking member of the US delegation. "While you're tromping around in the sand on your treasure hunt, we'll be losing valuable time."

Weinberg scowled. "Feel free to remain here and work with our bio-weapons experts, as they're the best in the business."

"How can anyone be sure?" Cutler shook his head. "There's no physical proof that what you seek is there."

The genius grinned. "Mr. Cutler, do you believe in God?"

"Of course I do, as the Bible provides plenty of proof." His eyes narrowed.

Weinberg canted his head as his eyes shined. "But where's the physical evidence other than the book itself? The el-Amarna tale is a vital part of our history, like the Bible. The only difference is that it was never recorded in a book. Who would've thought that Hassan could discover and resurrect a great plague?"

"Touché, Mr. Weinberg. I guess some things we have to take on faith," said Cutler, eyebrows narrowing.

"Okay, now that we've settled that, we should get down to business. The team has been chosen, but I have some good and bad news." The Israeli grinned.

Cutler groaned. "Let's hear it."

"The good news is that my government has arranged for rapid transport via tilt-rotor aircraft, and we can make good time and land right at el-Amarna, where we can get to work without delay."

"What's the bad news?" The CDC expert covered his eyes.

Weinberg stroked his chin. "The bad news is that we must skirt the Gaza Strip in order to streamline our flight path, so we have just enough fuel to get us there and back. The Israeli version of the V-22 Osprey is much smaller and stealthier. It just doesn't have the range of the larger V-22."

"So the Israelis improved our tilt-rotor aircraft."

"The Israelis are masters at reverse engineering." The doctor answered with a gleam in his eye. "And it's very kind of America to do all the testing and evaluation for us. That saved us hundreds of millions of dollars."

"What's new?" Cutler shrugged. "I wouldn't doubt it if the US government provided you the funding as well. I believe the term is fryers' or suckers. Isn't that what your fellow countrymen call us?"

"Don't take it personally, as we're America's biggest ally in the Middle East, and we're your strategic security partner in the region."

"That's a debate for another day," said Cutler, "we must concentrate on our critical work."

"Indeed. The vehicles are waiting for us. We'll fly at night, as the Egyptians haven't sanctioned our mission. Flying in darkness will provide us some cover for our operation. Let's go." Weinberg motioned to the front door.

The drive to Sde Dov Airport in Tel Aviv took the six-person team thirty-five minutes in light traffic. As eight o'clock in the evening approached, most of the work crowd had dispersed hours ago. Yet, the night owls had prepped to go out for the evening. Like many cities throughout the world, Tel Aviv sprung to life after ten o'clock. People would head to the restaurants and bars to celebrate living. The Israelis remained a resilient people, despite wrestling with terrorism and hostile neighbors since the country's founding. Having lost so much, they saw life as precious and celebrated each day with a zest that rivaled an Irish wedding reception.

As the van and accompanying security vehicle approached the main gate, a police car flashed its blue lights. An arm shot out of the police cruiser's passenger side window, motioning them to follow. Whisked through a seldom-used side entrance, the three-car procession drove between two large metallic hangars. The cars pulled into a small parking area and stopped next to a third hangar. The Minister of Health exited his vehicle and greeted Weinberg, walking him away from the group.

"Jacob, I've arranged special transport for you and your colleagues. I had to call in several favors to finagle it." The minister postured a bit, expanding his chest. Minister Yossi Barlov was a longtime Likud party hawk; his family name and personal wealth connected him to both the past and the present. Weinberg and Barlov went back several years.

Weinberg shook his head. "Yossi, you don't have to remind me about your importance. Our mission will be successful, as my word is good."

Barlov nodded. "I'm counting on you, so don't let me down."

Cutler scrutinized the conversation between the two Israelis and pondered the secrets they kept to themselves. He waited to board the strange looking aircraft, seemingly half plane and half helicopter. It would be his first time flying in something that appeared to defy physics and Sir Isaac Newton's law of gravity.

Cutler ascended the ramp on the tail of the aircraft; the crew chief directed him to an inward facing seat, made of nothing more than nylon straps. His colleagues trailed him, sitting down and fumbling with the craft's belting systems, so the crew chief intervened because of their time constraints. With several quick movements, the chief had them all strapped into their seats and ready for take-off.

Weinberg strolled into the plane minutes later, so the security team leader ushered him into a jump seat behind the two pilots. Cutler speculated that the scientist's handlers orchestrated it to segregate him from his American counterparts for operational security. Cutler adopted a sullen look as he knew the scientist couldn't navigate or fly the plane, but recognized the jump seat's added comfort. The American envied the man as Weinberg was treated like royalty.

After the pilots completed their preflight checklist, the engines kicked on, vibrating the aircraft. Cutler hoped his Dramamine kicked in soon rather than suffer a long flight. He watched the pilots don their night vision goggles. Their route would take them south along the Mediterranean coast; they would skirt the Gaza Strip, before passing over the Sinai and turning south to el-Amarna. The mission remained unsanctioned by the Egyptian government and violated their air space, so the pilots planned to circumvent Egypt's radar installations that cast a loose net. The Israeli Air Force often exercised with its neighbors, and practiced flying at sixty feet above the ground or the sea, which would pay dividends tonight. These tactical maneuvers served as another layer of protection, especially if the Egyptians had conquered their radar deficiencies.

As they skirted the northern section of the Gaza Strip, an alarm sounded, echoing throughout the small aircraft. Its high pitch rhythmic beep sent shivers down Cutler's spine. An Iranian-made Mithaq-II, man-portable, surface-to-air missile streaked skyward with its fire trail visible in the stygian night. Its source, a three-person Islamic Resistance launch team, scrambled to a nearby bunker.

Captain Ben Arzi pulled the stick hard to the right, as his copilot released a trail of flares. Cutler prepared for the worst, not knowing Arzi's experience as a decorated pilot. The captain evaded the missile and sent it out to sea, but the second Mithaq-II presented a problem for him as he looked for a way out. The pilot spotted a Palestinian fishing vessel and pushed the aircraft's limits by maneuvering it into a steep dive. He estimated the missile's direction and the boat's relative position to it, transitioning the aircraft from a plane to a helicopter and hovering behind the vessel as a shield.

Arzi's forehead wrinkled. "Hold on. We may take some splash from this one. It's going to be close." The decorated pilot gritted his teeth.

A second later, the Iranian-made missile slammed into the unsuspecting fishing vessel. A fireball and a plume of black smoke exploded skyward. Ben Arzi felt both elation and remorse for his maneuver, which spared his charges, but killed six innocent Palestinian fishermen trying to eke out a living. Not that he loved his Palestinian neighbors. He had lost many friends to militants, but appreciated the Palestinian plight and those moderates who wanted peace instead of war. Arzi wanted peace with his neighbors, so his grandkids could experience a lasting reconciliation unknown to him.

Simultaneously, an F-15 jet locked on to the militants' position and fired its sidewinder missile; the pilot watched the missile slice through the night air. Seconds later, a fireball erupted on the ground, culling the three-person missile team. Captain Arzi beamed. More than ever, he appreciated the Israeli Air Force's insistence on shadowing his aircraft, as they proved their worth tonight by making three more martyrs with a skilled counterattack.

Arzi started his reverse transition from helicopter to plane. Slowly, the aircraft gained forward momentum as the two tilt-rotors turned horizontal. Within thirty seconds, the aircraft had reached two-hundred miles per hour, showcasing its capabilities against missiles. Few pilots could have survived the back-to-back missile shots. Yet Arzi skillfully maneuvered the aircraft and his mission continued. He hoped the remaining flight would be uneventful and looked forward to delivering his cargo to the Egyptian desert.

Following the waypoints on the aircraft's GPS, he evaded radar detection while avoiding populated areas. He didn't want anxious citizens to report their presence to Egyptian authorities. Arzi soared just above the desert floor, adjusting his altitude to avoid small sand dunes. This would challenge a skilled pilot in daylight hours; however, he flew it in the desert's darkness with night vision goggles.

As he approached within twenty miles of the ruins, the pilot jerked back on the stick as he passed an Egyptian patrol. His catlike reflexes and flying prowess spared the ground force as he buzzed past them. Several of the soldiers fired their assault rifles at the swooping aircraft. Arzi sped away unscathed, blasting the scrambling troops with sand as his craft's twin props sparked a mini-sandstorm. The pilot would inspect his aircraft once he had landed.

Several minutes later, he transferred his tilt-rotors upward to hover mode, descending to the hard ground. As he touched down, the craft settled in the sand before coming to an abrupt stop. When the props stopped spinning, the crew chief lowered the rear ramp. Four Israeli soldiers exited first, fanning out and securing the area in seconds. Their two-thirty in the morning arrival guaranteed minimal interruptions to their mission. As Weinberg and Cutler stood, Arzi reminded them of their three hour deadline for their mission. They acknowledged their desire to be halfway home by daybreak.

The soldiers converged on the back entrance to the chamber and set a series of lights down the one-hundred foot corridor. The scientists followed as instructed, schlepping their equipment in small backpacks. Opening the chamber's door, the ranking Israeli soldier reminded the scientists to watch their steps. The expansive cavity held several sophisticated traps and other surprises.

Weinberg turned to Cutler. "The legend describes booby traps which rival the ones Indiana Jones faced throughout his adventuresome journeys. Watch your step, my friend, as this is it. Look for a small box similar to the one we confiscated from Islamic State's strategic base. It will have hieroglyphs on it."

"Good luck, Jacob. May God be with you."

The four soldiers, all explosive experts, had faced countless bombs throughout Israel and the Palestinian territories. They had together logged over one hundred successful deactivations. Terrorists hid their bombs in everyday items, such as loaves of bread, watermelon, and animal carcasses. The soldiers divided the chamber into four quadrants and analyzed the ceilings and walls for clues. By the skeletal remains and deceased bodies, the soldiers discovered five traps, and neutralized them with both ingenuity and explosive devices. In one instance, the soldiers tripped a pendulum trap, cutting off its blade and rendering it safe. With the chamber secure, the scientists began their search. The soldiers remained vigilant, reexamining their respective areas, and safeguarding the chamber.

Weinberg and Cutler scrutinized every inch of the chamber. The quantity and quality of the artifacts astonished them, as the chamber's contents rivaled the inventory of the world's best museums. Two other scientists trailed behind them to video the artifacts, so archeological experts could later analyze the extravagant relics from an age and place not well understood.

Cutler sighed. "I don't think it's here."

"It has to be here, as I can feel it." Weinberg said. "We need just a few more minutes."

"We've looked everywhere and should return to the lab, so we can develop our own vaccine and antidote." Cutler shook his head, throwing his hands up into the air.

Weinberg sneered as his face reddened. "We're not going anywhere. You're our guests and I need another minute."

"Okay Jacob, you're the boss." Cutler abandoned his search and instead examined his assistant's video footage.

· · · · ·

Captain Ben Arzi checked his watch as it neared zero-five-thirty; they would have to depart in another twenty minutes, with or without the treasure. Flying in daylight presented too much risk, particularly in proximity to some closer cities, like Cairo. He inspected his aircraft from top to bottom, but found neither bullet impacts nor fragmentation splatter from the Iranian missile that slammed into the fishing vessel. He contemplated his skill and luck, deducing he had a bit of both tonight.

As he sat in his chair, he reviewed his preflight checklist. He glanced to the east, spotting his copilot taking digital photos of the ancient ruins. Suddenly, he heard a muffled rifle shot, followed by a quick burst. His copilot scrambled back to his seat in the plane as the Israel soldiers returned fire.

Arzi radioed the Israeli soldiers. "Get the scientists to the plane now, as we're taking enemy fire."

"Copy that, we're coming now." An Israeli soldier replied.

A salty sergeant grabbed Cutler by the arm. "Come on, we have to go."

The CDC leader nodded. "You won't get any argument from me. I was ready thirty minutes ago."

Weinberg spun around. "Hold them off! I've found what we came for, but I need a minute to unearth it."

"Get to the plane," the soldier barked. "I'll get the damn artifact. No harm can come to you, doctor. Get back to the airplane at once and I'll bring the treasure to you."

Weinberg and Cutler followed another soldier back to the plane, running all out. They reached the airplane short of breath, as an adrenaline surge permitted them to leap into their seats in a few bounds. Having watched the crew chief show them before and motivated by gunfire, they fastened their seatbelts. They braced for their abrupt takeoff. Seconds later, three Israeli soldiers arrived at the ramp, one remaining outside to return suppressive fire.

Captain Arzi revved up the engines. "Where's Avi?"

"Let's go, the Egyptians are closing in on us." Cutler blew out a series of quick breaths to regain his composure.

The veteran pilot shook his head. "We're not leaving anyone behind. I'll shake the Egyptians up a bit." He yelled at the soldier on the ramp to climb aboard. The soldier complied while still firing on the approaching Egyptians. Arzi began his ascent at about forty-five degrees, accelerating his engines to full throttle. The resulting back blast sent a sandstorm at the Egyptian soldiers, temporarily blinding them.

"I bet they're all choked up over that move." The pilot said, chuckling. "Let's retrieve Avi at the cave's entrance."

Arzi maneuvered his craft to the chamber's secret exit. He hovered just two feet off the desert, sending sand in all directions. He rotated the aircraft ninety degrees to place the ramp facing the cave's exit.

Seconds later, Avi emerged from the cave, holding a gold-plated decorated case out in front of his body. As he reached the ramp, a bullet struck below his armpit, finding a void in his ballistic armor. The crew chief grabbed Avi by the forearm and swung his arm around to hit the ramp's button, sealing the occupants inside the aircraft.

Avi clutched the relic, moved forward, and delivered it to Weinberg. "Here you are, sir, just as I promised." Avi gasped. After fulfilling his word to Weinberg, he collapsed to the plane's floor seconds later. Blood dribbled from his mouth.

One of his teammates was cross-trained as a medic, ripped off his ballistic vest and shirt. The medic worked on his comrade for thirty minutes before giving up. Silence occupied the rest of the journey, as they had found the artifact, but at a tragic cost.

CHAPTER 31: Precision Strike

New York Bay, Atlantic Ocean

Six-foot waves crashing against the ship's bow masked the noise from a nearby freighter setting out to sea. The Arabian Star's captain brushed the crust from his eyes and squinted out at the early morning horizon. A light northwesterly breeze foreshadowed rain later in the day. A gentle, two-story-high fog yielded to the rising sun. Popandropolis savored the end of his journey, as he wanted to purge his ship's cargo, retrieve a load of electronics, and return to Egypt. His instincts signaled pending trouble, but he allayed his concerns, and his conscience, by rationalizing that the Americans had earned their fate; their imperialist ways had alienated many across the globe. His deep reflection kept him from noticing the futuristic vessel approaching from aft.

Lieutenant Jason Roberts loved the sea, as the ocean gave him a sense of peace, belonging, and now a higher calling. He grew up in a small township in northern Wisconsin and lived on Lake St. Croix. Roberts spent his summers swimming, fishing, and later scuba diving into the depths of the lake. After high school, he joined the Navy to follow in his father's footsteps. By doing this he merged his fascination with the water with his goal of serving his country. He rose through the ranks and simultaneously attended night school, graduating from college on the GI Bill. When an opportunity presented itself to try out for the SEALs, Roberts dove in headfirst and pushed his body to extremes, earning a position with one of the US military's most elite units.

Known for his ingenuity, strength and courage, Roberts quickly earned the respect and his teammate's trust. Their assignments propelled them to global hotspots, such as Afghanistan, Pakistan, Libya, and Iraq. They had all served with distinction in America's twenty-first century wars in remote lands. They found in ISIS, Al-Qaeda and its affiliates, a determined adversary. Not that the thought of death ever crossed their minds, but their favorite saying was "drive fast and take chances." They would do both today, as the motto seemed applicable to the task at hand, their mission's sensitivity, and their victory's importance.

Roberts commanded the sleek thirty-six foot vessel with precision, following his operational plan. He used a Panamanian freighter to mask his swift and stealthy approach. Arching around the front of the freighter, he entered the Arabian Star's wake. As the high-tech boat sped toward its target, Roberts addressed his men.

"If possible, we should take Hassan alive," said Roberts, glancing at his watch. "But don't take any unnecessary chances to keep these bastards alive. Remember, we only have eight minutes to finish the job. After that, the Joint Chiefs have one last option. The Arabian Star will never reach America's shores."

James stepped forward. "I'll stay out of your way, as my mission is to rescue Suhar Atallah. Once I have her, I'll return to the boat," he barked. His voice was barely audible over the boat's dual caterpillar, six in-line diesel engines' thunder and the waves crashing against its hull. The long narrow boat with a deep V-shape hull sliced through the water and could turn on a dime.

Roberts tilted his head back. "Lock and load," he said. "Prepare to board. Let's get it done."

The SEALs racked back the slides on their assault rifles outfitted with silencers and the latest optical equipment. Loaded and ready, they secured their equipment to their bodies in preparation to board the vessel. Only a handful of the nation's political elite knew the full nature of their clandestine mission. Having ordered the strike, the president trusted the veracity of the CIA's information. He desired a clean operation devoid of any political fallout.

As the two rigid hull inflatable boats edged up on the Arabian Star, two commandos raised their weapons to cover their team from any threats above; seconds later other SEALs raised their single-prong hook ladders skyward. The hooks landed on the top railing with its weight securing them in place. The SEALs shimmied up the rope ladder to the vessels railing.

Senior Chief Dan Hill reached the top first. He peered over the edge of the vessel, scanned the rear section of the ship, scaled the railing, and waved his teammates to advance. One by one, the SEALs climbed their separate ladders and formed two eight-man teams to prepare for a dual-prong assault of the ship. Roberts tasked Hill to secure the upper decks and the bridge, while he would hit the crew's quarters, cargo hold, and engine control room. Roberts had requested another attack element, given the vessel's size and the intelligence showing a fifty-strong opposing force; however, the requirement for a stealthy approach mandated a reduced force and the advantage of surprise.

Roberts signaled the two teams to begin their assault. Hill's men scooted broadside while Roberts' team scurried to a hatch leading to the ship's lower levels. James shadowed Roberts' team and glanced at a small laminated schematic of the Arabian Star. As he entered the hatch behind Roberts' team, Hill announced contact over his radio. Without firing a shot, Hill immobilized two unsuspecting crew members and used plastic flex-cuffs to bind their hands and feet to the vessel's railing.

As Roberts descended the stairs, he maneuvered right at a three-way hallway juncture, while his second in line veered left. The trailing SEALs alternately broke right and left, creating two four-man teams headed in opposite directions. James held his position at the foot of the stairs, using the hallway wall as a temporary shield. He covered the passageway with his submachine gun, and admired the fluidity of the SEALs as they swept room-to-room, neutralizing everyone in their path. Within seconds, the two teams rounded their corners as they hit room after room. James held his ground, securing the stairs and the middle corridor as the SEALs cleared all rooms.

James reviewed his watch; its countdown timer read six minutes and twenty-three seconds. The SEALs' efficiency astonished him, as they advanced through a quarter of the ship in under two minutes. He knew their trade didn't come easy. Each SEAL spent endless hours in individual and team training, firing thousands of rounds each day. They trained constantly for the worst-case scenario, using speed, surprise and violence of action. By sea or land, they remained American's strategic option as the tip of the spear on terrorism.

The howling wind from the deck above distracted James as he glanced skyward. A lull in the SEAL's radio transmissions compounded the awkward silence and his solitude. A creak emanated ahead of him; James snapped his head back toward the hallway and eyed a T-shaped corridor about fifty feet ahead of him. He shifted his gun toward the noise, as his eyes landed on two familiar ones. They momentarily transfixed on one another. Hassan raised his pistol and pulled the trigger, sending two hollow point projectiles at James. The agent kneeled, used the wall as cover, and pressed the trigger on his submachine gun, firing three rounds of his own. Hassan ducked behind the wall.

James clicked the button on his microphone. "Roberts from James. I'm engaging Hassan. I have him pinned down in the lower deck."

"Hold your position," Roberts barked. "I'll send back-up, so don't let him get by you."

"Copy that," James said, ducking back around the corner as Hassan fired another volley toward him.

He considered his options when Hassan whizzed across the corridor. The terrorist fled toward another stairwell and a potential avenue of escape. Hassan fired four rounds down the hallway. James aimed his gun at an exposed hand and fired another three-round burst as he moved toward him.

James approached the corner and allowed his submachine gun to hang by its sling while drawing his pistol. He prepared to round the corner and held the pistol at arm's length. Suddenly, Hassan sprang into view and thrust his pistol at his upper body. He instinctively struck Hassan's wrist, causing the terrorist to squeeze a round off before dropping his pistol to the ground. The shot ripped into the wall behind him.

"Don't even blink." James said, aiming his pistol at the terrorist's head.

Hassan raised his hands. "You've caught me," he hissed. "What will you do with me?"

James scowled. "I'm going to take you in to face justice. Get down on your knees and keep your hands above your head, where I can see them." James reached to his belt to remove his handcuffs while covering the terrorist leader with his pistol. Hassan's docility surprised him. James overheard on his radio that the SEALs had advanced to the bridge. The captain released his hands from the helm when a SEAL thrust him to the floor. The boat rocked abruptly. James wobbled and slammed back against the wall. Hassan sprang forward and grasped the agent's gun hand at the wrist. He pounded the American's hand three times against the wall until the pistol clattered to the deck. Hassan threw a knee strike to the agent's mid-section, which he blocked with his own knee. James jabbed his left fingers at his adversary's throat. Hassan's knees buckled, but he recovered in an instant and tossed James against the wall.

James slammed his right elbow down between Hassan's scapulae and reached over the man's head and cupped his chin. He sprawled out, thrusting his legs backward and unleashing his two-hundred pound frame on his opponent. Hassan fell to the floor, taking the agent with him. Hassan snapped his head up and nailed James on the chin, followed by an elbow to his temple. James' grip released. The two warriors scrambled to their feet, facing one another. Hassan kicked James' lower leg as a distraction; he lunged for the pistol, rolled to a kneeling position, and turned to point the weapon at the agent. James kicked, catching his opponent's hand as he fired. The round grazed his shoulder, but failed to slow the tenacious agent. Hassan spun to the right, executing a back kick into the agent's stomach.

Hassan scampered up the stairs and lunged for the hatch. James charged after him, determined to bury him. Midway up the stairs, he heard a muffled feminine scream. At that instant, two commandos approached surreptitiously.

"Hassan went through that hatch." James pointed. "He's all yours."

The two SEALs nodded and vaulted upward and disappeared through the hatch.

Scurrying down the hall, James pounded on each door while shouting, "Suhar, Suhar." At the fourth door, she responded. "Matt, I'm in here."

He took a half step back and kicked the door just below its handle. The solid wood door barely rattled. So he kicked it again. Wood splinters hurled through the air as the door snapped open. He entered, and there on a bed lay his target; she was stripped to her bra and panties, tied to the bed hand and foot.

"I hope that I'm not interrupting anything." James raised his eyebrows, as his fingers worked the rope's knots. He then grabbed the mic, holding it to his mouth. "Roberts, this is James. I've recovered the woman. I'm returning to the rally point, precious cargo in tow."

"Copy that," Roberts said. "We've pinned down fifty hostiles in the cargo area. We're taking fire."

Automatic gunfire echoed through his earpiece. "Copy that. Good luck. James out."

"What's going on?" Atallah hugged him.

"We've got to go. Our guys are taking down the ship and they've encountered fierce resistance."

She winced. "They can't do that. Those men are all infected with the virus. If they get too close, they'll be exposed to it. Call them off before something happens to them."

He tossed Atallah her pants. "Hurry and put on your clothes and shoes, as we've a deadline to meet."

He depressed a button for his microphone. "Roberts, Roberts, this is James. I've just been informed that the terrorists have injected themselves with a lethal virus. You should lock the terrorists in the cargo hold and get out of there. You're in a hot zone. This ship must be quarantined. Do you read me? Over."

"No worries, James," said Roberts, "we have all the exits covered. I'll tell my men to chain the doors and we'll head back to the rally point."

"Good. I'll see you in a few minutes. James out." He grinned.

He grabbed Atallah's hand and led her from the room and down the hallway. "Stay close to me." He squeezed her hand.

James retrieved his pistol from the floor and holstered it. He raised his submachine gun to cover his escape route. He retraced his route and navigated through several corridors and up a stairwell where they exited a doorway leading to the rear end of the ship.

Inhaling the salty air, he scanned the back of the ship. "It's clear. Follow me."

He gripped her hand and guided her to the ship's rear, arriving at the rail seconds later. James reached into one of his vest's front pouches and removed a set of gloves; he donned them before going over the railing and grabbing the ladder anchored to the top railing. Atallah climbed over the rail and slid down James' back, clasping him around the neck.

"Hold tight." He climbed down the ladder, landing seconds later on the bow of the boat below.

She hugged James as he let the ladder loose. "Thanks for rescuing me. Otherwise, I was going to be shark food."

He grinned. "It's not over yet. Let's get you to the boat's rear." He escorted her to a seat, as the SEALs descended the ladders and assumed their standing positions on the two boats. Within a minute, the helmsman revved the engines while the last of the SEALs let the ladder dangle in place.

The skilled driver slammed the boat into forward gear.

"Let's move," Roberts said. "Hassan almost got away on a jet ski, but my men shot him down. Watch the ship, as I think you'll find our next move inspirational."

"Are you sure he's dead?" James' eyebrows narrowed.

"Unless he's an Olympic swimmer, I'm sure he's fish food. My men checked out the area where he went down for three minutes."

James nodded. "Chalk up another one for the good guys. He was one ruthless bastard."

Roberts tapped James on the shoulder. "Look at those F-18 Super Hornets. They're locked on to their target. And we thought our jobs were fun." The lieutenant grinned.

James watched as the two jets screamed toward their target. The lead pilot released his missiles, as did his wingman. A brilliant flash and a black smoke plume now preceded each jet. An instant later the four missiles slammed into the Arabian Star, simultaneously hitting the upper and lower decks. A fireball erupted skyward as the ship engulfed in flames. James watched as the Arabian Star lost its buoyancy and disappeared beneath the crashing waves. The ship and, more importantly, its cargo failed to reach the shores of America. As the Super Hornets screamed on by, the two pilots dipped their wings in salute. James' skin tingled from the gesture.

CHAPTER 32: House Call

James' Condominium, Arlington, Virginia

The sun glistened off of the nearby Potomac River as a light breeze drifted in from the east, bringing unseasonably warm air to the nation's capital. James gazed into the eyes of his breakfast companion, as she tackled her honey dew melon with a knife and fork. His six-by-ten-foot balcony offered a sweeping view of Washington DC, a panorama that carried a stiff price tag. The nation's monuments lingered at his backdoor. Among them stood the sobering expanse of Arlington Cemetery, a field of white stones signifying the sacrifices that Americans had endured throughout their brief history.

Atallah interrupted his reverie. "What's bothering you?"

He turned toward her. "I was looking at the cemetery and thinking about the high cost of freedom, as Americans have sacrificed over the years, and I'm wondering how many more white stones will be added this year." He said, staring down at his plate.

"You're always so serious. When are you going to relax because you certainly deserve it, especially after what we just endured?" Atallah smiled.

He chuckled. "I'm relaxed and haven't felt this comfortable in years, so I could get used to it."

"We saw so much yesterday and I really enjoyed the White House tour. It's nice that you have friends in the Secret Service." She beamed. "The china room was magnificent with many spectacular pieces, spanning several centuries and presidents."

James had lived in the area for over a decade, taking the city's riches for granted; however, he remained familiar with Roosevelt Island, given his near-daily lunchtime runs. He appreciated the coalescing of a presidential tribute to nature, all in the nation's capital. American history was replete with great presidents; however, Teddy, of Rough Riders fame, was one of James' favorites, because of his love of the outdoors and athletic qualities. He also admired his directness and brevity, qualities that appeared absent from many of today's politicians. He had little time, nor patience for trivia.

They toured the Lincoln and Jefferson memorials, the Washington monument, and the Smithsonian over the weekend. The Georgetown seafood and nightlife enthralled the exotic beauty, but this didn't surprise James, who called in a favor from a buddy he had once saved in Iraq. His indebted colleague anchored his forty-foot houseboat off the promenade and waited for James to cash in his chit for a view of the DC lights at night. It left a lasting impression on Atallah, who enjoyed not only James' undivided affections, but America's good life.

"What was best about last night?" James looked deeply into her brown eyes.

She grabbed his hand as her eyes sparkled. "I enjoyed the splendid company and our romantic trip down the Potomac River, as DC looks so peaceful and beautiful at night."

He smiled boyishly and momentarily relived his passionate embraces with her from the upper deck of the houseboat. "The company was outstanding," he said, eyebrows rising, "particularly after we returned home for the evening, as you have a wild side that needed to be tamed."

She blushed. "Yeah, that was incredible too."

"The cuffs were unexpected, so it was lucky for me, I had a couple and a four-poster bed. I must admit, though, that was new for me." He said, turning a subtle shade of red.

"And did you enjoy it, Matt? How did it make you feel?" She fished for the desired answer.

He grinned. "In a word, it was exhilarating, sensual, and sizzling."

"That was several words. So you fancied it? She lifted his hands and licked his index finger.

"It was liberating." He said with his eyes wide and glowing.

Catlike, she left her chair and slid onto his lap. Her warm breath permeated his neck as her seductive powers tantalized him. The woman made his body quiver with a sudden adrenaline rush. And she was certainly a master at manipulating men.

A soft knocking at the door startled them, and he contemplated ignoring it when the doorbell rang, showing determination by the untimely visitor.

"Timing's everything," he said. "Mine seems to be bad."

"Just leave it." She kissed him again, only this time pulling his body tighter to hers. She could feel his heart beating through his shirt.

He eased her back off his body and looked into her eyes. "I'm on the job twenty-four seven, so I must get it."

She sighed and tenderly raised herself from his body, as her lips pressed together. She was used to getting her way. As he walked toward the front door, she studied his physique from top to bottom.

"This will only take a minute," said James, grinning over his shoulder. "We can resume where we left off."

Opening the door, he eyed Dr. Sherman. "Hello." His voice cracked. "This is an unexpected house call."

"I came to check on you, as I thought you might have some concerns about your exposure to the Ebola-Nile virus. It's not exactly as widespread as the common cold."

"Please, come on in." He held open the door for the CDC doctor to slide by.

Atallah stood there, arms folded across her bosom. For an instant, the two women stared at each other, and then Atallah nodded. "You'll excuse me," she breathed. "You two have things to discuss." She trudged toward the shower.

"Sorry," the CDC expert said, "is this a bad time..."

James shot an awkward glance at the bathroom door. "Don't be crazy. I'm glad you're here, and it's wonderful to see you again."

"And you as well." She flashed an enigmatic smile. "But I have to tell you, I'm truly worried and borderline panicked, as the intelligence isn't good. Can we talk somewhere privately?" She scanned the condominium.

He looked and pointed toward the balcony. "Can I make you anything? How about a cup of Columbian coffee? A friend of mine there sent me it."

She nodded. "That would be wonderful." Her eyes swept the room. "This is a beautiful place. You're full of surprises."

The agent chuckled lightly. "I can't take credit for it, as I used to date an interior decorator. She shared the place with me until she grew tired of living alone in it. I was always off on an assignment somewhere, so I can't blame her for walking away, but I'm just surprised she didn't do it sooner." He shrugged as his brows rose.

"I imagine your job is tough on a relationship." She said, knowing the answer.

"You pay a price for it, but it's worth it. Look at that vase?" His finger pointed to a delicate crystal piece perched atop a miniature white marble Roman column.

"It's beautiful." Her eyes lit up.

"I bought that in Romania. I like to bring back something typical from every country I visit, so it gives the place a worldly feel," he said, in a slightly self-mocking tone.

He vanished into the kitchen and emerged holding a handmade Peruvian mug. He handed it to the doctor, motioning her to his balcony table. "There's milk and sugar. Let's talk, as I'm guessing I'll not like what I hear."

"Have a seat. I can tell you, it's not good news." Her voice shook.

"It can't be that bad? You must've faced countless disturbing viruses in your work."

She crossed and uncrossed her arms. "The el-Amarna virus is one-hundred times more potent than anything else I've ever seen, and it's easily transmittable. We project it could spread across America in months as it travels lightning fast."

The agent gazed into the doctor's eyes. "Why are you bringing this up now? I've done my part to stop the plot, so get someone else to finish the job. That's if there's anyone left to save. His mouth crumpled.

She leaned forward. "Do you recall the scientific exploration of el-Amarna by the joint Israeli and American team?"

"I vaguely remember it. I believe they launched their expedition, but I heard nothing about its results." His smile wavered.

She gave a downcast expression. "They explored the site, and discovered a relic that could provide clues to a potential cure or a vaccine, but the news is mixed, so the American scientists are skeptical, but the Israelis believe they've found a cure."

"That sounds promising," James said, nodding. "Modern science is a wonderful thing, particularly when you concentrate your best minds and artificial intelligence on a problem."

"I wish it were that easy, as the Israelis aren't sharing their findings with us, and the speculation is that they're developing a cure or vaccine so they can safeguard their population." She scowled. "US intelligence experts opine the Israelis don't want to share their research, as they're afraid we'll give it to the entire world, including the Arab nations."

He slapped his forehead as his eyes widened. "Imagine that. I'm betting they view this as an excellent opportunity to rebalance the continents to ensure their survival. I don't blame them, as Iran is calling for their annihilation, and everyone knows that many other Sunni and Shia nations share the same feelings."

"You think so? I can't imagine our closest friend in the Middle East wouldn't cooperate with us." The doctor peered over the brim of her coffee mug.

He rolled his eyes. "Don't be naïve, as the Israelis use us like everyone else, perhaps even more so."

"I can't understand how any democratic nation would harbor this sort of belief, as humanity could be at risk." She tugged at her earlobe.

"I agree," he said, "but Israel has been fighting for its existence ever since their founding in 1948. So, you're saying that the el-Amarna legend is definitely true."

She shrugged. "History books allude to a great Egyptian city that was annihilated by something deadlier than one-hundred plagues. I don't know, but it certainly sounds plausible under the circumstances. Given your personal experience, I'm surprised you'd doubt it."

He sipped his orange juice. "Why are we even talking about this? My mission eliminated the threat, and it's over." James' mouth slackened.

"Let me show you something, Matt." She lifted her briefcase to the table and released its latches. Pulling out a manila folder marked Law Enforcement Sensitive, she opened it, revealing a report from the FBI's Detroit Joint Terrorism Task Force. She handed it to him. "You should read this."

He scanned the document, originating from a source that had infiltrated the Muslim community; it described an unknown resurrected virus coming into the country that would be unleashed in the days ahead. He finished reading the second page, displaying the caveats he had seen far too often, as they couldn't determine the source's authenticity and it would reach the US government.

"This could be dated information or circular reporting." He threw the folder down. "And this intelligence has been overcome by events, and I'm talking about those same events that we thwarted." His mouth turned downward.

She looked up. "You could be right, but can we afford to disregard it? Hassan's body was never recovered, so he could be out there now, waiting to strike a fatal blow."

"The SEALs claim they eliminated him; they're great shots and some of the finest operators in the business," he said, shaking his head. "Hassan's dead."

"You're one of the few people to have seen him. Listen to me, Matt. I've some theories, but I require your help. Please, just humor me."

He held up a restraining hand. "Bring me some hard proof," he said, "Then we'll talk."

Her shoulders sagged. "I can't really blame you and I must admit I'm winging it here, but Matt, I'm terrified as it's too risky to take any chances, no matter how small."

"I know, I know," he raised a cautionary hand. "Intelligence gathering's something you're very good at, so bring me more and we'll talk, Jill. How about we talk over dinner?"

Her eyes met his and lingered. "Okay, but I'll be back, and soon. You can count on that. If it's proof that you want, I'll get it." She gave a curt nod.

"I'm counting on it, but just don't make it too soon, as I'm entertaining a guest that I've neglected since your arrival." He said, again feeling a slight twinge of guilt at his attraction to the doctor. This resonated with him, especially with the breathtaking Middle Eastern beauty in the next room.

"And how's your weekend going?" She raised her eyebrows.

He grinned. "I've never been this busy in my life and spent so much time sightseeing, not to mention entertaining that I'm all tuckered out. The female archeologist is unique and an interesting, exciting woman."

Sherman blushed. "I think I've heard enough. I'm sorry that I asked. You really must excuse me though, as I must finish some important work."

He smiled. "I also have some serious work I need to address."

"You're incorrigible. I'll just let myself out, if you don't mind." She stalked stiffly away.

James trailed her to the door, while admiring her spirit, tenacity, and wholesomeness. He tried to deny his attraction to her, though she seemed too proper for his tastes, yet she still appealed to him.

The doctor turned to say goodbye, and she tried to deny to herself the growing feelings she felt for this cocky, yet charming man. Despite his cowboy exterior, he remained a sensitive, honest, and patriotic man.

"You take care of yourself, Matt. I'll update you in a week."

"I'll look forward to your call, and I hope you find the reassurances you seek. Keep me apprised and have a great day." James flashed a grin as he closed the door.

CHAPTER 33: Unseen Treasure

The alarm sounded at zero-six hundred, awaking James from its increasing high-pitched beep. He rolled over and hit the off button with the flick of his wrist. He turned toward Atallah and swept the hair out of her eyes to gaze at her angelic face. Her exotic look that melded eastern and western attributes fascinated him, and he looked forward to exploring it.

Not wanting to disturb her, he eased out of the bed, tiptoed to the adjoining master bathroom, and peered into an expansive walk-in closet built out of solid mahogany. His eyes scanned the petite dresses and other scanty apparel that hung alongside his suits and warmed his guarded heart. It prompted him to strive for a proper work-life balance. As he was raised with solid Christian values, he valued the sanctity of marriage, but his fast-paced, chaotic life limited opportunities to meet the right woman. Although he recognized its unreasonableness, he sought a woman who would understand his patriotism and altruistic desires, while stomaching her secondary role to him serving the country. He suspected the right woman may alter his behavior, while appealing to his paternal instinct. A reluctant part of him realized the difficulty of being with the Middle Eastern beauty. He doubted that, while her fearless, adventurous side made her an exciting and worthy companion, she would succumb to being the wife of a DS agent. She wasn't one to wait for anyone, he realized, and he wasn't one to stay home. Perhaps their likeness compounded matters. Still, he thought, he hated to give up. Maybe he had misread her and could wake up to that angelic face regularly.

James ran his electric razor over his face and then brushed his teeth. He removed and tossed his red, white and blue boxer shorts aside. Opening the door to his glass-enclosed shower, he turned the handle counter-clockwise, releasing a steady water stream. His hand adjusted the handle to hot until steam filled the enclosure. He stepped into the water and the showerhead's pulsating stream rained down on his face and upper torso, relaxing his muscles and invigorating his mind. His preoccupation with the shower's massaging action reduced his usual awareness of his environment.

The glass door snapped open, startling him out of his reverie. Atallah slipped out of her black lingerie and joined him in the hot shower. His eyes captured her gaze. He pulled her against him and passionately kissed her soft, full lips. The embrace seemed to last for hours. She clutched the soap from the dish and lathered his back. He turned back to the stream of water, as she sensuously slid the soap from his neck down to his ankles. She reached under his arms and brushed her body up against his, repeating the ritual. Her touch left him trembling as she swept the soap over his entire body. James grabbed the soap from her and reciprocated, starting with her front. He slid the soap over her neck and across the front part of her shoulders. While making his way down her body, the ring of his cellular telephone interrupted him.

"Just don't answer it, Matt. Please just leave it."

"I wish I had that luxury." He gasped. "It could be important."

He gave her the soap while turning to the door. She held his hand and placed it on her heart. He contemplated letting the world handle its own problems for now. He wanted to linger in the shower with her, but his instinct prevailed. "I'd like to stay, but just can't." As he turned from her, he silently cursed his overdeveloped work ethic.

James exited the shower and grabbed a towel off the rack against the wall; he wiped off his shoulder and right arm, lifted the phone, and hit the answer button. "Hello, James here."

"Hi Matt, this is Patricia calling. I hope I'm not interrupting you."

"I was just in the shower." He bit the inside of his cheek.

"Sorry to interrupt, but I think it's important. Please hold for Director Jacobs."

He glanced back at the black haired beauty and shrugged. Her face sank. She pivoted to the shower to wash her hair as he walked into his bedroom for some privacy.

"How are you managing, Matt?" The director asked.

"I'm doing well, sir." The sudden bypassing of the chain of command puzzled him. "What can I do for you?"

"We have an urgent situation, so you need to report to duty. We just received flash traffic regarding the mission you recently concluded," said the director, as he avoided disclosing anything to do with the virus over an open line.

"Say no more, sir." His heart quickened. "I'll be at the office in twenty minutes." The phone line went dead.

James finished toweling off and threw on his underwear, a white dress shirt, a blue custom fit pinstripe suit, and a blue tie. He looked more like a Wall Street broker than a federal agent.

He entered the bathroom. "Suhar, I have to go to work. Make yourself at home. I'll return around five o'clock, if all goes well." He vanished a second later.

James sprang out the front door, descended his steps, and walked to his parked car on the street. He unlocked the driver's side door with his key and opened the door, hopping into his car. As he turned the ignition with his key, the car roared as he pressed down on the gas pedal. After releasing the vehicle's hand brake, he placed the selector in gear and sped away.

· · · · ·

Meanwhile, Atallah stepped from the shower, dried off, and dressed in comfortable jeans and a white blouse. After drying her hair, she hurried to the bedroom and grabbed her purse from a nearby dresser. She dumped its contents onto the made bed. The bag contained over sixty distinct items, but she required only two of them. Tossing aside a pocket calculator, cell phone, and a letter opener, she sifted through the entangled mess of items and focused on a lipstick container and a lotion bottle an inch in diameter and three inches long.

She clutched the lotion bottle in her left hand, opening it and exposing a white creamy skin softener. She rubbed the moisturizing cream on her forearms, hands, and face, and eyed the container's Human Growth Hormone label. Her fingertips followed the seam and pulled on each side, causing the container to split open. She wiped off a half inch of lotion and now grasped a glass ampoule containing a clear liquid substance. Her concentration intensified as she turned the vial over, set it down on the nightstand and reached for her lipstick, twisting the top off it. She removed its false cap, pulled open a hidden compartment containing a small syringe, and rested it on the nightstand next to the vial.

Atallah snatched her purse from the bed and foraged for a loose thread in its handle. After locating it, she tugged the thread, but it didn't budge. She pinched the purse's handle and jockeyed a small, machine-made, metallic object toward her right. She tugged again and a fine two-inch needle appeared. The ease with which she evaded US Customs surprised her.

She threaded the syringe's needle, clutching the vial and plunging the needle into the vial. As she retracted the plunger, her eyes monitored the liquid as it flowed into the syringe; she transferred about one-half of the vial's contents into it because of its miniature size, but speculated it would suffice. She studied the vein on her forearm and opted against using it, anticipating that James might discover the resulting mark. His powers of observation surpassed all the men she had encountered over the years. She knew a needle mark would expose her to a series of questions, and she didn't want to admit that HGH helped maintain her youthful looks and muscle strength.

Atallah scanned her body for a reachable, but concealable position in which to inject the liquid. Her mind envisioned it would be easier and then recalled a movie where a drug addict injected herself between the toes to hide her track marks. She set her left foot on the bed's edge, picked up the syringe, stabilized her foot, took a deep breath and thrust the needle between her big and index toes, yelping as pain radiated throughout her foot. Just wanting to get it over, she pushed the plunger down and unleashed the liquid into her system. She considered injecting the remainder of the vial's contents, but opted against it because of the discomfort.

Atallah brushed the pain aside and now felt energized. Her eyes scanned the area to hide the vial and the syringe; she underestimated the task's complexity, given James' near compulsive cleanliness. She reflected upon her powers of manipulation and believed she could distract him from his daily routine, so she considered hiding both objects in plain sight. The bathroom seemed a likely place to hide the items. Her eyes panned the bathroom and then focused on the drawers centered between the vanity's twin sinks. She rummaged through the drawers, but they were too organized; a trait that would be unexpected in the typical bachelor's home, but not in James' well-ordered life.

She glanced at the mirror above the sinks and noticed a wall vent behind her. The vent would only be accessed during a thorough duct cleaning. She climbed into the bathtub to examine the vent cover's fastening mechanism. Four screws held the twelve-by-four cover in place. She looked into the vent and saw a limited ledge which would leave the items visible; she also couldn't risk discarding them down the shaft and damaging the heating element. This gave her an idea, though, so she walked into the master bedroom and searched for a floor vent. The room held two vents, so she opted for the one behind a corner stand supporting a large Sony plasma television. After sliding the stand aside, she jostled the vent that gravity kept in place. She lifted the vent cover, scurried over to the nightstand to retrieve the syringe and the vial, and walked to the vent. Her hand reached down the vent and felt a ninety-degree bend in it. She retracted her hand, grabbed the syringe and vial, and inserted the two items deep within the bend, withdrawing her arm to regain her balance. She kneeled over the vent and peered down into the void where the items remained invisible.

Atallah replaced the vent cover, slid the television stand into its previous position, and brushed the carpet to conceal any indentations. She stepped back a couple of feet and admired her work. Not even James could detect the temporary disturbance of his furniture.

CHAPTER 34: Watchful Eyes

Northern Virginia

James tapped his hand against his thigh while waiting for the light to turn green. His peripheral vision noticed north and southbound traffic congestion. Situated first in line, he expected the lights to change as a racecar driver would at the Indianapolis 500. He punched down on the accelerator to unleash the engine's horsepower; an abrupt jolt occurred as he entered the on-ramp to the George Washington Memorial Parkway. His car did not let him down, hitting the speed limit only seconds later. He grinned in childish delight at the car's performance. As he merged onto the parkway, he released the accelerator to enter the morning rush hour traffic that flooded the roads.

He preferred the parkway, even though US Highway 66 was a more direct route. Literally chiseled through parkland, the route provided a brief respite from the heavy congestion in the nation's capital. This proved true in the fall when the trees turned myriad colors covering the spectrum of a rainbow. Orange, yellow, and shades of brown lit up the morning sky, replacing the nearby steel and cement structures. It reminded him that some simpler things in life provided the finest pleasures. Many ignored the scenery as they rushed to work.

James dialed his stereo to his favorite country station, while noticing three deer grazing just outside the tree line. Toby Keith's "Courtesy of the Red, White, and Blue" was just starting, so he cranked up the volume over the car's six strategically placed speakers. He appeared in his element now, enjoying nature and country's best. Born into a different era, he could have been a cowboy, as he preferred the country to the city with its peaceful environment of nature. It also was devoid of the stresses of fast-paced urban living.

The light commute shortened the drive time to the Diplomatic Security Training Center (DSTC) in Dunn Loring, Virginia. The DSTC, as insiders knew it, played home to DS' Office of Training and Performance Standards, the Office of Mobile Security Deployments, the Office of Anti-Terrorism Assistance, and the Washington Field Office. Its four offices comprised about one-eighth of all DS agents, or at least it did on paper. Most agents spent a disproportionate time away from their home base. This proved true for MSD agents, as they frequently responded to global hotspots, as flashpoints littered the Middle East, Africa, and South Central Asia. If you wanted to see the world, these offices were a DS agent's gateway.

James drifted off into deep thoughts, as his mind always seemed to race, processing the day's events or planning future ones. He smiled, recalling Atallah's fragrance, her passion, and the excitement she brought with every touch. As he commuted, his thoughts wandered to Dr. Sherman, who possessed an entirely unique beauty. He respected her intelligence and warmth and wondered about their compatibility. Atallah appeared exciting, but in a forbidden, slightly off kind of way. Not that he minded, as the handcuff incident would warm him through many a chilly night. Sherman appeared to be someone you could bring home to your parents; someone whose natural grace and integrity swept a room. He compared the two women, realizing that Atallah's stature paled in comparison. James gave himself a mental shake and vowed to find something special to surprise his exotic guest for his disloyal thoughts.

James reflected upon the doctor's suspicions of the female archeologist, and speculated she might be interested in him, although perhaps he gave himself too much credit. He understood the efficacy of a woman's intuitive powers. Laughing internally, he recognized the difficulty in understanding any woman given their complexity. Despite himself, he became more and more morose as he more carefully examined his days with Atallah. He recalled her rescue on the Arabian Star, and how he may have interrupted the two childhood sweethearts in a tender moment, as the knots and ropes appeared too loose to be effective for restraint. His mind continued to analyze events, reflecting upon the strategic ISIS lab in the Sinai Peninsula.

She appeared fearless, despite a loaded syringe at her neck. And, although he had a healthy amount of belief in his ability to attract women, if he was going to follow his thoughts to their conclusion, he had to wonder how an Arab woman, no matter how westernized, could have thrown herself so wantonly at a man within hours of meeting him. She either was powerless to resist the chemistry between them or an effective actress. As much as he wanted to believe in her, he would need to silence his doubts before he could move on.

James reached into his suit coat, clutched his cellular phone, and pressed the menu button, navigating to his contact list. He scrolled through myriad contacts until he arrived at his newest entry and punched the call number.

After three rings, a feminine voice answered. "Hello, Dr. Sherman speaking."

"Hi Jill, it's Matt, Matt James."

"This is a surprise," she said. "How can I assist you?" Her voice energized.

He cleared his throat. "Can you help me? I doubt you're right about Suhar, but there's enough suspicion that we should allay any concerns. After we spoke, I reflected on past events, and I must concede there are several inconsistencies. I can't explain the specifics over the phone for operational security reasons. Can you meet me near my place in the Starbucks parking lot on the corner?"

"What time and how will I find you?" She said, glancing at her wristwatch.

"Right now. I'll be driving a Dodge Stealth, so you can't miss me."

"I can be there in fifteen minutes, but I'm at the Pentagon, so this better be good, as I'm briefing military scientists on the Ebola-Nile virus. My deputy can brief them for me, so I'll see you soon." The CDC doctor hung up.

Almost halfway to work and knowing that there would be hell to pay for disregarding the director's recall order, James darted off to exit at the CIA's off-ramp. He maneuvered the overpass and turned left, now heading east on the parkway. Traffic surged into the city, but he would make it in fifteen minutes. He followed the normal flow of traffic, exiting at Rosslyn, and then heading west on Route 50. After negotiating a few turns, he entered the parking area and backed in next to a mini-van; it provided partial concealment, but still allowed a visual of his front door to his condominium.

Now, he would just have to wait. Unlike the glamor portrayed in most shows, he found surveillance boring, but a necessary part of the job.

He analyzed the area for anything unusual. Several minutes later, a dark blue four-door sedan paused in front of him; it then backed in alongside his car. Sherman rolled down her window, as did James.

"Are you having fun yet?" She jutted her chin while smirking.

"It doesn't get any better than this. Do you want to join me? I have room for two." He swept his hand back toward his body.

She smirked. "You want to conduct surveillance in that flashy sports car. We'll stick out like whores at Sunday mass."

"And your government-issued sedan would blend in much better? We only have two choices." He shrugged.

"I vote we take my car," she said, "trust me, growing up with older brothers gave me some excellent skills at avoiding detection. I won't be spotted."

"Then it's settled. We'll take your car, so I'll need to transfer a few items." He rolled up his window, vaulted from the car, and went to the trunk. Opening it, he pulled out a cooler, a pair of binoculars, and a Northern Virginia map. His hand slammed the trunk door down, locking it.

James approached the government sedan and peered through her window. "You want something to eat or drink?" He held up his cooler.

"Get in cowboy and bring your goodies. I see you know how to show a girl a good time." She chuckled.

"Wait for our second date." He winked. "We'll have twice as much fun."

James opened the sedan's door and stowed his binoculars on the dashboard; he placed the cooler on the back seat before sitting down. He shut the door and turned to his new partner. "Some men will do anything to win a lady's heart."

"So what's going on?" Her eyes widened.

"All joking aside, things just don't add up. Suhar seems fine on the surface, but a couple of things bother me. She reacts when it's something little, but's expressionless when you'd expect a major reaction. She hardly blinked when she was held hostage by Hassan at the ISIS base. The more I think about it, the more I feel that I'm being manipulated." A sinking feeling emerged in his stomach.

"Why would she be using you?" The doctor rested her hand on his forearm.

He rubbed his forehead. "I'm not sure, as it could be she's still involved with Hassan and he's using her to learn our moves."

"That would make some sense. Although now that Hassan's out of the picture, I don't see how it matters." She wrinkled her nose, deep in thought. "You don't think she could be another of his human weapons, do you?"

"I can't see him risking a woman he cares about. And if they aren't still an item, I can't imagine she would volunteer for the job." He drummed his fingers against his thigh.

"So," she looked at him, "what's our next move?"

His eyes narrowed. "If I'm going to confront her, I have to catch her in a lie. I need proof that she's up to something."

"What kind of proof? I'm not sure that you'll be able to uncover anything." Her face tightened.

"Why's that?" He peered at her.

She grinned with a knowing gleam in her eyes. "A woman carries many secrets. Sometimes they're simple and other times very complex. The problem is getting them to admit any of it. Many women, particularly in the Arab culture, will take their secrets to the grave instead of revealing them."

"I don't suppose you're a doctor of psychology as well." He squinted and gave a hard smile. "You seem to know many things."

She felt a lightness in her chest as she looked into his eyes. "I've spent a lifetime learning about people. Their bearing, demeanor, and body language always yield clues as to their truthfulness. And with women, although we're trained to hide our genuine emotions about men, it's easy for another woman to read them."

James' stomach fluttered. "They may be simple for you to read, but they're a mystery to me. I'll never understand them."

The two spoke for an hour, touching on politics, religion, crime and punishment. He admired her conservative views on the issues of immigration, national defense, smaller government, welfare and drugs. However, she remained somewhat liberal in education, woman's rights, and gay marriages. She impressed the seasoned agent by her worldly views and her logic, as she exhibited both passion and compassion in her thoughts about human nature. Engrossed in their conversation, they nearly missed

Atallah emerging from his condominium. She shuffled down the steps and hopped into the back of a local taxi.

"Okay, here we go. Let's see where she's going." His eye twitched. "Let them get out in front and be careful with your distance."

She sighed. "Don't worry; tailing a car is child's play, so you leave the driving to me. I'll stalk her like a cat does its prey."

James unfolded his northern Virginia map and placed it across his lap. It would be important to identify an alternate route should they lose the taxi. Any delay could mean losing the Jordanian woman, and they could not afford to lose her.

"Put that map away." She touched his hand. "You're such a dinosaur." She clicked a button on the dash and pulled open a small digital monitor with GPS. "We won't get lost with this baby."

"I'm not worried about getting lost, but concerned about losing that taxi." His eyebrows drew together as he rubbed his pant legs.

The doctor grinned. "Just sit back, watch, and learn from the master. You've nothing to worry about." She saw the taxi drive northbound on Lynn Street. Placing the gear selector in drive, she tailed the cab, leaving four car lengths between them. She understood mobile surveillance's intricacy and the requirement for multiple vehicles in an operation of this magnitude. Approaching a series of traffic lights, she gripped the steering wheel as her face turned pallid; she edged up on the taxi, but left two cars and one lane between them. The heavy traffic provided plenty of concealment. Sherman stopped at the first red light, steering her car to the left lane; she expected the taxi would head west on either Route 66 or the George Washington Memorial Parkway, and her instincts proved her right. As the light turned green, the taxi's left indicator light blinked. The driver skirted to the far left lane.

After passing through another light, the taxi turned left onto the Route 66 access road. Sherman trailed from a distance, turning left and coming to an abrupt halt after the light changed. "Don't worry, Matt. These lights are synchronized, so the taxi is stopped at the light ahead of us. You see it up there?" She pointed to the taxi, maintaining her hand below the dashboard.

He nodded approvingly as her surveillance skills impressed him. He realized her complex nature, which the casual eye could overlook. The lab didn't occupy all her time. He soon relaxed as his new partner took control of the situation.

"Okay Jill, I'm sorry I doubted you. It's obvious you've tailed targets before." James nodded.

She smiled. "Yeah, but it's been a long time. I guess you never forget some things. Now I'm used to tracking the plight of a pathogen as it works its way through a village, town, or large metropolitan area in some remote country."

"That sounds a lot more difficult than this operation." His voice softened.

"Sometimes it's impossible. I was in the Congo last year trying to isolate and contain a Marburg virus outbreak, which culled a small village and then vanished just as fast. Viruses are a strange and complex phenomenon, as they require the right conditions to survive and thrive. My parents often questioned why I chose this profession. They wanted me to go into general practice. I must admit, there are many days when I ask myself the same thing." She pressed her lips together into a crooked frown.

He nodded. "I know what you mean. Suddenly, the job consumes you and you forget the importance of family and life's other finer things. It's a lesson that I only recently learned, but I'm glad that I discovered it, as it's never too late."

She admired his wisdom. His sensitive side intrigued her, so she reminded herself to probe it later. "We should continue this conversation when we have more time, possibly over dinner." Her impulsive forwardness surprised her.

"That would be great." James lifted his head. "I know some quiet places with magnificent views."

Heading west on Route 66 in light traffic, she remained four car lengths back to avoid detection. Upon seeing the taxi exiting onto Leesburg Pike, she closed the distance, expecting a series of lights. The cab followed the off-ramp and then headed north at a steady pace.

"I bet we're going shopping, as Tysons Mall is just up the street." She said with gleaming eyes.

James sulked. "I hate malls, as they're often overcrowded with overzealous people shopping for deals. I prefer the Home Depot. Now that's my type of mall."

"This will make it difficult for us to follow her, so we better step up our game." The doctor said, as she turned right into the Macy's parking lot.

The cab pulled up to the mall's entrance, as Sherman jockeyed her car in between an oversized truck and a minivan hugging the line. James watched his Jordanian companion pay for the ride and waltz into the building. As they vaulted from the car, the two pursued the exotic beauty. They knew it would be difficult to find her unless she loitered. Upon entering the building, they spotted her in seconds, combing through men's dress shirts and ties in Macy's.

"I wish we could've tagged her to follow her electronically." Her mind raced through other possibilities. "That way we could keep our distance without the fear of losing her."

James nodded as he ducked behind some kitchenware. "It's simply a matter of time before she spots us. I realize she only got one glance at you, but she knows me intimately, so I'm going to back off. You need to take the lead."

"You're right." Sherman's voice shook. "But I won't last long before getting burned." She wrung her hands.

James vaulted ahead and walked through the store into the general mall. He recognized the high ground's advantage, so he ascended the escalator and stood near the overpass. Five minutes later, Atallah emerged with the doctor trailing and admixed with countless shoppers. He shadowed Atallah from above and could see both of them. He watched Atallah turn into a jewelry store while the doctor pretended to window shop on the other side; Sherman used the glass' reflection to spot their subject browsing through several items.

Atallah emerged from the jewelry store with a small bag containing a gold bracelet. Her affluent upbringing and self-indulgence surfaced in the city. She meandered through the mall, stopping periodically to browse a store's items, as the latest gadgets at Brookstone's captured her attention. James watched her enjoy a full massage chair, trying every button. He never understood the appeal of this sort of shopping, and avoided lollygagging, as he valued his spare time.

Atallah stood, entered the mall, and walked briskly, glancing back over her shoulder. Her dilated pupils skipped around the mall. She stopped in the food court, took a calming breath, and then perused a Chinese restaurant menu before exiting the line and walking to the restrooms behind the court. Sherman waited for her partner to catch up. They pondered their next move. Vaguely familiar with the area, the doctor recognized they would be exposed in the alley.

Sherman rocked in place while licking her lips; they waited a couple of minutes before venturing into the back area. The CDC expert walked into the woman's restroom, scanning the four stalls and other areas, but encountered only one other woman. She emerged to find James loitering near a water fountain.

"She gave us the slip." Sherman surveyed the area.

James scowled. "Well, you're right, there's more to her than meets the eye. Atallah knows what she's doing, as she executed her stroll through the mall with real purpose. She most likely entered the stairwell and trotted away, so we'll never find her now given the mall's size."

The virologist shrugged. "Shouldn't we try to find her again, as we need to discover what she's doing?"

The two wandered downstairs to the ground level and reentered the mall near a convergence of halls. They scanned the various stores in the vicinity, noticing multiple avenues of egress. The two lost hope on reacquiring the Jordanian archeologist, so they strolled toward their car; they walked on opposite sides of the walkway, browsing all the stores along the way. Each store received a cursory glance as the countless stores and people left too many areas to hide.

After their fruitless search, they exited the mall, walked across the lot, and hopped into Sherman's vehicle. Unbeknownst to them, they passed within a stone's throw of Atallah upon exiting the mall. Seated in a nearby restaurant, she sipped a glass of Chilean wine while waiting for her lunch companion.

Before putting the car in gear, Sherman turned toward the agent. "Matt," she said, "I'm sorry. I know you didn't want to find anything."

He shrugged, maintaining a deadpan face. "Hey, perhaps she's just a shopaholic and she'll tell me about her bargaining in excruciating detail. Anyway, better to know now than later, right? Let's go." He fiddled with his watch and gave a heavy sigh.

Sherman reversed out of her parking space, but slammed down on the brakes, nearly clipping a man skirting by them in a hurry. "The dumb ass never even looked." Her facial muscles tightened as she watched the man walk away.

James snapped his neck around, glimpsing at the man from behind. He pondered his familiarity before turning to the doctor. "Great reflexes, speed racer."

She ignored the jibe and retraced the route back to James' condominium. The ride remained awkwardly quiet for the first ten minutes, as their uniform disappointment over losing Atallah riddled their faces. The two shared a competitive spirit, which often pushed them to the edge and contributed to their success in their chosen careers. Both of them seldom lost.

James reached over the seat and grabbed his cooler. "Can I get you something to drink? I have sodas and juices."

"I'm parched. Do you have anything stronger than juice or sodas? I can't believe we lost her. I'll take the orange juice." She pressed her hand to her abdomen.

He opened the eight-ounce container and handed it to Sherman, who guzzled it in one breath. "Thanks."

"Wow, that was impressive. If you can swig beer similarly, then you're the perfect woman for me." His posture stiffened.

She laughed. "You work up a thirst conducting surveillance, particularly with all that walking. How could we lose her, as we were right there?"

"We needed more resources, as it was impossible with only two of us. We're good, but no one could've done better." He nodded.

She glanced at him. "You'll just have to interrogate her tonight to see what types of lies she feeds you."

"I'll talk to her tonight, but I'll wait for the right opportunity to spring it on her. She won't even know what hit her." His eyebrows rose. "We should get back to work. Could you drop me off at my car?"

"Absolutely," she said, leaning in.

Sherman made excellent time, dropping him off at the parking lot ten minutes later. He thanked her for her patience and support, advising that he would call her tomorrow. The doctor acknowledged his appreciation and thanked him for his trust before driving off.

As he headed towards the door, the unwelcome thought of Atallah's duplicity crossed his mind. Maybe I'll give her a full body search, he thought to himself. He smiled at the absurdity of the idea. Well, at least I'll have fun looking, he laughed to himself.

CHAPTER 35: Payback

Jeddah, Saudi Arabia

Nightfall loomed as a shadowy figure parked his white Toyota Land Cruiser on the dark side of the street. He now sat about a block from the decrepit al-Jabbar hotel on the outskirts of Jeddah. The small family-owned, brick three-floor transient hostel catered to the lower-middle class. Its peeling paint, shattered fluorescent hotel sign, and trash piled up on the corner left a blemish on an evolving part of the sprawling city as urban renewal took root. A prescient land developer bought the eyesore and its neighboring properties, envisioning a western-style mall. Progress had a way of reshaping the landscape, and Saudi Arabia was not immune to this phenomenon.

Haim Rubinstein peered down at his watch. His eyes narrowed as he scanned the streets. He tapped his palm on his thigh and glimpsed at a plastic grocery bag fluttering in the mild breeze. Scrawny cats riddled with parasitic infections rummaged through a nearby dumpster; their wails interrupted the night's quietness. He watched a car round a corner as its headlights hit his face; yellow spots danced in his eyes for a few seconds. The car skidded to a stop at the hotel's entrance. The Israeli scrutinized the two men, as they exited the yellow and orange taxicab, paid their fee, and entered the hotel's reception area; it doubled as a waiting room and a small restaurant. After shadowing the two men for the past several days, his patience waned as his senses heightened.

The passenger door slammed shut as a stout man entered. "Look at those two pricks. I can't believe they're wandering around this earth worry-free and unremorseful. They should've been assassinated years ago in a slow, excruciating fashion, and then dumped in the desert for the vultures to eat," said Ofer Ziv, scowling.

"The birds would've died eating that garbage. You'd have all the animal rights activists after us. You must be patient, Ofer." The lanky man grinned.

Both worked for the Israeli Mossad for over fifteen years. They had differing physical characteristics, seeming more like the odd couple than a pair of top Israeli spies. This obscurity contributed to their real world success and unblemished records. Ziv appeared stocky, while Rubinstein stood lean and tall. A formidable team, their vast skills complemented one another. Ziv was as strong as an ox and specialized in weapons and tactics, while Rubenstein's linguistic abilities in Arabic, English, Russian, and French aided their operations in many parts of the world; his skills in technological espionage, tactical satellite communications, and physical security resulted in countless successful missions.

They scanned the hotel to determine their target's room and eyed the lights throughout the hotel's three floors. Five minutes later, a light emerged on the third-floor, the second window from the left, as two male silhouettes stood in front of its scanty curtains.

Ziv smiled. "I got them. Now we wait for them to fall asleep, and then we'll do our work. The two terrorist leaders won't escape this time."

Rubinstein did a double take. "You're such an old fart, Ofer. Is that the right room? That technique is so dated. Besides, there's no way to verify that you're correct other than sheer luck. It would be disastrous to enter the wrong room, especially if we surprised an unsuspecting couple doing the nasty." The geeky spy said, lifting a single eyebrow.

"Sometimes the simplest ways are the best. Do you think you can do any better?" Ziv folded his arms over his stomach. "I'll bet you dinner that I'm right. I've worked an entire career with the old techniques and I've never been wrong."

"You're on Ofer. I hope you brought your wallet this time because I'm starving. Watch and learn how the tech-savvy pros do it." Rubinstein broke out a small computer, opened its lid, and powered up the Panasonic tough-book, which ran its warm-up cycle in under two minutes. The tech-savvy Israeli began rattling off keystrokes and inputting commands. Within three minutes, he now scanned the hotel's registry. "What a surprise? There's no

Zuhar or Rantisi registered in the hotel, so let's find out what names they're using."

"They're not amateurs, and they may be scum, but they're not stupid. You should stick with the techniques that are proven. Sometimes the old ways are the best. You owe me supper and I'm famished," said the stout man, snickering.

"Not so fast, Ofer." Rubinstein reviewed the check-in times. "I've got them in room 316, using the names of Muhammad Atif and Abdul Abed. I guess you owe me dinner."

"Perhaps we're both right as we equally identified the room. Let's go check in and get ready, Haim."

The two grabbed their small suitcases, locked the car, and activated its complex alarm system with a click of a button; two quick chirps stirred the silent air of the backstreet. A pungent odor from a nearby dumpster saturated the area. They entered the hotel, scanned the lobby area, and found it deserted except for a front desk clerk, a server, and a bus boy. Rubenstein approached the counter to exercise his Arabic tongue. "Good evening. We would like a front-facing third floor room farthest away from the elevator."

The clerk scanned his computer screen before looking at the two men. "I'm sorry. The end room's occupied, but three-one-four is available, which is two rooms from the end."

The Israeli looked over the rim of his glasses. "That's fine."

As the Mossad operatives entered the elevator, their faces changed from relaxed to staid as they closed in on their targets. Approaching room three-fourteen, Ziv analyzed the area, identifying the stairwell for a hasty escape. Rubinstein entered the room, knowing it would be hours before they could execute their critical mission. The virtue of patience blessed him.

Ziv closed the door behind them. "I guess we're both right. Room three-one-six is the second room from the end. It's definitely your turn to buy dinner, anyway."

"I always buy." Rubinstein shook his head.

"You're the wealthy one. Playing spy is just a hobby for you. I only have my meager government salary and I'm supporting a family with four kids, two of them in college." Ziv gave a quick, disgusted snort.

"Okay, you set up the equipment and I'll call room service." Rubinstein spoke in Arabic and requested a smorgasbord of meat and chicken dishes, along with some fried potatoes. Neither of the spies drank coffee, so he ordered four cokes, as the soda's caffeine would help them stay awake.

Ziv removed the mirror from the wall adjoining their neighbors and then rummaged through his suitcase to remove an old hand drill. As he opened the drill bit set, he grinned at its simplicity.

"What are you doing, Ofer? You're such a dinosaur. You should organize your tools, so you can find them when needed. Your case looks like a female's purse, as there's shit everywhere." Rubinstein fingered his collar.

"Now what's it, Haim? I know what I'm doing, so just let me work in peace," Ziv grumbled, shrugging his shoulders.

Rubinstein pointed to his left. "Look at the room's corner, as it used to be a suite with our neighbors. They sealed it, but they left the door. Their crude patch work's visible at the seam and around the door knob."

"So what?" Ziv frowned as his nose crumpled. "I figured you were a spy, not an interior decorator."

Rubinstein's mouth slackened. "They left the space underneath the door, so the carpet covers it, but there's still a small groove. You must work smarter, not harder."

The technician opened his suitcase. Hard foam separated his expensive and sensitive equipment. Rubinstein lifted out a book-sized gray instrument, depressed a switch to activate its monitor, and pointed the affixed fiber optic cord at his partner.

"Only a mother could love that face." Rubinstein slapped his thigh.

Ziv's mouth quivered. "Give me that damn thing." He snatched the device from his partner and crept to the false door. Ziv kneeled down and slid the fiber optic lens under the door. The pencil-thin optic hugged the floor, so he pivoted it and caught the men sitting at a table. The small five-by-five inch monitor displayed the two playing cards; one's straight was no match for the other one's full house.

Rubinstein adjusted two dials on the device and began recording. "We must document our work. This operation's unprecedented and will be taught at the academy" Rubinstein's eyes glimmered.

Ziv looked down and away. "We shouldn't record anything, given the potential repercussions. A secret can be kept by telling no one; this wasn't the type of operation meant for outsiders, particularly the press. Governments have fallen for less."

"You're too paranoid, Ofer," Rubenstein shook his head. "Our superiors want this mission documented and I'll give them their wish."

Their current predicament highlighted additional differences between the two spies. Ziv remained a pragmatic man, filled with skepticism and privacy, willing to take his secrets and sins to the grave. Conversely, Rubinstein, a man of truth and righteousness, believed in the system and the hierarchy. Ziv admired his colleague's spirit, even the naivete behind it, as he had once felt the same way until life's hard lessons taught him otherwise.

The Mossad agents watched their suspects while eating their dinner. As a man of action, Ziv lacked patience, and thrived upon the climax of an operation, while his partner found the chase and build-up exhilarating. Despite their differences, the two collaborated productively. Rubinstein gained the requisite information, while Ziv's ability to improvise meant they could contain an evolving situation.

The two men traded turns monitoring their targets as time seemed frozen. Shortly before midnight, the two terrorists retired to their single beds and turned off their bedside lamps. Ensuring their targets hit a deep sleep, the Mossad operatives waited for a respite in the hallway activity. Ziv looked at the alarm clock on the nightstand; three more hours had passed since the two terrorists fell asleep. Their mission's success depended on the aspect of surprise. They both napped in between watches.

Ziv took the next shift. Midway through his watch, his eyes closed for a second before snapping wide open. He looked at his watch again; it read zero three-hundred. "Haim, wake up. It's time to work."

Rubinstein wiped the sleep from his eyes. "I'm on it. Let's make Israel proud."

The two threw their equipment into their respective cases. Rubinstein walked to the door, peered through its viewer, and listened. Only the slight buzz from the hall's florescent lights could be heard. "It's clear."

Rubinstein opened the door; its rusty hinges screeched and echoed throughout the hallway. Ziv stepped behind him with his lock pick and torque wrench, trotting to the target door and taking a knee facing it; his partner's eyes scanned the entire hallway. Calm and focused on the lock, Ziv inserted the pick and tension wrench into the keyhole. He worked the ancient lock like a concert pianist playing a keyboard. His music appeared just as sweet as he manipulated the lock's last tumbler and it clicked.

Ziv glanced over his shoulder at Rubinstein, raising his eyebrows twice. Within seconds, they moved from the doorway to the beds; they pointed silenced pistols at each of their respective targets and awoke them with blows to their heads. Startled and stunned, Rantisi and Al-Zuhar trembled from both fear and uncertainty.

Rubinstein spoke in perfect Arabic. "You make one noise and it will be your last. We're going to take your valuables and leave. Do as we say and you won't be hurt." Ziv holstered his weapon and swept the room for valuables, retrieving a Rolex watch and almost two-thousand dollars.

After pocketing the valuables, Ziv removed a small preloaded syringe from his shirt pocket. "We're going to put you to sleep. When you wake, we'll be long gone. Now be still while I inject you." Ziv withdrew the plunger and pierced the needle through Rantisi's forearm, unleashing the sleeping agent into his blood stream; it knocked him out seconds later. Ziv then discarded the syringe into his coat pocket and removed another one from his shirt pocket.

"It's your turn, Al-Zuhar." Ziv grinned. As he pulled back the plunger, Al-Zuhar kicked and screamed. Ziv blocked one arm and covered Al-Zuhar's mouth with his other hand. He silenced him with a frontal choke; his grip released as the man's eyes rolled back from a lack of oxygen to his brain. He injected him with the sleeping agent. Al-Zuhar's body wilted.

Rubinstein holstered his weapon while Ziv disposed of his trash. They left nothing to chance, subduing their prey in under a minute.

"It's payback time. This is for the homeland." Ziv relished the moment before executing the ultimate phase.

"These bastards are getting what they deserve. I've waited too long for this precious moment," said Ziv, nodding. "Hand me the gray case, so we can finish and depart."

"Do you think that it's as bad as they say? I can't imagine something so contagious that it could spread like wildfire in days."

Ziv opened the gray case by pulling a zipper from its back to front, and flipped the lid open, exposing two loaded syringes. He turned on the lamp on the bed stand, desiring to see his subjects more clearly. His eyes scrutinized Rantisi's forearm, as he needed to stick the needle into the recent wound. Ziv buried the needle into Rantisi's arm and pushed the plunger down, releasing the el-Amarna virus into him, as the Mossad operative savored the irony. Rantisi now rested as a human time bomb set to wreak havoc on his fellow Muslims. He alone could kill more people than all the terrorist bombs planted to date around the world. Ziv repeated the process, infusing death into Al-Zuhar's body.

The two spies looked at one another, as they completed their mission in Jeddah, starting an unstoppable chain reaction, which would devastate the world's population, decimating Muslims and indiscriminately killing many others. The coronavirus and its many mutant variants paled in comparison. They both understood Israel's ability to safeguard its populace while the virus systematically cleansed the world. It explained the vaccination they received prior to their mission. The two men only hoped their plan didn't backfire, as they recognized the virus contained no boundaries. They also silently prayed for God's forgiveness, as they understood that many innocent people would fall as they rebalanced the earth. It seemed a bittersweet mission for them; they remained good to the Mossad motto, "by deception, thou shalt do war." They were about to deceive humankind in the biggest war of all. More lives would be erased with this single act than all the wars that preceded it. And done correctly, Hassan would be blamed for it.

The two operatives retrieved their cases. Ziv led his partner down a side stairwell. Both of them remained solemn and poised, cognizant that they had just performed the largest sin of all. They would exit the premises and head straight to their car. Rubinstein removed a phone from his briefcase and traded the antenna for a longer, more powerful one in order to boost his signal. He needed to apprise his superiors about their operation. Rubinstein inhaled before dialing a number he had recently memorized. After four rings, a relatively unfamiliar voice answered. He recognized the voice of the Mossad director.

"Is it done?" Israeli's chief spy tapped his heel against the ground while pulling the receiver tight to his ear.

Rubinstein's voice cracked. "Yes, the disease has been placed in the rats and they'll soon deliver it to the nest. We'll track them to ensure a successful delivery."

"Excellent work, Haim. Tell Ziv to visit me when he returns to Tel Aviv." The Mossad chief vanished off the line as fast as he came on. The deed was done. Now they would all have to wait as the virus took root.

CHAPTER 36: Discovery

Arlington, Virginia

Darkness came earlier and earlier this time of the year, as people embraced the holidays, turkey, and football. James enjoyed seasonal shifts and the fresh crisp air and vibrant colors that came with the changing leaves; however, he hated leaving for work under obscurity and returning to his home in the same state. Things appeared different now, as he had something very real to come home to again and relished the feeling. He just wanted to ignore the cloud of suspicion that Atallah's daytime activities had sparked, but he knew he couldn't commit to her until he had silenced the alarms ringing in his head.

As James approached his front door, he took a deep breath; he remained resigned that his finely tuned interrogation skills would understand her recent spree. He hoped his fears would prove baseless, and that his discretion wouldn't jeopardize the fragile relationship he was developing with this mysterious and seductive woman.

Opening the door, he could hear the faint murmur of the television off in the background. The six o'clock evening news had just started. An incredible aroma permeated the air, spreading the flavors of Italy throughout his small condominium. Atallah abandoned her care of the pan on the stove; she balanced a wooden spoon in her white cream sauce as she heard James enter the room. She approached him with a carnal saunter that left him momentarily stunned by her sensuality. He fleetingly lost his train of thought as he savored the moment. He remained wary of this mystical power that she possessed over him, recognizing she was a man-eater and pondering whether he appeared on her menu.

"How was your day?" She kissed him.

He dropped his briefcase, pulled her to his body, and reciprocated the kiss as the room became hot. He pulled his lips back from hers briefly to answer. "It was mundane. I spent the bulk of the day writing reports about our recent adventures. I still haven't finished. It's difficult to describe what we've endured these past weeks and reads more like a fast action thriller."

She beamed. "I enjoy this type of job." She relished the adrenaline, travel, and fast-paced action.

"I understand how you feel, as it takes an expensive toll on your body and catches up to you." He stroked her hand. "Eventually, your body gets used to these regular adrenaline surges, and then has difficulty adapting to a more normal pace. The more you expose your body to adrenaline, the more your body craves it for regular functioning."

"You sound more like a psychiatrist than an agent." She smiled.

"I've been known to play one. I studied the subject after losing my last girlfriend to work. That's when I discovered this unusual medical diagnosis." He thrust his head back.

"You're serious about this?" She caressed his arm.

"I wanted to understand it, so I could better live my life at home. I desire a meaningful relationship, so it's important to recognize what's going on inside. A man should know his limitations." He smiled.

She reached for him again. "I've not seen any limitations so far, as you're a woman's dream, a manly man with a sensitive side. You're a rare and terrific catch, and now that I have you in my net, there's no escape."

"You're not wrong, but it's more like a web. Either way, I'm one lucky guy being caught by you." The tension lines in his face relaxed.

James realized her skill in eliciting information about him, so redirecting her questioning proved vital or she would discover all his secrets.

"So, did you do anything exciting today?" He leaned forward.

"I watched television, walked to the grocery store to grab some items for tonight's dinner, and napped. I'm still suffering a little from jetlag." Her eyes blinked.

He analyzed her face and body language; her demeanor appeared calm while her eyes stayed focused on his and displayed a regular blinking pattern. She also maintained an open posture, and her sentences appeared straightforward and uninterrupted, with no sign of any deception. He noted to avoid playing poker with the exotic beauty. His spirits plummeted. He had met many intelligence officers over the years; however, none possessed the talent of the lady standing before him. He doubted he could crack her story, and he questioned wanting to, given his attraction to her.

"Let me change out of this suit and I'll help you finish dinner. I've dabbled in the kitchen and once turned down a cooking show." He chuckled, needing time to regroup.

Atallah returned to the stove, sprinkling extra garlic salt into her linguine sauce. She chopped and added a generous amount of diced onions to her salad. She strolled into the living room and perused the wines in the agent's solid mahogany bar. His collection impressed her and seemed to be a compilation of all his travels. The labels reflected red wines from Spain, Argentina, Chile, Italy, and other places strewn across the globe. She also unearthed a trove of white and zinfandels.

James reemerged from his bedroom dressed in a solid navy blue V-neck sweater and khakis. "I've got more in the chiller; however, I would recommend the Australian white, as it's extremely smooth."

"I'm sure it is, but I wanted a red wine for my dish." Her voice softened. "Besides, studies have proven that a glass of red wine is good for the heart. At least that's what the doctors are preaching."

"Well, you're in the right section. I'd recommend the Chilean red. It's fantastic." He swung the side bar door open, joined her, reached under the front bar, and pulled a fine red from his international stock.

"I'll defer to your expertise. I'll go finish the food while you pour us a glass." She beamed, kissing his cheek.

He peeled back the foil wrapper around the neck and cork of the wine bottle, and inserted the corkscrew, while eying her graceful walk and fluid movements in the kitchen. He admired her and loved the feelings she stirred within him; it reinforced the importance of physical, spiritual, intellectual, and emotional connections. Her warmth now penetrated his guarded heart. He felt love once before, but abandoned his feelings to preserve his pureness in thought for his critical missions. Distraction could cause an operation to nosedive, and he feared failing his country, even if it meant his soul and a lonely existence.

James removed the cork and set the bottle on the bar, allowing the aged grapes to coalesce with the outside air. He ambled over to the dining room, taking special care in setting the table in this seldom-used room. He removed select pieces of his grandmother's china from the cabinet for the special occasion. James placed the china settings and etched colonial-era silverware on the delicate hand-woven placemats from Iraq. He lit two tall white candles held in place by fine Romanian crystal, creating a romantic ambience fit for the evening. He retrieved the wine, positioned the aerator, and poured two glasses. She joined him, carrying three decorative bowls containing a garden salad, white linguine sauce, and pasta noodles.

James approached her, carefully lifting the salad bowl balanced between her forearms. He placed it on the table between their seats, but before he could provide further help, she had already placed the two other dishes on the table. He walked behind her, kissed her on the neck, and withdrew her chair. She followed his cue and sat down, so he slid her chair inward before sitting opposite of her.

He raised his glass. "I'd like to offer a toast. Here's to new friends and a future of prosperity and great happiness. Suhar, I'm glad you're a part of my life and I hope this is a new beginning for both of us, one that lasts a lifetime." He swigged his glass of wine, bolstering his social courage. He refilled his glass and placed the wine bottle back between them.

"What's bothering you, Matt, as you seem tense." She gave him an arch look. "I can relieve that tension."

"I bet you can." James winced. "Nothing, I just have a lot on my mind and I'm having problems with the director. He's upset that I kept our mission secret from him and detested the way I conducted my work in total secrecy. I was cautioned that I must be compliant if I want to advance in his organization." He stared down at his plate.

"Don't worry about him. The secretary knew of your mission. If he wanted the director to know about it, he would've informed him. Obviously, he didn't need to know." She grasped his hands.

"That's what I told him, but he disliked the response. Imagine that." He grinned. "We should eat this delicious dinner before it gets cold."

As they consumed their three-course dinner, they discussed delicate subjects, ranging from politics to religion. He understood the contentious nature of the topics, but pushed the limits because these areas often torpedoed relationships. He recognized that any irreconcilable difference would eventually surface and opted to disclose such differences of opinions. There seemed to be little divergence in these issues, which complicated his task. He valued matching wits with another, but not now, as he couldn't imagine having a relationship with a deceitful woman. He detested his current predicament of having to interrogate her to satisfy his concerns.

James poured his dinner companion a second glass of wine, topping off his glass in a sweeping motion. Even though wine normally induced sleep, he required additional social courage to question her activities. He opted to preserve the precious moment and postpone the questioning until later. He enjoyed his effortless conversation with her. This only added to his distaste over what he had to do later; they had developed an excellent rapport and shared so many common interests. He often guarded his conversations at work, knowing the difficulty of trusting people. His experience taught him that very few colleagues merited total confidence. Workplace gossip appeared to be the norm, rather than discussions on strategic initiatives.

The dinner conversation lasted over ninety minutes, but it seemed like only minutes to him. Perhaps the bottle of wine contributed to his calmness, but he doubted it. He recognized the answer, probably lied with the beautiful lady across from him. By now, he disregarded the doctor's unfounded doubts. After all, her shopping spree proved nothing. Still, her deceit required explanation.

James collected the dishes when she placed her hand on his to halt his actions. "I'll get them later. Why don't we relax in your Jacuzzi tub? I've been eying it ever since we arrived. I can remove all your tensions in there." She winked.

"I'm sure you can." He licked his lip with cautious hope. The woman appealed to his manly needs. Although he relished the feeling, he cautioned himself. He couldn't afford to let his guard down or fall any further for the woman, at least not until he understood her excursion to Tyson's Corner.

"You go draw the bath while I clear the table. I'll be there momentarily." She nudged him toward the master suite.

He sidestepped, arguing with the convincing exotic beauty. He recognized the unique opportunity the bath presented to check her more closely, just to be sure.

"Don't be too long, as we should get to bed early. It's a monumental day tomorrow," he called out.

"I'll be there in a flash." Her eyes sparkled in the low candle light.

James ambled to the bathroom, kneeling and twisting both the hot and cold water handles. He adjusted the water temperature to over one-hundred degrees. Turning to grab a hand towel off the rack, he froze, mesmerized by the backlight-produced silhouette. Unbeknownst to him, she had strolled into the room, stood there silently and gracefully behind him. Angelic in appearance, the light captured her incredible essence and her long, glistening, flowing black hair. The heavenly sight silenced him.

"You've never seen a naked woman before?" She smiled, knowing that the backlight magnified her sensuality. She enjoyed his awestruck expression as he gazed upward.

He sprang to his feet. "I've seen no one so beautiful like you. I felt I was dreaming for a moment."

"Flattery will get you anywhere." She approached him with a seductive saunter.

He reached forward and caressed her cheek. "Is it flattery if it's the truth? You make Aphrodite look like an average woman." He smiled.

She beamed as she relieved him of his pants, which fell to the floor an instant later.

As James removed his boxer shorts, he turned to observe her pouring a blue colored liquid into the tub. "Stop, it's not good for the filter."

"Relax Matt, this is from the Dead Sea and is rumored to heal the body. If it can do that, I'm sure it won't hurt the filter. Get in the tub. That's an order." She turned, walking back to the bathroom counter. She retrieved two candles that she had found in the kitchen, lit them, and placed them near the tub. The candles' flickering light softened the atmosphere. Switching the light off, she approached the tub.

The agent complied with her instructions as he sat in the tub. Wary of displacing the water over the rim, he rested his back against the backside of the Jacuzzi. She entered a second later, laying her back against his chest. He pushed the play button on a control panel to turn on the stereo in his bedroom; it played the soundtrack from the movie "The Fabulous Baker Boys." The combination of piano, saxophone, and stringed instruments enhanced the mood and romantic setting.

His fingers gently squeezed her shoulders and back. He started at her hairline and worked his fingertips down her neck to her back.

"That feels great. Your hands are wonderful, but I was planning to massage you." She sighed.

"You don't think that I find touching a beautiful woman relaxing?" He said, examining every inch of her exposed body. Between the suds, high water level, and dimness, he realized its futility. It proved impossible to distinguish anything on her body, other than it appeared toned, smooth, and near-perfect. He wouldn't get any additional clues regarding her intentions and happenings, nor did he really care. He would start again, fresh in the morning.

They stayed in the tub for an hour, trading turns on the massages. He hadn't been so relaxed in years. Her wandering hands had released all his tensions, as she promised. He felt the effects of the wine and her soft and welcoming touch.

"We should go to bed, as I'm getting tired. I'd like to be well-rested for tomorrow's event. You get out first and I'll be right behind you." He stood up and helped the beauty to her feet, wrapping a towel around her petite frame.

She dried herself as he glanced fleetingly at her shapely figure. A small tattoo on the right part of her back, just above her buttocks, captured his attention. "What's with the tattoo on your back? It's so small, but looks like a red five-pointed star with olive branches, and there's some sort of black marking centered in it." He brushed his fingers over it.

She looked back at him over her shoulder and smiled. "It's a teenage indiscretion that embodies my roots. It represents hope for my people, nothing more and nothing less. I'm going to change into something more comfortable. Come join me." She wandered into the bedroom.

The emblem appeared familiar to him, recollecting it belonged to one of the Palestinian groups. He would research the symbol in the morning.

James finished toweling off, threw on his boxer shorts, and walked to his bedroom. He froze in the doorway to see Atallah slipping into a black corset. He walked around the bed and slipped under the covers.

She stood up, posed, and turned around gracefully. "Don't you love it?" She beamed.

"Is that a trick question? You look beautiful and very sexy." He gazed at her.

"I'm glad you like it because I got it for you." She kneeled on the bed next to him and peered into his eyes. "What's bothering you? Your mind's elsewhere. You can tell me anything." She stroked his cheek.

"I called home several times today, and you were gone for over two hours. You had to go somewhere else other than the local grocery store. You could walk there, shop, and return in less than thirty minutes." He looked away.

"Well, I wanted to surprise you. If it's bothering you, I'll relieve your curiosity so you can relax. I went shopping at Tyson's mall and I picked up this corset and one other item." She vaulted out of bed, walked over to the five-drawer walnut dresser, opened the bottom drawer, and rummaged through some of his old clothes. A second later, she lifted out a small neatly wrapped package and presented it to him.

"This is for you. I wanted you to have something special for tomorrow's ceremony. I hope you cherish it." She hurried over to the bed and passed it to him.

"This is very thoughtful, Suhar." He shook the package to find out its contents, and speculated on a tie by its size, weight, and feel of the package. He didn't want to ruin her surprise by guessing, so he removed the ribbon and gold bow. Starting in one corner, he inserted his finger under the paper and pulled it open, exposing a box. He lifted the lid and unearthed a light blue silk tie with an intricate, royal pattern.

James set the tie on the nightstand. "Come here. I love it." He kissed her and drew her close to his body with an enduring hug. He then lay down, resting his head on his pillow and pulling her on top of him, and lovingly kissed her again, only this time without being plagued by his suspicions of her. James drifted off to sleep, content with his relationship and optimistic about his future with the Jordanian beauty.

CHAPTER 37: Vital Link

NSA Listening Site, New Mexico Desert

Jack Dawson's stomach churned as it approached lunchtime. Even though he pulled a night shift, the day seemed to be beginning for him. He had worked for the National Security Agency (NSA) for nine years, gaining a reputation as a key player. His career serving his country spanned three decades, and it was long and distinguished. He had been recognized with prestigious awards on over two dozen occasions. A true patriot, he finished a twenty plus year career in the Army conducting signal's intelligence. His transition to the NSA appeared natural; he melded his love of the country with continuing to protect its citizenry. But unlike his past in the field, he now operated from the comfort of a desk. He found it refreshing, as he preferred the office's air conditioning instead of the dust and dirt in some desolate third world country. Dawson had earned the comfort of his leather chair as he meticulously managed and maintained his systems.

Dawson enjoyed tracking spies, terrorists, insurgents, and traitors. He valued and appreciated America for the vast opportunities it gave him. No matter how critical world events seemed, he always remained positive and sought the answers. His job made finding critical solutions possible. Even though it appeared to be a gigantic computer game to him, losing would be disastrous, and he hated to lose, which meant that he worked harder and longer than others. Failing to deter a terrorist attack or detect a spy could have catastrophic damage on America's security, so he recruited some of the most energetic and brilliant minds that America offered.

Fiber optics advancements and satellite communication had revolutionized spying. Fortunately, the US government provided him with the best equipment that money could buy. His twenty-five antennas wired to a supercomputer captured signals from anywhere in the world. The sheer power at his disposal amazed him, as his high-power antennas could snatch conversations from their targets and send them to a supercomputer which would analyze the communications for key buzzwords, sentences and phrases. The fast pace of his work was far from routine. His team analyzed terabytes of information every day. It was only with the supercomputer that this became possible. It could tie unrelated information together in a credible and understandable fashion. His teams often uncovered national security information of the highest priority.

Space's airwaves heralded vast riches beyond the mind's imagination. People spoke without regard to the reaches of disparate intelligence services. They could track a phone conversation across the globe, not to mention separate code in ostensibly unbreakable encryption. Violating people's privacy occurred routinely from the edge of space. Signals intelligence dominated everything from organized cartels to boardrooms to government centers. Even insurgents and terrorist organizations sought this ability. Information equaled power, and there were many who would pay generously for its fundamental value, which could give them a critical edge in today's competitive society or during complex negotiations. It didn't surprise him that the US government had the greatest hunger for such information.

Dawson looked at his monitor's screen before punching several keys. His supercomputer came to life, running a series of diagnostic checks of its systems. He periodically ran these checks to guarantee the billion-dollar supercomputer's operating integrity. His systems processed millions of conversations each day in over thirty-five distinct languages. His painstaking work had proved its worth over one hundred-fold. America's leaders had a ravenous appetite for his intelligence reports. The decaying human intelligence capabilities elevated his work's importance.

Concentrating on the Middle East, Dawson searched the airways for anything of strategic value. Message transmissions flooded in from all countries in the Middle East, making it difficult for his team to monitor all the significant traffic in real time. Several more Middle Eastern countries had recognized Israel's right to exist. Yet, there were several holdouts, one being the Iranian regime. Although they hid behind a fragile nuclear deal, they smartly hid their nuclear ambitions. Their scientists had enriched enough plutonium to build multiple bombs. US intelligence still assessed Iran as being years away from a nuclear weapon. However, the Israelis insisted that Iran already possessed several of them, which threatened their very existence. The Iranians had another unknown secret nuclear facility in the mountains in Northeastern, Iran. Israel became increasingly concerned as the Mullah's threatened the Jewish State with annihilation. Israel couldn't afford to wait any longer. Their long-range bombers appeared ready to strike.

With tensions rising throughout the Middle East, Saudi Arabia now feared the renegade Iranian regime. Iran's closeness with the Russians and the Chinese exacerbated the situation. The axis of evil had banded together once again against America and its allies. The president now needed clarity, and he would look to his intelligence agencies to provide it for him. This left Dawson in a bit of a predicament, so he combed and sifted through millions of pieces of information gleamed from his supercomputer. His attention included many countries, but today focused on Iran, China, Russia, North Korea, Israel, and Saudi Arabia. Of course there were many others, so Dawson had to have his ears open to anything that could spark World War III. Taiwan-China territorial disputes, new Artic shipping jurisdictions, and biological warfare were just a small sampling of the issues that plagued the world. The Doomsday Clock stood at two minutes for a reason, and there was no shortage of disputes or crisis that could spark the next regional conflict or world war.

Dawson had to prioritize any messages regarding the Palestinians and Israelis. Brokering peace between the two had eluded past presidents. Yet, peace stood closer than ever with more and more countries establishing diplomatic relations with Israel. Dawson also sought anything that could provide senior policymakers leverage in the ongoing Palestinian and Israeli peace talks. The battles fighting extremism required peace in the region. The long plight of the Palestinians often served as a rallying cry throughout the Muslim world. He focused another team's energies on Israel's Arab neighbors, the Egyptians, Syrians, Jordanians, and now ISIS. An alert from Saudi Arabia surprised him, given all the other flashpoints in the region.

"Jack, you should look at this information coming in from Jeddah." Lori Taylor said with a gleam in her eyes, while drumming her feet against the floor.

She had worked for the NSA for the past four years. A gifted linguist, she spoke Russian, Arabic, Hebrew, and French. This, combined with her deductive reasoning, made her a top asset at the agency. Her unique ability to decipher the intricacies of a conversation allowed her to break many encrypted messages. Even using encrypted systems, many still spoke in code to disguise their clandestine dealings. This resonated with the Israeli Mossad, who had cracked many codes over the years. They knew the vulnerabilities of communications systems, even ones that were secure. An expert at analyzing dialects and nuances, Taylor had listened to thousands of Middle Eastern conversations over the years.

He approached her desk. "What have you picked up? I hope it's good." He peered over her shoulder at her computer screen.

"Do you remember the flash traffic we received from H-Q warning us to keep an ear out for a possible biological dispersion? I think I've found something of that nature." She gave a knowing grin.

Taylor tapped a few keystrokes on her computer. Her monitor displayed the conversation she had flagged minutes earlier. The computer's screen flashed the important transmission:

"Yes, the disease has been placed in the rats and they'll soon deliver it back to the nest. We'll track them to ensure a successful delivery."

"We could only capture one side of a conversation from a Mossad field agent. I presume he was communicating with his superiors." She said, holding her chin high.

"Excellent work Lori, can you run this to the ground? This could be something big, like when you discovered clues reflecting the Coronavirus came from Wuhan." Dawson stood with his hands tucked in his armpits, thumbs visible and pointing up.

Taylor sighed. "Haim Rubinstein is the man on the ground. According to our database, he's a clandestine operative of the Israeli Mossad. We captured another conversation of his yesterday, showing they were tracking two Hamas terrorists. These terrorists were identified from other communications. We triangulated them in essentially the same locations over the past couple of days."

"What are their names?" He squinted.

"Their names are Mohammad Al-Zuhar and Abdul Rantisi. Do they mean anything to you?" She turned to her boss.

"Oh my God, it can't be." His eyes enlarged as he covered his mouth with his hand. He knew all the major players in the Middle East like the back of his hand.

"Why, what is it? Who are these people?" She stared at her supervisor, waiting for his answer.

Dawson shook his head in disgust. "They're the two terrorist commanders who ordered an attack on Israeli children near Jerusalem. Their men carried out an operation in Israel in 2002. They ended up driving a bus full of children over a cliff, killing them all. It was an unforgivable and heinous crime. Mossad is finally going to avenge those poor children and their families by taking Al-Zuhar and Rantisi's lives."

Taylor rubbed her eyebrow and cleared her throat. "It serves the two terrorists right. The only problem's that they're going to be carrying some sort of biological weapon. That's what I think poison means in the conversation we captured. I also think the nest refers to the Gaza Strip. It's where they just came from and where they've operated with impunity for many years."

"What else can you deduce?" Dawson pushed his glasses up. He felt it would be speculation, but he trusted her instincts. Her prescience remained a remarkable gift and a powerful guiding force that was consistently on target. It had frequently linked innumerable intelligence bits that shaped high-level negotiation strategies.

"Yeah, it will kill them and many more. Al-Zuhar and Rantisi are making their annual pilgrimage to Mecca for the Hajj. They'll return home, spreading whatever virus they're carrying across their homeland. The Gaza Strip is one of the most densely populated places on the planet. The Israelis contain it. Its prison-like atmosphere and overcrowding make it the perfect environment for the virus to flourish. It will spread from north to south and from west to east in days with catastrophic effects." She scowled.

"How sure are you?" His eyes wandered as he scratched his cheek.

"It's hard to predict, but I'd say that it's about an eighty percent probability." She stated. "We could run a computer analysis to find out how precise. Even then, it's just a calculated guess based on our input."

He scowled. "How long will it take?"

"Just a few minutes to input the data and the supercomputer will do the rest." She clasped her hands behind her neck.

"Do it." His hands tapped his thighs.

"You got it, boss. I'm on it. Just give me a few minutes."

Within minutes, she inputted the data into her special software program. The supercomputer's immense processing power calculated the answer even faster, spitting out an eighty-seven percent probability of being correct. "That was fast. It doesn't get much better than that."

"That's outstanding and a high probability. We must get this information to Fort Meade and the White House. Please relay the captured transmission and your analysis ASAP. This must go to the president and his top advisors at once." Dawson bounced on his feet. "Great job, Lori." He nodded and waltzed back to his desk.

His top analyst had once again stumbled onto something big. He found capturing signals transmissions both exhilarating and alarming, but biological weapons horrified him. He feared that a lethal pathogen could cause widespread destruction, pain, and suffering. The mutant strains of the Coronavirus-19 had already unleashed much pain and casualties on the world. He feared the pain and deaths this biological weapon would wreak if not stopped.

Taylor assembled her analytical product in less than twenty minutes, compiling all the information for her superiors. The information had to be simplified and summarized to foster understanding. Policymakers limited their amount of time for reading classified product given their schedules. The trick involved balancing the narrative with the requisite facts to support the claim. Her experience taught her that intelligence recipients often desired the facts behind the critical revelation.

She sent her report and attachments to Dawson. He printed the report out and thumbed through it in minutes. She impressed him with the accuracy and speed of her product. The agency needed others like her. He remained proud of her continuing accomplishments. She always produced quality, factual reports, no matter the priority or time constraints.

"Lori, this is outstanding work, as always. You should teach others your abilities and craft, so we're expanding your work requirements to teach others your analytical skills; I'll cite this as an example." His eyes twinkled.

People drove the mission. He enjoyed taking care of his people with awards and promotions. It was a supervisory quality often lost by today's leaders, who often tended to their own personal ambitions and monetary advancements.

Taylor beamed. She enjoyed working for a boss that appreciated her talents. "I welcome the opportunity to teach others my skill set. I'll send the report now."

Dawson knew the terrorists deserved death deep down inside. He prayed he could provide the information to the policymakers in time. It was their job to act correctly and decisively with the intelligence he provided them. Their timely interdiction could spare humanity another awful catastrophe, so he focused his team's efforts. There would be no sleep until this event was laid to rest.

CHAPTER 38: Extreme Measures

Washington, DC

The clamor of the power elite echoed throughout the White House Situation Room. Like their predecessors, these select government executives assembled to solve an emerging crisis. They analyzed, discussed, and developed strategies to address the nation's most pressing problems of this or any century. In the last couple of weeks, the group had dealt with five key crises. The Israeli bombing of Iran's nuclear facilities and the third Palestinian intifada against Israel presented ongoing dilemmas. They also assembled to discuss Syria's chemical weapons use, an ISIS homeland threat, and a growing Chinese-Taiwanese conflict.

The council bellied up around a rectangular eight-by-eighteen foot mahogany table. The president, who chaired the National Security Council, sat prominently at the head of the table. He faced a fifty-inch digital monitor; he routinely held secure video conferences with other key officials or government leaders. Besides the eleven cabinet secretaries seated at the table, another outer ring of chairs encircled the table. There sat other important officials who attended on an as needed basis. They realized the insignificance of their presence as the true players sat at the president's side. Everyone knew the president's lifelong friend James Jackson had his ear and trust; the head diplomat always spoke his mind.

The room supported a dozen large monitors that could display the latest situation or crisis. Over twenty critical flashpoints littered the world's stage today; many would have to wait. Digital displays reflected the time differences around the world, zoned to twelve separate geographic areas.

Even with advancing technology, people still made the crucial decisions. Technology only simplified the process; it streamlined the vast amounts of information that appeared at their fingertips.

The National Security Council's usefulness often depended upon the president's management style. President Baker valued a diversity of opinions, so he empowered the group. America's top diplomat, Secretary James Jackson, appeared the most vocal and noteworthy participant and often led the conversations and brought them to a crucial decision point. He would then turn to the president, who would decide the course of action.

As the president entered the room, everyone stood to pay their respect to the commander-in-chief. "Please be seated." President Baker gestured with his hands. "I appreciate all the work that you and your teams have done. Never have so many flashpoints plagued us. It's a very troubling time, which demands our resolve and work be at its best in order to protect our great nation. We've seen some impressive accomplishments and feats in the previous week. I'll ask, though, that you all redouble your efforts. My national security advisor just briefed me on some very disturbing news developed from the NSA. I'll defer to our director of National Intelligence to brief us on this latest crisis. Please give him your undivided attention." The president sat and scanned the group.

The DNI director scanned his prepared talking points. A career intelligence officer, Director Robert Whittington presented only the facts and allowed his esteemed colleagues to deduce their own conclusions. The NSC was full of members who understood intelligence, so he didn't have to spoon-feed it to them, like some politicians who sat on the various congressional committees. A true orator, Whittington always knew his audience and tailored his presentation directly to them. His long and distinguished career in intelligence had taught him this valuable lesson.

"The CIA has developed information derived from multiple sources, which shows that the Israelis have developed a biological weapon from a mummified bat discovered at el-Amarna. This basically corroborates the same facts that a DS special agent got from a key informant. The source said that the reward money was used to fund an excavation operation that involved the resurrection of an ancient, extremely lethal, and easily transmittable form of the Ebola virus. We neutralized the ISIS threat when

US Navy SEALs took down the Egyptian freighter, the Arabian Star. It appeared in the media as a routine drug interdiction gone bad."

The DNI director guzzled some water. "We received a critical intercept several hours ago from our listening site in New Mexico. It reflects that the Mossad delivered the el-Amarna virus to two unsuspecting Hamas terrorists. The terrorists are currently in Jeddah and we believe that they're traveling to the Hajj."

The chairman of the Joint Chiefs of Staff pulled his glasses down and looked over its rims. "You mean to tell me we thwarted this threat once before from ISIS, and now we must ramp up for this contingency after all, thanks to our closest Middle Eastern ally. Politics aside, when are we going to learn. They're only our friends when it's convenient for them." The four-star general sighed.

"That's a discussion for another time, Ben. Let's resolve the problem at hand." Jackson smartly refocused the group's attention. He knew Israel's best interests weren't always aligned with Americas, adding to the complexity of the relationship.

"Can somebody refresh my memory? What are the spread rates, lethality projections, and countermeasures we can take to safeguard Americans from this threat?" President Baker glanced at the chairman.

"Mr. President, the el-Amarna virus decimated the ancient Egyptian city with a one-hundred percent kill rate. It's extremely contagious and spreads like wildfire. Just like Coronavirus-19, it will spread globally in less than two months, instead of two years like the Spanish flu. If we're lucky, it will leave five percent of the world's people on this planet. This is what our computer-generated spread and casualty projections reflect." The chairman of the Joint Chiefs advised with a deadpan face.

"How did the Israelis develop the biological weapon so quickly?" The president's eyes narrowed.

"That was the simple part for them." The chairman motioned. "ISIS launched a biological attack against the Israelis by infecting members of their border police. Fortunately for the Israelis, they contained the virus to their base in the Negev desert, so this minimized the virus' spread and casualties. So the terrorists essentially hand delivered the virus directly to their doorsteps."

Jackson lifted his chin. "Our agent was at the Israeli base briefly with a CDC bio-weapon's expert. He was rushed to the base after his assault on the strategic ISIS hide out in the Sinai Peninsula. The CDC doctor overheard some classified conversations that showed the Israelis were developing both a vaccine and antidote to the el-Amarna virus."

"Then it's obvious the Israelis believe they can deploy the weapon and either vaccinate or cure their populace." The president stated rhetorically.

"Mr. President." The DNI director peered at the commander-in-chief. "It appears so. They're a tiny country and can easily seal their borders and ride out the cleansing of over six billion people. We, however, are less fortunate given our expansive borders and large population. It's nearly impossible for us to develop sufficient medicines for all our citizens. To anyone left alive, the Israelis will merely blame this catastrophe on the terrorists. They'll underscore that ISIS developed the virus, and it backfired on them. Just look at the recent plague deaths of Al-Qaeda in Afghanistan; over forty perished because of a lab accident. We must stop this at all costs."

The president's hands formed a steeple as he reflected; his members looked to him for guidance. "How long do we have before the two Hamas terrorist become contagious?"

The DNI director glanced at his notes. "It will take the virus between twenty-four and forty-eight hours to become active and contagious, so we've roughly eight to twenty-four hours to intervene. The terrorists will arrive in Mecca today and join over three-million worldwide Muslims. Given the congested environment, the virus will disperse quickly amongst them; they'll carry the virus to all continents and countries around the globe, including America."

"The clock's ticking. What's our course of action?" The president scanned his council for an answer. Not surprisingly, his eyes ended up on Jackson.

Jackson nodded. "Make no mistake; it's essential that we or the Israelis interdict these two before they reach the Hajj."

The secretary of state glanced at Whittington. "Correct me if I'm wrong, Robert. Our military cannot locate and neutralize the Hamas operatives in time. The two terrorists will reach the Hajj and start the virus' global spread. Our only option is to drop a thermite bomb on the Hajj, as it will vaporize all its participants and the virus itself. It's not an excellent choice, but given the time parameters, it may be our only one. Imagine the repercussions, as it would solidify ISIS and Al-Qaeda's Jihad. This would create a world war from which we'd never recover."

The president scowled. "So, we can save six billion people by vaporizing three million. And exactly how do you propose we do that?"

"We could launch our bombers out of Basra, Iraq. They can be outfitted with the latest high-tech weaponry that would incinerate everything within a mile radius." The four-star general stated confidently.

The DNI director tapped his pencil, thinking. "Can we disguise the bomb to make it look like it was a terrorist attack, or perhaps the Israelis who conducted the bombing operation?"

"Once the truth surfaces, the situation becomes uncontrollable." The president voiced his reservation with the operation.

Jackson turned in his chair. "There's another option. But it would require some luck, a masterful bluff, and an extreme threat. Only the Israelis can stop the pandemic without tremendous collateral damage. Mr. President, you must contact the Israeli prime minister to advise him you're aware of their plan. The prime minister will undoubtedly deny the accusation, but you'll need to press him hard, and underscore if they don't abort their mission, you'll make it known that they're responsible. We should clarify that without their cooperation, we'll have to eliminate the threat by extreme measures. And we'll be forced to rethink our alliance with Israel."

"What do you mean by rethinking our alliance? You mean I'll cut off all funding and military aid to them, while exposing them to the world as the next perpetrators of genocide, for that's what they're attempting. How much of a threat is that? They're willing to wipe out six billion people to ensure their way of life." The president shook his head, supporting a downturned mouth.

Jackson nodded. "That's what you must do. We must be harsh, and they must believe us, or we'll be required to send in our bombers and God save us from that action's ramifications."

The president scanned the room. "Are there any other options?" The room remained quiet, overwhelmed by the weight of the decision they faced. There appeared no good options, unless the Israelis played ball.

The president stood up. "I must prepare for this epic call. Prepare the bombers for their mission."

The general nodded curtly. "Yes, sir."

"Whatever happens, I'll require speeches to address the American people and the world. Let's get cracking." The president walked out the door to let his chief advisors handle the specifics. They all rushed out to handle many contingencies. It would be another hectic day in the White House.

CHAPTER 39: Hardball

Oval Office, White House
Entering the oval office, the president trudged over to his desk. The el-Amarna virus briefing and its ramifications diminished his enthusiasm. Although he was gone for an hour, his work had piled up. America's endless problems surfaced and would not wait. He sat down with an expressionless face and unleashed a heavy sigh. The president picked up his phone and ordered fried eggs, three strips of bacon, and an English muffin. He would eat his breakfast while reading briefs and preparing for his conference call with the Israeli government head.

The buzzer sounded on his phone. His secretary advised him that the chairman of the Joint Chiefs of Staff was on the line. The president picked up the phone. "What do you have, Ben? I hope we're ready on your end."

"Mr. President, we've a problem. ISIS has launched a major attack on Basra, damaging our munitions. We'll have to fly out of our air base in Turkey. Their route will take them over the Mediterranean, above Israel and the Sinai Peninsula, down over the Red Sea and then east toward their target." The four-star Army general paused.

The president rubbed his forehead. "We'll be spotted flying in broad daylight. What aircraft will you use for the mission? Are they outfitted with the requisite munitions to ensure absolute success? I'm not willing to start a world war — a war of religion — unless we know our plan will eradicate the virus and its transmission."

"Yes sir, we have two B-1 Lancers ready to go. The munitions are being loaded as we speak. They'll be able to evade all radar in the area, but they'll be visible flying in daylight."

The president scowled. "Sometimes I hate this job. When President Truman dropped the atomic bombs on Hiroshima and Nagasaki, he killed a quarter million people in wartime, but ended a war. I'm preparing to give the order to kill over ten times that amount and start a world war." He massaged his temples.

"I don't envy your position, sir." The veteran general tried to assuage his commander-in-chief's concerns. "You may not have a choice," he said. "If the virus spreads into the populace, it will decimate most inhabitants on this planet. By taking this difficult, but necessary course of action, you'll save the planet from near extinction. Six billion lives will be spared. Now, we can live with that."

The president glanced at a picture of his wife and two children displayed on his desk. "There's always a choice. Sometimes it's the lesser of two evils. I'll have to live with this decision for the rest of my life. And believe me, Ben, it will haunt me my entire life."

"Genuine leaders make the tough decisions, not for expedience or popularity, but for the good of humankind. Your leadership's needed more than ever. We'll get through this, Mr. President. Americans will understand you made the right choice." The general raised his head.

"I appreciate the kind words Ben, but it doesn't simplify the decision." The president reseated his reading glasses on his nose.

The general laughed. "If it were easy, then anyone could make it. Being the 'Leader of the Free World' comes at a hefty price."

The president contemplated his decision. "When will you have to launch our bombers?"

"Given the flight time, I'll give the go order in two hours. It will take them a couple of hours to reach the target and then they'll deliver their payload. It will be over in seconds." The chairman said with a deadpan face.

"Okay general, proceed with the operation. Let's hope I can talk some sense into the prime minister of Israel. I'll talk to you after my phone call with him. God help us all."

The president hung up the phone, feeling sick to his stomach. He opened the top drawer to his desk and pulled out a small bottle of Pepto-

Bismol. He twisted off the top and gulped a mouthful before returning it to the drawer. The president would call on its services again, and sooner than he would like. The pressure of the job would literally shave years off his life.

He contemplated the number of tough decisions that had taken place from this unique office. All his predecessors had to make hard choices, which would define their presidencies and form their legacies. It was now his turn. His decision would affect generations of Americans and last for decades. The nation was already in a war on extremism. This decision would only strengthen the dividing lines while giving the extremists a watershed event to rally additional people into the fight. He edged back in his ergonomic chair, recognizing the virus' spread must be stamped out. The lethality projections spoke volumes. The decision's logic did not make it any easier.

A knock at the door aroused him from his deep thoughts. His secretary delivered his meal, setting it on the side of his desk. The president thanked her and returned to his briefing notes to prepare for his discussion with his Israeli ally. After finishing his briefing notes and his breakfast, he sipped his green tea while his secretary called Israel.

A minute later, a familiar voice landed on the receiving end of the line. "Hello, Mr. President. To what do I owe this unexpected call?" The Israel prime minister said.

"Mr. Prime Minister, should we forgo with the pleasantries and discuss the approaching crisis? Our time's valuable."

"Please Sam, call me David," said the prime minister.

"You must abort your mission to infect the pilgrims at Mecca. I know all about your plan, using two Hamas terrorists as the delivery mechanism. They'll deliver the el-Amarna virus to the Muslim world." The president sipped his tea.

"Your accusation is unfounded. Where did you get that information? I can assure you..." The prime minister's voice boomed.

The president interrupted him in mid-sentence. "There's no time for this nonsense. Don't deceive me or patronize me. We understand what you're up to and why you're doing it, so you better abort this dangerous mission now or I'll invest the rest of my Administration in isolating Israel for your actions. I'll eliminate all our foreign aid and tell the world your responsibility for unleashing this terrible pandemic."

"Don't threaten me. You'd better be sure of your accusation before you point the finger at Israel. We've been persecuted for thousands of years. Besides, we both know that ISIS developed the lethal Ebola strain from the el-Amarna virus using modern science." The prime minister glanced at his assistant.

"I'll destroy you for this. Need I remind you that thousands of American-Muslims attend the Hajj? They'll become infected and then they'll carry the deadly virus back to America. The virus will move like wildfire, wiping out most of the country. I've seen the lethality and spread projections. You won't get away with this. I implore you to handle it now or I'll do the unthinkable. But make no mistake, Mr. Prime Minister, I'll take decisive action. And if I must do the unthinkable, I'll reveal Israel's role to the world."

The prime minister grumbled. "I resent these accusations; however, I can understand your concerns, Mr. President. We have a long history of friendship and cooperation, so I'll instruct our intelligence services to do whatever they can to resolve the situation."

"Just get it done, David, or I'll have to conduct a targeted strike on the Hajj. I've my jets on standby to deliver a bomb that will neutralize the virus at Mecca." President Baker said, knowing that a bluff in poker only works when you have the attention of your opponent and he believes that you have the cards to back your wager. Only this wasn't a bluff. The president had just upped his wager, and he had the prime minister's attention now. He peered at his notes while an awkward pause transpired.

The Israeli leader's jaw tightened. "I'll have an answer in four hours, given the difficulty in locating and identifying these terrorists. It was only a matter of time until the terrorists unwittingly infected themselves as they experimented with biological weapons. Remember when al-Qaeda terrorists exposed themselves to the plague in Southeast Asia, and they lost forty of their personnel. It serves them right."

"Can we dispense with the bull, Mr. Prime Minister? We don't have the time and it insults my intelligence. I've compelling evidence of Mossad's operational involvement to spread the virus throughout the Muslim world. I know you have a vaccination and a cure for it; you got your sample of the virus from your base in the Negev, when ISIS attempted to spread it across your nation by infecting several border police. You can easily lockdown your borders and vaccinate your populace. The US borders are much too expansive for this and we cannot vaccinate our entire populace in time, nor could we develop enough serum to treat our three-hundred and thirty million people." President Baker barked.

"If you know so much, why don't your operatives locate and neutralize them?" The prime minister twisted his head to the speakerphone.

The president exploded. "Damn it! You have only four hours to dispose of the problem. If not, I'll handle it and then we can expect WWIII. You better put your military on alert, as the situation will rapidly deteriorate. And I want to make it clear, Mr. Prime Minister, that you'll be on your own. The United States will be preoccupied safeguarding its own interests and people."

"As always, Mr. President, you make your points clearly, delicately and diplomatically." The prime minister's eyes widened.

"I'll get back to you within four hours; the Mossad's very professional and can handle the problem."

"I don't care what you do, David. Just finish the job, so we can move on. And get it done in two hours or I'll launch my bombers; then only God can help us."

"I'll let you know, Mr. President, and call you when it's done." The prime minister grimaced as he directed his attention to his Mossad director, who was monitoring the conversation. His nod assured him it could be done.

The president cleared his throat. "I'll await your call, but don't be late. Goodbye David." The president hung up and looked at his national security advisor, who joined the conversation at its beginning.

"Will we really bomb Mecca if the Israelis don't neutralize the virus? She captured the president's gaze.

The president nodded. "There's no alternative; the virus cannot escape into the world's population. It will be catastrophic. We're not ready to return to the Stone Ages, if I can help it."

"I know, sir, but the American people aren't ready for this sort of sustained war. Our economy is stable, people are gaining in their purchasing power, and they need something to provide them continued hope. This just makes everything worse." The veteran advisor cautioned.

"Americans have always risen to the challenge throughout history, so we'll do it again. This differentiates America from other countries and makes it a beacon of hope." The president nodded curtly.

"I hope you're right, Mr. President. This will be the ultimate test of our resolve and mettle, and it will challenge us for decades."

"Yes, it will," said the president, picking up the phone. "Margaret, get me the chairman of the Joint Chiefs on the line."

"Yes sir, right away." His longtime assistant said.

It was show time, and the president wanted to instill his confidence in those he led. He decided he would lead with absolute resolve. His cabinet and others needed to know the state of play, so he called an emergency meeting of his National Security Council. They had spent a lot of time together. The president recognized the ramifications of his decision. The council would meet daily if he had to do the unthinkable. He prayed he didn't have to drop the bomb.

"Mr. President, how did your call go with the prime minister?" The chairman pressed the receiver to his ear.

"It went like expected. The prime minister advised that he'd neutralize the threat in hours, while denying any culpability in the plot." The president laughed. "Imagine that, the Israelis are denying all responsibility in this Armageddon plot."

"The Israelis have been masters of their own fate since 1948, and they don't have to play by international rules. It's a small country surviving in a rough neighborhood, one that would prefer that they disappeared off the map. After Iran's repeated calls for their annihilation, it doesn't surprise me they would take this sort of extreme measure, particularly with Iran's nuclear developments." The general said.

The chief executive in the Oval Office grunted. "You'd think that they just would've targeted Iran to make a point, instead of jeopardizing all of humanity."

"We could sit here and second guess Israel's actions, but it won't change the situation. Simply, it is what it is." The general stated fatalistically.

"You've got a unique way of simplifying a complex problem, Ben." The president chuckled.

"Have you made a final decision, Mr. President?"

"General, on my authority, you can begin the countdown on operation Clean Purge. You must stress to the strike leader the mission's importance, and that a decisive target hit is required to vaporize the virus. The virus must be eliminated." The president ordered.

"Yes sir, Mr. President. Consider it done. It's the right decision," said the chairman before the president concluded the call.

The president glanced back to his family photo on his desk. He understood his decision's logic and knew it would impact three million people in Mecca, all with family and friends. Even when explained by the networks, the distorted truth would make it look like America purposely attacked Islam. The president knew that many, particularly the uneducated, would believe the worst about America, joining radical groups in masses to wage holy war on it. US embassies, consulates, and American businesses would be the first places struck. The jihad would intensify, and America had to be ready. He would make sure of it.

The president lifted his phone's receiver. "Margaret, please assemble the NSC and get my press secretary, as we have another long day ahead."

"Right away, Mr. President. Your wife and daughter are here. Can I show them in?"

"Absolutely, it may be the only opportunity to see them today."

The door to the Oval Office sprang open. The first lady glanced at her husband, and recognized the strain on his face, although he tried to hide it. They had been together for too long, so she could read him like a veteran skipper could read the sea.

The president's stern face lightened to a smile as his four-year-old daughter trotted to his side. He loved his little girl, who could brighten the darkest of days, and this was one of them, despite the bright sunshine gracing the nation's capital. He lifted her into the air while the first lady admired him from the doorway.

"I missed you this morning." The president's youngest fan said. "How's your day, daddy? Are you coming to the park with us this morning?"

"I'm sorry, pumpkin. I can't today, but I'll walk you to the garden." The president set his daughter down, and held her hand as he led her to the door, stopping to kiss his wife.

The first lady embraced her husband. "Has it been a tough day?" She knew the answer, but asked him anyway.

The president smiled wearily. "It's been my toughest day, but the worst is ahead. A world crisis is brewing in hours."

The first lady smiled back at him. "Then we should just enjoy a few minutes with our daughter." She clasped his hand as they walked by his secretary and were joined by his secret service agent-in-charge. It was another day in the job of jobs.

CHAPTER 40: Jackpot

Arlington, Virginia

Daylight glistened through the curtains, as James' deep slumber left him invigorated and smiling. He credited his surge in rest to his onslaught of exercise and fresh air. He gazed at Atallah, who lay quietly in his bed, and contemplated another possibility for his disposition. She swept into his life, reminded him of life's other pleasures, and re-energized his soul, providing him a greater perspective on his future needs and desires.

James crept away from his bed to the adjoining bathroom. Her brilliant essence captivated him, and he preserved the image in his head. He removed his underwear and tee shirt, tossing them into the hamper in his walk-in closet. The cold Virginia night air lingered in the room, as he awoke before the thermostat's heat activated. Twisting the shower's dial, he dispensed a stream of hot water into the glass enclosure; its warm mist permeated the room. He stepped into the shower and felt relief as the warm water defrosted his cold bones. The showerhead's pulsating shiatsu jets massaged his shoulder and neck muscles.

After lathering his body and washing his hair, the lean muscular agent rinsed his entire body. He turned off the water, toweled off, and wrapped the soft, damp cloth around his waist, which covered his mid-section down to his knees. James combed his hair, shaved with his electric razor, brushed his teeth, and gargled with mouthwash. He shuffled to his closet, scanned his array of suits hung and arranged by color, and opted for a blue pinstripe suit. He threw on his pants, white dress shirt, and grabbed the silk tie given to him by Atallah. Putting on his jacket, he strutted to the bed to eye an awaking exotic beauty. She revealed her petite frame and sleek legs from beneath the sheets and comforter.

"So, what do you think?" He smiled, eying her legs.

She brushed the sleep from her eyes. "You look fantastic. The new tie looks great on you, making you look rather sophisticated and political," she said, beaming. "Someone has exquisite tastes."

"I need to be both to survive in the State Department, as it's a major balancing act." He chuckled.

"I imagine so; I like that part of you. You're many things." Her eyes twinkled.

"Thanks, I have to leave for work to handle several issues before the awards ceremony. I'll return around noon to pick you up."

He bent over and kissed her soft, moist lips. A second later, he vanished into the wind, leaving the mesmerizing woman to fend for herself. He knew she would manage just fine without him given her independence, reflecting her willing adoption of western ways. He had traveled the world and encountered no one as intriguing as her.

As he dashed down the stairs leading from his front door, his mind raced about work. James looked forward to the Secretary of State's award ceremony and his dinner plans with Atallah to celebrate. He inserted a key into the ignition and turned it, firing up the horses; his vintage car roared to life. He tuned his radio to a country music station, while waiting for the car to warm up. James shifted the car into gear and sped off a second later through the parking lot and into the morning's rush hour traffic.

Meanwhile, Atallah showered, ate, dressed and scampered out the door, turning to check the door handle. Her mind wandered to the upcoming ceremony. She walked down the stairs and arrived at the curb. A black BMW zipped out of a nearby parking space and pulled up curbside. Her intense brown eyes scanned the lot before opening the passenger door to climb into the vehicle.

Lifting her binoculars to her eyes, Sherman struggled to see through the windshield, but the car's tinting and the sun's glare obscured the male driver's face. She shrugged it off, recognizing her pursuit of discovering something more sinister. She sensed the Jordanian beauty's deceit, driving her resolve to prove it.

Once Atallah drove out of the complex, the CDC expert radioed her colleagues; her booming voice over the radio stirred them out of their restful state and into action. Two large hazardous materials vans rounded the corner to the complex and rolled up seconds later. She ran across the parking lot, signaling with her hands where to stop.

She scowled, glancing at her watch. "Let's move it, people. There's little time and the suspect could return soon. We must comb this place without knowing what exactly we're looking for."

A five-person team piled out of the van, dressed in light gray, one-piece clothing. They trotted in unison to the front door. Their silver biohazard suits' impermeable plastic-like material crinkled with each flex of their appendages. The team leader used the manager's master key to open the door. They disappeared inside a second later, closing the door and waiting for their instructions.

"I need you to divide up and conquer this place like you own it. Search each room for any sign of a bio-weapon. If you find something, call it out and another colleague will help document the discovery by taking photos. We have only a brief window, so let's get moving." She said, panning the room. She radioed the drivers to move the vans to the rear of the complex.

The doctor walked into the kitchen. She enjoyed rummaging through someone else's belongings. An individual left many clues to their nature by the way they maintained their house. James aroused feelings deep within her and piqued her curiosity. She hoped to learn something more about the intriguing federal agent. In opening all of his cupboards and cabinets, she noticed his clean and meticulously arranged items. She admired his anal-retentive ways.

Opening his refrigerator, she noticed everything was organized by category. Vegetables, fresh fish, poultry, free-range eggs, and a medley of fresh fruit filled the shelves. His healthy food choices surprised her, as she admired his low-carbohydrate, organic diet. It strayed away from the standard bachelor's diet of pizza and beer. She recognized his uniqueness and complexity. Perhaps she would view him differently based on these revelations. After an hour of scouring the place, the seasoned virologist sat at the bar. She studied the pictures displayed of James with former presidents, world leaders, and other notables. Her eyes studied a picture enclosed in the bar's glass cabinet; it showed the DS agent posing in his tactical gear with Yasser Arafat. She laughed at the irony of the picture. James would give his life protecting a reformed terrorist who took the life of innocent people, including Americans. She wondered whether he would have taken a bullet for Arafat. James' smile surprised her, highlighting his neat and white teeth.

She rushed to the master bathroom sink, finding two toothbrushes placed in an upright stand. Pulling out two small sandwich-sized plastic Ziploc bags, she placed each toothbrush in a separate bag. She barreled out to the hazmat van, her heart racing from the discovery. She recognized the answer could lie in the contents of the two Ziploc bags. The doctor entered the back of the van, as her colleague exited the driver's door to join her.

Kent LeBrock recently graduated from John Hopkins medical school. He served America instead of establishing a practice in a small town that signified his roots. She speculated he joined the CDC for similar reasons as her. She valued and enjoyed serving the country, traveling the world, and discovering new and exciting viruses. The revelation revealed that she required a life outside of work. Inside the CDC's mobile lab, Sherman tossed the bags on the counter. She opened a drawer with several metallic tools and an assortment of reactive agents.

"Dr. Sherman, what are we looking for in these samples?" LeBrock eyed the Ziploc bags.

"We're going to analyze the remnants on these toothbrushes for the Ebola-Nile virus. Modern science resurrected it to be the worst imaginable bio-weapon on the planet. It wiped out an ancient city of el-Amarna with one-hundred percent efficiency." The virus specialist grimaced.

LeBrock laughed. "I was just asking. If you don't want to tell me, there's no need to create such a fantastic story. I don't have to know."

She swayed her head with a twisted mouth. "Kent, just watch and learn. Please set up the electron microscope."

As LeBrock prepared the microscope, Sherman followed a standard protocol for conducting an analysis of the samples. She reached into the drawer, extracted two Petri dishes, and donned a protective mask and gloves to prepare for opening the bags. She removed the first toothbrush and cut off several bristles from the brush, placing them in the dish. LeBrock expected her requirements and had already printed a label as sample one and affixed the label to the dish. Careful of cross-contamination, she used a fresh scissor with the other toothbrush and labeled it sample two.

LeBrock focused on her solemn, intent demeanor, and stepped back. "You're serious about our purpose. We're dealing with a previously unknown virus that's deadlier than anything we've ever encountered. It's even more deadly than the Ebola-Zaire virus?"

"That's correct." She said while applying the reactive agents to each sample. "Now we'll wait a few minutes while these chemicals react with our samples. We'll then place them under the electron microscope to see if we have our evidence."

"It's such an exciting discovery. Part of me wishes we uncovered a new virus to document, but the other half wants this to be a bust. I can't imagine having a society wiped out by this thing," said the rookie doctor with widening eyes.

"We both agree on that. I only hope there's a sufficient sample to make a definitive determination, so we can advance forward." She closed her eyes, sighing.

LeBrock looked at his mentor. "What if we can't find evidence of the el-Amarna virus?"

"We start over again and continue our search, only redoubling our efforts. Persistence is the key to solving many great mysteries, but my stomach is churning over this one. We'll find out in minutes though." She tilted her head back.

Sherman placed a sample from the first Petri dish under the electron microscope. Her fingers dialed the lens to increase the magnification and clarity. She scrutinized the sample and recognized the commonly found mouth bacteria. Her face remained stoic, as she asked her apprentice to examine it in order to assess the skills of her protégé.

"Look at this Kent and tell me your opinion." She stepped back from the microscope.

LeBrock placed his eyes on the scope's viewing platform. He squinted because of the magnifier's brightness and adjusted it for greater clarity. He paused, examining its shape and movement. "This is a common bacterium that's found in everyone's mouth. I'm sorry, doctor." The rookie shook his head.

"There's nothing to be sorry about. Let's look at the second sample. Perhaps we'll have greater luck with this one." She winced.

She exchanged the first sample with the next one on the microscope, peered down at it under magnification, and studied it. Her eyes narrowed, puzzled by the mix of bacterium and a wormlike virus attacking any cell in its proximity.

Her pulse quickened as her eyebrows furrowed and then released. "Have a look, Kent. Tell me what you observe."

He examined the sample through the lens. His eyes widened while he watched multiple thriving organisms fighting one another. He pulled back from the lens.

"What is it? Is that what we're looking for?" His eyes protruded as he looked at his mentor.

She gave a hard, obvious swallow. "I'm not sure what we're looking at here. It looks like a virus attempting to invade and dominate other cells. This sample possibly contains the el-Amarna virus, so we need to let the sample mature for a couple more hours. It's inconclusive, and I can't even make a calculated guess whether James or Atallah is infected."

"What do we do now, boss?" LeBrock stroked his chin.

The squelch of the radio interrupted her thoughts. "Dr. Sherman, we need you back here now; you have to see our discovery."

Entering the agent's condominium, a colleague directed her to the master bedroom where a CDC technician handed her a bag containing a small syringe that had been tagged, cataloged and photographed. A small volume of an unknown substance left in the vial surprised her. She eyed the vial's Human Growth Hormone label.

"Where did you find it?" She read the vial's label.

The veteran technician pointed over his shoulder. "I discovered it in the floor duct for the HVAC system. I had to reach deep, but I found it in a bend and was lucky that I didn't stick myself. Fortunately, my hand reached the plunger end of the syringe first."

"This is painstaking work, and it's probably the exact evidence we require. I doubt a decorated special agent would use HGH. Let's clear out and head to the mobile lab to test it." She motioned to her team and led them out the front door.

The team backtracked through each room, returning everything to its proper place. Within minutes, the CDC specialists filed out the front door, locking it behind them. Sherman directed her team back to the van and instructed them to test the sample from the syringe. She reached into her pocket, pulled out her cellular phone, and scrolled through her contact list, landing on James' entry seconds later. She pressed the call button.

The phone rang twice. "Hello, Matt James here."

"Matt, it's Jill Sherman. Where are you now? We have a major problem and I need your help."

His eyes sparkled as heat radiated through his chest. "I'm at work. What are you so excited about?"

"I'm at your residence. We've found a vial with an HGH labeled on it and a syringe." She felt a fluttery feeling in her chest.

"Why are you at my residence? Did you talk to Suhar?" He barked as his face turned red. His exclusion from her clandestine operation troubled him, as he had nothing to hide.

"I don't owe you an explanation for the CDC's operation." She read the time on her watch. "We have a serious situation, so you must trust and assist me. There's a high probability that Suhar infected herself with the virus. My results are inconclusive, but I'm confident the test will yield positive results in a matter of hours. Where's Suhar? She's not at your house."

"She should be there. I was supposed to pick her up at noon today, as we're scheduled to attend the awards ceremony at the US Department of State," said James, puzzled by the virologist's revelation. He hated playing the fool.

"She stepped into a black BMW an hour after you left, but I don't know where she went. We didn't have another unit to follow her." She sighed.

James pondered her information, but an incoming call interrupted his thoughts. "Jill, can you hold a minute? I've another call." Not hearing her answer, he pushed a button on his phone and another one to answer it. "Hello, Matt James here."

"Hi Matt, It's Suhar. I hope you're having a brilliant morning." She inquired.

James contained his anger over his betrayal. He struggled to find an alternative explanation for the syringe. "I'm having a fantastic day so far. I can't wait for the ceremony. Are you dressed yet? I may come home a little early to pick you up." His voice remained steady.

"That would've been great, but a friend took me clothes shopping and I'm getting a magnificent dress for tonight's celebration. How about I meet you at the State Department's diplomatic entrance at a quarter past noon? My friend will drop me off," she said, rubbing her hand.

He eyed his wristwatch. "Okay, I'll meet you in about an hour, so be ready to go. We have to be in our seats around twelve-thirty, because the secretary's security detail follows strict protocol for guests."

"Yes, I'll be there on time and I can't wait to see you." She checked her email while looking at the cashier. "I have to pay for this dress, but I'll see you soon." She hung up.

James punched another button on his phone to reengage the CDC doctor. "Are you still there, Jill? That was Suhar on the other line."

"What did you tell her?"

"I played along with her charade and I'll join her at the State Department in about one hour. She purportedly went shopping with a friend."

Her posture sagged slightly. "You don't believe her? She's a liar."

"You may be right and I'll assume the worst-case scenario; she has infected herself to target the US secretary of state. We'll stop her or I'll die trying." His mouth turned downward.

"You have to isolate her from the public without causing panic. She mustn't be allowed to spread the virus to anyone. Do you understand?"

"You've made yourself perfectly clear, but I'll do what I can." James looked downward.

"Do you know what that means? You'll be infected with the new Ebola strain, if you get too close to her."

"This day just keeps getting better and better." He muttered. "It's a good day to die as any. I'll do what's necessary to protect the State Department and its employees."

"You won't die; it takes the virus one to two days to incubate. You'll then have several more hours after that, as it depends on your resistance and your original level of exposure." She nodded once.

James winced. "That's a comforting thought. Do you have more good news to assuage my concerns?"

"Don't worry, the CDC's working on a cure. The finest minds in government will solve it."

"That's reassuring that the best minds in government are going to save me? Good thing I upgraded my life insurance policy." He snickered.

"We also know that the Israelis are way ahead of us. They reportedly have a vaccine and a potential cure. I'll ask our liaison to get several doses of it, so we can duplicate it and make as much serum as possible in a short time." The doctor glanced at her watch.

"Alright, we've talked enough. I'm going to the State Department now and can get there early to interdict her getting out of her car, so I can keep her away from the crowds."

Sherman glanced at her team. "We'll meet you over there. I'll alert the Metropolitan Police Department to place a lookout for the black BMW. Perhaps we can interdict her before she gets there, so I'll have the police position themselves at all bridges into DC. They'll be given specific orders to stop and not approach her. I'll just advise them it's an emergency quarantine situation."

"That's a good plan. I'll see you there. Don't be late." James hung up as he entered a dark blue Ford Crown Victoria government vehicle. He hated her treachery, given the wide-reaching effects. He recognized his responsibility to foil the plot before it metastasized.

The DS agent sped down Idlewood Road toward Route 66 and lifted the microphone to contact the DS Command Center. "Enterprise, Enterprise, this is Agent Matt James. We have an emergency that should be relayed to the DS hierarchy, our uniform division, and the special agent-in-charge of the secretary's detail.

"Agent James, this is Enterprise. Go with your message."

"Enterprise, we have a biological threat directed against Falcon. Can you alert everyone that the suspect terrorist is named Suhar Atallah? She's expected to observe today's awards ceremony." His voice remained steady.

"Standby Agent James. We're relaying the message now."

Turning right onto Leesburg Pike, he floored the gas pedal. A patch of rubber remained behind on the pavement, as thick black smoke wafted skyward. He entered the eastbound ramp to Route 66 and eased off the gas pedal to glide around the subtle one-hundred and twenty degree turn; his fingers flipped a toggle switch on the center console. The vehicle's emergency blue lights flashed as his siren wailed. He smiled as he hit a straightaway leading to Route 66 and let the horses loose. The car shuddered as the engine growled; its speedometer reflected eighty miles per hour seconds later.

Enterprise came over the radio. "Agent James, you're patched through to the DSS director, so go ahead with your message; you're operating in the encrypted mode."

James raised the microphone and depressed its transmission button. "Sir, we have a bio-terror plot unfolding against Falcon, which involves a female named Suhar Atallah. CDC informs she has exposed herself to the el-Amarna virus, and she is scheduled to attend today's awards ceremony."

"Damn it, why am I just hearing this now?" The director barked. "This is serious, as Falcon won't be the only one affected; the president will make a surprise visit to present the awards himself, so I'll have to alert the Secret Service at once."

"I just learned about the plot myself. CDC reps are headed to the Department of State right now with their mobile hazmat lab. They've alerted the Metropolitan Police to be on the lookout for a black BMW. I'll be arriving there shortly to interdict the suspect before she gets inside the building. The CDC has instructed me to isolate her, if I can."

The director scowled. "You have my full support, so do what's necessary to deter this plot. I have to brief the assistant secretary." The director hung up.

James punched the accelerator further to ninety miles per hour, as he needed to get there in advance to shut down the terrorist operation. At his present speed, he would arrive at the Department of State's diplomatic entrance in under ten minutes, so he focused on the path ahead and its sparse pre-lunch traffic. The ultimate decisive moment for him neared, but would he prevail? Only time would tell.

CHAPTER 41: Abolition

Saudi Arabia

As the sun approached the horizon, Haim Rubinstein's mind vacillated between his family and his mission. The sun's glare pierced through the car's windshield, causing his eyes to water and narrow. Even his prescription sunglasses did little to shield his eyes from the intense rays. He sensed the vehicle's presence a couple of car lengths ahead of them. Its faint outline flickered as Rubinstein concentrated on the road and vehicles around him. Ofer Ziv's head bobbled while drifting in and out of sleep in the passenger seat. He found trailing a vehicle tedious and prepared for its next phase by recharging his body. The Mossad agents shadowed the mini-bus to ensure that the infected terrorists remained on course. The highway teemed with Hajj goers making their Islamic pilgrimage to Mecca to fulfill their mandatory religious duty.

A ring from their satellite phone broke the droning silence. Ziv awoke from his slumber, scowling at the interruption to his dream state.

"Ofer, answer it. I can barely see with the sun's glare hitting my eyes." He clenched his teeth.

Ziv grumbled, picking up the phone and pushing a button. His ear pressed firmly to the receiver as he received their new instructions. "Yes sir, we'll take care of it now." He hung up.

"Damn it." Ziv threw the phone aside as his cheeks reddened. "I don't believe it! The prime minister ordered us to abort the mission and neutralize the threat and the virus. We're to make them disappear and we must act quickly."

"Are you sure?" Rubinstein scratched his jaw. "That has to be wrong. Why would they abort the mission so late in the game?" He rubbed his brow.

Ziv's shoulders slumped forward. "The P-M advised that the Americans discovered the plot and they've directed the operation to be aborted."

"Since when do we take our orders from the Americans?" Rubenstein's face tightened.

"The Americans advised our prime minister to take care of the threat, or they would. The director stressed it would get terrible for our homeland if we failed to neutralize the problem." Ziv rubbed his neck.

"This isn't right, so we should disobey this order and let God decide the world's fate." Rubenstein flapped a hand in dismissal.

"As much as I agree with you, Haim, we can't disobey this order; we'd be outlaws and the Mossad would hunt us down. Do you want that hanging over your shoulders for the rest of your life? We've both worked too hard to let this be our fate. Besides, think of your family. They shouldn't be burdened with that legacy."

"No, I don't want that. You make a notable point, Ofer, so what should we do next?"

Ziv grinned as he relished thinking on his feet and pondered their options. "They'll need gas soon, so let's tail them for a bit. When they stop, we'll execute our abort plan."

"What plan? Will you tell me or will you keep it a secret?" Rubinstein's nose crumpled.

"I'll fill you in when we arrive at the bus stop, but I should review the map first." Ziv grumbled while unfolding his roadmap.

They drove for another thirty minutes before the bus pulled into a rest area for gas and food. Rubenstein tailed them from a distance, pulling off to the station's side to avoid detection. They both watched the occupants of the bus offload and walk into the store. Ziv directed his colleague to open the trunk and then resume a watchful eye on their targets, while he pulled out a set of spikes from his go kit.

"Watch my back, Haim. It's crowded, so we must execute our plan away from here. I'll make it happen." He took a calm breath.

The stout agent ambled toward the mini-bus, as the driver stood unaware of his presence and pumped gas into his vehicle. Ziv crouched, pretending to adjust his shoe. A split-second later, his right hand slipped the spikes under the rear tire. He strolled back to his car while Rubenstein scanned the store, and minutes later, the hordes, including their two Hamas targets, returned to the bus and entered it.

"Well, that should do it." Ziv brushed his palms together to remove the dust.

"Now what do we do?" Rubenstein grimaced and cracked his knuckles.

"You must have patience, my friend. We'll resume following them and when they pull over, we'll make our move. Just follow my lead, as it will become clear." Ziv gave a playful grin.

As the bus continued on its journey, Rubenstein steered his car back into the heavy traffic. The congestion masked their position, but also made it difficult to tail the vehicle. The dense traffic elevated their concerns about losing the bus, so Rubenstein pulled into the other lane to edge up on the bus.

"Careful, Haim, you mustn't alert them to our presence. Besides, where can they go?" Ziv said with a sense of calm and ease.

"They won't escape me; I've been tailing people for decades, and many much harder than this," said Rubenstein. His eyes combed the road and surrounding cars. The chaotic driving habits of the Saudis made his fellow countrymen look passive. Suddenly, a red aura permeated the roadway. Rubenstein slammed on his brakes, screeching to a stop and avoiding the four car pile-up.

"Damn it, they're getting away, while we're blocked in. What do we do, Ofer?"

Ziv shrugged. "There's nothing we can do, but let the traffic clear."

After about ten minutes, Ziv recognized their stalled state and traded places with his partner, taking the helm of the car. The roadway remained jammed, so he shifted into reverse and stomped down on the accelerator. Ziv navigated to the breakdown lane and glided backwards amid inquisitive looks from those he passed, albeit in a different direction. Rubinstein fumbled with his seatbelt while his bulging eyes glanced at a haze of vehicles they passed. After about one-quarter of a mile, Ziv saw his opening and shifted the gear selector into forward. He drove down hard-packed ground leading over a small embankment. His vehicle slid sideways and downward. The car sprang up on two wheels.

Rubenstein gripped the dashboard. "We're going to flip."

"Calm down, Haim. I got this," said the accomplished anti-terrorist driver, grinning.

After seconds of jarring and fishtailing in the sand, Ziv landed on a path that paralleled the highway. He sped onward for about six-hundred meters, and then he turned off, heading up a small incline. The car sputtered while cresting the incline. Ziv chuckled as their car hit the highway's pavement, well ahead of the accident. He slammed the accelerator pedal to the floor and sped off. After ten minutes, the two operatives' faces tightened as they looked for the bus. Fortunately, they spotted the bus on the curb of the highway two minutes later. Its passengers encircled the rear tire while Al-Zuhar and Rantisi stood by the engine of the bus.

"Here's the plan. We'll pull off the roadway and approach the driver. You'll ask the driver if he wants help to fix his tire. He'll say no, so you'll advise him we're going to transport our friends, so they won't be late. We'll take the two terrorists at gunpoint and get them into our car. Then we'll take care of business." Ziv's fists tightened.

Once the vehicle stopped, Rubinstein shuffled to the driver who was jacking up the bus. His Arabic tongue raised no concerns with the driver who refused help and relinquished his two Palestinian passengers. Ziv met Rubenstein midway between the bus and his vehicle, where they discreetly drew their silenced pistols. Ziv shielded his pistol with a local newspaper while Rubenstein tucked the pistol underneath his armpit. As they came face-to-face with their mortal enemies, Rubenstein asked for a smoke, and when Rantisi reached into his pocket, the two spies brandished their weapons.

"You both have a choice. We can shoot you or you can walk to the car and get in it without making a scene." Rubenstein rushed his words.

"Who are you?" Rantisi cocked his head to the side.

Rubinstein leaned forward. "We're Saudi intelligence, so follow our instructions, and you won't be harmed."

The two Hamas commanders nodded and trudged back to the car. Ziv thrust his pistol's barrel into the small of Rantisi's back. "Get in the front seat, drive the speed limit, and do nothing foolish, as I'd hate to shoot you accidentally."

Rantisi drove at the speed limit while Al-Zuhar stared out at the horizon. Neither said a word. After driving several miles, Ziv ordered them to turn right onto a dirt road that ran into an expansive field. They drove for another two miles in silence.

"Pull over here." Ziv said, pointing to some scrub brush. "Get out now." The two Mossad operatives leveled their guns at the terrorists' heads.

"Walk to the trunk of the car." Ziv motioned. "Now open the trunk and grab the two shovels. I have a job for you before I release you into the desert." Ziv scanned the area.

He pointed his finger at a patch of scrub brush. "Haim, take them over there to dig two holes. I'll join you, but I have to get two things first."

Rubenstein pushed the two terrorists to the scrub brush. Ziv opened a hard plastic gray case and grabbed a gas can and two golf ball-sized grenades. He shut the trunk and adjusted his watch, knowing he owed the Mossad director a phone call in just a few minutes. The repercussions of his tardiness evaded him. Not that he cared, as the seasoned spy never let things bother him and stuck to his plan; he had already rehearsed it several times in his head. He rejoined his partner, setting the gas can down at his feet.

"We don't have all day, so dig faster. We'd rather do other things than entertain you two bastards." Ziv thrusted out his chest while giving them a harsh squint.

The two Hamas terrorists dug two rectangular holes approximately eight feet long and three feet wide. Fortunately, the semi-firm sand made the job go by quickly.

It took them thirty-five minutes to dig three feet down. Rantisi stopped, glancing up at his captors. "Who are you? We have done nothing to you and complied with all your instructions."

Ziv glanced at his colleague. "We're Israeli Mossad. You're responsible for the deaths of many Israelis, including children. We're here today to render justice, so it's time for you to pay for your heinous crimes."

Rantisi shook his head. "We didn't kill those children. Yes, we've killed some of your countrymen, but that was war. We're now politicians and we can return home to work toward a peace deal with Fatah and then with Israel."

"Yeah, that's likely, as you both vowed to annihilate Israel. Since when have you adopted a softer heart? I doubt you'd ever seek peace with us," said Rubenstein, snickering.

"If you're going to kill us, just get to it. Allah's great and we've no fear of death." Al-Zuhar scowled and spit at the Israeli's feet.

Ziv smirked. "You deserve a painful death for your sins against Israel. Unfortunately, there's no time, as I have to report back to my headquarters."

Al-Zuhar glanced at Rantisi as if to communicate to him by telepathy. The two terrorists raised their shovels to strike the two Israelis. As they swung their shovels, Ziv fired several rounds into their legs. The terrorists wobbled and then crashed to the ground. Rubenstein watched in shock while his partner executed his plan with ruthless precision. Moving to the side of the grave, Ziv removed the shovels from the two fallen terrorists, and then reached down and grabbed Rantisi's leg, dragging him backwards from his seated position to rest him flat on his back. He admired the grave's fit with a twinkle in his eye and then stepped over to the other hole to jostle Al-Zuhar into a similar position. The Hamas commanders' eyes rolled back as blood poured from their legs.

"Are you boys comfortable? You look a little hot from your workout." Ziv smirked.

"You can get rid of us, but you'll never kill our spirit. We're just another pair of martyrs and our deaths will rally other warriors to the cause." Rantisi said as spittle launched from his mouth.

"Is that so? Let me make it clear. You'll never be found, and we'll advise our sources in Gaza that you ran off with western women. How do you like that?" Ziv spit on him.

"Why do you dignify the two bastards by acknowledging them? Let's just finish the job and notify our headquarters." Rubenstein disliked his partner's ruthless side.

"No problem," Ziv said, picking up the gas can and showering both Hamas men with gasoline. "This will eliminate the virus and leave no trace of it."

The terrorists gagged on the gasoline's pungent vapors. They both bled profusely from their gunshot wounds, but they wouldn't succumb to them. Ziv had another plan for their deaths, and one that would equal the fate of their victims.

"You'll die a quick death by fire, just like the pain you inflicted on those kids on the outskirts of Jerusalem; your minions mercilessly ran their bus over that cliff. It's said that several of the children survived the crash and were screaming as the bus was engulfed in flames." Ziv said dispassionately.

Rantisi could barely speak, beset by the immense pain that radiated up from his knee. "Go to hell, you bastard."

Ziv grinned. "You first," he said, retrieving two small metallic grenades from his jacket pocket. "These are your sleeping pills." He released the pins on the grenades and tossed them into each hole.

Rubenstein, silent until now, caught on. "Let's move." The Israeli operatives hurried towards the car, as the thermite grenades exploded. Flames shot skyward, turning the recently created graves into incinerators. Both Israelis felt the intense heat generated from the two fire pits. The howling desert winds quickly replaced the terrorist's screams. Their bodies burned for ten minutes before the two agents could approach the graves. The flames morphed to embers. Grabbing a shovel, Ziv covered the remaining bones and ashes with dirt.

"That wasn't so bad." Ziv gave a wide grin while walking back to their sedan.

Rubenstein speechlessly followed his partner. He had never seen death so close and personal, realizing it would haunt him as long as he lived. Although he despised the crimes the Hamas commanders committed, he also pitied them. It troubled him that his partner enjoyed this type of work, and he hoped to never experience this side of him again.

As the two carried out their work, they remained unaware of the consequences of their delayed operation. The prime minister paced back and forth in his office, wearing a hole in his Iranian handmade carpet. Across the Atlantic Ocean, the US president ordered Operation Purge; two B-1 stealth bombers now screamed toward their targets in Mecca.

Rubenstein reached into the passenger's side of the car, removed his satellite phone, and punched its redial feature, receiving a busy signal. "That's strange. I can't reach our director's office." He depressed the redial button again and received the same busy tone.

"Let me try." Ziv yanked the phone from his associate's hand.

Ziv dialed the telephone number to the Mossad director, but received no dial tone for his efforts. After repeating the process and receiving an automated voice, he tossed the phone to his wiry colleague. He bit his lip, perplexed by the low signal strength given the countryside's barrenness. He scanned the landscape for an elevated point to try again.

"Let's get moving; we don't want to keep our director waiting any longer. We're already fifty minutes late, so he'll be wondering if we completed our mission." Ziv twisted his wedding ring.

"I'll drive. We should follow the road to Mecca. We'll need to find a landline if we can't get a signal." Rubenstein patted Ziv on the shoulder.

"Whatever we're doing, we must do it fast. The clock's ticking." Ziv's eyes widened.

The two retraced their route back to the highway as nightfall approached. People scurried about, rushing home to prepare for the evening prayer hour. The two pulled their vehicle back into some horrendous traffic. Ziv's patience waned while they sat in bumper-to-bumper congestion.

"I could run faster than this. I wonder what the hell's going on here; we're going to miss our deadline." Rubenstein bellowed.

"We already missed the deadline, Haim. We must get a message to our boss, and fast. Can't you think of another way to message them?" He gave him a silent look.

Rubenstein looked up as his eyebrows narrowed. "I could use my laptop to relay a message to him, but the signal would travel through regular commercial lines, so it may be subject to interception; I'll have to talk cryptically."

"Pull over and message them." Ziv barked.

Rubenstein steered the car to the breakdown lane. Reaching into his soft black day bag, he removed his laptop computer. The computer booted-up in minutes. He logged on, brought up his email by hitting an icon on his desktop, and typed in code: *"The rats have been neutralized and buried. Operation Purge has been successfully aborted. Rubenstein out."*

Rubenstein pressed the send button. The electronic highway would deliver his message, but would the Mossad director get it in time to inform the US president? If not, disaster would befall both countries.

CHAPTER 42: Extreme Exposure

James drove into the tunnel and emerged from it a few seconds later. He saw Rosslyn through his peripheral vision while he focused on his target across the Potomac. The nation's capital usually inspired him, but his mission overshadowed it. His eyes swept the roadway while weaving through traffic at speeds approaching seventy miles per hour. He switched off the siren and kept his flashing emergency lights on as he raced toward the State Department.

Approaching the Roosevelt Bridge, he drifted into the left lane to avoid the traffic merging from the south. He jockeyed to the right, raced over the bridge, and descended a small incline to Constitution Avenue. The light turned red, so he slowed to a stop. His fingers flipped the toggle button; his flashing lights ceased. After minutes, the light turned green, so James drove with the flow of traffic for a block and stopped to make his last turn. Once the oncoming traffic subsided, he turned left and cruised up the block. A guard manning a booth halted him. He rolled down his window to greet the uniform guard, displaying his vehicle placard and employee identification card. The guard glanced down at the badge and signaled for his partner to lower the mechanical barrier. "Agent James, we've been expecting you. We have a guard holding a parking spot for you just to the left." The security officer motioned with his hand to a parking spot and his colleague.

The Delta barrier descended to street level a second later. James drove over the flattened barrier, turned left, and parked about a quarter of a block from the diplomatic entrance. He exited his vehicle and scanned the building's facade before closing and locking the car door. His eyes darted back and forth from the parking area to the diplomatic entrance.

James walked toward the front entrance while his eyes searched the area. A diplomatic motorcade sat staged in a covered circular driveway. He bypassed a side screening area and stopped under a covered area, where he met Special Agents' Bishop and Clark. James extended his hand. "It's great to see you guys. Thanks for the help." He glanced at his wristwatch, noting his early arrival.

Bishop rubbed his forearm and looked around the area. "I wish we could've been of more help. We arrived as fast as we could, but Atallah had sweet-talked her way in because of the cold. Her lobby isolation was the best we could do, but we have two guards monitoring her."

"That is helpful, but you'll need to have the screening guards pulled and quarantined." James held his hands loosely behind his back. "They could've been exposed when they touched her items. The CDC team will arrive shortly. Please have them interview and talk to the guards that may have come in contact with Atallah. Close the screening area and decontaminate it thoroughly. I'll go meet and isolate her somewhere in the building. Keep a trained eye on me so you can clean up behind me. I'll do my best to keep her away from others or touching things. I'll talk to you later."

"Good luck, Matt." Clark scrubbed a hand over his face and winced.

A steady flow of employees entered and exited through the entrance's glass doors. James walked through the glass doors and glanced to the left, where Atallah stood near some turnstiles. Capturing her gaze, he returned her smile and walked toward her after using his ID to pass through a controlled access turnstile. She embraced him and gave him a kiss on his cheek, mindful of the public surrounding them.

James felt a quiver in his stomach. "I was waiting for you outside for five minutes." He released her embrace, consciously forcing his limbs to relax, recalling the doctor's virus precaution.

She beamed. "I was a little cold from the breeze and the guards suggested I wait inside, so I took advantage of the opportunity and checked-in, receiving my visitor's ID, so we can go right in to the awards ceremony. I've been looking forward to meeting the secretary of state."

The poker-faced agent held back his smirk. "I bet you have. We're running a few minutes early, so let me take you somewhere private. I have this sudden urge to kiss you."

"Lead on, I'm all yours." She seized his hand.

His mind raced, cognizant that she had out maneuvered him by checking in and accessing the building. Quarantining her in his car appeared no longer possible, so he considered his options and escorted her through a set of double doors controlled by two uniform guards. They strolled down a wide corridor flanked by an array of the world's flags. After about one-hundred feet, they passed a wall with the names of fallen department personnel. He stopped, looked down, and pointed to his uncle's name inscribed on the wall. "He was killed in the line of duty." His voice cracked as his eyes darkened.

She gazed at him. "I'm sure he meant a lot to you, as I can see the pain in your eyes."

James nodded. "My uncle was the best and died in the prime of his life. I probably joined the service because of him, his fantastic tales, and wild adventures. I remember him telling them, as a kid."

"You know what they say, only the good die young." She caressed his hand.

"Then I've got nothing to worry about. I'll live until I'm in triple digits. Won't I?" He peered into his companion's eyes and grinned.

She glanced away. "Inshallah (God Willing)."

"Well, that's not good, as I can say from my experience in Iraq that Inshallah means god willing or never, forget it. More often than not, it meant the latter." He laughed.

"Allah works in mysterious ways, so when it's your time, there's nothing you can do but embrace it." Her face tightened.

The undeterred agent bit his lip. Her statement proved very telling. "Follow me; I've something I want to show you and I bet you'll like it."

James led her by the hand past a bank of elevators and walked down another lengthy corridor. They passed several offices on each side. People flooded by them on their way to lunch. He searched for a place to isolate her, needing to prevent the State Department from becoming ground zero. He veered leftward and walked down another less traveled passageway.

"Come here," he said, leading her to a nearby bathroom and locking the door to it. "You look so sexy. I want you now."

He guided her to the bathroom counter, turning her to face the mirror. "Look how beautiful you are. You have so many outstanding qualities to offer like beauty, talent, intellect, wit, and warmth."

She demurred, focusing on her mission. "Do we have time? You're making me so hot, but we must be on time for the ceremony."

James glided his hands up her back and then slid his right hand down to her buttocks. He watched her eyes close as she concentrated on his touch. He retracted his right hand from her waist and reached around his back, removing his handcuffs.

"Matt," she said. "While I appreciate the sentiment, don't you think we should save this for later?"

He slid the metal cuff around her back and down to her right wrist. With one quick motion, he handcuffed her to a towel rack. "That should tame the tigress. It's a damn shame."

Her smile changed to disbelief as James backed away from her. "What are you doing, Matt? I love you."

"Save it for someone who believes you." His fiery eyes pierced hers. Her deception haunted him; he prided himself on his unique ability to read people, and this experience left him questioning his judgment.

She dropped her mask, turning to glare at him. "You're as good as dead; you're tainted with the lethal disease now."

"I have no fear of death, and I guess you were correct about the good passing before their time. Why did you do it, Suhar? You have so much." He rocked his head with a pinched expression.

"You Americans just don't get it. You continue to spread your so-called democracy all over the world. What you don't understand is that it's not always welcomed; it's a disease similar to a virus because it kills and corrupts. You should learn from other cultures instead of thrusting yours on others." She sermonized.

James nodded in resignation as the adrenaline surge left him. Less angry than saddened by the loss of the future he had briefly imagined, he looked at her. "I thought we shared something special that's a rarity in life. Are you telling me you have no feelings for me? Be honest with yourself."

"I enjoyed my time with you, but you were always a means to the end and it could've never worked. We're from two different backgrounds and cultures."

"It didn't have to end this way, Suhar. In America, our differences enrich life. People overlook their religious differences and live and work together." He removed his cell phone and turned away to notify the CDC that he had secured the suspect.

"What gave me away?" She stalled.

James turned back to her. "Several things didn't add up, but your tattoo was your critical mistake, as I later realized it was the Democratic Front for the Liberation of Palestine emblem."

"I should've removed that damn thing years ago. I can't believe it gave me away, and I should've known that you would catch that." She said, looking down.

With one quick, but forceful tug, she harnessed all her energy, ripping the towel holder off the rack. She lunged forward and smashed the agent's head, knocking him to the hard tile floor. She ran into the hall and headed to a nearby stairwell to search for an escape route. He rose and dashed from the bathroom and into the stairwell. Her footsteps echoed from below and revealed her downward path toward the basement. The tenacious agent pursued her, thrilled that her path would take her into seclusion.

Exiting a basement door, she found herself in the State Department's underground parking garage. Unfamiliar with her environment, she vaulted through another door and landed in a labyrinth of vehicles. Awkwardly clutching the towel rack, she scanned the area, looking for a way out; she heard the door slam behind her. Without looking, she sensed the dogged agent and ran away, seeking to evade him.

Her bulging eyes looked ahead, where she noticed a black Cadillac pulling in front of a guarded entrance, which included a private elevator. She sprinted toward the car as its rear right door open. Secretary Jackson emerged from the vehicle, reaching back into the car to retrieve his briefcase. He had just returned from a National Security Council meeting at the White House, where he got the specifics of the president's negotiation with Israel's prime minister, the Mossad's success in neutralizing the threat to Mecca, and his recall of the bombers. Now, he had to rush upstairs for the ceremony.

James expected her path toward the secretary and plowed his own shortcut to America's top diplomat. He couldn't beat her to the secretary, so he drew his pistol and aimed at Atallah.

"Freeze Suhar." James barked.

She stopped as an agent went to interdict her for approaching the secretary.

"Stay away from her." James pointed as his eyes looked through the agent. "She's infected with the lethal Ebola-Nile virus. Get the secretary out of here." Three members of the detail sprang into action; they encircled the secretary and formed a human shield to safeguard him.

Atallah shifted, causing James to tighten his grip on his firearm. "Don't even think about it, Suhar, or I'll shoot you."

She smiled, looking back over her shoulder. "You wouldn't dare, not after all that we've been through. You don't have it in you." She taunted.

"You're wrong, as my country will always come first, and I'll always carry out my duties."

She swung the towel rack at the approaching agent and hit him on his temple, causing him to wobble and then fall to the ground. She bounded over the agent and charged towards the secretary, as his detail rushed him inside the holding area. James readjusted his sights, but couldn't fire and risk the chance of hitting one of his fellow agents, so he sidestepped to the right, aimed at her leg, and fired one round that sliced into her upper thigh. She teetered and then fell to the cold, hard concrete floor.

"Get the secretary upstairs," yelled James with a strained voice. He pointed at the shaken agent. "Back away from her and seal the area." James approached the fallen woman, aiming his weapon at her chest. He wouldn't again underestimate her resourcefulness.

She rolled onto her back to face him. "I can't believe that you shot me, especially in the back."

"What are you talking about? I shot you in the leg. I could've used lethal force, which meant I should've shot you center mass, armpit level." He sighed.

"I wish things ended up differently between you and me. This isn't how I envisioned dying." She moaned.

"This could've ended differently. We all make choices Suhar. You made yours and now you'll have to live with it."

"But you don't understand, Matt. Hassan kidnapped my mother and father and threatened to kill them if I didn't cooperate."

"I wish I could believe you. I would've rescued them myself. If you succeeded in your plan, then we would all be dead, including your family. The Ebola-Nile virus has no boundaries, but of course, no one knows that better than you. I have to say, I admire your tenacity, but even manipulating me won't help your plan now." He tossed her a triangle bandage from his coat pocket. "You must apply direct pressure on the wound to slow the bleeding."

"What for? I'm dead anyway. This will save me from an agonizing death." She clenched her jaw.

He smiled as he raised his chin. "Not necessarily, as I believe we now have a cure for the virus. We received it from the Israelis, so you'll recover to face a trial."

"I'll get off, as there was no overt act. Your judicial system will find me innocent."

"We'll see about that. We found the syringe you tossed down the vent. I think that our friends from the CDC will be very convincing, and I'll tell my story." His eyes widened.

"What will you say?" The archeologist groaned while applying pressure to her wound.

He grabbed his cellular phone out of his pocket. "I'll tell the truth. Stick around, help's on the way."

James walked a few steps away from her, turning to monitor the fallen woman. He scrolled through his phone's contact list, stopping on Sherman's number and depressing the redial button.

After four rings, the CDC doctor answered. "Hello Matt, where are you? I have my team standing by at the diplomatic entrance."

"I'm down in the building's basement parking area. Head east on C Street, turn left at the guard booth, go down the ramp underneath the building, and turn left. Drive straight forward for another one-hundred feet and then you should see me." He gulped.

"Okay, hold tight. We'll be there in three minutes." She hung up.

Sherman ordered her team to the garage entrance, and walked to the guard booth, presented her credentials, and solicited his help in quarantining the area. The guard called his supervisor, who responded in seconds. Within minutes, a complement of officers joined the CDC biohazard team, so she briefed them on the gravity of the situation. They all listened as she explained the lethal nature of the virus and its spread rates. The officers relished their perimeter assignments, smiling as they transferred jurisdiction to the specialists. The CDC hazmat van drove down the ramp and into the garage.

"Follow me," she said, leading the guards into the quarantine zone, while supplying them with surgical masks. "You must secure all the entrances and exits, while ensuring that nobody enters unless you have my permission. I'll keep your supervisor near me for communications." She flipped her protective hood down, covering her head. After ensuring an airtight seal, she approached James, who sat next to the secretary's Cadillac. "Are you alright?"

He crossed his arms. "Are you kidding? I probably only have a few days to live.

"You should've practiced safe sex." The CDC doctor quipped with a broad smile.

James rubbed his eye. "She kissed me on the cheek. So I'm certain that I'm infected with the virus, or do I call it the Ebola-Nile virus. You should just shoot me now. I saw the spread projections."

Sherman grinned. "Don't you trust me? I'll save you; however, we must quarantine you, Atallah, and the agent she smacked on the head. How close was the secretary to your lady friend?"

"She came as close as eight feet when I shot her. I ordered her to stop and when she failed to comply, I shot her in the leg." James' voice shook.

"Nicely done, as the secretary is safe thanks to you." Sherman raised her hands skyward, forming a V.

He shook his head in disagreement. "He wouldn't have been in jeopardy if I hadn't brought her here."

"Or if you listened to me." She nodded with a glint in her eyes.

"I owe you if I survive." He gave her his trademark cocky grin.

She grinned back. "I'll hold you to it, but I expect a fantastic dinner, a cruise down the Potomac, and then we can call it even." She signaled for her team to bring two airtight containers, which melded a stretcher with a bubble. The team set one next to Atallah and dropped the other one next to the doctor. Sherman kneeled and opened the hard plastic enclosure. She snapped her fingers. "Get in, Matt."

"It's a good thing that I'm not claustrophobic; this is tighter than a doghouse." He grumbled as he slid in.

"Just be quiet and get inside so I can move you to Bethesda Medical Center." She shut the container as he laid flat on his back. Her assistants whisked him into the van. A few minutes later, they placed Atallah's container next to him. He glanced over at the sleeping woman, and couldn't escape her power, even knowing she had plotted to kill him and his government's leaders. She had touched his heart and then broke it in the course of a month. It would take time to get over her.

Sherman jumped into the van to accompany the two to the hospital. Another CDC vehicle arrived in the garage to begin decontamination operations of the entire area. She prayed they had thwarted a major pandemic, but only time would reveal humanity's fate. They would have to monitor area hospitals closely. She instructed the van to depart, leaving diplomacy in the wind.

CHAPTER 43: Renewal

Bethesda Medical Center, Maryland
James' eyes darted around his sterile room while sitting up in his bed. A calendar marked by ten red X's sat on the door just above another, more troubling sign. The yellow biohazard sign with a black circle in the center which was eclipsed by three outward facing black crescent moon shapes joined at the center. Bethesda Naval Medical Hospital's sterility and his quarantine state stymied his creativity. Its solitude and austerity allowed him to reflect upon his career and his many life choices. His mind shifted from his personal life to his work with the federal government. He considered its organizational failures and the urgent requirement for pioneering reforms. An organization's survival needs should never eclipse its responsibilities for protecting its people.

Over the years, James' frustration with interagency rivalries, duplication of effort, and gaps in critical areas had grown. He believed that government should be efficient and effective. The government had to recruit and keep the best people to ensure the nation's future. Although they had thwarted a homeland bio-terror plot, he recognized the components of both luck and skill, and knew the next attack on America could be more robust and catastrophic. The government had to be ready for it, so he stood ready to take a stand, as the opportunity had presented itself to him on a silver platter. In hours, James would address the senators that could overhaul the system, but first he needed his discharge. But by taking a stand, he also knew the career he had worked to build could be sabotaged. It stood time to make a choice, and he knew his choice would coincide with the nation's best interests.

A rhythmic knock came at the door, shattering his reverie. "Come in." He turned toward the door and welcomed the interruption.

Doctor Sherman shuffled into the room for the first time without her protective suit, bearing a luminous smile. "I've got splendid news for you, Matt. You're not infected with the el-Amarna or Ebola-Nile virus, as our last tests confirmed it."

He returned the smile. "That's a great relief, so thanks for informing me. By the way, how is Suhar? Did the Israeli treatment cure her of the virus?"

"She's responding well to it, but we'll have to watch her for another week to ensure the cure's effectiveness. Would you like to see her? I can arrange it."

He felt a slight chill. "I don't think so; there's no sense in dredging up old feelings. She decided her fate and now she'll just have to live with it. I'm moving on."

The doctor hesitated. "We found her parents, safe and sound at home. It looks like her story of coercion was just another desperate attempt to lower your guard. Once she knew it was over, she confessed she masterminded the plot, and that she brought el-Amarna to Hassan's attention. His martyrs were just a diversion. She had planned to escape from him and use you to access the cabinet. You just made it easier by rescuing her. She had some twisted idea that by eliminating our cabinet, Arab women would be treated with more respect."

The solemn agent shrugged, trying hard to hide the sudden stab of pain the revelation caused him. "I knew it was a desperate act. I examined the past weeks while enjoying this hospital's luxuries. She manipulated me; so much for my keen judgment and ability to read people. It could've been disastrous and I would've been to blame." He looked away fleetingly, unaccustomed to revealing so much of himself. "Plenty of lessons learned," he finished, giving the CDC expert a weak smile.

The doctor gave him a stony expression. "Matt James, you can't hold yourself accountable for her actions! Believe me, no man could've resisted that intensive of an onslaught. They executed their plan and there was no way for you to have known."

He glanced at the physician. "Ah, but you knew, didn't you?"

She chuckled. "Well, yes, but I'm a woman."

James changed the subject and eyed the petite doctor. "Am I to infer from your lack of overalls that I'm now free to go?"

"Yes, and I brought you a suit, underwear, tee-shirt, socks, shirt, and a tie from your apartment. I selected a dark blue suit that will make you shine, as it's your big day." She grinned.

"Indeed it is. Let's hope I can make a difference."

"I'm sure you will. The intelligence committee wants to hear your thoughts on the thwarted attack. They want to know how to prevent such an attack in the future, so it's your chance to effect significant change while making our government more effective." The doctor's eyes widened. "This lifetime opportunity only comes around once."

The humbled agent frowned. "I received a call from the director about a half-hour ago. He suggested I stick to the script that they'll hand me. I already received the first draft. As expected, it just relays the facts surrounding the event, so it's the standard government whitewash."

"Tell me they're not sanctioning what you can say. This is unproductive and plain wrong." Her face reddened as her mouth downturned.

"I'm not sure what I'll do. The director implied that if I cooperate, then I'll get my choice of an onward overseas assignment." His brow rose.

She nodded. "So what happens if you unload the truth? What will they do to you then?"

"They'll send me to the far reaches of the planet or give me an undesirable position. This will end my promotion prospects. It's often the position that drives the promotion." James gave her an easy nod.

"You'll do the right thing. I'm sure of that." The veteran doctor winked.

"I should get ready. We depart for the Hill in thirty minutes. Thanks for bringing my clothes. You have excellent tastes."

Sherman held her hands loosely behind her back, believing in the quality of his character, which excluded selling out; she would bet her life on it. As she walked to the door, she glanced over her shoulder. "Would you like me to accompany you to the Hill? I've got time, and I'd like to see you testify."

"That would be fantastic. I'd welcome your company." Perhaps he had misjudged the woman. He admired her professionalism, intelligence, and patriotism, and lately he had seen a lot of her softer side, too. The doctor appeared witty, friendly, and warm when she let her hair down. He smiled, watching the doctor saunter out the door.

After he finished showering, shaving, and brushing his teeth, he dressed in his dark blue suit. A light blue tie and black dress shoes finished his look. He found an item he failed to recognize and read its inscription, *"The truth will empower."* The agent smiled and slid the tie tack on.

James retrieved his black travel bag with several other personal items and strolled to the room's exit. As he swung the door open, an awkward silence emerged, as the department's legal advisor and the DSS director halted their conversation with the CDC doctor. The two greeted him, congratulating him for interrupting the terrorist plot.

"Here's your three-page statement that you need to read. This has been cleared by all the appropriate DS and Department personnel." The director said, eying the agent.

James scanned the prepared statement. "This only outlines my mission and the results of it. I'd like to provide my thoughts on how to thwart this type of attack in the future." He said with narrowing eyes and a pinched expression.

"Just stay on script and leave the other stuff to Assistant Secretary Chen." The legal advisor leaned forward.

James bit his lip at the apparent order. He disliked the prospect that defiance meant being stationed in West Africa or any of the Stans. Pakistan, Tajikistan, Afghanistan, or Uzbekistan didn't appeal to him, nor did an isolated place like Papua New Guinea, where cannibalism could still be encountered deep in the country's heart.

James smirked. "Don't worry about a thing. I'll take care of my part." He glanced at the doctor and winked.

She smiled, eying her gift affixed to his tie. "The tie tack completes your outfit. You look very honorable and professional, perfect for facing a bunch of senators." Her eyes sparkled.

"Thank you. That was very thoughtful. Every time I wear it, I'll think of you." He smiled.

"Then you should wear it every day." The enchanting woman returned the smile.

The four figures strolled out of the medical center. They entered a four-door dark blue Crown Victoria parked curbside. The legal advisor doubled as a driver with the director riding shotgun. James opened the back door for Sherman, displaying his chivalry. She sat and slid across the back, making room for him. The drive to the Hill remained quiet, as the legal advisor doled out more unsolicited advice to deal with the committee.

James had no trepidation and stood unimpressed by the hordes of senators and congressional representatives. They paraded themselves around the capitol and too often around the world. The DS agent had protected many of them throughout the years. He neither appeared enamored, nor made anxious by them. He had a better understanding of the terrorist problem that America faced in the years ahead. His newfound celebrity status also buffered him. Political correctness would spare him from a senator's jibes. After all, he risked his life for the nation; however, he would prepare for the worst, as someone would always play politics.

Sherman grabbed his hand. "You'll do great by just telling the truth."

He smiled. "The truth is the straightforward part. It's the questions that could sting. I'm sure they'll want direct answers, and I'll give them what they want."

"Just stick to the script and everything will be cool." The advisor interrupted, glancing back at the agent through the rearview mirror.

James gritted his teeth as the advisor had a knack for irritating people. The counselor took his orders and answered to the department's hierarchy, and he couldn't fault the legal advisor for that. James had been to the Hill myriad times to discuss Iraq and other Middle Eastern issues. Each time, one of the state's handlers accompanied him to report on the meeting, its outcome, and any deliverables. Yet, their primary duty involved keeping him on the message, something that he resented. Still, he gave the advisor the benefit of the doubt.

As they turned left onto Independence Avenue, the Capitol stood prominently against the cloudy skyline to the east. James admired the magnificent white structure, both in design and symbolism. On the eastern end of the National Mall, the Capitol serves as the central point of the district's four quadrants. It stood since 1800 and was partially destroyed in 1814 when Washington was burned. Its restoration took five years and later it received a facelift which included its large prominent dome and elongated wings. Enduring over 220 years, James brushed aside the hordes storming it in 2021. Democracy seemed under attack, and James valued the Constitution and its principles; something he vowed to uphold, even if it took his life. Unfortunately, five hundred and thirty-five congress persons forgot their vow to the people. Their reckless spending, partisanship, self-serving and power-hungry nature, and influence peddling jeopardized the country and its founding principles.

He understood these hearings' importance and wanted to forge the outcome. He expected one senator would serve him a softball and he would hit it over the fence.

"You've testified before grand juries. Imagine this as a larger one and you'll be fine." The advisor pointed out, breaking the silence.

"Sure, no worries." James reflected momentarily before gazing out the window at the splendor of the Jefferson Memorial. He valued this part of DC the most. He had spent many afternoons in the area pondering world events or just lost in reflection. The monuments inspired him, as they represented influential Americans, the price of freedom, and important events in the nation's history. He despised the cancel culture that tried to minimize the country's greatness.

As they made their last turn into the expansive premises, a police officer stopped their vehicle. The officer identified the occupants and found out the purpose of their visit. Satisfied by their justification, the uniformed officer directed them to a nearby parking area reserved for official visitors. The advisor maneuvered and parked the vehicle curbside. A flock of journalists engulfed the car for a shot at the headline-breaking story. James remembered his protective missions when the media swarmed his dignitaries, requiring him to clear a path. He cringed at being the target of their cameras and microphones. The legal advisor turned from the front seat and cautioned the agent about speaking; the media required containment, and it was the legal advisor's job to do it. James sighed as his pending testimony preoccupied him. Facing the press never appealed to him.

Fortunately, a longtime friend and colleague converged on his location. Special Agent Jack Ford pushed his way through the overzealous reporters to block them from the sedan's door. Ford served as DS's protective liaison agent assigned to the Hill and knew every nook and cranny in the Capitol. More impressively, he knew most of the congressional representatives who frequented it. James laughed as Ford pushed the press back; the clever agent imprinted his thumb on the lenses of their cameras in a classic maneuver.

Upon exiting the car, reporters on the hunt obstructed his path. The advisor expected this move, bolting out the door to provide additional help. Along with the Capitol Police, they escaped the press unscathed. Ford whisked them across the visiting parking area and through a side door. The reporters dropped their pursuit at the entry point.

"Good to see you, Matt." Ford extended his hand. "How long has it been?"

James shook his hand. "It has been too long, my friend. Thanks for bailing me out back there from that mob."

Ford leaned in. "It's the least I could do, as I owe you my life."

"You don't owe me a thing," said James, cocking his head. "We've known each other for years. Besides, you piloted me down the Potomac to make us even." He motioned to his new friend. "I'd like to introduce you to Doctor Jill Sherman of the CDC."

"Oh, so you're the famous Jack Ford. I've heard so much about you. I look forward to seeing your houseboat." She beamed.

Ford reciprocated the smile. "I'll take you out whenever you want and it will cost you a mere hug, but we can talk about that later. Let's get Matt to the hearing. We can't be late." Ford escorted the contingent through a few corridors, and stopped to point out some antiques, famous paintings, and other symbols of American history. Ford appeared more like a senator given the congressional representatives who greeted him while walking to the committee floor.

Today's closed session excluded the public and press from the senate floor, as the committee desired to maintain the sanctity of the hearings. Often, sensitive testimony had fallen to the impetuous press that smeared it on the front pages, disregarding the consequences. The committee chair vowed to prevent leaks, particularly given today's hearing on weapons of mass destruction.

James' unfamiliarity with the building left him completely dependent on Ford for guidance and directions. Ford led them straight to the committee floor, holding them inside a plush waiting area. After a lengthy delay, Ford showed them to their seats where James sat after being sworn in. Following his opening statement and minutes into his proposed solution, a fire alarm sounded, forcing the building's evacuation. His full testimony would have to wait for another day.

CHAPTER 44: Loose Ends

As they evacuated the capitol building, the cold air reinvigorated James. At least it countered the need for two aspirin, if only briefly. Walking down a path, the director swept him off to the side, lambasting him for deviating from his department-cleared statement to propose a revolutionary reorganization of the service. He berated him for circumventing the chain of command, blustering out threats of disciplinary action. James ignored the idle threats, as politics kept the director at its mercy. He would use his current elevated status to match swords with him.

"I understand your concerns, but I seized the opportunity to outline what's in the country's best interests." James raised his chin.

The director scowled. "I'm in charge, so I'll create policy and recommend to the hierarchy future courses of action or directions for the service. That's not your job, so you had better conform. I can ruin your life."

James glared. "Are you threatening me? I've done nothing wrong. In fact, my boss is putting me in for the department's heroism award."

"Yeah, but I ultimately approve or disapprove it." The director's face flushed as a vein on his forehead bulged.

"This sounds like a threat. Do you have a problem with my actions or me during the mission? At least tell me face-to-face instead of playing these games. I think you owe me that." He stared back at the director.

"You were a loose cannon from the get-go, James, and I needed you to keep me apprised of your activities and you should've blown off the CIA. You overstepped your authorities. DS doesn't get involved in these types of covert activities." The director bellowed.

"So this is the problem? The secretary allowed my involvement, and it's not my fault that he elected to keep you in the dark." He barked back.

The press spotted James and rushed towards the group. The director recognized the danger of the approaching press. "I order you to come to my office first thing tomorrow, and we'll address your insubordination then."

His skin tingled as light beads of sweat formed on his forehead. "I'll be there. Now, if you excuse me, sir, I think I'll find my own way home." James turned to walk away, nearly bowling over the CDC doctor, who had quietly emerged at his elbow.

She smiled. "I'll accompany him. It was a pleasure meeting you both." She trotted off to catch up with James.

As she approached him, she clutched his hand. "It will be fine; you did an outstanding job in there. Your director will cool off. He probably just feels he had no control over the potential change to his service. Besides, I'm sure that he'll have to report to his command what transpired. It wasn't exactly a little solution that you proposed." She shrugged.

James smiled feebly. "I guess you're right that I shouldn't be surprised by his reaction. He thinks I orchestrated it all."

"Wow, you let loose in there and your testimony opened their eyes. She chuckled.

"I certainly did." He smiled. "I wonder if the advisor pulled the alarm, as he disappeared briefly. It doesn't matter now. I'm hungry, so let's eat. I know a place close to here." He inhaled while admiring the view of the National Mall.

She beamed as her stomach growled. The two wandered out to Independence Avenue, where they hailed a cab to take them to the National City Brewery Company. He liked the establishment's nice semi-upscale ambience, which would make a good place for a happenstance date and an ice-cold beer. The prospect of spending time with the doctor delighted him. Her reticence and business-like exterior, wrapped up in an intelligent and capable package, bolstered her appeal. He enjoyed watching her personality unfold and felt honored that she had revealed herself to him. He liked her refined sophistication and dry sense of humor. Her gentle and persuasive demeanor could diffuse any situation before it metastasized.

Following a ten-minute taxi ride, James opened the restaurant's door for his companion and followed her in; a hostess seated them immediately as it was the tail end of the lunch hour. The two sat down and chatted about his testimony, ordered their food, and demolished it when it arrived. Her intuitive academic and tomboy side fascinated him, causing him to lose track of time. Clearly, she could keep pace with him, and he relished her ability to spar verbally with him. He never met a woman so straightforward, and he finally understood how interesting life with her could be.

"I enjoyed the day with you." He said, smiling.

The CDC doctor laughed. "You probably like me as much as Senator Johnson."

"Did it show that much? She gets on my nerves, but I admire her tenacity." He said, grinning. "I still can't figure out her agenda, but she had a vendetta against me."

"My gut says it's something else. I just think she's a firm proponent of the FBI because she's not up for reelection. She's just trying to break out of the cloud she's operating under as a junior senator. I bet she's trying to make her mark, and for whatever reason, she picked this venue as the time to do it, so I'm sure that it's just business."

"Yeah, I'm sure you're right. We should go now? Why don't we grab a cab back to my place? I can drive you home from there, or if you like taking a risk, I could cook you dinner." His eyebrows rose.

"Let's play it by ear, but I'll take the ride to my place." She nodded once.

They stepped out the front door and scanned the area. A yellow cab sat parked a half a block up the street, so James walked to the cab and gave the driver instructions. His accented English captured his attention.

"Where are you from as your accent sounds familiar?" James canted his ear toward the man.

"I'm from Erbil. Do you know the city?" The driver puffed out his chest.

"I thought I recognized your accent, as I was there in the spring of 2009. Erbil was a fascinating place, but it was a little colder than I imagined, though. I hear Sulaymaniyah's nice. I was disappointed that I never made it there."

"It's the nicest place in the region."

"Are you Kurd then?"

The driver sneered and switched the radio to some jazz station. James shrugged it off; it seemed they encountered the only cab driver in DC that appeared at a loss for words. The rest of the ride remained quiet, and five minutes later, they arrived back at his condominium, paid the driver, and exited the vehicle.

He glanced at the CDC expert. "Did you find that driver odd? He sure shut up when I mentioned his ethnicity. What do you suppose that was about?" He peered at his companion.

She chuckled. "He was of Iranian origin. Didn't you notice the subtleties of his accent? Perhaps he was originally from a place near the Iranian and Iraqi border. But it's hard to tell, though. He could come from a mixed background."

"That's impressive." He contemplated her regional knowledge or her bullshitting ability. He would explore them both in the future.

"Can we go inside for a minute? I'd like to change my clothes before I take you home. I may look good in a suit, but I'm more comfortable in jeans." He smiled.

Walking up the stairs, his scalp prickled as he checked the landing. He pondered the stress of constant travel or the recent emotional changes within him. His arthritic knees awoke from the damp air and the trek, so he dialed out the pain and refrained from limping. Right now, it wasn't the doctor part of her he wanted to interest.

"Stairs are tough on joints. Where do you hurt? I'm guessing it's your knees or hips." She eyed his legs.

"It's my knees today, but I think the walking aggravated them. I used to run marathons, and now I'm lucky to walk several miles."

"It doesn't appear to slow you down, so what's your secret?" Her nose wrinkled.

"I pop Ibuprofen like most people take vitamins."

The doctor shook her head. "That's going to eat up your stomach and take its toll on your liver. I know a great specialist who can help you, so I'll arrange for you to see him."

James nodded, thrusting his key into the deadbolt lock. After unlocking two deadbolts, he opened the solid wood door and motioned for the doctor to enter, holding the storm door open. He followed her into the entryway and then punched in an eight digit code to deactivate his alarm.

"Please make yourself at home. If you want anything, the kitchen's to your left, and the bar's straight ahead." He motioned with a flick of the wrist.

She grinned. "I could use a drink." She walked toward the bar and froze.

"What's wrong?" He trailed her into the room and realized the cause of her reaction.

Hassan sat behind the bar, drinking a glass of orange juice and aiming a pistol at her head. "Come in and have a seat. We've some things to discuss."

"I thought you were dead. The SEALs said they pumped you full of lead and sent you to the bottom of the ocean. It's a pity that they missed." He taunted the terrorist while looking down the barrel of his pistol.

Hassan grinned. "Sometimes an illusion is best. They grazed me in the head and shoulder, but all my endurance training paid off. I held my breath for over three minutes and then swam off under the morning sunlight."

The agent sat on one of the bar's four stools. "What do you want from me?"

"I'm here to even the score. You denied me my victory and you have something that belongs to me, and now you must pay." The terrorist glared at him.

"Your insane. I've nothing of yours?" James glared back.

"You have Suhar and I want her back, so you'll bring her to me or I'll kill your lady friend."

"And how can I do that? She's safely tucked away at a medical center, under heavy guard." He gritted his teeth.

Hassan smirked. "Your modesty surprises me, as this should be easy for you. After all, you infiltrated my strategic base without a problem and killed some of my most capable warriors. Perhaps your time with Atallah has softened you, as she can have that effect."

He steeled himself to ignore Hassan's goading, recognizing that this was no time to play that game. "To the contrary," he said, "Suhar was clear in her admiration for my manliness. Just this morning she commented on how much she would miss that. Apparently, she hasn't known many men who could please her like I did."

"Just do it or I'll kill her now." Hassan cocked the hammer back on his pistol and thrust the barrel at the doctor's head.

Sherman reacted instinctively, redirecting the pistol away from her head as the weapon fired. The round ripped through James' upper torso near the collarbone, knocking him backwards and slamming his head against the hard wood floor. She chopped Hassan's windpipe and then smashed his elbow, causing him to release his grip on the pistol.

The stout man yelped, but grasped her head and slammed it on the bar counter. "You bitch; I'll kill you with my bare hands, and I'm going to make you hurt so bad that you'll beg me to kill you."

The determined agent struggled to his feet to assist the doctor. His shirt turned red as blood drenched it from a major artery. James needed to do something before he collapsed. He couldn't leave her alone with this maniac, so he scanned the area as she went toe-to-toe with the killer thug. Hassan would soon overpower her, given his size and strength advantage. It looked like a tiger fighting a stork.

She stood full of surprises, so James watched with amazement as she balanced on one leg while raising her other knee. Hassan swung a powerful right hand toward her face, and she deflected his punch, using his power and momentum against him. She smacked him with the backside of her hand on a nerve center on his neck. The doctor then landed a kick to the inside of his thigh. Releasing a powerful elbow strike to the crown of his head, she sent him crashing to the ground. Her thumb, index and middle finger pressed together, so she then struck the upper portion of Hassan's back, hitting a nerve center. His eyes rolled back as his body wilted.

Sherman rushed over to James' side, sitting him in a nearby love seat. She assessed his wound, feeling the back part of his shoulder to identify the exit wound. The doctor reached for her purse, pulling out a triangle bandage and her cellular telephone. She called her assistant, apprising him of the situation and requesting an ambulance and local law enforcement. She set the phone down and returned to her patient, determined to control the bleeding and save him.

James smiled. "That was incredible. You were so graceful in your fight against him. Your style was obviously of Chinese origin. You moved like a stork, particularly when you were on one leg. You're an intriguing woman, Dr. Sherman, and I sense you have many interesting stories in your past."

"That was the White Crane style I learned from a master when I was assigned to Wuhan, China, to study the coronavirus," she said, eying the blood-soaked bandage. "It's a fluid, agile, and powerful martial art when executed correctly."

"Can you teach me? I can show you some Jeet Kune Do. I've learned to take the best from a variety of systems." He coughed.

"Let's heal you before we start our training, shall we? You'll need to stay quiet until help arrives." The doctor pressed harder down on his wound.

His eyes widened, so she turned to see what alarmed him.

The terrorist had regained his consciousness and picked up the gun. Staggering, he raised it toward the pair.

Sherman drove her right foot backwards, hitting him in the chest and sending him backwards to crash against the bar. He slumped forward and hit the ground.

She grinned. "White Crane plucking fish."

"Remind me not to fish with you." He smiled widely, as sirens wailed, converging on the scene. Within minutes, medical personnel, Arlington police, and FBI agents swarmed his condominium.

She directed the FBI to Hassan, while taking charge of James' medical care. She recognized his dire condition and vowed to keep him alive, given all he had endured. The sparkle in his eyes faded as the ambulance crew worked on him, starting an IV while monitoring his vitals. James pivoted his head and his blurred vision captured two FBI agents handcuffing Hassan and whisking him out the front door. He smirked at tomorrow's headlines, emphasizing how the FBI caught and foiled another attack. He shrugged it off and realized the importance of getting Hassan into custody to protect America and its citizens.

As James exited the front door on a stretcher, he witnessed the media converging on the FBI, as they prepared to give a press conference. Even on a stretcher and half dead, a local reporter swarmed him, thrusting a microphone into his face and inquiring about Hassan. The weakened agent waved off the reporters and pointed them toward the FBI.

The medics lifted James into the ambulance and placed him in the back, locking him into place, while the CDC doctor jumped in beside him.

"So why did you direct the media to the FBI? You could've told them the truth. DS should receive recognition for arresting the master terrorist." She rolled her eyes.

James winced, turning to his right. "You should get the credit for capturing him since you disarmed him, but I just wish you'd aimed his gun in another direction other than at me." He winced.

"Yeah, I'm sorry about that, but my reaction was instinctive. So, why let the FBI grab the headlines for his capture?"

"Knowing the FBI, I'm sure they're taking full credit for their exhaustive manhunt that resulted in Hassan's apprehension. I told the committee that the bureau seeks publicity, often taking credit for the work of other agencies and local law enforcement. The truth about this will surface to reinforce my testimony to the committee." His eyes rolled back.

The medic scrutinized his patient's vitals, as the CDC expert shifted in her seat. James' sudden loss of color alarmed her. "His blood pressure's dropping, so we should get a move on it or we'll lose him." The medic shouted to his partner.

Sherman gripped the agent's hand. "Hold on. Everything's going to be fine."

He struggled to keep his eyes open, as the medic injected his arm with some pain medication and checked his I-V. His eyes glazed over as the light faded. He concentrated on the doctor's face; his pulse slowed as his energy and vitals plummeted. He closed his eyes and disregarded the high-pitched tone. The line flattened on the cardiac monitor. The medic worked frantically on the agent, trying to revive him. He charged his defibrillator in preparation to jumpstart his patient's heart. Sherman watched helplessly as he faded before her eyes. She held her hands to her face, sobbing in disbelief.

·   ·   ·   ·   ·

The sound of an ear-piercing pitch awoke him. It was a sound he had grown accustomed to, the sound of another hotspot boiling over somewhere exotic. He had learned that exotic appeared relative to the individual.

"What happened? I feel like a sledgehammer hit me in the chest."

Sherman canted her head. "We thought we'd lost you. You lost so much blood, but the medic and I saved your life. For a while, we didn't think that it was possible, but it's a miracle you're alive."

"How long have I been out?" He wiped his eyes with his fingertips.

"You've been unconscious for three days," she said, grabbing his hand.

"I finally got some much needed rest. It has been some time since I've slept this well." He reached for his iPhone off the nearby nightstand. He clicked the message. "*Flash traffic in from overseas. Return to the office immediately for an urgent deployment.*"

Sherman rocked her head. "No, you don't. You just let that one go. You're going to require at least six weeks to recover."

She removed a pen from her pocket and scribbled a note. "I'm quarantining you to this room. You can't go anywhere and you're in my hands now." She grinned wickedly, and his heart skipped a beat.

ABOUT THE AUTHOR

Mark J. Hipp was a 29-year veteran with the Diplomatic Security Service who has served as Chief of Security in London, Baghdad, Tel Aviv, Lima, and Tirana. As a former Deputy Chief and Team Leader of the Mobile Security Division (MSD), the author has spent eight years with DSS' elite antiterrorist unit responding to exigent situations in over 70 countries on five continents, as well as wrote numerous manuals on protective tactics and emergency response. He has been featured in three documentaries, but most notably in the Discovery Channel's *MSD: The Unknown Protectors*. He has also appeared on news interviews with ABC, CBS, and CNN.

NOTE FROM THE AUTHOR

Word-of-mouth is crucial for any author to succeed. If you enjoyed *Rogue Pursuit*, please leave a review online—anywhere you are able. Even if it's just a sentence or two. It would make all the difference and would be very much appreciated.

Thanks!
Mark

We hope you enjoyed reading this title from:

www.blackrosewriting.com

Subscribe to our mailing list – *The Rosevine* – and receive **FREE** books, daily deals, and stay current with news about upcoming releases and our hottest authors.
Scan the QR code below to sign up.

Already a subscriber? Please accept a sincere thank you for being a fan of Black Rose Writing authors.

View other Black Rose Writing titles at www.blackrosewriting.com/books and use promo code **PRINT** to receive a **20% discount** when purchasing.

Made in the USA
Coppell, TX
16 December 2021

68981294R00194